Enjoy the journey!

Phyllis Bohonis

Tomorrow's Promise

A NOVEL

PHYLLIS BOHONIS

www.3rdseason.ca

Tomorrow's Promise
© 2015 Phyllis Bohonis

First 3rd Season Publication April 2015

Front cover photo © 2014 Mick Bohonis
Author's photo © 2015 Kuzphotography
Cover Design © 2015 Crowe Creations

Interior design by Crowe Creations
Text set in Palatino; headings in Abadi MT Condensed Light

3rd Season
ISBN: 978-0-9920616-5-4

To Joyce White, my tutor and mentor all those years ago, who taught me to "write as if no one is reading."

Also by Phyllis Bohonis

Fire in the Foothills
The Wilderness

ACKNOWLEDGEMENTS

As always my heartfelt thanks to Ray, Mick, Sharon and Lynda for their patience, love and encouragement. And to my "other daughter" Mari-Lou for her constant support. I thank my son, Mick Bohonis, an award-winning photographer, who once again has provided me with a spectacular cover photo which encompasses both the story and William Shakespeare's quote about a golden sunset. I thank my talented editor, Sherrill Wark, and her company Crowe Creations for the excellent editing and preparation and design of both the print and electronic versions of the book. She is editor, designer, publisher all rolled into one. My gratitude also goes to the Centrepointe Writing Circle members in Ottawa whose critiques and suggestions always add strength and credence to my writing. I can't leave out my good friend, Maxine Tenander, who read the first rough draft and encouraged me with the words "it's definitely a book I'd buy." And to my readers for buying my books and keeping me on track by insisting I not keep them waiting too long for the next one.

The weary sun hath made a golden set,
And, by the bright track of his fiery car,
Gives token of a goodly day to-morrow.
— from Shakespeare's *William III*.

PROLOGUE

T his time death had not been the horrendous, gut-wrenching shock it had been before. This time it had been painfully slow. Was one easier than the other? She was too numb to know. Why was she always the one left to mourn?

He had been a good man. The priest said so. His family said so. All the cards and flowers said so. Her heart said so too. And now, once more, her heart had to heal. God, she was going to miss him. Given a line-up of men, he was not the one she would have chosen. He had been persistent, she would give him that. She had thanked him over and over for his persistence. How would she have survived without him? How will she survive now? He had taught her how to enjoy life. How to find sunshine where she saw only clouds. How to find music where there was chaos. How to love. More importantly, how to accept love. Even in his suffering he had exuded peace and acceptance. He had comforted her.

The last mourner and grandchild had left. She moved through the kitchen to the patio behind. Their family had tidied the kitchen, making sure the leftover casseroles and baking were labelled before storing them in the freezer. All the rooms were neat and clean. The only evidence of death was the myriad of flower arrangements displayed throughout the house.

Now she could enjoy, if that was the right word, the quiet time she needed. She took her drink of vodka and orange juice out to the patio and sank into a big old wicker chair. His big old wicker chair. When had it begun? When had life gone from hell to normal … and back again?

Her toe caught the leg of a footstool and she pulled it close. It felt good to

1

rest her feet on it. There were several plastic patio glasses floating in the pool. A smile warmed her face as she remembered her grandsons' guilty looks when asking if they could swim in the pool. Amy was aghast even as Jo had told them to jump right in, reminding her daughter-in-law that funerals now were called celebrations of life. What better way to celebrate than enjoying a swim in the pool their grand-dad had enjoyed so much. The older boys were almost finished university and the younger ones were in high school and middle school.

She sipped her drink as her thoughts went back to the beginning. The real beginning. It had started during the second year after another funeral. Was it really over twelve years ago they had met? Life had been complicated for so many years, starting with the death of Stu.

She closed her eyes and remembered …

ONE

"Damn wires. Do they just assume everyone's a master electrician? When they charge a king's ransom for a display booth, you'd think they would supply easy-to-use, basic electrical hook-ups." Jo Henderson voiced her frustration.

"You'd think so, but I've not seen too many females setting up their own booths at these shows."

Jo glanced up to see an attractive male, probably in his early sixties, peering over her display counter. Embarrassed she had spoken loudly enough for a passerby to hear, she immediately went on the offensive.

"The fact that I am a female has absolutely nothing to do with it. My contract clearly states that booths would be display-ready, complete with electrical outlets. It mentioned nothing about untwisting ten kilometres of cable while figuring out which connections are mine and which belong to the booth behind. I would appreciate some help untangling this mess. I'm assuming that's your job?"

She didn't mean to sound so testy but it was somewhat unnerving the way this handsome fellow was just standing there with that … that outrageous smile. His plaid flannel shirt and blue jeans enhanced a lean muscular body that said he either worked hard physically or enjoyed countless hours at a gym. She guessed "job" as he dressed and looked the construction type. He stretched his long body over the counter and surveyed the array of wires. Turning smoothly, he headed for a nearby door after assuring her he would find someone to assemble everything for her.

Jo busied herself setting up her audio/visual equipment within the booth for easy use by potential customers. Once the equipment was organized to her satisfaction, she tackled the containers of postcards and brochures, the marketing tools so proudly designed by Stu, her late husband.

After several minutes, the fellow returned with a young man in coveralls who was carrying an enormous yellow toolbox. He showed the younger man the problem with the wires then quickly backed away saying he was overdue in the stage area at the other end of the building. Before Jo could thank him or even apologize for snapping at him, he flashed a heart-stopping smile and promised to come by later.

Glancing down, she noted that the young man was accomplishing in minutes what would have taken her hours. When finished, he labelled the electrical boxes with the booth numbers then turned his attention to the electronic equipment. She thanked him for his prompt assistance and apologized for "any problems I may have caused by barking at your employer." Tim, as his name badge showed, explained he was part-time help sent over by the union to do everything necessary to keep the booths and stage area running smoothly.

Jo continued readying her space for the first onslaught of visitors expected at the opening that evening. It was extremely difficult to focus. Her thoughts kept returning to previous outdoors shows when Stu was working beside her. His excitement had grown with each successive year. Red Sky Lodge had certainly been his pride and joy. He had lovingly driven every nail into every board himself. He had fished every square inch of Sunset Lake and had hunted every logging road within a 75 kilometre radius.

Twenty-eight years before, it had consisted of four rustic cabins planted on some cleared waterfront property. A ribbon of sandy beach broken only by a long rickety dock. A ramp thrown together from logs and rough concrete was used for boat launching. The absentee owner had hired a real estate agent in Thunder Bay to oversee summer rentals.

The first time they had rented a cabin, Jo remembered the squeals of delight from their sons when they first discovered the beach. These had been followed by groans of disappointment upon returning to the city after a whole glorious month communing with nature. Fond memories of shore lunches with freshly caught walleyed pickerel and marshmallow roasts every night were rehashed continually over the long winter. The following year they had reserved a cabin for the entire summer. It was a two-hour commute to Stu's office where he worked as a forestry engineer which necessitated his remaining in the city for work and joining his family only on weekends after his scheduled four-week vacation. The Friday before Labour Day, they bade goodbye to the cottage, already having made the decision to reserve it for the following summer. When Stu stopped at the real estate office that year to return the key and arrange the next summer's rental, the agent informed him that the owner had commissioned him to sell the cabins. He offered Stu first right of refusal. If Stu and Jo were interested in purchasing the little cottage they'd been renting, the present owner was willing to take back a mortgage.

The young couple discussed at length the possibility of purchasing the cabin on the lake they loved so much. At noon the next day, Stu made an unprecedented drive home at lunchtime. He slowly opened his briefcase and removed several papers with figures carefully penciled in columns. He confessed he hadn't been able to concentrate on his work; his mind kept returning to Sunset Lake and those cabins. After spending the morning working out figures, he decided to come home and bounce an idea off her.

"It won't work, it just won't work," she argued, first with Stu then with their lawyer, accountant, and eventually their banker, each disagreeing with her. Finally she relented, and the following twenty-six years at the lake were the happiest of their married life. They had purchased the whole property, not just one cabin. They built more cabins and a main lodge. Cleared land and built a proper boat launch and dock. The boys had grown up spending every summer at the lake until they were grown and moved on to follow their own dreams.

Then the unthinkable happened. Her soulmate was taken from

her in a tragic accident. A late spring snowstorm had swept in. High winds driving heavy snow had forced Stu off the highway through a guardrail and down an embankment. Jo was devastated.

Their older son, John, was married and living in Mississauga with two young boys of his own. Mark, their unattached younger son, had wanderlust and a career as a plant biologist that drew him to remote areas of the world. Both their sons had their own lives.

When her sons returned to their respective homes after the funeral, the pain of being alone was almost unbearable for her. She and Stu had worked side by side annually from May until October since the boys were youngsters. In recent years, when the hectic pace of summer was behind them and the colours of autumn first reflected in the waters of the bay, they spent their evenings sitting on the deck watching the sunsets together. When the last faded leaves had fallen and the nights became cold, they would reluctantly close up shop and head back to town. They always stayed in their Thunder Bay condominium until Christmas. Then, after sharing the holidays with their grandchildren in Mississauga, they would enjoy a month-long vacation on a tropical beach somewhere. By the beginning of February, it was time to start setting up their displays at the outdoors shows throughout the midwestern United States. This bit of marketing usually filled the few vacancies not reserved each year by returning customers.

Even before Stu's funeral, she had experienced her first doubts about continuing to work the resort alone. Over the years, she had become a well-rounded, knowledgeable hostess, but Stu was the businessman, the brains behind the operation. There was no way she could continue running the resort without him. She could see no way around placing it on the real estate market.

After the funeral, there were only two weeks until the first guests of the season were expected. She had no alternative except to persevere until a suitable buyer could be found. An older bachelor renting one of the trailer sites had been returning faithfully every year since the very beginning. He paid annual fees and left his trailer on his chosen spot year round. During the winter, while enjoying ice fishing, he would always inspect the buildings making sure everything was secure for the Hendersons. In the summertime, if Stu had needed a hand with anything, it was Barney McGuire he relied on. When Barney learned of Stu's death, he came promptly to Jo's condominium and volunteered to get the boats and the grounds ready for the season. What a blessing that was! With the combined help of Barney and her experienced cleaning and cooking staff, Jo limped through the first month.

About midway through the second month, the real estate agent informed her he had a developer interested in the resort. The next day, the agent, the prospective buyer and a contractor arrived and together they examined the property with a magnifying glass. Two weeks later, Jo had an offer-to-purchase in front of her. It was a completely fair and generous offer. The buyer would even allow her to complete the current season if she wished to do so. However, in further conversations, she learned he wasn't interested in renewing the rentals for the camping and trailer sites. He had plans to expand the business with a three-story luxury resort complete with airplane landings, Jet Ski rentals and high-powered boats equipped for water skiing. Her first thought was of Barney. This would not be his cup of tea. Their current clientele included young families who couldn't afford the cabin rentals, but could enjoy two-week vacations in their own campers and trailers. After giving more serious thought to the noise and how the fishing would be affected, she telephoned him to refuse the offer. She and her husband had worked hard to maintain a quiet fishing lodge for families with middle-class incomes.

"Well, little lady, I don't think you've given this enough thought. Maybe you need another couple of weeks." Jo could hear the condescension in his voice. "If your husband had received an offer like this, I'm quite certain he would have accepted it."

"And what would possibly make you think that? You didn't even know my husband." A nerve twitched just above her jaw line.

"That's true. That's true. But the men who are interested in developing your property are active in the business world. Women in your situation don't usually know what sells and what doesn't in the world of recreation." He took a deep breath and slowly released it, not even bothering to muffle the sound. "These guys have done their research and know there are more vacationers looking for luxury wilderness retreats than there are people wanting to sit around a campfire toasting marshmallows. Nowadays, they want spas, Jacuzzis, and the ability to fly from the larger urban centres in a couple of hours. You've probably been busy preparing the meals and worrying about the social aspect of your business and not aware of what's happening in the business world." She could actually hear his smirk. "I'm sure your husband would have understood the direction tourism is taking. You impress me as an intelligent woman wanting to get out of a male-dominated business … maybe you should talk this over with someone before you make a hasty decision."

"Well, Mr. Sanders, I may be just a woman but I own this property and I'm rather partial to my uninformed guests who are too ignorant to know they're not enjoying themselves. I am so sorry. I just lit a campfire with your offer-to-purchase and the marshmallows are waiting. You have a great day now — in your business world."

After refusing two more offers, she realized she was being possessive about Stu's resort — their resort. She knew she could not, would not, sell it — to anyone.

Subsequently, here she stood, in this building in northern Illinois, after having been in Minnesota and Iowa the previous weeks. Where the hell was Barb? Her best friend was supposed to have joined her by now. Barb Atwood had promised to lend her moral support as well as physically assist her through these gruelling shows. Jo and Stu both had valued Barb's help in the past whenever she could join them. Perhaps she had gone straight to the hotel. Checking her watch, Jo realized she had better hurry if she were to change, eat and be back before the opening ceremonies.

TWO

Jo's friend was indeed waiting for her at the hotel. Barb explained how she had missed her connection in Chicago because of weather delays at the Toronto airport and had to arrange alternate transportation. Having just showered, and still wrapped in a terrycloth bathrobe, Barb ordered their dinner from the room service menu. When Jo was cleaned up and changed, the two women headed back to the pavilion to begin their marketing.

During the taxi ride, Barb gave her friend a sideways once-over. "Has the format for the show changed?"

Puzzled, Jo lifted her eyebrows. "Why do you ask?"

"Oh, I don't know. It just seemed to take you a little longer than usual to dress. I've never seen you make so many costume changes. If I didn't know any better I'd think you're trying to impress someone." A sly smile tugged at the corners of Barb's mouth.

"Don't be ridiculous. You know I always try to make an impression. Impressions sell my resort."

Her friend was absolutely right, however, and that really annoyed her. She had indeed wondered about the impression her appearance might make on a certain silver-haired man. What had come over her? It couldn't be those haunting blue eyes and that charming smile. She had to admit she'd given those eyes more than a passing thought since they'd locked on hers that afternoon. She shrugged it off. He would probably be far too busy overseeing all the mechanical operations of

9

the show to even give a second thought to a middle-aged widow from Canada. *Okay, maybe slightly past middle-age.*

They reached the building in good time to tour the pavilion and view the competition. Stu had always chosen a booth at the opposite end of the building to the stage and entertainment. He maintained that the quieter atmosphere lent itself to the peace and tranquility they portrayed in their videos and photos. Jo and Barb wandered through the hundreds of booths and eventually worked their way to the front stage area. Not all of the displays were for fishing and hunting lodges. Many were promoting outdoor products such as boats, tents, trailers, barbecues, and other products. If a product was manufactured for enjoying outdoor wilderness living, it could usually be found somewhere at these shows.

"What are you looking for?" Barb asked.

"I'm not looking for anything. Why?"

"Jo, you're definitely looking around for something. Or maybe someone?"

Feeling embarrassed again by her friend's uncanny insight and frustrated by her own inability to locate the blue eyes she was searching for, she retorted, "Well, if you must know, there was a worker, a supervisor I think, who helped me find an electrician this afternoon. I really chewed him out about the display setups. After he found someone to assist me, he left before I had a chance to apologize and properly thank him."

"Well, don't throw your neck out. We'll be around for two more days and I'm sure you'll run into him again." Barb smiled. "He wouldn't be the reason for all the wardrobe changes, would he?"

"Barb, he's just a worker here and you're right I will run into him." Embarrassed by her friend's perception, she turned quickly, head down, checking her watch … and stepped on a man's beautifully shined dress shoe. In that same instant her head hit a chin and she heard a sharp curse. The owner of the shiny shoe lost his balance and went flying backwards, landing half under the stage, Jo falling right along with him. After knocking over a lighting pole, she found herself on the concrete floor straddling a man's body. All she could see was the headless, well-shaped form of a man in a tuxedo, lying on his back — underneath her. Embarrassed, she immediately scrambled to her feet, apologizing profusely. She vainly attempted to free the man's head and shoulders from under the stage. When he finally sat up, tuxedo smudged from the concrete floor, all she could see were those beautiful blue eyes. Her heart sank when she noticed his charming smile had been replaced with a scowl.

Again feeling foolish and going on the offensive, Jo asked inanely, "What are you doing in a tuxedo?"

Rising as he dusted himself off, he replied. "Well, I do have to work tonight and I always try my best to look good. Putting my ... *best foot forward* you might say." To her embarrassment, he was rubbing his scuffed shoe on the back of his other pant leg. "You never know who you might *run into*."

Then she noticed his mouth lifting at one corner and that the eyes looking down at her were doing so with amusement. When he smiled, she noticed a little spot of blood in the crease of his mouth and she asked if he was badly hurt.

"Not mortally," he replied. "My lip just got in the way when you cracked my jaw. Of course, I probably shouldn't have opened my mouth when you stepped on my foot, but I'm not as fast as I once was, nor am I wearing a mouthguard."

Feeling this was not going the way she would have liked, Jo took a deep breath and attempted a fresh start. "Of course you're not wearing a mouthguard, but I wouldn't expect you to be wearing a tuxedo either. Anyway, I just wanted to thank you for taking care of my needs earlier today."

Oh my gosh, did I really say that?

"And I'm sorry for making your lip bleed."

Oh no! Why wouldn't her mouth work right? It was that smile and those eyes, damn it. How could she be expected to think and talk at the same time while the most beautiful man in the world stood grinning at her?

Just when she thought her humiliation was complete, she heard another male voice saying, "Well, Mike, just what kind of need did this pretty lady have that made your lips bleed?"

Where the hell was Barb? Jo just wanted to escape. Unfortunately, Barb was nowhere in sight, so Jo backed away as graciously as she could, mumbling something incoherent and then hurrying off in the general direction of her booth. Thank goodness there was a group standing in front of her display, reading pamphlets. She immediately busied herself answering questions to which she knew the answers.

A few minutes later, Barb appeared with a paramedic in tow who immediately questioned Jo about the possibility of pulled muscles, bruises or sprains. After giving her a quick once-over, the paramedic was satisfied she had no injuries requiring treatment and left. Barb immediately bombarded Jo with questions about the gorgeous man involved in the "incident".

Jo, totally embarrassed, threw up her arms. "Barb, let's just forget the whole thing. I made a fool of myself and I'd rather not talk about it, OK?"

Several hours and several bookings later, the two weary women began shutting down for the night. Jo's body was somewhat sore and she realized she probably had pulled a few muscles during her tumble earlier.

There had been a stage show performing all evening. While they couldn't actually distinguish the music or various events from their end of the building, they could hear the muffled noise in the background. She'd be happy to return to her room and have a quiet relaxing drink with Barb before they retired for the night. There were two more eight-hour days ahead. Thank goodness this was the last show for the season. *I'm getting too old for this. It's just too much of an undertaking. Thank goodness for Barb.*

Maybe she should give the idea of selling the business more thought. Oh well, she'd pull a Scarlet O'Hara and worry about it tomorrow.

When they finally dragged their weary bones to the exit, there was a long queue for cabs. Just when they reached the front of the line, there was a bit of commotion near the door and they could hear male voices shouting "Coming through." Jo turned to see the man called

Mike and his friend work their way through the crowd and reach for the door of an approaching taxi. She kept her sarcastic comments to herself. She had voiced her opinion enough today even though it was inconsiderate of these workers to push themselves into a cab while others were still waiting. However, she relented and gave them the benefit of the doubt. Maybe there was an appreciation party for the workers and they were late. Why else the tuxedo? She really didn't care. She just wanted to soak her weary body in a soothing bubble bath. As Barb signalled for the next cab, Jo glanced up in time to see Mike smiling and waving from the rear window of the preceding vehicle. She did a double-take when he winked flirtatiously as his car pulled into traffic.

THREE

Two more days of working the crowds proved beneficial as they almost filled the reservation book for the season. It was becoming increasingly difficult each year. Ever since the 9/11 disaster in New York, many American tourists were no longer crossing the border into Canada. The increased security sometimes meant delays of several hours and in some instances almost a whole day. Even after a year and a half when the delays minimized somewhat, the price of gasoline increased significantly. It took an incredible amount of selling to entice the Americans to visit Northwestern Ontario.

Jo had noticed the absence of Mike during the past two days. There certainly appeared to be enough workers in coveralls around, so there was probably no need to call in the supervisors on weekends. She was surprised to find herself somewhat disappointed by his absence. He was a good-looking man and he had stirred feelings that had been dormant the past year. Working in a man's world, she invariably found herself in the company of some nice-looking males, however, none had affected her quite this way.

Finally, all their paraphernalia was packed and waiting for the truck to pick it up for shipping home. She and Barb had decided to remain an extra night in the hotel to unwind before flying back to Thunder Bay. After feeling sluggish all day, she was relieved they didn't have to rush right home. Barb commented on her friend's melancholy mood. Jo passed it off as loneliness, reasoning it was because this was her first season attending these shows without Stu.

Trying to shake the feeling, she concentrated on having a leisurely dinner with Barb. The approaching tourist season would not offer many opportunities to share quiet evenings with her long-time friend. Jo was happy with the decision to eat dinner in the hotel dining room rather than venturing outside into the late winter weather blasting off Lake Michigan.

The women enjoyed their dinners while they talked about their plans for the next couple of months. Jo intended spending some time in Southern Ontario with John and his family before opening the lodge. She was always reluctant to intrude too much into her children's lives but she did enjoy visiting with her grandchildren.

She was deep in conversation when she noticed a silver-haired man, his back to them, sitting a few tables over. She felt her stomach flutter and momentarily lost her train of thought. The man turned slightly and she sadly noted it was not the handsome profile she had anticipated.

"Jo, I'm more than a little worried about the way you look."

Startled, she rebutted. "Thanks, Barb. *You* look beautiful as usual."

"I don't mean it as an insult. I'm not being sarcastic. I mean the weary look about you. I hope this business isn't proving too much for you."

"I'm sorry. I guess I am a little on edge. These shows are very tiring, Barb, and the marketing is getting tougher and tougher. However, when I'm at the lake, I can't imagine being anywhere else and I realize all the effort is worthwhile. This is my first round of shows without Stu so I guess I've spent a good part of this weekend reminiscing. I miss him terribly."

"I can understand your melancholy. If these shows are going to pull you down like this, why don't you just skip them and do your marketing on the Internet?"

"That seems to be the way to go now, but surprisingly, people still want to see and talk to the resort owners. Only a small percentage of our cabins are booked from our website. Something else that attracts me to this circuit is the opportunity to check out the competition. And the new products available. Maybe next year I'll have more experience and it won't be so stressful."

"I couldn't help but notice the way the hunk in the tuxedo was giving you the eye. Another woman might have picked up on it and taken advantage of an opportunity to become acquainted with a handsome man."

"I'm not another woman and I definitely don't need a *handsome man* in my life right now. After thirty-seven years of marriage to the most perfect husband a woman could want, I'm not interested in becoming acquainted with a man — any man. Subject closed."

As though in harmony with her wishes, the waiter arrived to suggest another round of drinks. They declined, deciding to call it a night.

The flight home the next day was without incident and Jo was home in her condo in Thunder Bay by mid-afternoon. She was still suffering from the melancholy that had engulfed her and try as she might, she couldn't seem to shake it.

After unpacking and doing laundry, Jo went through the never-diminishing stack of mail. After checking and answering several e-mail messages, it was time for dinner. Jo had never become accustomed to eating by herself, but she enjoyed cooking and tried to make her meals as nourishing as possible. This evening, she decided to warm a casserole from the freezer and eat while watching the evening news on TV.

Impatient, she cursed having to sit through the sports news while waiting for the weather forecast. After muting the usual hockey scores and baseball trade announcements her stomach did a complete flip when she glanced once again at the television set. There, in living colour, was Mike the handyman, attired in an expensive-looking suit and apparently being interviewed.

"Where in hell did I put the remote?" She couldn't hear what he was saying.

She cursed while fumbling to turn the volume up. Why in the world would he be interviewed on TV? By the time the sound returned, all she caught was that Mike Talbot had signed a one-year contract to broadcast some football games. The sports newscaster was giving previous statistics and Mike's face was held in a still shot on the screen. He looked a little younger on TV and even more handsome than she remembered him.

Giving her head a shake she admonished herself for acting like a besotted teenager. She still didn't know why he would be broadcasting televised football games.

Her telephone rang and she could hear Barb's laughter before the receiver was halfway to her ear. "Did you catch your Mike on TV?"

"He's not my Mike. What was he doing on TV anyway?"

"He's Mike Talbot. *The* Mike Talbot. I thought he looked familiar, but I never associated him with being at an outdoors trade show. As soon as I saw him, I recognized him."

"Who in hell is Mike Talbot?"

"He used to be a running-back for a couple of NFL football teams. In his day he was quite a catch, both on and off the field. He retired early, maybe thirty or thirty-five years ago, and went behind the cameras to do some colour commentating. Then he travelled the talk show circuit for a number of years. If I remember correctly, he even acted in a TV movie once. He dropped from the scene about ten, maybe fifteen years ago? God. He still looks great."

"I'll call you right back."

Jo quickly delved through all the brochures from the show they had just attended. Finding the advertising she was looking for, she quickly slid her finger down the list of guest celebrities. There it was. Opening night guest celebrity: Mike Talbot, retired professional football player.

Oh my gosh. The man must think me a complete idiot. How in the world could I possibly have mistaken him for a handyman? Well, it was his own fault. He never identified himself as being anything else and he did bring an electrician when I needed one. He knew I had him tagged wrong and never let me think otherwise. No wonder he was dressed to the nines on opening night. And receiving preferential treatment at the cab queue. What a fool I am. She looked at the brochure again. *Oh well, not to worry, I'll never see the man again.*

Why did she find that thought a little disconcerting?

When she dialled Barb's number, the phone was picked up on the first ring.

"Barb! I found the advertising for the show. You're right. He's one and the same. I feel like such a fool. However, that's the end of it."

Her friend laughingly agreed and before closing the connection, they made tentative plans for lunch several days later.

After missing the local weather report, her thoughts kept going back to those blue eyes and that smile, those blue eyes and that great body, those blue eyes … period. Realizing she was behaving like a lovesick teenager, she decided to forget this foolishness and get back to business.

The next morning she was kept busy organizing her reservations for the coming season. Then there were the staffing requirements to deal with. Needing to call Barney about the outboard motors which were supposed to have been serviced over the winter, she was reaching for the telephone when the business line rang.

She quickly answered. "Good morning, Red Sky Lodge. How may I help you?"

A vaguely familiar voice asked, "Would the boss lady be around by any chance?"

She hesitated. *Could it be …? Why would it be …? No. It couldn't possibly be …*

"Hello? Can you hear me?" The strong male voice sounded slightly amused.

"I believe you're referring to me," Jo answered.

"Are you Jo Henderson?"

"Yes. May I ask who's calling, please?" As if she didn't already know, and why was she having difficulty breathing?

"This is Mike Talbot. You might recall we *bumped into* each other at an outdoors show last weekend. Did I catch you at a bad time? You sound short of breath."

She could almost picture him grinning at the other end of the line. Again, feeling somewhat embarrassed by the whole uncomfortable chain of events at the show, she immediately went on the offensive.

"Sorry, I'm not short of breath, merely short of time. Is there something I can do for you, Mr. Talbot?"

"Well, I'm crushed. Not even an 'Oh Mike, it's so nice to hear from you!' or 'Oh, this is such a pleasant surprise!' We're even forgoing the personal health inquiries and weather comments." Laughing, he continued, "All right, I won't waste your valuable time, I'll get right to the point. While you were wrestling with your wires at the show last weekend, I picked up one of the folders from your counter. I used to enjoy fishing when I could find the time. Your place looks real comfortable and you do promise some big walleyes. I was hoping maybe you'd still have a cabin available early in the season, maybe during the last part of May? I just signed a contract that will keep me really busy right through the summer."

"What did you say?"

"Do we have a bad connection? Shall I repeat myself? Sorry. I know I'm using up your valuable time. Could we just book me into a cabin at your lodge and then you can get back to whatever you were doing?"

She could almost picture the sardonic smile on that gorgeous face.

Smarten up girl, what are you doing? Don't blow this. This man is not the first celebrity to reserve a week at the lodge. Her stomach tightened and breathing became difficult. On the pretext of perusing her reservation book, Jo forced herself to calm down and speak normally.

Finally she asked, "How many will be in your party, Mr. Talbot, and for how many nights?"

"I'm coming alone and I'd like to stay a week if possible."

"Will you require a housekeeping cabin or would you prefer staying in the main lodge?"

"I'll require privacy and just some nice quiet fishing. How you go about that, I'll leave entirely in your hands."

"I'm sure we can accommodate you, Mr. Talbot. Fortunately our honeymoon cabin is available. It has a very private setting with its own dock, a complete kitchen, and a large bedroom with an en suite bath. Your neighbours won't even know you're there unless you want them to. It's available the fourth week in May, very soon after the opening of fishing season. The temperature should be quite pleasant. The water will be too cold for swimming but the walleye fishing should be at its best. Shall I book a guide for you as well, Mr. Talbot?"

"That all depends."

"On what?"

"On whether you're the guide."

Her breath caught and she was almost at a loss for words. As was her habit when feeling cornered, she became abrupt. "Oh. I'm usually too busy to do much fishing. I'm sure you would rather have someone more experienced than I anyway."

"Well, that's disappointing. Maybe it's just as well if you say the water is that cold. I sure wouldn't want to be knocked overboard accidentally. Just arrange a boat and a license. I'll worry about finding the fish. Ready for my credit card number? Then, perhaps, you can give me directions for getting there?"

The sarcasm didn't go unnoticed but she knew from experience that an endorsement from one important celebrity could lead to many other bookings. She would have to swallow her pride. Besides, it might be quite enjoyable to go fishing one evening when her chores were finished.

After they completed their business, Jo informed Mike which airlines flew into Thunder Bay airport and instructed him to notify her after he knew his flight number. She would make arrangements for him to be picked up and chauffeured to the resort.

"I'm looking forward to having you as a guest at our lodge, Mr. Talbot. We'll see you in late May." She tried to sound businesslike even though her stomach had a thousand butterflies in it.

"I'm really looking forward to being your guest, Jo, and I'm hoping before I leave your place that you might start calling me Mike." With that he disconnected.

***

"Yes!" Mike was very pleased with himself. He had anticipated learning that the lodge was fully booked for the spring season. Lady Luck was working with him. Unable to understand why, he had a gut feeling that this little woman with her ginger-coloured hair might finally bring some happiness into his cheerless life. In his business, the opportunity for meeting an honest, unaffected woman was almost nonexistent, especially at his age. Alone for so many years, he was beginning to accept the reality of never finding a companion to share his "golden years" with. Who would have guessed he would encounter such a fiery beauty at an outdoors trade show. Of course he had no way of knowing if she was involved with anyone. He had noticed she was listed as the proprietor on the lodge brochures. Why would a delicate little thing like that be involved in the hunting and fishing business? He would be disappointed if there turned out to be a male partner somewhere near the scene. Jo. A little name for a little lady. *She sure flustered easily, and man, those light brown eyes surely caught fire when she did. They went from golden brown to blazing amber in a matter of seconds. Yes sir, this is going to be one interesting fishing trip.*

FOUR

Jo wasn't sure whether she would share this exciting turn-of-events with Barb or not. Mike did say he wanted … no, *required* … privacy, so the fewer people aware of his planned visit the better. She felt delightfully wicked as she anticipated Barb's response when finally told after Mike Talbot had come and gone. Her friendship with Barb dated back to early childhood. They had been bridesmaids for each other and godmothers to each other's firstborns. During their dating years, Barb had always been the popular one. Intimidated by Barb's flawless complexion and vivacious beauty, Jo had always felt she was living in her friend's shadow. This would have surprised her friend who, in turn, had always envied Jo's natural amber curls and petite figure. In all honesty, she was still a little jealous of her friend's good looks. It was with only a small amount of guilt that she decided to keep Mr. Talbot's fishing vacation to herself.

For the balance of the week, she found it increasingly difficult to concentrate on anything. Her thoughts kept going back to that gorgeous mouth and those sexy blue eyes. She felt nineteen instead of fifty-nine.

Later, when dusting the pictures of Stu in the living room and bedroom, she experienced a real pang of guilt. This past winter, some of her well-meaning friends had offered male friends to escort her to concerts or to make up a foursome for dinner. However, the thought of keeping company with another man just didn't appeal to her. Stu had been the singular love of her life and she considered it a waste of time feigning interest in anyone else, even for an evening. Yet, here she was, barely able to concentrate on her work because her mind kept wandering to the image of an extremely handsome man she knew only slightly.

***

After everything was under control for the opening of the lodge, she flew to Mississauga for a few weeks and enjoyed some time with her grandchildren. They thought it was really neat having a grandmother who operated a fishing lodge. The walls of the boys' bedrooms were covered with pictures of prize-winning fish that had been caught by the guests at her lodge. Their grandmother, wearing blue jeans and a flannel shirt, was always somewhere in the pictures. Of course they had pictures of their grandpa, too, but somehow pictures with their grandma seemed that much cooler. Usually John and Amy brought the boys up north for a week sometime over the summer holidays. Their schedules didn't allow them a lengthy vacation, so they came only long enough to enjoy some incredible fishing. These family excursions usually brought back some cherished memories for John from his own childhood. Jo tried several times to have them leave the boys with her for a longer stay but their soccer and baseball schedules always interfered.

John was employed as a financial planner for a major firm in downtown Toronto. Amy was a supply teacher in Brampton and the two boys were in elementary school in Mississauga. Jo knew they enjoyed having their grandmother visit, but she was more comfortable staying in a nearby suite left vacant in winter by a snowbird friend. She kept a few personal items in the suite's storage room for her visits.

By the time Jo returned to Thunder Bay, it was time for hiring staff and getting supplies ordered. Things would be different this year, as she had *chosen* to operate the lodge on her own. Last year, her hand had been forced at a time when she was emotionally not ready to deal with the responsibility. She was rather proud of the successful season the lodge had experienced, although it never would have happened without Barney's assistance. She would be eternally grateful to the wiry little guy for doing all that he did. After him balking at first, they had come to a mutually agreeable financial arrangement where he paid no rent and all his meals were supplied in return for acting as caretaker and looking after the guiding and docking needs of the resort.

After stopping at the wholesale warehouse to pick up her cleaning supplies and minimal groceries, she headed out the highway. Two of her long-time cleaning staff would be arriving the same day to assist her in readying the cabins and main lodge for occupancy. Barney and one of the dock boys would get the fish house, dock and boats in readiness. A glance at her watch reminded her it was almost time for an appointment with a painter to estimate the cost of refinishing the wood trim on the cabins.

Turning off the highway onto their access road, she was compelled to stop and take a few minutes to compose herself. Last year at this time, Barney had handled most of the lodge business. She had been in no mental shape to make many of the decisions. This year, feeling rejuvenated after her success at the sportsmen shows, she was looking forward to pouring herself completely into the business. All thoughts of selling were far removed. She alone was responsible for satisfying the requirements of the guests she had booked for the season. The reservation book was completely full except for the occasional days here and there, and those would fill up before long. Every weekend during July and August was completely sold out and the cancellation list was longer than usual. She couldn't keep from smiling when she thought of Mr. Sanders and his "luxury resort".

Everyone was complaining about gasoline prices but apparently it wasn't keeping anyone at home this year. She noticed their vehicles were getting larger and larger. Dollar for dollar though, a summer resort vacation was much more economical for a family than travelling to large centres and paying top dollar for hotels and meals. Of course there were fancier resorts than hers available, complete with tennis courts and nine-hole golf courses, but they were out of the price range of most families.

She had survived last season even though she saw Stu every time she turned around. One night last September after sliding into bed, she realized that until that very moment, the whole day had slipped away without her thinking about him even once. She felt almost guilty, as if by not remembering him she was forgetting him, when nothing could be further from the truth. She sat in her Explorer allowing herself one final thought about what Stu might have done when he arrived at the lodge. She squared her shoulders allowing a half sigh, half sob to escape, then started down the road. Completely unaware of what was awaiting her, she knew that whatever it was, she would handle it.

Molly and Diane had been housekeeping at the lodge for eleven and twelve years, respectively. They knew what was expected of them before they were even given direction. When Jo arrived they had already opened most of the windows to allow fresh air into the cabins and rooms. Barney had the pumps for the well going and the water heaters and the furnace were running. Hydro had been installed a number of years before, but the stand-by generators had to be serviced every year. The new dock boy, Russ Langen, came over to help unload the Explorer and introduced himself to Jo. Barney had done the hiring in this case as he knew what was expected of the lad. Everyone seemed to have a chore to do and was engaged in getting it done. She moved into the kitchen and started organizing things there because she'd be doing the cooking for the next week or so. Josef Vanderploeg, lovingly referred to by all as "Cook", usually arrived a week ahead of the opening of fishing season. He would then prepare the menus and supervise the grocery purchases for that first week.

Once Jo had the kitchen in order, she decided to take a tour of the cabins. They all seemed to have survived the winter exceptionally well, no roof leaks and no dead birds or squirrels in the fireplaces. She wandered over to the honeymoon cabin and found herself eyeballing it a little more critically than the others.

Would he find it welcoming and comfortable? Or simply adequate? She had never noticed before how faded that braided rug in front of the fireplace was. A plumper, newer quilt on the bed might give it a little more class but then the curtains on the window would look faded. Realizing what she was doing, she reprimanded herself. *Who is this man anyway? He's just a retired football player coming for rest and relaxation before starting a new job. As long as everything is clean and fresh, does it really matter what type of comforter adorns his bed? He'll probably be surprised to find the "en suite" has running water and an indoor toilet.*

The physical activity over the next couple of weeks proved to be sufficiently strenuous to make everyone fall into bed exhausted at the close of every day. It felt really good. The sun was getting warmer; they even experienced some days in excess of 20 degrees Celsius. The warmth was enabling the painters to get all the cabins looking clean and bright. Clouds rolled in and rain cooled the air again. It also washed away the last traces of winter and everything began to smell fresh with the new growth noticeable in the forest. The lawns, framed by the multi-coloured tulips and bright-purple crocuses in full bloom under the windows, were starting to turn varying shades of green.

Miraculously, on opening day, the sun appeared, while the fresh breeze from the lake whispered promises of a summer like none other. That same day, Jo received a long distance phone call from Mike. She loved the slight drawl. He was calling to give her his flight arrival time and number. She assured him someone would meet him at the airport and would deliver him to the lodge.

A newly married couple was renting the honeymoon cabin during the first week of fishing season so Jo made a mental note to give the cabin a very thorough going over herself once it was vacated. She wanted to make an impression — correction, she wanted the lodge to make a big enough impression on Mr. Talbot that he might recommend it to some of his sporting acquaintances. She mentioned to Barney, Molly and Diane that a celebrity would be staying in this cottage for a week and had requested absolute privacy. Molly and Diane were to be responsible for keeping it clean.

Jo realized with some uneasiness that she was wishing the week away. Always in good condition from the outdoor physical activity of working around the lodge, she couldn't help giving herself the once-over every time she passed the mirror in her bedroom. She found herself sucking her tummy in, checking her waistline and wondering whether she was still even the slightest bit attractive to the opposite sex. She had never given it much thought before. Stu had always commented on what a great shape she had, but with a wink would add "for an old broad." Jo remembered how firm Mike's body was. God knows she certainly felt every sinewy inch of it when she fell against him. She was surprised that a man in his sixties would still be that hard and muscular. Many athletes, after they retire, became soft and started fastening their belts a little lower under their mid-section. Not Mike.

She asked Barney if he would take the company SUV and pick up Mike at the airport but was reminded there was a large group booked for that weekend requiring several boats and guides. They agreed Barney would be better left to tend to their needs. Cook needed some special ingredients for the next week's menu so Jo decided she would drive into Thunder Bay to run the errands then continue to the airport.

Later Friday morning, after a shower — and several wardrobe changes — she headed into town. The drive to the city normally took about ninety minutes through some of the most beautiful country east of the Rocky Mountains. The sun was shining brilliantly as she turned the volume up on the car stereo and sang along with Eddie Rabbitt. The temptation to press harder on the accelerator was hard to control while tapping out the tempo of *Rocky Mountain Music*.

***

Molly's instructions had been to make sure the honeymoon cabin was extra clean and supplied with their best towels and linens. A bowl of fresh fruit was to be placed on the coffee table along with complimentary bottles of red and white wine. The two housekeepers began to speculate who this mystery guest could be. They had entertained other important people at their lodge without Mrs. H. getting all in a dither about it. Molly would do her best to make certain this guest would leave with a yearning desire to return, and maybe recommend the lodge to some of his friends.

***

After completing her errands, Jo had found time to slip into her favourite beauty salon for a cut. She still pulled into the airport parking lot approximately fifteen minutes before Mr. Talbot's scheduled arrival. She had freshened her makeup at the beauty salon but she re-checked her reflection in the glass doors at the airport entrance. As she walked toward them, she was pleased she had chosen her rust-toned windbreaker with the name of the lodge embroidered on the front. It enhanced her ginger hair and it didn't hurt to have the name of the lodge displayed just in case Mr. Talbot had forgotten what she looked like.

Studying the flight monitor, she happily noted that Mike's plane was arriving right on schedule so proceeded to the waiting area for international flights. It wasn't long before the first passengers began striding through the double doors. In no time she noticed a distinct head of silver hair above the crowd coming down the passageway. She caught her breath when he spotted her and started moving toward her. He was even more gorgeous than she remembered.

"Well. I didn't expect the top brass to come for me. Not that I'm complaining." His mouth parted in greeting and curved into a genuinely friendly smile.

Before Jo could answer, a young man passing by tossed his duffle bag over his shoulder. Misjudging the weight of it, he was thrown off balance, bumped into Jo and sent her flying forward right into Mike's stomach. She crumpled to the floor with her foot caught underneath her.

FIVE

"I'll measure you for crutches to help you keep your weight off that ankle. Keep your foot elevated as much as possible and alternate hot and cold packs on it for the next forty-eight hours. I'll see you in my office in about a week."

Jo stared at the doctor as if he were speaking in a foreign language. "Larry, I can't stay off my feet. This is the beginning of fishing season. Do you know how many guests are registered at my lodge right now?"

"Well, Jo. As I recall from my last vacation, you have a pretty competent staff. Just let them do their thing. Relax in your chair, threaten them with your crutches, and I'll wager that lodge of yours will run just as smoothly as if you were on your feet shouting instructions."

"Don't worry, Doc," said Mike. "She'll stay put if I have to sit on her to make her do it. You wouldn't have a problem with her stretching her legs in a fishing boat for several hours a day would you?"

"I'd say that's the best medicine for her right now." Turning to Jo he continued, "You're lucky it's just a sprain and no bones are broken, but it still requires the same care, or you might do some serious damage. Remember, at your age you don't heal as quickly as you did at twenty or thirty. Now, get yourself home. Let your friend take care of you and while you're forced to sit, you might just as well be in a boat enjoying the sunshine."

Before Jo could say anything more, the doctor ordered her to follow him down the hall to get her crutches. She glared at the floor as Mr. Talbot slid an arm around her waist and she hopped one-footed down the hall. She couldn't even look him in the chin, let alone the eye. She could just sense the amusement in those blue eyes and she could almost hear that grin he surely must be sporting. When she finally glanced up, she was surprised that it was concern rather than amusement she saw in his eyes, which only made her feel worse.

Outside in the parking lot, settled begrudgingly in the passenger seat of the Explorer, she turned to him and stated sadly, "Welcome to Thunder Bay."

He returned the look and without missing a beat replied, "This is the first time I've walked into an airport and had women literally falling all over me. I think I'm going to love Thunder Bay."

Without a comeback, she gave him directions out of the city and onto the highway. Jo had called the lodge from the emergency room at the hospital, so the staff was aware they would arrive a couple of hours late. She had also given them instructions to keep something aside for Mr. T. to enjoy for a late dinner when they finally arrived.

At this time of year, the sun set very late in the evening, so Jo knew they would arrive before dark. She wanted Mr. Talbot to enjoy the drive to the lodge during daylight, enabling him to truly savour the scenery in all its natural beauty. With an abundance of wispy clouds trailing across the sky, she knew the sunset was going to be spectacular. Small talk was relatively easy during the drive. He described his flight from Minneapolis on the small plane and related stories of some of the places he had visited after the sportsmen show in Illinois.

Jo had noticed her doctor do a double take when Mike walked in with her. When she introduced him only as Mike, a guest at the lodge, he didn't ask any more questions. She hoped Mike would enjoy a quiet vacation without anyone hounding him for autographs or intruding on his privacy.

After turning off the highway and travelling a few kilometres on the blacktopped road leading to the lodge, they were just coming over a rise when Mike gasped and pulled the vehicle over to the shoulder of the road. The expression on his face said it all.

"Now you know why we call it Red Sky Lodge."

"I thought Wyoming had spectacular sunsets but, lady, they can't hold a candle to this. I hope the fishing is as great."

After all these years, Jo had not lost her appreciation of the extravaganza she was privileged to witness on so many evenings. The sky was absolutely ablaze. Many hues of gold surrounded the blushing clouds that faded into softer pinks. They became brilliant again in the glow of purples, mauves and oranges reaching like flames streaking across the horizon. She suggested he continue to the lodge and if they were lucky, they would catch the last act of the show when the giant red globe would settle into the water.

He manoeuvred the vehicle onto the travelled portion of the road again and continued the short distance to the lodge. Jo could hear his breath catch as they turned into the driveway overlooking her property and the lake beyond. True to her word, the fireball was just starting to submerge into the red-black water. The streaks of cloud had turned crimson as well, setting the entire sky ablaze. Looking at it, one could almost hear the water sizzling as it slowly put out the flame.

"I think I want to cancel my television contract and stay all summer. I'll scrub pots, mow lawns, clean outhouses. Anything. Just don't make me leave."

"I'm glad you're impressed, Mr. Talbot. This is something that can't be captured and incorporated into our advertising. The gods have chosen to honour you with this display on your very first evening. I hope you'll find everything else, including your cabin, to your liking as well."

"Cabin? Hell, just string a hammock between two trees. I don't want to miss any of this by being indoors."

"In another ten or fifteen minutes you'll be happy to be inside. At this time of year, no matter how high the temperature climbs during the day, as soon as that sun sets, the air cools down considerably. In fact, I gave instructions for the staff to have a fire going in your cabin so you would find it cozy and comfortable upon your arrival."

Just then, Barney caught sight of the Explorer and came hustling up from the dock. "Good evening, Mrs. H. Molly told me you had an accident. Glad to hear you didn't break any bones. Evening, sir." He nodded toward Mike. "Now, Mrs. H., you just make yourself comfortable inside and leave me to settle our guest in. Afterward I'll bring the supplies inside too."

"Barney, I'm not a complete invalid and I want to make sure that everything is done up right in Mr. Talbot's cabin."

Mike spoke up then and introduced himself to Barney and turning toward Jo, insisted that the two men were quite capable of getting his gear into the cabin. "You go inside and get off your ankle. Trust me. I've had some experience with sports injuries. I'll come in and check on you later."

Jo assured him there would be a hot meal waiting by the time he was unpacked. She instructed Barney to show Mr. Talbot to her private quarters where she would instruct Cook to bring their food. She knew the wait staff would be in the process of giving the dining room its final cleaning for the night before setting up for breakfast.

She hobbled up the steps to the reception area of the lodge and went inside. Jo hadn't wanted them to see how eager she was to get her foot elevated. The two-hour ride with her leg stretched as best she could in the cramped quarters of the vehicle had proven too much. She greeted all her staff as each came over to offer a different bit of advice about the care of her ankle. After thanking them all, Jo went through the kitchen to see about Mike's dinner. She was immediately shooed into her own place with a promise it would be served piping hot as soon as her guest came up from his cabin.

After freshening up a bit, Jo manoeuvred the hassock in front of her favourite chair and found the remote for the television. Easing herself into the chair, she made her leg comfortable on the footrest. Only then did she allow herself to think about what a complete shambles she had made of Mike Talbot's arrival. The only redeeming factor so far had been the sunset. It was as if someone was taking pity on this poor woman.

Looking at her watch after a while, Jo assumed Mike must have gone to bed early, only to hear a knock on her door. Barney poked his head through the opening and announced that Mr. Talbot had arrived for something to eat. Starting to rise she heard a deep voice booming for her to remain seated or she would be sat upon. Barney left to inform Cook the two were ready for dinner.

"Why don't you have a cold compress on your ankle?"

"Because when I sat down, I didn't feel like getting up again."

Cook came in from the kitchen pulling a small cart behind him bearing two covered trays. He promptly set up two TV tables nearby and placed the contents of the trays on them.

Mike asked, "Is there anything in the kitchen that we can use for cold compresses?"

Cook replied. "I can wrap up some ice cubes in plastic and towels."

"Do you have any frozen vegetables? Peas? Corn? They work better. More pliable. Just refreeze and reuse. I'll come with you."

The chef assured Mike he would deliver some and then returned to the kitchen. Mike moved Jo's TV tray closer to her chair so she could eat more comfortably.

"I don't want you spilling any of this hot food in your lap," he said with a hint of a smile.

"I know you'll find this hard to believe, Mr. Talbot, but most of the time I do manage to stay upright on my *own* two feet. I usually talk in a manner that doesn't cause too much embarrassment to anyone, and I generally manage to behave like a pretty sensible businesswoman. And most importantly, you will see I normally do not require a bib."

"Well, I am delighted to hear all that." Leaning forward he whispered, "I wondered whether you suffered from a disability of some kind. It's reassuring to learn you're perfectly healthy. I can only assume that I literally swept you off your feet, not once but twice. I'll be happy, though, when you start referring to me by my given name and even happier when you stop barking at me every time you address me."

Just then Cook returned with two packets of frozen peas and handed them to Mike. When asked, Jo assured the man they wouldn't need anything else, adding she would make coffee herself later. After

Cook left, Mike placed one of the packets in the refrigerator freezer in her little kitchen. He found a dishtowel and wrapped it around the remaining packet and placed it gently over her ankle. Jo thought his hand may have lingered just a second or two longer than necessary when he gave her a little foot rub.

Their previous conversation forgotten, they enjoyed the fresh-caught pickerel that Cook had pan-fried in his special beer batter. When she asked if his cabin was comfortable enough, Mike answered with a straight face that he was pleasantly surprised to find hot running water in his faucets. She noticed the blue eyes twinkling with amusement.

"I hope you were equally pleased, then, to realize you don't have to go outdoors to relieve yourself. Would you like a cup of coffee or perhaps a cold beer, Mr. Talbot?"

"I don't drink alcohol, Mrs. Henderson, but it would be my pleasure to make some coffee. I'm still on Pacific time so if I'm keeping you up just send me on my way."

"I don't usually go to bed much before midnight and I always enjoy a coffee after my dinner. I'm not an invalid, however. I can make it for us."

"Oh, but indeed you are an invalid. You were instructed by your doctor to stay off your feet as much as possible. Remember he cautioned that 'a woman your age' doesn't heal quickly?" The corner of his mouth twitched. "Besides I make a pretty passable pot of coffee."

After a wink and a chuck under her chin, he could almost see the smoke billowing from her ears. They stared each other down before both burst into laughter.

It wasn't hard to find everything he needed in her little cubbyhole of a kitchen. Stu had built a few cupboards and crafted a counter enclosing one corner of their rather large living room. The apartment-sized refrigerator, stove and microwave oven were quite adequate for her simple culinary requirements as she usually ate in the dining room or kitchen.

***

She sat admiring the strong back and trim waistline as Mike filled the pot and got the coffee brewing. While it was dripping, he retrieved one of the trays Cook had brought in and arranged sugar, cream, mugs and spoons on it. When the coffee was ready, he flipped open the top compartment and dumped the filter full of hot used grounds into a plastic baggie he found in a drawer. He sealed it, carried it to Jo's chair and removed the cool packet from her ankle. He took that towel, wrapped it around the hot packet and gently laid it on her ankle.

"What are you doing?" Jo asked, bewildered.

"Don't you remember the doctor said to alternate hot and cold packs on your ankle? No point in wasting these nice hot coffee grounds."

"You really have done this before, haven't you?"

"I played football back when dinosaurs roamed the planet and believe me, I suffered more than my share of injuries. When you're on the road, you improvise any way you can. In the dressing rooms, there's always state-of-the-art equipment but in hotel rooms you used your imagination. Tomorrow I'll make you a couple of hot packs from rice. You can just heat them in the microwave for a few seconds and they'll stay hot for a long time. Now, I shall pour our coffee."

He filled the two cups and brought the tray over to the coffee table.

"One lump or two, madam?"

"None."

He held one of the cups just beyond her reach. "There is a price for this deliciously aromatic brew."

Startled, she was reluctant to ask what the price could be. Almost barking again, she demanded what he wanted. He met her eyes and replied, "From now on you must call me Mike. I really dislike this Mr. Talbot business."

"I guess I can manage that … Mike." She felt foolish for suspecting he wanted something more.

Mike enquired if there were any sports stations on TV, then asked if she'd mind if he caught up on the day's games. Her breath caught when she watched him settle into what had been Stu's favourite chair. When he slid his shoes off and lifted his feet onto the hassock almost touching hers, she felt a strange warmth course through her. She wasn't sure whether she should welcome this easy familiarity, but after the day's events and his patience with her, she felt she owed him a little "creature comfort".

When the sports scores had all been reported, Mike used the remote to shut off the television, then wandered toward the kitchen and returned with the coffee pot. Without asking, he poured each of them another cup. After rinsing out the pot, he returned to the chair and looked around the room, his eyes finally coming to rest on Jo. "This chair and some of the furnishings in this room have the feel of a man about them. Is there someone in your life, Jo?"

She hadn't been prepared to talk about Stu with him. She didn't feel she should. She really didn't want to open that door. He sensed her hesitation and remarked that it really wasn't his business and he shouldn't have asked such a personal question.

"My husband died when his vehicle went off the highway just over a year ago," she stated with a calm she'd never experienced before. "His name was Stuart, everyone called him Stu. We built this lodge together twenty-seven years ago. This is my second year operating it by myself. This was my first year attending the outdoors shows without him." Her sentences sounded short and choppy, but she realized this was the first time she was able to utter all the words without her voice breaking.

"I am so sorry." He sounded genuinely concerned. "How did his accident happen?"

She explained that near the end of April the previous year their region was blasted by a surprise late snowstorm. Stu had decided to precede her to the lake to get everything in readiness for their scheduled season opening three weeks later. She was to meet him out there the following week. The storm had been forecast as a light snowfall and ended up breaking weather records for the next thirty-six hours. Unfortunately, Stu's Suburban was no match for the eighty-kilometre-an-hour winds that appeared from nowhere, driving the snow into whiteout conditions. On a stretch of highway with steep embankments on either side, he lost control of his vehicle and wasn't found until the ploughs came out late the following day. A portion of broken guardrail was discovered and subsequently investigated. When pulled from the vehicle it was determined he had died not long after his SUV had hit a large rock at the bottom of a forty-foot embankment. He was still strapped inside when rescuers reached him, with no indication he had ever regained consciousness.

"At first I wanted to sell this place, but when it came right down to it, I couldn't relinquish ownership. Barney has been such a tremendous help to me. If it weren't for him, I would have been forced to give it up whether I wanted to or not. Now, I really can't think of any other place I'd rather be or anything else I would rather be doing. This lodge is my whole life."

***

Mike slid his feet off the hassock and leaned forward, elbows resting on his knees. He wanted to put his arms around her and offer her comfort but realized he couldn't do that. What a gutsy woman. No wonder she was having trouble setting up her booth; it was the first time she had done it alone. He had been amused when she thought he was an employee of the building. He had wondered where her male counterpart could be, never thinking that a woman would be running a fishing lodge by herself. Mike figured she would surely be upset knowing he was qualifying that thought by adding " woman her age". He had hoped to return to her booth before appearing on stage but time had run out. There was something about her that had sparked his curiosity, making him want to know her better. All the stage celebrities had been invited to a function in the private boardroom right after the show. He'd managed to excuse himself with just barely time to be whisked away to the airport. When he settled the contract to provide the colour commentary for the football games, he decided to take some time for a short holiday before the season would start. And he knew exactly where he wanted to vacation.

***

"Do you not have any family to help you?"

"My two sons live elsewhere building their careers. John, the older one, is a financial planner in Toronto. Mark is the younger one. He's a plant biologist currently working in eastern Asia. We had our dream and they have theirs. I want to continue with this, and I want it badly enough to do it alone. I'm not ready for retirement nor will I enter a retraining program — at my age ..." She smiled. "... to work in an office or a flower shop. I have to admit I did find the shows very difficult. I asked a girlfriend of mine to give me a hand and keep me company but I realize now I should have had Barney with me. I believe I'll take him next year. I felt I needed moral support more than physical, but as you witnessed, it didn't take long to learn I was out of my league."

She paused in thought for a minute. "I believe next year will be easier for me emotionally as well as physically."

"How did you and your husband choose the fishing and tourist business? Were you brought up in it?"

"No, it started with a family vacation."

Before she knew it an hour had passed and she had shared more with Mike than she had been able to share with anyone. He added a comment here or asked a question there but mostly he just listened. It was strange, but she didn't feel depressed the way she usually did after talking about Stu. It seemed as if by talking, she had shared her grief and the load had lightened.

Mike noticed that Jo was looking tired, and felt guilty about keeping her up so late. He was being entirely selfish, but he wanted to know all about her, the heartaches as well as the happiness. He loved the sound of her soft, husky voice and while she was talking he felt something warm growing deep inside him.

He stood up while commenting that Barney had offered to have one of the young dock boys guide him to a fishing spot where the fish had been biting the last few days. Mike added he was holding out for his own personal guide, perhaps later in the morning? Lifting an eyebrow he waited for her reply.

Unsure how to respond, she replied that the best fishing is usually very early in the morning and she wouldn't be able to leave until her work was finished. He knelt on the floor beside her and took her foot in his hands, massaging it tenderly. He reminded her that if she hadn't come personally to meet him, she never would have suffered this accident. He felt responsible and would not enjoy going fishing by himself knowing she was disobeying the doctor by working instead of resting.

Not sure whether he was literally pulling her leg or not, she decided to accept his declaration at face value. "Okay, Mike, I'll go fishing in the morning, but not at sunrise."

A grin lit up his face. "How's that for luck? Not only have I progressed to a first name basis with the boss lady but I have a date to go fishing with her as well. And all accomplished over two cups of coffee.

"I better leave before you change your mind."

Taking the now-tepid compress off her ankle, he advised her to wrap a cold one around it before going to bed, reminding her not to leave it on for more than twenty minutes.

"I'd offer my help with that but a smart man knows when to quit." He winked.

After assurances he needn't do anything with the dirty dishes, she accompanied him to the door. As he was about to walk through it, he turned and said softly, "You know, Jo, if I don't catch a fish all week, I've already had my money's worth. That unforgettable sunset this evening and the couple hours relaxing with you are more than I had hoped for." He brushed her cheek with his lips and started down the path to the cottage before she realized what had happened.

When she was lying in bed with frozen vegetables on her ankle, it occurred to her she hadn't asked him about his breakfast plans. "Oh well, he's a grown man. I'm sure he'll manage," she murmured to herself.

She fell asleep dreaming about the bluest eyes she had ever seen in her whole life and lips kissing her foot, while strong hands smoothed away the hurt from her ankle.

**

Mike followed the path down past the stand of trees that separated him from the other cottages. Upon his arrival, he had been pleased with the seclusion of the cabin. After spending the last couple of hours with Jo, he wasn't entirely sure it was seclusion he wanted after all. The bowl of fruit and the wine had not gone unnoticed. In fact a pear and banana had kept his stomach appeased until he had changed and walked to her quarters. If that pickerel was a sample of what he would be eating for the next week, he just might cancel his contract and stay all summer.

He threw another log into the fireplace, stoked the embers a bit and sank into the rocking chair to enjoy the fire. He had stayed in some pretty fancy hotels over the years but this place somehow had a homey feel to it. He loved the slightly worn rug in front of the fire, thinking it gave the room an ambience even the most expensive broadloom couldn't accomplish.

After losing himself for a while rehashing some of the conversation he had just shared, he realized he was somewhat envious. If he and Trish had shared the kind of love that Jo and Stu had, life would have been so different. He wasn't blaming her. He remembered they both had done their utmost to salvage their marriage but they finally admitted you couldn't force love. If it's not there, it's not there, and loneliness can drive people to do things they wouldn't normally do. He had been extremely bitter after their "bad time". He realized he had Shannon to consider and managed to pull himself together. Poor Shannon, his daughter had been his salvation in the end.

Everyone was surprised when he went into retirement at the peak of his broadcasting career. Those close to him knew his reasons. He retired to his ranch in Wyoming, raised horses and tried to salvage a life with Shannon. Last year, his old buddy, Jack Freeman, came looking for him. Jack had been asked to join the public speaking circuit which included sportsmen's dinners, shows and roasts. Wanting his old partner back, he asked Mike to join him. The opportunity to give it one more try was pleasing to Mike, a second chance. Nothing was etched in stone. If he found he didn't enjoy it after one season, he just wouldn't return. He agreed to tour with Jack for one circuit and see how it worked out. In no time, their schedule was fully booked. It seemed there were many people who hadn't forgotten what a great entertainer he used to be. Hell, he had even been a movie star. He never guessed it would lead to signing a broadcasting contract within the year.

When he had walked by Jo's booth at that outdoors show and heard that little lady in distress, his soft-hearted nature wouldn't allow him to just stroll away. When he saw the mess of wires she was trying to untangle, he remembered the guy with the toolbox a few rows over and went to fetch him. After grabbing a folder off the counter, he noticed the woman was the manager of a fishing lodge somewhere in Canada. She certainly was full of spit and fire. The cute little package was topped off with a mass of short curls in a real warm ginger colour that matched the spark in her eyes. He found the fellow with the toolbox and told him he was badly needed a couple of aisles over. Mike was supposed to have been up in the stage area fifteen minutes earlier so he just left the young fellow with her and promised to come back later. He would explain to her then in what capacity he was working the show. Complications setting up the sound equipment barely gave him and Jack time to return to the hotel, grab a bite to eat and get changed. He could never figure out why tuxedos were required at a show everybody attended in jeans, but he was being paid well enough to oblige without argument.

When they had returned to the coliseum, he had checked the sound system one more time. A glance at his watch verified that if he moved quickly, he might have time to squeeze in a visit with that little lady in the booth. Why did she have to be so far away from the stage? Going down the steps, he had just kicked a loose wire under the stage when someone stepped on his foot. As he let out a yelp, a curly head lifted up and caught him in the jaw. The force made him bite his lip as he was thrown off balance. The next thing he knew he was flat on his back staring at the underside of the stage. Wasn't this just great — he probably had holes in his tuxedo. He tried to get up and realized somebody was straddling his legs. The guilty culprit scrambled off him; next he could feel someone pulling his arm. He managed to stand with some dignity, and began brushing off his tuxedo examining the fabric for rips. Mike couldn't believe he had just been bowled over by the little redhead who couldn't possibly weigh more than a hundred pounds soaking wet. She seemed equally surprised to see him and immediately started jabbering some fool thing about him in a tuxedo. In the next breath she was concerning herself over his bleeding lip. Before he knew it she had disappeared and Jack was taking him backstage for repairs to his tuxedo. The next time he saw her, they were rushing into the limousine supplied by the cab company to catch their plane. When he saw her frustration at being bested at the taxi queue, he made up his mind then and there that he wanted to see her again, if only to straighten out the mishaps between them. He knew where to find her and he couldn't help but smile looking at the fire in those eyes as the limo took him away. He had wondered if something other than anger might bring that same spark …

It was going to be a real pleasure finding out.

SIX

Mike was smiling as he undressed and slid into his bed. He ran one hand over the covers as he pulled them into place, thinking how nice it was not to have one of those heavy quilt things that were always on hotel beds. What a waste. You only ended up kicking them off anyway because they were too warm. Mike could have sworn, as he was drifting off, that he could hear Eddy Rabbitt singing a duet with some raspy-voiced female.

***

Jo's throbbing ankle awakened her around 7:00 the next morning. Her hopes of ignoring the painkillers the doctor had prescribed for her were dashed when she stepped on the floor. She immediately slumped back upon the bed and avoided putting her weight on her foot for as long as she could. When the pain subsided a little, she hobbled to the bathroom and back. Unhappy at having to do so, she dug into her purse and retrieved the prescribed medication then swallowed one tablet. She eyed her crutches with distaste, but realized they would be a necessity after she lost her balance and accidentally landed on the wrong foot. Jo returned to the bathroom and filled the tub with warm, lightly scented water. She unwrapped the tensor bandage from around her ankle and eased herself into the bathtub. Half an hour later, wrapped in her fluffy white terrycloth bathrobe, and with a fresh-perked cup of coffee in her hand, she opened the door to her deck and counted the number of boats that had already left their moorings. There was a light knock on the door from the big kitchen and Molly called her name softly. Jo opened the door to welcome her cheerful housekeeper who was standing with a tray of juice and oatmeal with brown sugar and cream — Jo's favourite breakfast.

"I heard you running your bath water earlier, Mrs. H., so I thought I better get your breakfast ready before you start wandering around trying to fix something for yourself."

"Molly, I'm not totally helpless."

"Mr. Talbot told us that the doctor wants you completely off your feet for several days."

"Mr. Talbot has a big mouth."

"He was really concerned about you. He's already filled some plastic bags with rice that Cook gave him. Mr. Talbot said they'll make excellent hot packs for your ankle. Imagine that. He also wanted to be informed as soon as you were moving around."

"Just who's giving the orders around here? And why does Mr. Talbot have to know when I'm awake?"

"Because my guess is, you haven't had a hot pack on your ankle since last night." Mike sauntered through the door and steadied her as she limped to the chair. "Perhaps I should've followed my intuition and stayed here overnight. Let me take a look at how the swelling is."

He sank onto the hassock in front of her, and then eased her foot across his muscular thigh. He touched, squeezed, and massaged with gentle pressure, then instructions followed for Molly to heat one of the pouches of rice in the microwave for sixty seconds. Mike located Jo's tensor bandage and carefully wrapped it around her ankle. By then the rice had been warmed and he placed the towel-wrapped plastic bag on her ankle. She admitted to herself that the heat felt wonderful.

Molly arranged Jo's breakfast on the TV table that was still in place from the night before. When Mike asked if there might be any more coffee, both women immediately expressed concern about his breakfast.

"What a way to start the day. Two beautiful women worrying about my stomach. You will both be happy to know that Cook is preparing something for me. As we speak."

Molly excused herself saying she had rooms to clean, but enquired if Mr. Talbot had found everything to his liking in his cabin. She grinned when he commented he was as snug as bug in a rug.

Cook brought a tray in for Mike and while the two men discussed the sausage, Jo scrutinized Mike and decided he certainly looked well-rested. This morning he wore a checked flannel shirt that was a deeper blue than his eyes, and dark blue jeans. She noticed his feet were bare inside deck type shoes.

After the door closed behind Cook, Jo asked, "Are your feet not cold without socks?"

"A little. I normally don't wear socks with casual shoes, but I didn't realize your mornings would be so nippy. Did you sleep well?"

"I slept very well. Although I realized when I woke up that I definitely needed something for the pain." When she saw the concern on his face, she quickly added, "but I'm feeling just fine now."

"Do you always eat porridge for breakfast?"

"Most of the time."

"I remembering reading somewhere that women your age need their fibre."

She was flabbergasted at his rudeness until she saw the smile working the corner of his mouth. "Yes, regularity is important. Otherwise we get downright nasty, sometimes knocking over old geezers just for the sport of it." She watched a real smile tugging at both corners now and remembered how those lips had brushed her cheek the night before. "How did you sleep, Mike?"

"Like a newborn baby. I could hear country and western music as I was dozing off. It was rather pleasant. The female had a husky voice similar to yours. If I didn't know better, I'd swear you and Eddie Rabbitt were right outside my window."

They ate breakfast in relative silence, surprisingly comfortable with it. They even shared the morning paper delivered earlier from Thunder Bay. Mike commented on the promise of a beautiful day and wondered aloud how long the fish might continue biting.

"Pickerel — or walleyes, as you Americans call them — are usually early morning and late evening feeders, but in the past, we've caught them all day. It takes slightly longer to catch your limit, but at this time of year that shouldn't prove too difficult. If you have a good guide, anything is possible."

"Will I have a good guide?"

"The best. I know every square inch of this lake and exactly where the fish are, at any time, on any given day. I'll guarantee it."

"Then why are we sitting here making small talk? Tell me what needs to be done. I'll get everything ready and come back for you."

"Did Barney bring a boat around to your dock?"

"Yes. Complete with a spare tank of gas."

"I believe I noticed you carrying a fishing rod."

"Yep. The best one K-Mart sells!"

"Mm hmm, best for what?"

"Listen here, darlin'. I ain't no fishing dummy. While I don't profess to be an expert, I've been around the lake a time or two."

"OK, OK. If you can find Barney, ask him to bring a bucket of minnows and my fishing rod to your dock. Give me a few minutes to slip into some shoes and grab a jacket. We really should take something to eat."

"I've already arranged for a cooler of fresh fruit, some snacks and cold drinks."

"Well, aren't you a regular Boy Scout. You must have been pretty sure you had yourself a guide."

He smiled as he went through the door. While Mike tracked down Barney for her fishing equipment, Jo hopped to the bathroom and made a valiant effort at running a brush through her unruly hair. She had to keep it short or it would be totally unmanageable. After fighting with it for a few minutes, she fitted a slightly soiled baseball cap on her head, one with the lodge logo embroidered on the front. She quickly shed her bathrobe, donned a pair of shorts, and then slid a pair of nylon jogging pants over top. When she attempted to put on her shoes, she realized her foot was swollen enough to allow only a sock — no shoe. She grabbed a windbreaker that matched her pants and, using her crutches, hopped back into the living room. Mike was waiting to open the door and allowed her through to the deck. He surprised her by scooping her into his arms then suggested she leave her crutches behind, explaining that she wouldn't need them in the boat. Ignoring her objections about having to be carried, Mike pointed out that her crutches were too difficult to manoeuvre in the sand.

"Besides, knowing you're off your feet, I'll feel more confident about remaining on mine." He gave her a squeeze as he said this and started along the path that wound past his cabin.

He parked her on his veranda, then went inside and returned with the small cooler he'd borrowed from the kitchen. He carried it to the dock then loaded all their equipment into the boat.

"You've done this before," Jo said as she looked around at the efficient way everything was stowed neatly underneath the seats and in the bow. Mike lifted her easily onto the narrow bench up front and rested her injured foot on the middle one. After untying the bow rope, he stepped nimbly onto the rear bench, freed the stern rope, and pushed off.

Starting the motor on the second pull, he slowly eased away from shore and after testing the depth of the water, he eased the motor down into running position. Smugly he commented, "I don't think you believed me when I told you I'm an experienced fisherman."

"As a matter of fact, I didn't. I'm impressed."

She settled back and gave him directions to a bay in the southwest area of the lake into which a small river emptied. Pointing to the mouth of the river, she suggested they anchor just at the edge of the faster moving water for a while and try their luck. When Mike manoeuvred the boat into position, Jo let the anchor drop and allowed it enough slack to hold the boat exactly where she wanted it. While Mike was an experienced fisherman, he had never used minnows as bait so she showed him what type of hook to use and how to attach the minnow. They cast their lines out either side of the boat and worked them slowly back. It wasn't long before Jo had landed one. She explained the catch-and-release system, so Mike joined her in this. He had no intention of taking fish home. He just wanted to enjoy the sport and the company, especially the company. They did agree to keep a few for dinner that evening.

Before long the sun was quite high, the temperature was rising and they shed their jackets. When the bites slowed, Jo suggested they lift anchor and head across the bay to a relaxing area along the shoreline and just drift while they enjoyed their lunch. When they reached the protected side of the bay, Mike cut the engine and they loosened their lifejackets. Jo decided to enjoy the warm sun on her legs. Several attempts to remove her long pants proved difficult, if not downright impossible, because of her inability to stand or put weight on her bad ankle. Mike watched her futile efforts and offered his help. While she lifted her hips from the bench he then easily worked them down past her hips.

She noticed his eyes roaming over her legs and hips as he did this. Slightly ruffled, she hoped he damn well liked what he saw. She was embarrassed and could feel the skin on her neck tingling. Her voice sounded tight and slightly high pitched when she attempted to ask what was hidden in the cooler. Very efficiently, Mike laid the cooler lid on the middle bench to form a tabletop then arranged some ham-and-cheese sandwiches on the surface followed by two apples, two oranges and two bottles of iced tea.

"With you around, when does Cook have time for my other guests?" she asked sarcastically.

"I never bothered Cook at all. It was Molly who fixed the sandwiches."

"I think you've done a number on Molly. I've never seen her respond to anyone in such a manner before. She normally likes to be left alone to get her cleaning done."

"If you must know, I promised to get her into show business if she treats me right," he whispered as he leaned forward. "I hinted that the Green Bay Packers are looking for a new poster girl."

Jo almost choked on her sandwich as she laughed. "I had *my* heart set on that job."

"Listen, sugar, when you can make a sandwich as good as this, I might consider you."

"I'll certainly work on it."

They finished their lunch, saving some of the fruit for later. Jo instructed Mike to troll slowly along the shoreline. She pointed out a new-growth area where a forest fire had burned dangerously close to the lodge eight years earlier. The guests had had to evacuate and were relocated to a motel in Thunder Bay for two nights until the winds changed. Fortunately, the fire moved in another direction and eventually it was brought under control. They circled a small island some of their first guests had named Table Island. It was just big enough to sustain a few trees. A number of summers ago, Stu had placed a picnic table under one of the trees so families could enjoy coming ashore and stretching their legs while eating their lunch in the shade.

They passed a beaver dam where a shallow creek joined their lake with another smaller one. Beyond that, a short portage eventually brought a boater to another large lake where the walleye and northern pike grew to trophy size.

Travelling around another point of land, Jo showed him a crumbling old building, the weathered logs turning grey. Some rotted out and lying on the ground. "Story has it that at the turn of the twentieth century, a trapper started building this log home for his new bride. He was in his thirties and she not even twenty. A beautiful Métis girl he had met in Fort William. Sadly, she succumbed to tuberculosis before it was completed. He was so heartbroken, they say, he never finished. A year or so later another trapper found his remains on the ground beside a grave marked with a beautifully carved wooden cross. Authorities buried him beside his love. Apparently, if you know where to look, you can find the two markers but there's kind of an unspoken rule to leave the lovers in peace so everyone admires this token of love from the water." She stared quietly for a moment then smiled. "We have our very own, more romantic version of White Otter Castle."

"White Otter Castle?"

"That's another story in another place a couple of hundred kilometres from here. I'm sure there must be hundreds of such stories across Canada and the United States."

All during the previous season, Jo had difficulty visiting these sights that she and Stu used to cruise, but being with Mike seemed to ease her anxiety. He appeared to be genuinely interested and to sense the difficulty for her, never pressing for information. He was content to let her talk without interruption while he enjoyed the surrounding countryside.

Before long, she felt some pain in her ankle returning. He immediately apologized for selfishly keeping her out too long. Mike turned the boat in the direction of the lodge and they headed for home. Travelling across the open water, she found the cooler air once more uncomfortable on her legs. She unsuccessfully tried to tuck her pants around them. Mike noticed her discomfort, cut the engine back, and assisted her with them once again. As he tugged the pants over her hips, he was leaning so closely, his breath was actually tickling the side of her neck. Feeling somewhat disappointed when he moved away, she was comforted a little when he lifted her swollen ankle onto his lap. He steered with one hand while massaging with the other. She was uncomfortable with her reaction to his closeness.

Easy girl, don't get too carried away here. After all, he's only staying for a week. Besides, he probably dates women half your age routinely sliding their pants on and off their tight little butts.

When they returned to his dock, he picked her up effortlessly and strolled toward his deck. A porch swing with a padded vinyl seat was tucked into one corner. He gently set her down then brought a cushion from inside and placed it under her head. After elevating her swollen ankle to the armrest, he offered to get her painkillers from her apartment. Moments later, he returned with her prescription pills and a bottle of water. When she had convinced him that she was comfortable, he went back to the dock and unloaded everything from the boat.

Jo was dozing lightly when Mike, trying to be quiet, carefully sat on one end of the porch swing, easing himself under her legs. She felt him lay something cool on her swollen ankle. *This feels so wonderful, I could stay like this forever.*

"Well, you stay like this just as long as you want, darlin'. If my legs cramp, I'll live with it."

She didn't realize she had given voice to her thoughts and immediately felt the blush creeping around her neck again. Mike continued, "I took the liberty of telling your staff you were down here and that we'll deal with our own supper." She knew she should have scolded him for taking liberties but it felt good to be pampered just a little.

"Maybe my forever could last at least until suppertime."

They continued to swing in silence for about half an hour while he lightly stroked her foot and ankle. She wasn't sure if it was his magic touch or the medication, but before long she was pain free.

Jo guessed the circulation in his legs must be slowing and started to sit up.

***

He felt a slight twinge of regret when she removed herself from his lap. Mike couldn't ever remember being so content. Even at his horse ranch he could never relax completely. He continually suffered from a compulsion to be doing something, finding something, always on the move. For once, following his instincts had paid off. On this lake in a remote northern wilderness, he had found total relaxation with this beautiful little woman. He hoped it wasn't too soon after her husband's death for her to welcome the friendship of another man. He didn't expect anything more than friendship right now. He wasn't sure how far he was prepared to let his own feelings develop. He was certain he wanted to know her better, acutely aware that he had only one week to win her friendship, if not her affection.

Jo sat up and stretched her arms straight over her head. She arched her back and lowered her hands to massage her lower back with a kneading action. "I think I should walk around and stretch my legs. My whole body is stiffening."

Mike reached under the swing and handed her the crutches he had brought with her medication. After watching her hobble across the deck a couple of times, Mike reminded her about the hot tub located on the little deck on the other side of his bedroom. He explained that whenever he and his teammates had a muscle injury, the trainer usually ordered them into the whirlpool in the locker room.

Jo remembered she was still wearing shorts underneath her

jogging pants. A soak in the hot tub couldn't hurt and certainly might do some good. Mike turned the heater on and gave her some towels. She wandered through his bedroom and out the back door. Once the temperature of the water was correct, he again helped her slide out of her track pants and lifted her easily into the hot tub. He went inside and returned, dressed in swim trunks, and carrying two soft drinks. He handed her one then eased himself into the water, directly opposite her. As they drank their sodas, Jo once again realized how comfortable it was to share quiet moments with this man. It wasn't necessary to talk. It seemed enough merely to be together. She felt his eyes on her almost constantly, but instead of making her uneasy, it comforted her. Whenever she glanced at him he would wink or smile. After they finished their drinks Mike stood, stating time was up. "I don't want you getting weak in the knees and falling all over me again."

He lifted her from the water and wrapped a bath sheet around her. She experienced a wonderful feeling of being totally dependent on someone and loving every minute of it. When she was completely dry and her wet clothes were removed, Mike offered her one of his long-sleeved sweatshirts to wear with her jogging pants. He seemed reluctant to say goodnight just yet.

***

At sixty-six, he hadn't held much hope of experiencing the warm and fuzzy emotions he was feeling at the moment. He had always seen his future as settling down on the ranch, doing the odd bit of travelling, and just enjoying leisure time with Shannon and his grandchildren.

He wondered what Jo's plans were for her golden years. He really couldn't see her retiring anytime soon. She was too vital, too active and he thought, somewhat reluctantly, too young.

She couldn't be more than fifty-five and here he was practically an old man — a pensioner. He knew he had looked after himself, keeping trim and physically fit. Looking at her, he wondered what her physical needs might be. It had been quite a while since he'd taken a woman to bed. Would he still be able to? Would he have the opportunity to find out? *Get your mind out of the gutter oldtimer and start thinking about supper.*

***

Jo had been watching him, wondering what had him so deep in thought. She realized this fishing furlough wasn't going the way he had probably planned it to go. She had thoroughly enjoyed the quiet morning of fishing and sincerely hoped he had too. When he had requested at the time of his reservation that she guide for him, she knew he had not anticipated playing nursemaid to an old woman whose middle name should be Calamity. He probably longed for male companionship and someone to swear and laugh with when the "big one" got away. She hoped he didn't think she was clinging and taking advantage of him. Maybe she would be selfish and enjoy dinner with him tonight and then, uncharacteristically, feign ankle pain tomorrow and insist on being left alone. Then he'd be forced to utilize one of the regular guides and hopefully have a great day.

After changing clothes, she was pleased when he began heating the barbecue. Mike admitted his plans included stealing a couple of steaks from the kitchen as well as a couple of potatoes. Jo laughed and whispered, "You might just as well do a complete job and swipe some salad fixings, too."

With that, he disappeared in the direction of the main lodge and left her to study the cloud formations and speculate on what kind of sunset they might enjoy that evening.

"You cook a mean steak, Mike!"

"I raise my own beef so I know how to appreciate a good cut of meat."

"Well, cowboy, keep this up and Cook may never touch the grill again."

He turned, started to speak, and apparently thought better of it. She wondered if he was hesitant about telling her he might not be here long enough to do any more cooking. A melancholy swept over her as she realized this man she was so comfortable with would soon be leaving. Jo decided not to let her feelings throw a damper on the rest of the evening. Instead she began clearing the dishes and stacking them in the sink for washing.

"Uh, uh, uh. You're not doing those dishes, Jo. You are my guest this evening and it would be extremely bad manners on my part to allow you to clean this up." Wrapping his arm around her shoulder, he led her back to the porch swing. "Now, let's just get comfortable and wait for the sunset." Once she was settled, he went inside to make coffee. It wasn't long before he returned carrying a tray with coffee, cookies from the fruit basket, and her jacket. He hoped he'd covered all bases and there would be no interruptions once he had her firmly ensconced in his arms. Mike positioned her so that she was leaning across him with her head resting on his arm and her legs over the other armrest. When she felt him slide his muscled arm around her shoulder, she decided she liked this. She liked it very much.

They sipped their coffee while she asked him about his ranch. She wondered if they still carried out roundups and whether he had real cowboys working for him. She said she had never visited a ranch and cringed when he suggested she come to see his. Realizing it must have sounded like she was pushing for an invitation, she changed the subject.

"I don't believe the sky will be quite as spectacular as last evening. There aren't as many clouds lingering tonight."

***

Mike believed, colour or not, this was the most spectacular sunset he had ever experienced. It was a warm spring evening after a day of great fishing. He was watching the sun go down over a scenic bay while sitting on a porch swing and drinking coffee with a beautiful woman in his arms. What could be more perfect?

Jo was right, however. After the brilliance of the night before, this evening was great, but not quite as colourful. Soon they heard the lonesome cry of a loon carried forlornly across the water. Quite overcome, Mike leaned down and placed his lips on her forehead. Words were inadequate. His kiss spoke for him. This was going to be a short week. An extremely short week.

Jo nestled deeper into his arms. Mike held her closer, thinking she was finding the chilly evening air uncomfortable. Thoughts of other ways of warming her were surfacing when he heard someone walking down the gravel path. Mike felt like a schoolboy thwarted by the return of his girlfriend's parents just when he was about to cop a feel.

***

It was Barney, apologizing profusely for intruding. Another group of guests had experienced motor problems with their boat. Barney wondered if they could borrow Mr. Talbot's boat if they brought it back before noon the next day. Mike readily agreed saying he wouldn't be going anywhere early.

Forgetting her resolve to be indisposed the next day, Jo suggested she could give Mike a guided tour of the surrounding area in her vehicle the next morning. He accepted her invitation wholeheartedly.

By this time, it had grown quite dark and she was feeling tired. After commenting she should return to her own place, Mike handed her the crutches, picked her up once more, and started up the path. The trail had somewhat of an incline but it posed no problem for him. Again she marvelled at his fantastic shape and silently hoped he didn't notice her soft flab. Try as she might, she could never motivate herself to work out although she knew that at her age, exercise was needed to keep muscle tone.

He lowered her to her feet when they arrived at her apartment and waited while she unlocked her door. Always a gentleman, he then opened it for her and switched on the inside lights. As she hopped inside, she thanked him for lunch, dinner, and the much-appreciated therapy in his hot tub. He brought one of her hands to his mouth and kissed the inside of her palm, those gorgeous blue eyes lingering on hers. She thought she was going to faint. The effect couldn't have been more dizzying if he had kissed her on the mouth. Anticipation was followed by disappointment once again, though, when he turned and walked silently out the door.

SEVEN

Jo slept fitfully that night. Finally, in the predawn hush, that time when all the night creatures are quietly tucked away in the shadows and morning is nothing more than a timid promise, she peeked through her window toward the honeymoon cottage.

What in the world was she getting herself into? At first, she thought Mike was just being overly friendly out of sympathy for her. Maybe he thought himself somehow responsible for her accident. However, the look in his eyes when he had kissed her palm the night before was anything but sympathetic. What were his intentions? How could she be sure? He doubtless was accustomed to having any woman he wanted. Possibly this hand kissing was just a ploy he used. In fact, now that she really thought about it, the possibility became more of a probability. Not being experienced with men and games, Jo felt frustration at her vulnerability. Perhaps she should keep her distance. That would be the best plan. After all, he had travelled all the way up to relax and fish before he faced the football season, hadn't he? Well, no more games. She would see to it that he got exactly what he wanted — solitude.

She had been wrong in offering to take him through the country-side today. Now he was obliged to travel around with her for half the day. Maybe it wasn't too late. She could still play invalid. If she didn't, he certainly wouldn't be going home regaling his buddies with stories about the great fishing. Somehow she had to correct this, to arrange for one of the guides to take him out. Even if he were stuck with her for one more monotonous day, she'd be well enough by then to return to work and allow him the opportunity to enjoy his fishing. Guilt free.

***

When Mike awakened before sunrise, he couldn't resist peeking up toward the lodge. Through the sparse spring foliage, he could see a light burning inside Jo's apartment. Was her ankle keeping her awake? He shouldn't have kept her out all day. She should have been sitting comfortably at home with a pillow under her foot, changing the hot and cold packs regularly. What a selfish bastard he was. He had insisted on having her for a fishing guide, giving no thought to her injured ankle. Now she was offering to give him an escorted tour today just so he wouldn't be bored. As much as he desperately wanted to be with her, he knew in his heart it would be better if she stayed off her foot. He had brought some background information on football teams with him to study. He could catch up on homework today. What better way to work than sitting outside on a porch swing enjoying a pitcher of iced tea, watching the boats go by?

That's exactly what he'd do. It would be damned hard knowing she was resting just a few hundred feet up the path, but that poor little woman didn't need him underfoot another day.

I'll arrange to have my meals brought to my cabin today and have the staff pass along a message thanking Jo for her kind offer. I'll use the excuse of not having a boat to spend the day getting some work done. He didn't trust himself to talk to her directly; it might weaken his resolve.

When Mike reached for the water to make coffee a short time later, he noticed Jo's pain killers sitting on the counter where he had left them yesterday afternoon. No wonder her light was on in the middle of the night. She'd probably been up all night suffering terrible pain with no meds. He decided it wasn't too early to sneak up to the lodge, the kitchen staff would already be on duty. He quickly wrote Jo a note and marched up the path to the lodge. He spoke with Cook about his meals for the day and asked if someone could give the note and the medicine to Mrs. Henderson later. He then trudged back to his cabin and glumly sorted through his reading and video material.

***

Jo managed to doze a bit in the chair after she'd put some heat on her ankle. She hoped her excuse for not spending time with Mike today wouldn't make her sound like a wimp. She decided to give Molly a note for him when she brought her breakfast. Then either of the women could deliver it to Mike's cabin.

After soaking in a warm bath for twenty minutes, she pulled on a pair of baggy track pants and a loose pullover then made herself comfortable on the sofa. It wasn't long before Molly knocked on the door and brought Jo's breakfast tray in. Jo gave her the note for Mike and told her she'd return her own tray to the kitchen later. She explained she hadn't slept well and perhaps had overdone it the day before. Molly agreed with her that a day off her feet probably was the best medicine. She would ask Diane to deliver the note with Mike's breakfast.

When Jo unfolded the newspaper on her tray, she was surprised to see her bottle of Tylenol beside her juice glass. Then she noticed an envelope with her name on it tucked under her flatware. After reading Mike's note, she had difficulty eating her breakfast. How foolish she had been. He was polite. She'd give him that. He really was a gentleman, saying he realized he had taken advantage of her yesterday, forcing his company on her when she should have been resting. He had noticed her light on earlier and remembered he had forgotten to give her back her pain medicine.

Promising to leave her alone to rest for the whole day, he made some excuse about having work to do and that he'd probably talk to her tomorrow. What did "probably" mean? Did that mean he may *not* talk to her tomorrow? Well, she would ask Barney to have someone take him fishing this evening — maybe down to the far end of the lake where he might catch a trophy fish. Or see a mermaid. Or the Loch Ness monster. Anything that might make an interesting story for his buddies. Babysitting the aging lodge owner didn't make for repeat business. In the meantime, she would stay out of his way and maybe he would come to realize he didn't have to entertain her for the balance of his vacation.

She picked at her breakfast while attempting to concentrate on the news stories in the morning paper. After reading for the fourth time about the protest to stop the garbage movement from the Toronto area, she finally decided it was useless. She kept thinking about those soft lips that had so warmly caressed the palm of her hand. If he was bored with her company why did he look at her so intently when she talked, and why did he keep asking her questions about herself? And why, oh why, did he insist on sending her into such a tailspin with those little brushes of his lips?

She turned the television on and tried, unsuccessfully, to concentrate on one of the morning shows. Not used to being idle, she limped out to the front desk to see if anyone had picked up the mail. Delighted to see her basket full, she returned to her sofa to sort through it.

Around eleven o'clock, experiencing cabin fever, she brewed a fresh pot of coffee and took some of her paperwork outside to the deck. It was the sunniest day yet, promising to reach the high 20s by mid-afternoon. She went inside and changed into a pair of shorts and unwrapped her ankle to get some sun on her legs. Setting her work aside and with her coffee mug on a nearby table, she stretched out on a chaise and closed her eyes.

***

Mike spent the better part of the morning watching videotapes. The research department had been very good about supplying him with statistics; however, he could offer much more "colour" if he knew the style and personality of a coach or a player. Finally feeling the need for fresh air, he wandered out onto the deck and was surprised to see how much the temperature had risen. He pulled off his t-shirt and slowly walked bare chested around the porch to the shaded side. About to sit down, he noticed a slight movement through the trees. He peered toward Jo's place where he could see her lying on a chaise on her deck. He watched her for a while, feeling like a real creep for having selfishly tired her out yesterday. He hoped he hadn't blown it — that she'd be strong enough to share lunch or an iced tea tomorrow.

***

From where Jo lay, she could make out the frame of Mike's cottage and part of his porch through the sparse foliage. Dozing off and on, she noticed him leaning against the railing. He was drinking something and he appeared to be looking right at her. He stayed there for a moment, then shook his head and walked back out of sight.

He must be bored silly. A man as healthy and vital as he is probably wants companions who are just as physically fit. I must appear so damned helpless to him. He's been patient while carrying me, cooking for me, fetching my medication, dressing me, undressing me. It's a wonder he didn't put my pyjamas on and tuck me into bed for goodness sake. What an impression he must have of me! Tomorrow I will try to walk normally.

In frustration she started to rise, lost her balance and knocked over a ladder which had been left leaning against the deck. It hit the ground with a resounding crash just as she landed squarely on her bottom between the table and the chaise.

Mike, who had been pacing the porch, walked around the corner in time to hear the crash. He immediately looked in the direction of the sound and saw Jo trying to raise herself from the floor of the deck. He hurdled his own porch railing and went racing up the path, reaching her just as she pulled herself to her knees. Sliding his hands under her arms he lifted her until her face was even with his. "Are you all right?" he asked with real concern.

"What are you doing here?"

"Dammit, Jo. I heard a crash and thought you'd fallen down the stairs with your crutches."

"No. I just tried to get up too fast and lost my balance. That damn ladder shouldn't have been there. When it fell, it startled me and I lost my footing."

With that, he moved one arm under her legs and settled her back down on the chaise. "Oh, Jo, I thought for sure you were seriously injured." He was stroking her temple and cheek with one hand as he knelt beside her. "Can I get you anything?"

"No you can't get me anything. I'm perfectly capable of taking care of myself. I'm not an invalid you know. Just … just … Oh, just go back to your cabin, Mike, and stop coddling me!"

Absolutely astounded, Mike stood up and looked at her. He opened his mouth to speak but nothing came out. He backed away, turned and hastened down the stairs. When he was out of sight, Jo covered her face with her hands. She immediately wanted to call him back and beg him to put his arms around her again. What had possessed her to snap at him like that?

She wanted to hike up to Twin Pine Lookout with him. She wanted to take a picnic lunch to Table Island and enjoy the soft breezes wafting through the pines. She wanted to portage with him into Second Lake and take the canoe that was stowed there to the weed bed where there were really big northern pike. All these things she wanted to do with him. Instead, she was stuck on a chaise with him asking if he could get her anything.

***

Mike walked quickly to his cabin and went inside. *What the hell just happened?* He knew she wasn't feeling well, but she had scared the devil out of him. All he had intended was to make sure she was OK. Christ, she must have thought he was sitting here watching her and just waiting for an opportunity to pounce. *What a pathetic fool you are, Mike Talbot! Well, you might as well pack your bags and leave right now because there's no way you're going to get back in that little lady's good graces!*

He sat for the balance of the afternoon trying to work but his mind kept going back over the events of the morning. There must be something he could do to redeem himself, but what? He couldn't even send her flowers. He felt totally helpless once again. Maybe if he just left her alone for the rest of the day, she might be more receptive to an apology in the morning.

Mike noticed Barney bringing his boat back to the dock. He waved from the doorway and the little guy came over and asked Mike if he wanted to try some evening fishing. Mike's first thought was to refuse, but maybe this would work out. If he were out on the lake, he would be totally out of her hair. She could fall from her roof right onto his doorstep and he wouldn't be there to get in her face.

He and Barney made plans to go out right after Mike finished his dinner. That would give Barney time to get all the gas cans filled for the morning and to take a run to the dump with the garbage.

Right on time, as Mike was cleaning up after his dinner, Barney came down the hill with a minnow bucket and his own fishing rod. The two men decided to go across to the far end of the lake where, according to Barney, evening fishing sometimes produced some pretty big ones.

***

Jo went inside after her episode with Mike and put a fresh cold pack on her ankle. "Please," she prayed, "please, let it be much better tomorrow."

She stretched out on the sofa again and tried to answer some of the mail but she just couldn't concentrate. Why couldn't she keep her mouth shut when she was embarrassed instead of always going on the attack? She wanted Mike to see her independence, not her incapacity. "Can I get you anything?" she said out loud in mocking tones. "Yes, my cane, my slippers, my pills and my false teeth from the glass beside my bed!"

She knew she owed him an apology but was feeling too ashamed to face him right now. Maybe after dinner she would work her way down to his cabin to try to undo the damage. What could she possibly say to him? "I'm sorry" didn't seem adequate. She decided to watch a movie. Maybe she could lose herself in something light. She stretched her leg across the ottoman and within minutes she dozed off. It was Molly who woke her when she came in with dinner. "Your friend Barb called earlier, but I told her you were resting so she's going to call back this evening."

"Did you mention my ankle to her?"

"No, Mrs. H. I know you don't like us telling anybody anything."

"Thanks, Molly. I don't want to worry her. The next thing you know, she'll be arriving and fussing over me, too."

"Is your ankle feeling any better? Now that you've had a chance to rest it a little?"

"Yes, thank you. I think tomorrow I might be able to do a little work. I'm going crazy sitting around."

"Maybe you and Mr. Talbot can get fishing again. He seems like a nice gentleman, hard working even on vacation. He might need a break, too."

"He's reluctant to mix with the other male guests in case anyone recognizes him. He just wants some down time before reporting for work. It would be wonderful if he could catch a ten-pounder."

Jo ate her dinner and remembered the expression, "A hero faces death but once, a coward a thousand times." She squared her shoulders and decided it was time to face the foe. After running the brush through her hair and changing into a pair of jeans, she managed to get both shoes onto her feet. Shoes would give her a little more traction she hoped. She was determined not to fall, or even give the perception of falling. The slope was more gradual from the front door of the office, which gave her more confidence about remaining firmly planted on both feet. The driveway was designed to wind gradually around, giving vehicles better leverage and traction pulling the boats out of the water. Mike's cabin was at the very end of the driveway, hidden behind a stand of pines. A sign marked PRIVATE PROPERTY hung from one of the trees so guests would assume it was part of the owners' quarters and not venture beyond that point. Jo regained some of her confidence when she reached the foot of the driveway without losing her balance. She followed the path beyond the sign and around the trees, carefully placing her crutches with each step. Calling out Mike's name she ventured up the front steps and onto the porch. The inside door was closed so she knocked, and knocked again. When there was no answer, Jo followed the porch around the side of the building and leaned over to look out back — no sign of him there, either. Wandering once again around the beach side, she noticed the dock was boat-free. She was left wondering whether Mike was out fishing, or whether Barney hadn't brought it back yet. Feeling both deflated and relieved at the same time, she decided she would just have to leave things till morning.

Slowly, she made her way back up the hill and as she opened the door to her quarters, she heard her phone ringing.

"What's this about taking naps in the middle of the day? You? The world must be coming to an end."

"Nothing like that. I just didn't sleep well last night and things were all under control so I snuck a nap. It's no big deal."

"Honey, when you don't sleep well, there's something wrong. What's up?"

"Nothing's up. If you must know, I slipped and twisted my ankle a couple of days ago and I guess I overworked it yesterday. It's fine now. In fact, I just walked back up from the beach and came in the door as the phone rang."

"Are you sure it's nothing more?"

"Honest. Now, how are things with you? Are you just calling to say hi?"

"Well, not exactly. I know it's a bit premature for you to be making vacation plans for next winter, but a friend of mine has offered me her condo in Florida for the whole month of January. Are you interested?"

"Oh, Barb, that sounds divine, but I can't make plans until the calendar of shows comes out later in the summer."

"That's what I was afraid of. I have to let her know very soon. If I don't reserve it she has a waiting list of friends."

"Well you go right ahead and accept it. Don't let my schedule stop you from going."

"But if the shows are scheduled for that time, I won't be able to go either. You'll need my expert assistance."

"Darling, please don't be hurt, but I've decided Barney might be more helpful than you. I really felt quite useless a couple of times on the road last winter. I guess I'm just getting too old for it and a man can accomplish so much more without assistance. You saw how I made a complete fool of myself a couple of times."

"How about that! Thrown over for a little Irishman. I'll live with it only if you promise you'll come if you're free."

"Promise."

"I'll hold you to it."

After catching up on gossip, Jo was relieved to hang up without Barb pressing her about the twisted ankle.

It would be great to relax in sunny Florida for a while. She had really missed her winter vacation last year, especially after she and Stu had made a practice of going south every January.

Flicking channels she realized there was nothing on TV but reruns. Feeling out of sorts, she went out into the lobby and worked her way through the videos on the shelf. Finding a recent Kevin Spacey movie, Jo went back to her apartment, put some popcorn in the microwave then grabbed a can of ginger ale from the refrigerator. Goodness, this invalid business was for the birds. Settling into her chair with popcorn and a soft drink, she was determined to enjoy this movie whether she liked it or not. Halfway through it, she glanced out the window to see that the sun was setting. Thinking about last night and the night before, she suddenly felt forlorn. Shutting the movie off, she wandered onto the deck and reclined in a chair, staring at the reddening sky.

***

Barney pulled the boat up and Mike slipped the bow rope over the dock cleat, then he jumped out and grabbed the stern rope from Barney. Once the boat was secure, Barney offered to take the minnows and gear up to the shed.

"Thanks for a really great evening, Barney. I'm glad I brought my camera along. My buddy wouldn't believe my fish stories without pictures to back them up."

When Mike carried his tackle to his cabin, he noticed holes in the sand near the beach and in the dirt around his steps. On closer inspection, he realized they were the marks made by Jo's crutches. Is it possible she had walked down here? He followed the marks and saw they came from the path on the opposite side of his cabin, continuing up the driveway.

He and Barney had caught some great fish, but he was quite disappointed at the thought of missing Jo, if she had indeed been down.

He leaned his fishing rod against the building and stowed the lifejacket in a little wooden box on the porch. He unlocked his door and went inside. After removing his fishy-smelling clothes, he stepped into the shower. When he wandered back outside he was blown away once again by the magnificent sky and wished he could turn the clock back to the previous evening. He sat for a moment but realized that watching this scene unfold only made him lonelier. He decided to continue working and to pick up some soft drinks from the office vending machine to enjoy while he watched a game on video. The path that meandered by the back of Jo's was the shortest route. He was coming up the path, glancing over his shoulder at the setting sun from the higher angle, when he heard his name called.

"Pardon me? Is someone talking to me?"

"Yes, Mike. I said I had just wished for a tall handsome man with whom to watch the sunset and like magic you appeared."

He couldn't believe his ears. "Were you down by my cabin earlier?"

"I came down to apologize for my behaviour this morning. It took me all day to build up my courage but when I arrived on your doorstep, you weren't home. I didn't know whether to be relieved or disappointed."

"What won out?"

"Disappointment."

"Why?"

"Because I knew I had to face you sooner or later and I didn't want to go to bed with this between us."

"I don't understand why you feel the need to apologize. It was I who invaded your privacy after you made it abundantly clear you weren't feeling well and wanted to be left alone."

"Mike, you've treated me with nothing but kindness and I repaid it by shrieking at you when you were only trying to help."

"Kindness isn't what I'm feeling."

"I don't blame you after the horrid way I treated you. I've ruined your vacation and acted like an inconsiderate old witch."

"How have you ruined my vacation?"

"By making you play the nursemaid, hover over me, and tend to me when you would rather be out enjoying the fishing in the great outdoors."

"And who told you I would rather be out fishing?"

"Mike. That's the reason you came all the way to Canada. It's not your fault that I was knocked off my feet at the airport. That accident was exactly that, an accident. As much as I enjoy the attention of a great-looking guy and appreciate being carried around in strong arms, it's embarrassing. Especially when I *can* take care of myself. When I knocked that ladder over this morning it just added to my mortification when you came and picked me up off the floor. So I took my humiliation out on you. I am so sorry for losing my temper."

"Jo, it looks like we started off on the wrong foot — no pun intended." He grinned as he glanced down at her tensor-bandaged ankle. "I'd like us to start all over again or at least turn the clock back to last night. We have another beautiful sunset tonight and I don't want to watch it alone, either. I was just heading up to get some soft drinks. Can I get you anything? Oops, sorry. Forget I asked."

Laughing, she told him to go inside and grab one from her refrigerator.

***

Mike noticed the half-eaten popcorn and the video case by her chair and made a mental note to leave as soon as the sun had completely set. He was not going to overstay his welcome. Sunset. Home. Grabbing a soda, he went back outside, pulled a deck chair around beside Jo and eased into it. He wanted the whole cake but was not above settling for whatever crumbs fell his way. If twenty minutes of sunset was his allotment for today, he was already convinced that twenty minutes of heaven was better than a whole evening of lonely hell.

***

Jo knew the cloud conditions had to be just right to achieve anything as spectacular as the sunset a couple of evenings ago, but she was always overcome by the uniqueness of each evening. It was one of

God's glorious wonders that she was given the opportunity to enjoy so many sunsets over the years and never see two exactly the same. She knew without a doubt she would never watch another without thinking about Mike. Glancing at his strong profile, she could see his genuine awe at the unbelievable beauty of the evening sky. She felt the urge to run her fingers along that square jaw, then over those fantastic earlobes, and around to ... *get a grip, girl.* She turned her gaze back to the lake.

***

Mike felt her looking at him and wondered what was going through her mind. She seemed genuine in her apology and invitation to sit. Of course he was a paying guest and as a good hostess she must feel obliged to make him feel comfortable whether he was right or wrong. Did she really think he was handsome? A great looking guy was what she had said. Well, that was certainly better than some things she might have called him — another crumb falling his way.

***

They sat in silence, each wanting to make physical contact with the other, both afraid of ruining the mood. When the bright reds had faded to pale pinks and then soft greys, Mike stood up and thanked her for the soft drink and the company. He hesitated as if wanting to offer her assistance, then very slowly extended his hand. She took it willingly, not wanting to offend him further. He slid his hand under her elbow then moved his other arm behind her back guiding her smoothly to her feet. Commenting that she appeared to be standing on her foot better, he continued with his observation that the day's rest seemed to be what she had needed. She raised her hand to his chest, commenting that it appeared to have done wonders for her mood as well. She leaned into him, lifted her face somewhat shyly, and brushed her lips lightly against his. Enjoying the sensation, she returned for another taste and lingered a little longer, parting her lips slightly. Then, embarrassed by her own boldness, she turned and reached for the door.

***

Once inside, she stood trembling. She couldn't believe she had actually done that. Outside of a couple of unsatisfactory teenage episodes in the back seat of a boyfriend's car, Stu was the only man she had ever known sexually. He had been an excellent lover, so she had never been physically attracted to another man. Until now. *This has to stop. You are fifty-nine years old. This man is here one week, gone the next. He lives in a different world and comes into contact with younger, more beautiful women every day. Smarten up before you make a complete fool of yourself, Jo Henderson!*

***

Mike stood on her deck for a few seconds, not believing the incredibly big crumb he had just been thrown. She had seemed almost bashful in the way she moved away from him after that lingering kiss. Could that be it? Could it just be that she's extremely shy, or nervous? Damn. He needed more from this woman than just these goodnight kisses. He wanted the whole freakin' cake.

EIGHT

The next morning when Jo stepped on her bad foot, the slight discomfort immediately reminded her to take it slowly. However, she was surprised at how much stronger it felt. *I guess the doctor does know what he's talking about.*

She quickly showered then dressed in rust-coloured cotton pants and a sleeveless button-front blouse a shade lighter. She gave a little more attention than usual to her makeup application. Happy she could slide both feet into shoes finally, she grabbed her crutches "just in case" and moved off toward the main dining room.

Jo noticed more than the usual number of people eating inside as she made her way through the room, greeting everyone as she passed. On weekdays, most guests were the extended-stay variety who tended to bring a week's supply of groceries which they prepared and ate in their own cabins. The weekend crowd usually was enjoying leisure getaways and preferred eating in the dining room. Even though no one appeared to be waiting unduly for their meal, she thought she had better check the staff schedule and make sure all areas were adequately covered. Most of her cleaning staff could help serve in a pinch but she didn't want the rooms neglected either. She grabbed a cereal bowl and a box of cold cereal and hobbled through the swinging doors into the kitchen.

"Well, look who's back among the living." Cook took the bowl from her and broke open the cereal. He motioned her over to the table in the corner where the staff always enjoyed their meal breaks. While he poured milk into her bowl, Jo grabbed a spoon and a juice glass. Cook set her breakfast on the table and went to get the orange juice for her. After questioning her on the progress of her ankle, he commented that her Mr. Talbot should be arriving momentarily for his breakfast as well. She wondered if she ate quickly enough whether she could be finished before he arrived. Still feeling foolish about her boldness the night before, she decided she needed more time before facing him again.

"Good morning, Mrs. Henderson."

Too late.

"Don't you look gorgeous today? How's your ankle?"

"Good morning, Mr. Talbot. My ankle is quite a bit better today thank you. I'm finally able to wear both shoes with no problem."

"Great! Maybe in a day or two we'll be able to take that tour you promised me. Do you prefer to eat alone or can I join you?"

"Please sit down. It's too bad you're not comfortable in the dining room, it has so much more to offer in the way of ambience."

"I don't know this for a fact, but I've noticed in some movies that, in the great Italian restaurants, you are nobody, absolutely *nobody*, until you are invited to eat with the owner in the kitchen. One knows one has truly arrived when welcomed into the hallowed space of the kitchen. Are you going to take that honour away from me merely by offering a little ambience?"

"Well, when you put it that way, I should think not. Cook, please bring this gentleman whatever he wants, after all — he has arrived!" Beckoning the chef to her side, she leaned to him and in a mock whisper said, "Don't embarrass him by mentioning this is not an Italian restaurant. The poor man seems confused."

A few minutes later, Mike had a plate of Canadian back bacon with two eggs over-easy, and two slices of French toast placed in front of him. "When a man can start a day with a breakfast like this and finish it with the most gloriously coloured sky you could ever imagine, how can he possibly fill the in-between?"

"A successful day of fishing perhaps?"

"Maybe. But, I have it on good authority," he leaned over and whispered, "I'm good friends with the owner here you see," sitting upright he continued, "that one only needs to fish for a few hours out of the day to catch his share of fish. The rest of the day can be passed doing other enjoyable things."

"For instance?"

"For instance — picnicking, going sightseeing, or taking garbage to the dump."

Jo started to choke on a mouthful of juice at the last suggestion. Then, she couldn't stop the tears, she was laughing so hard.

"Laugh if you must, but things experienced in the company of a beautiful woman are all moments to be treasured."

"Who in the world even suggested taking garbage to the dump?"

"I overheard two young boys wishing they knew where the dump is. Apparently, when they used to visit their uncle's camp, the best part of the day was when they were driven to the dump to see the bears."

"So you want to go to the dump to spot a bear?"

"It would be the highlight of my visit, ma'am."

"Then the dump it shall be. Barney and the boys will gladly let us take over that duty any day of your choosing."

"With you just getting back on your feet, I'm sure you have a million things to catch up with, so you let me know when it's convenient. I'll just be hanging around waiting for you to crook your finger."

"Well, I haven't done any work for several days so I don't even know what's waiting for me. I'll check around and let you know shortly. I understand there may be some rain moving in. We may want to do our sightseeing and dump-visiting early this afternoon."

"You know where to find me."

"I can ask Barney to have a dock boy take you out fishing for a couple of hours, if you like."

"Thanks, but I, too, have things to do and for some reason I'm inspired today. I'd better take advantage of that and stick with the paperwork."

With that, Jo left to check with the cleaning staff to see if they required anything. She was pleasantly surprised to see that everything was running smoothly. The cabins and rooms were being cleaned, the laundry was sorted and being washed and the dock area was running like clockwork. Jo wandered around back to the greenhouse to check on her bedding-out plants. She wouldn't be able to plant most until after the next new moon when chances of a late frost were past. That was about a week or so away. She trimmed the multicoloured tulips in the beds under the windows, and decided the ground was warm enough to plant a few of the hardier flowers. She saw the painter's van coming down the driveway and went to talk to him about stowing the ladder safely away when not in use.

By the time she had completed her rounds, it was almost lunchtime. She was beginning to feel tenderness in her ankle so decided to heed the warning by preparing a sandwich for herself and taking it with her into her apartment. She left instructions with Cook that if Mr. Talbot came in for lunch, she wanted to chat with him before he returned to his cabin.

She stretched out on the sofa, placed an ice pack on her ankle and turned on the midday news. Before long there was a knock on her door.

"Who's there?" she called out.

"The bogeyman," Mike warned.

"Come in. I'm just giving my ankle a rest."

"I was picking up some snacks to take to my cabin. Molly keeps me well-supplied with fruit so I don't need a full meal at lunch time."

"Sit and eat it here if you like. I thought I'd elevate my foot while I ate my sandwich. I don't want to overdo it my first day back on the job."

"Smart woman. Jo, it's great seeing you mobile again. Are you sure you're up to doing anything else today? We can wait until tomorrow if you like."

"One of the thunderstorms we're famous for is supposedly moving into our area tonight. If it's true to form, it will last through most of tomorrow also. Consequently, I will have nothing to do tomorrow but rest. You can probably get plenty of your work accomplished then, too. If I just relax for another half hour or so, I'll be almost as good as new and we can sneak away. The painter tells me he wants to finish before the storm comes. He'll be working around my door and windows for the rest of the afternoon so I'm sure he'll appreciate me making myself scarce."

"I'll finish my lunch and continue with my notes. I'm trying to prepare a couple dinner speeches I'll need next month. The office staff is pretty good about helping with them, but I need facts firmly planted in my head for the question periods that follow. Should I come back in about an hour?"

"Sounds good."

Things seemed to be going OK. Mike didn't appear to consider this an afternoon of babysitting. Even better, he definitely wasn't carrying a grudge about her snapping at him the day before. She mapped out in her mind the sights she would show him today. If all went well, who knows, maybe after a couple of days when the weather improved, they may be able to portage to Second Lake. She would see to it that his vacation was memorable one way or another.

***

Mike couldn't believe the way circumstances had changed. From thinking all was over and he may as well return home, he was getting the grand tour and spending the whole afternoon with Jo. She had to be the most confusing woman he had ever met. He figured the safest way to handle it would be to let her set the mood and hopefully it wouldn't be too difficult to follow along. He wasn't going to tire her out by demanding too much of her time and energy and by all that was holy, he wasn't going to offer to *do* anything for her either. He might be slow but he wasn't stupid, as the saying goes. Right now he would finish up the notes he had been making and hopefully, if the cards fell right, he would be too busy to return to them any time soon.

Trying to concentrate was proving to be impossible. *Get a grip man, you'd think you were going out on your first date instead of going to the garbage dump with your hostess.*

He pictured again how she had looked the first time he saw her.

The fire in those eyes warned she was ready to do battle if he had proven to be uncooperative. He recognized she was a spitfire even while looking so delicate. He speculated she could hold her own with any man, on just about any subject — except football. He had never encountered a woman who piqued his interest like this one. Well, he was determined she would become just as interested in him, even if it killed him.

He willed the hands of the clock around and immediately when the hour was up, he was on Jo's deck, knocking at her door.

"Come in," he heard her call.

"All set? Were you able to rest?"

"I kept my foot elevated for as long as I could. I think I just about have this thing licked. Mike, would you mind bringing the *Explorer* around to where the garbage bins are located across the driveway? If you sound the horn, one of the boys will load the bags in the back for us. I'll meet you out front. Barney ran out of time and didn't take the garbage yesterday so he'll be pleased we're taking it today. And I guess you'll have to do the driving. I'll be the navigator."

Once the garbage was stowed, Jo climbed into the passenger seat and they took off down the driveway. The sky was beginning to darken slightly but the rain wasn't supposed to start until evening. She cautioned they had better get rid of the garbage first or they would end up having to drive with the windows open. They turned onto the main highway and travelled about five kilometres before reaching the dump sign. When Mike reached the edge of the dump, he swung the vehicle around and backed it up as far as he dared. He was about to get out when Jo cautioned him to look around first to ensure there were no furry visitors enjoying a smorgasbord. He had forgotten about the possibility of bears, the very reason for the visit to the dump. Looking around, he didn't detect any movement so jumped from the running board and quickly went around to the back of the vehicle. After tossing the last bag into the pit, he strolled around to the passenger side, opened the door, and took Jo completely off guard with a warm kiss planted firmly on her lips. He closed the door and strode back around to the driver's side and climbed in.

"May I ask what that was all about?"

"Well, you see, I've always been somewhat of an opportunist. I probably never, in my whole life, will ever again have the opportunity to kiss a beautiful woman in a garbage dump. So I thought I better take advantage of it. Do you mind?"

Why did he have to ask, and how was she supposed to reply? She tried to skirt the question. "Well, I've always said, 'when opportunity knocks, you better answer.'"

"I'll take that as a 'no, I didn't mind at all.'"

They sat in the vehicle keeping a lookout but when no bears appeared, Mike turned the van around and headed back to the highway where he stopped, waiting for directions. Jo was still thinking about how nice the kiss had felt and didn't notice he had asked which way to turn. When he nudged her, she was embarrassed at having been caught in her own thoughts. She instructed him to turn left and continue on the highway for about another three kilometres. She showed him a dirt road that looked more like a private drive and motioned for him to turn in. She explained it was an old logging road and wound upward into some higher terrain. There, they would enjoy an outstanding view of the surrounding countryside. They rode mostly in silence until Jo asked about the countryside around his ranch in Wyoming. He drew a mental image of how the hills were not as densely treed as in this area, explaining it was more rolling pasture, needed for the cattle.

"But," he continued, "there's a lot of wild game such as deer, some elk, grouse, pheasant, even wild turkeys. I have to confess, I'm an avid outdoors man and enjoy nothing more than riding my horse through the hills, with Sherlock, my yellow Lab."

They executed another turn onto a dirt road that only trucks or jeep-type vehicles would be able to traverse. Finally, it disintegrated into nothing much more than a path. After they stopped and he helped her out of the vehicle, she told him they would have to walk a few hundred yards. He worried about her ankle. Of course, he knew better than to say anything. Taking her hand, he hoped he might keep her from falling on the uneven trail.

The forest was not thick because a good portion of it was new growth from seedlings planted about ten years before by the Ministry of Natural Resources. The cost was borne by the logging companies that harvested the timber in these areas. Mike could hear the sound of rushing water. They came upon a fast-moving creek, still swollen from the spring runoff.

They followed the creek upstream for a short distance, the sound of the water getting louder and louder. Soon he could see a magnificent waterfall ahead of them, the kind one sees in wildlife posters and postcards. It wasn't really high, but with several rocky outcroppings at the crest, the dramatic result was much more picturesque than if it were smooth all the way across. He commented about the possibility of good fishing in the pool at the base of it, and she suggested they could come back another day with rods to try their luck.

"Why don't we sit for a while and listen to the water?" he suggested.

"We can, but the slight climb to the top isn't difficult and the view from the lookout is well worth the small effort."

When he commented on the danger to her ankle, Jo threw him a reassuring look over her shoulder and started up the path. It was a much easier climb than it first looked. As he scrambled over the rise, the view took his breath away.

Before him stretched a panorama of kilometre after kilometre of rugged hills. The colours ranging from dark to light yellow greens were the result of the mix of boreal and deciduous forest. It gave the landscape an almost brooding quality when mixed with the black water of several lakes. Jo gave Mike the binoculars she had taken from the glove compartment and pointed out the landmarks for him. There was an old abandoned forest ranger's tower perched precariously on a distant hill farther upstream. Where the ground rose into shallow cliffs, he could see an eagle's nest tucked into the rocky surface with the eagle clearly in residence. Jo pointed to a large body of dark water, explaining that it was the western end of their own lake. Farther off in the southwestern sky, they could see the approaching storm clouds rolling in, making the water appear even darker. Thunder could now be heard far off in the distance, sounding like bombs dropping in old war movies.

After sitting for a long time listening to Jo tell stories about different incidents at the lodge, Mike reluctantly agreed they probably should be heading back. Listening to her tales, he became well aware of the almost idyllic life she and her husband had experienced over the years. He tried to ignore the pang of envy tugging at him.

The return trek was a little more difficult because they had to go down some of the decline backwards and it was almost impossible to see where they were stepping. When they reached the bottom, Mike grasped Jo's hand firmly in his while they took their time walking back to the vehicle.

"Jo, I can't tell you how much I've enjoyed these couple days with you. The fishing, the sunsets and now the spectacular scenery would be enough to make any man think he's died and gone to heaven. Sharing it with you has made it much more special. When I upset you yesterday, I was just sick at the thought of spending the rest of the week thinking you were angry with me. I was so furious at myself, I was ready to pack up and go home. Do you mind if this grey-haired old guy tells you that you're the best thing to happen to him in a long time?"

Taken totally aback by this declaration, Jo was at a complete loss for words. She certainly was enjoying his company too. Would she be making any commitment, even a small one, by saying so? Was she reading more into this than what was intended? She had never given a thought to being romantically involved with another man — ever. What she and Stu had shared together had been so wonderful, she had never given another relationship even the remotest thought. She could survive forever on her memories. What should she do? What should she say? Certainly, yesterday had been anything but enjoyable thinking he might return home early. Well, maybe it wouldn't hurt to take some pleasure from the company of this handsome man for a few days, and in doing so, add a few more slightly romantic, if silly, memories to her collection.

"Mike, it's been very enjoyable for me as well. I know I won't ever watch another sunset without thinking of you, and maybe feeling just a little bit lonely."

"Just a *little* bit lonely?"

"Well … maybe more than a little." She gasped when she felt his arm slide around her waist, drawing her close. "Well, OK, maybe *very* lonely."

His lips almost cut off her words as well as her breath when he pulled her to him and wrapped his other arm around her. She hesitated for a moment. A very short moment. Then she gradually slid her arms over his shoulders and around his neck His kiss was gentle but warm, softly passionate, if that were possible. He parted his lips slightly but didn't force more from her than she was willing to give. He kissed the tip of her nose, then her forehead, then a light brush on the lips again.

***

Christ, he couldn't believe the warmth of her response. He had kissed her without thinking about the consequences. Too late, he realized his arms were around her. He had expected her to push him away. When he felt her arms around his neck, he knew he was done for. She seemed to hesitate at first, surprised perhaps, but then she was responding to his lips with her own. *You don't toy with this kind of woman, old man*, he told himself. *You just don't kiss her and run, so you better figure out where you're heading before it's too late. Shit, who am I kidding? It's already too late!*

NINE

Mike lifted her carefully into the vehicle and went around to the driver's side without saying a word. He threw the vehicle in reverse and backed up a considerable distance before finding a suitable spot for turning around. Once he had the vehicle headed in the right direction he looked at her, lifted her hand to his mouth and winked at her. She started to blush like a schoolgirl. God, what was happening in his stomach, it couldn't be butterflies now, could it? He felt like a teenager with raging hormones.

***

To keep herself from chattering like an idiot, she opened her CD case and slipped a Johnny Mercer CD into the player. To her embarrassment and Mike's amusement, the first song was "Fools Rush In". Realizing they would have to sit and listen to the words, she hoped he didn't think she had chosen it on purpose. She turned to stare out the window before he could notice her blushing again.

Mike assuaged her unease by asking if she was a Johnny Mercer fan. Her relief at the broken silence was evident and she quickly replied that she was a Kevin Spacey fan and loved the music from one of his movies. When she had learned it was mostly written by Johnny Mercer, she bought one of his CD's and thoroughly enjoyed it. After asking her about the types of movies she enjoyed, he was delighted to find out she had quite an eclectic collection. They agreed if it rained tonight, she would make popcorn and they would enjoy a movie night. He started singing along with the music, and surprisingly, knew the words to most of the songs. He responded by saying, considering his age, it shouldn't surprise her, as most of the music was his vintage. It was on the tip of her tongue to ask exactly the year of his vintage but thought better of it.

Too soon, they were back at the lodge, where she knew she had some mail to take care of before dinner to ensure it would get posted tomorrow. Besides, she really didn't want Mike to know that the hike up and down the falls had taken its toll on her ankle. A quick glance at the slight swelling above her shoe indicated the throbbing wasn't the only symptom.

***

Being a patient and wise man, he decided he would let her make the final decision about sharing dinner and a movie. As he started down the path toward his cabin, she remarked she was going to grab a quick bite and put her foot up for a while, but reminded him they had a movie date. A bit disappointed that he would be eating alone, he at least knew the crumbs falling his way were getting bigger and bigger, and looking more like a cake with each passing hour.

He wandered down by the water's edge where he removed his shoes. A few steps into the cold water confirmed there definitely would be no swimming. He had thought because of the way the days had warmed perhaps it might be possible, but he remembered Barney telling him that the ice didn't go out of the lake most years until the first or even sometimes the second week in May. The clouds were getting quite dark now and the drum roll of thunder was not that far off in the distance.

Feeling rather listless, he went inside and put another football video in the VCR. It wasn't long before he realized he wasn't able to concentrate enough to work effectively. His mind kept wandering to how a certain slender little body had felt when held close to his. She was so small and delicate and yet he knew how strong spirited she was. He thought about spending the evening with her watching movies and looked at his watch.

What would she be expecting? What if she wanted, needed, more than he could give? Who the hell was he trying to kid? He knew he could never satisfy her, not totally. His last few experiences he'd found that getting the old motor started wasn't a problem, but keeping it running was. He might only end up embarrassing her and himself. Well, maybe she wasn't even ready for sex yet. Maybe it was too soon after her husband's death. Besides he had an image to maintain. A number of women still told him he was really sexy looking, although lately they seemed to add or prefix it with "for someone your age." He'd rather she think him a man of character and restraint, rather than run the risk of finding out he may be a sexual dud. He shook his head. *Well hell, I'll cross that bridge when I come to it. In the meantime, she sure felt good in my arms, and she wasn't a bad kisser to boot.* He smiled. *And who knows, maybe she's just the right spark to keep my fire going.*

***

Cook had a plate of veal medallions and roasted baby potatoes ready for him soon after he made his presence known in the kitchen. Deep-dish apple pie with fresh whipped cream and hot coffee finished the meal to perfection. Mike looked at his watch again and saw it wasn't even seven o'clock. As eager as he was to knock on Jo's door, he knew she probably wasn't yet ready for him. He went for a short walk down the road. He was surprised to see a number of driveways and realized the cottages must be well-hidden from the lake as he hadn't spotted them from the boat. Most of the owners, he surmised, probably didn't come out until the water warmed up a bit. After walking for the better part of an hour, he decided it was time to go visiting. When Mike reached her deck, he noticed the inside door was open and called her name through the screen.

"Come right in, Mike."

He sauntered through the door with an armful of pussy willows, and grinning like a schoolboy. As he moved closer to the sofa, he noticed the cold compress on her ankle, the swelling, and the discomfort on her face. Not wanting to make a fuss he asked, "Does this mean doing the jitterbug is out of the question?"

"How are you at hand-jiving?"

"Not bad, but I much prefer holding hands while watching movies with a beautiful woman."

"Well, too bad for you. I'm afraid you're stuck with one cranky old lady."

"Oh? I thought I was spending the evening with you."

"You're smooth, Mike Talbot. The movies are out on a shelf in the main lobby. Oh, sorry. I keep forgetting about your celebrity status. I'll grab a couple for us."

"It's OK, I'll get them."

"No, I would hate for someone to recognize you out there. I'll go."

He sat on the edge of the sofa and put a restraining hand on her shoulder. "You know if there's anything I hate, it's an argumentative woman." He kissed her forehead and went through the door leading into the lodge. In a few minutes, he was back with *Message in a Bottle* and *Murder at 1600.*

"And I didn't even tell you which ones I haven't seen."

"Didn't I tell you I'm psychic?"

"Strong, handsome and psychic too. Wow!"

"There's something else about me you still don't know though. I'm the world's greatest popcorn maker."

Mike found a milk pitcher in her cupboard and filled it with water before dropping the pussy willows into it, then looked for the popcorn kernels. After cooking them to perfection, and seasoning with just the right amount of salt and a touch of Parmesan cheese, he brought a big bowl of delicious smelling popcorn to the coffee table. After placing ice cubes into two glasses he poured them each soft drinks. He then turned the video on and the lights off, before sitting on the floor and positioning himself against the front of the sofa near Jo's pillow. He wanted to ask if her ice pack needed changing before the movie started but was determined not to open that can of worms again.

Now with the room darkened, the odd flash of lightning could be seen through the windows. The rumbling of thunder was getting louder as well. Mike asked if there could be any danger of the power going out and Jo assured him if it did, Barney would wait for a short while to see if it would come back on of its own accord before starting up their gas-driven generator. They had lost a freezer-full of food one year when the power went off and stayed off for several days due to the Hydro lines being taken down by the high winds. She didn't feel this storm was going to have the severe winds, but there was always the danger of lightning knocking out a transformer or two.

Grudgingly admitting his popcorn was the best she had tasted, she ate more than her share before the first movie was halfway finished. Jo decided it was time for a Tylenol but didn't want to alarm Mike so she made an excuse for a washroom break. After making her way back to the living room, she found he had exchanged her ice pack for a fresh cold one. She was silently grateful. He fluffed up the pillows under her foot and let her get comfortable again before he restarted the movie.

The end of the movie left her in a melancholy mood and Mike, sensing it, wished he had known how it ended before he chose it. He offered to get her a fresh drink. Jo really wanted some hard liquor but remembered that Mike never touched alcohol so thought better of it. She wondered whether he might have developed an addiction to it at some time. Watching him stretch his legs and bend from side to side, she realized the floor couldn't be all that comfortable for him.

"My back's getting stiff from lying on it for so long. I think I need to sit upright for a while."

She put a pillow on the coffee table and moved her legs out in front of her, patting the sofa beside her. He thanked her and went to the door, peering out at the sky where lightning danced like a display of fireworks.

"In Wyoming, the country is more rolling and you can see a storm coming for miles before you actually hear it."

Jo got up and limped over to watch the light display with him, neither of them mentioning the wisdom of his returning to his cabin before the rain should start. He put his arm around her shoulder as if it were the natural thing to do. She unconsciously leaned into him, with her arms folded in front of her. The air was still and very close as the air pressure built under the looming clouds. When the wind started to pick up and the first raindrops were felt through the screen, he kissed her forehead and moved her away so he could pull the glass window down to keep the floor dry. Jo asked Mike to check her bedroom and bathroom windows while she did the same in the main kitchen, to make sure all was secure in there.

After everything was closed tight, they settled back on the sofa and Mike put the second movie in for them to watch. As the wind howled and the rains came down, they tried to figure out who the murderer was until, all of a sudden, everything went black and the only noise came from outside.

Without any hesitation, Mike leaned over, put his arms around Jo and kissed her passionately. After sliding his lips to her neck he whispered huskily, "How much do you think it would be worth to Barney *not* to turn the generator on?"

Laughing, she replied, "Probably just his job."

"Hell, it must be time for the old guy to retire anyway."

Grudgingly, he loosened his hold on her when she said she had emergency candles in a cupboard. Jo grabbed a flashlight from a drawer in the end table, and started rummaging through one of the cupboards in her little kitchen. Mike took two large pillar candles from her, set them on the holders she laid on the coffee table and lit them.

He couldn't help but notice how the soft dancing light enhanced her beauty, caught the sparkle in her eyes and made the brown appear much darker than it really was. He knew he had never felt this way about anyone ever before, he wished time could stand still, that he could hold the next week at bay — and the several-thousand-mile separation looming.

He felt her hand on his cheek and heard her soft voice asking, "What's taking you so far away, Mike?"

He started, thinking he must have spoken out loud, until he realized she was talking about his thoughts.

He took her hand and brought it to his mouth where he kissed each of her fingers tenderly. "I'm afraid if I tell you where my thoughts have taken me, I might frighten you away."

She looked at him with a warm curiosity and then to his surprise, she kissed him just as tenderly on the lips. "Try me."

He didn't trust himself to speak and just kissed her palm again, and gently rubbed it across his cheek then whispered, "Not yet."

He went to the window and looked out. She got the impression he suddenly felt trapped, and wondered whether the storm and the candles had given him urges that he seemed afraid to act upon. She smiled thinking that maybe he wasn't the sexy playboy she had surmised he was. Perhaps he had old-fashioned morals after all and she couldn't help feeling relieved. She and Stu had reached a stage in their marriage where sex was not a priority. They were comfortable in their togetherness and didn't need the passionate lovemaking they once had to keep their love alive and strong. In fact, she couldn't remember how long it had been since they'd had sex before Stu's accident. It may have been months. Would she be comfortable having another man in her bed, becoming familiar with her body? Not just another man, but this one in particular? Again she had feelings of inferiority about the shape of her body. She was just as slender but certainly not as firm as she had been, even ten years ago, and certainly not as firm as she knew his body was. It probably was just as well if they didn't pursue the more physical aspect of their relationship.

With this thought in mind she asked if he would like some coffee. Tempting him even further, she suggested, "I could raid the refrigerator in the main kitchen and maybe steal some deep dish apple pie for us if there's any left."

"You have no idea what a very weak man I am, especially where apple pie is concerned."

He agreed to join her only if he could have a double dollop of whipping cream. Then he asked, "How can you make coffee when the power is out?"

With a sly laugh, she showed him the little metal percolator she had stowed away inside her cupboard. "All I need from you is to throw a couple of logs into that Franklin stove sitting over in the corner."

Once the fire was going and the perking coffee lifted off the heat to slow the rising bubbles, they took the flashlight and sneaked into the kitchen. To Mike's pleasure there was about half a pie left. He cut a healthy portion but expressed his disappointment when Jo, deciding mentally she'd better start watching her waistline, wouldn't join him.

Back in her apartment, he savoured the aroma of fresh perked coffee, a smell he'd always enjoyed. He settled back on the sofa to let her wait on him. *Mm, mmm, it just can't get any better than this.*

***

Watching the satisfied grin on his face, Jo sat back in her chair and childishly decided not even to think about next week. She would just enjoy each day with Mike and build memories to treasure after he had gone. When his cup was almost empty, she gave him a refill and sat down beside him again. He put his arm around her and tucked her in close to him while they leaned back and watched the lightning through the skylight. After a while, Jo could hear his even breathing and realized, in spite of the coffee, he had fallen asleep. She slowly and reluctantly pulled herself away from him, successfully lifting his feet from the coffee table onto the sofa. He stirred and made himself comfortable without waking. She then covered him with an afghan, blew out the candles and went to bed.

She awakened to the smell of freshly brewed coffee and thought she was still dreaming of last night. Then she heard a male voice singing "This Time the Dream's on Me" and realized she wasn't caught in a dream ... She was living a dream and she decided to enjoy every minute of it. At her age, dreams could be short-lived and she knew this one in particular had a life span of only a few more days. She stole into the bathroom unnoticed, washed her face and brushed her teeth. Because she was wearing tailored cotton pyjamas, she carefully checked to make sure everything was covered and all buttons were closed. Then commenting about being awakened by someone singing off-key, when she had hoped to sleep till noon, she walked into her living room.

He apologized for waking her prematurely. "My first thought

when I woke up was to quietly leave for my own cabin but I decided the polite thing to do would be to have coffee ready for you when you decided to open those beautiful brown eyes. Besides, what do you mean 'somebody singing off-key'?"

"Actually, off-key's okay, off-key's good. Some of my best friends sing off-key. I can't think of another sound I would rather be awakened to than off-key."

As he turned his lips out in an exaggerated pout, she slid her arms around his waist and kissed his chin. He kissed her forehead and gave her a bear hug as he commented, "I really should shower, shave and brush my teeth."

As she took a full cup of coffee from him, the realization dawned that the power had returned. Jo made a mental note to check the clocks and to check with Barney to see how long it had been off and whether there was any damage. A glance out the window told her it was still raining, but now a steady downpour rather than the windy sheets of the night before.

"There are a couple of new, unwrapped toothbrushes in the medicine cabinet and Stu's razor is in the vanity under the sink if you want to freshen up here. The rain might ease a bit before you have to venture outside."

"I need a shower and change of clothes as well, but I would love to come back and have breakfast with you. If you have time."

The night before, she had made a mental decision to only do the minimum work required by her to allow her the time to fully enjoy the remainder of Mike's vacation.

"Give me an hour to check the lodge and then we can enjoy a leisurely breakfast together."

He borrowed a hooded rain poncho and ran out the door and down the path. As soon as he was gone, she showered and dressed. A tour of the kitchen, dining room, lobby and laundry room proved nothing seemed to have been affected by the power outage. Barney, dressed in rain gear, let himself in and assured her that everything seemed to be in order as far as the cabins and boathouse were concerned. "In fact, Mrs. H., I'm kind of amused by the fact that most of the guests probably don't even know there was a power outage."

When the rainfall was quite heavy, the staff enjoyed a breather as boats didn't go out and the guests tended to stay in their cabins. The kitchen wasn't as busy, either. It was usually a time for catching up on cleaning and minor inside maintenance. The season was fairly new so there wasn't too much required. Jo told the staff she was going to catch up on some paperwork and then relax in her quarters, but to call her if she was needed for anything. No one was in the dining room so she told Cook that she and Mr. Talbot would have a late breakfast in there.

When Mike came in, she seated him facing the window overlooking the bay. With his back to the room, they enjoyed a long, slow meal together talking about his upcoming season of football travels. He confessed. "I'm a little nervous about getting back into it, but I've only agreed to a one-year contract so I think I can live through that."

Secretly, he knew that the year's contract now would seem like a life sentence keeping him from Jo. Her season would be over much before his but he was afraid to ask about the possibility of her meeting him somewhere over the winter.

When the waitress came to fill their cups for the third time, they declined and pushed themselves away from the table. Jo walked with him through the deserted lobby then opened the door into her apartment. She opened one of the doors in the wall unit that housed her television set and pulled out a Scrabble game.

"What do you say, Mike, are you up to taking on the Red Sky Lodge's undisputed champion?"

With tongue in cheek, he replied, "You probably haven't played any worthy challengers … Until now. Lay out the playing field."

It didn't take too long before he realized she was taking advantage of both the Canadian and American spelling of certain words. Calling "foul" because he didn't know which words could have an extra "u" in them or when "er" could become "re". He warned, "I'm going to register an official complaint with the gaming commissioner. In the meantime, I'll finish the game under protest."

Agreeing to a second game using only American spelling, she bet him she could still win by at least twenty-five points.

"I'll accept your bet only if you agree that the loser buys dinner in Thunder Bay before I leave for home on the weekend."

She won easily and declared winner's choice for her favourite restaurant, but warning she would have to reserve ahead of time, that it was very exclusive and very expensive.

She laughed. "That's favourite, spelled 'favo **u** rite' and you are going to pay big time, Mike Talbot, for doubting me as champion — in any language."

TEN

Jo decided to take advantage of a rainy afternoon and another pair of hands. "Do you like to cook, Mike?"

When he replied in the positive, she asked if he liked potatoes and dumplings.

"Almost as much as deep dish apple pie."

"In that case, I'll give you a big pot and you can ask Cook to fill it with potatoes for me."

When he came back, she had newspapers spread out on her kitchen counter, stools pulled up on either side of it, a paring knife and a potato peeler lying on top. She told him to choose his weapon while she put the sound track CD from *Forrest Gump* in the player.

He chose the peeler and asked, "Is this going to be another contest? Because if it is, with all my KP experience in the Marines, this one I'll win for sure."

Laughing, Jo assured him, "It's no race. That means you better peel them cleanly, no dark spots will be left and absolutely no wastage is allowed."

He said he only had one question. "What in hell are perogies?"

Cautiously, she asked, "What did Cook tell you?"

"When I asked for a big pot of potatoes, he laughed, shook his head, and said when he saw the rain, he knew he should have warned me at breakfast time. When I asked what I had to be forewarned about, he said that every time we get socked in for a day or more with rain, you get the perogy urge, and anyone who crosses your path automatically gets drafted. Jo, what am I getting myself in to? Something tells me I should be begging off with a headache."

Jo put down her knife and said under her breath, "Well, when Josef Frederik Vanderploeg, our beloved Cook, comes begging for some perogies to have for his own dinner, I'll remind him of his warnings!"

"Is *that* his name?"

"His name will be mud if he's not careful."

"You still haven't answered my question. What rare delicacy am I learning how to make?"

She patted him gently on the cheek. "Just keep quiet and keep peeling. You won't be sorry."

Later, when all the potatoes were peeled, cut and put into the pot to boil, Jo pulled a small block of sharp cheddar cheese out of her refrigerator and asked Mike to cut it into one-inch cubes. She took the enormous stainless steel bowl that Cook had sent with Mike, too, and started measuring flour into it. When Mike finished cubing the cheese, she looked at him and asked, "How are you with chopping onions? If you don't like doing it, I'll do it."

"Are you kidding? I'm not about to refuse you anything. I noticed the size of the rolling pin in the oven drawer and I sure as hell don't want to be on the receiving end of it."

He surprised her by chopping them quite finely and uniformly. After melting margarine in a large frying pan, Jo dropped the chopped onions in and sautéed them until they were transparent and just starting to turn a light golden colour. They both agreed that was one of the finest kitchen aromas a person could experience. After checking to make sure the potatoes were cooked, Mike drained them for her, saving the water as instructed, into a smaller vessel with a lip on one side for pouring. When finished putting oil into a large measuring cup, she added hot potato water then kept adding ice water from the fridge until the mixture was tepid. She poured some of the liquid into the flour and started working the dough, continuing to add liquid as she worked until it was the right consistency. Jo cut off large pieces of the dough and put them in clean plastic bags, and set them to one side. Mike in the meantime was mashing the hot potatoes and cubed cheese together.

They took a coffee break while her ingredients "worked". He was thinking, she could have asked him to help her clean toilets and he would have followed her about like a puppy dog. Content, that's what he was, just by being with her, no matter what they were doing. He couldn't imagine playing scrabble or making "perogies" with any of the women he knew, whether in Wyoming, Texas, Green Bay, Los Angeles, or anywhere. They all seemed to have this preconceived notion he had to be entertained, had to be going "somewhere" or doing "something". Consequently, he always felt that he had to allow himself to be entertained. If someone had told him a month ago that he would be this content just by being in a kitchen peeling potatoes with a woman, he would have laughed in his face.

He sat singing and rolling dough, cutting out circles and filling them with the potato/cheese mixture for most of the afternoon, squeezing the two edges together tightly right around the half moon and then back again for insurance. God forbid that one should come apart in the boiling process. He wondered if he should be looking over his shoulder for the perogy police who might be watching, ready to pounce if one of these little floured patties wasn't sealed properly.

When he started to laugh at his own silly thoughts, Jo asked, "Are you going to share your joke or is it private?"

In answer, he just put down the little dumpling he was working on, picked her up and swung her around, planting a big kiss on her mouth before setting her back on her chair again. Asking him what that was all about, she burst out laughing when he thanked her for making his dreams come true.

"Years ago," he said, "a fortune teller told me that some day I'd find a beautiful woman who would soon have me rolling in dough. I concede that I have now fulfilled my destiny."

They finished the perogies, all fifteen dozen of them, and after smothering them in fried onions and butter, Jo bagged them, sealed them and put them aside to cool before they could be placed in the freezer. All except for a few dozen, which she kept out for their dinner, and if Cook begged properly, he may possibly have some too. She put a warm, freshly boiled perogy on a plate with melted butter and a dollop of sour cream and gave it to Mike to taste. The expression on his face said it all.

"Well, I can see I have another man wrapped around my finger just because of my perogies. Cook tried making them, but they weren't the same. I told him he didn't hold his tongue at the proper angle while filling and pinching them."

They decided to watch the rest of the movie that had been playing when the power went out the night before. By then it would be dinnertime. Mike started the movie and sat on the floor again rubbing Jo's ankle and foot. He noticed swelling, she had been on her feet all afternoon. He kissed each of her toes and started working his way up her foot and ankle. Just when she was starting to feel an old sensation in the pit of her stomach, someone knocked on the kitchen door. Mike pressed the pause button on the remote control and answered the door.

There stood Cook. "Mrs. H., do you want roasted spareribs for your dinner?" While asking, he peered through the door, trying to sneak a good look at Jo's countertop.

Jo replied, "If you are talking about your own world-famous recipe, they would be the perfect companion to our perogies."

He whispered to Mike, "Did you make very many?"

Mike winked at him and said there was enough to go around.

Cook smiled. "The spareribs should be ready in about an hour and a half." He started to whistle as he closed the door to return to the kitchen.

Jo sat up and started the movie again, patting the sofa beside her. Instead of sitting where she had indicated, he leaned down, picked her up, sat where she had been and turned her so that she was sitting across his lap. He asked, "So what are you going to teach me tomorrow if it's still raining?"

She commented that she hoped it wouldn't be raining. "I still have so much to show you outdoors and time is running out."

He started to speak and then stopped.

She hesitated then asked, "What were you about to say?"

Instead of answering, he pulled her to him so quickly and with such force that she almost lost her breath. He kissed her on her mouth, and cheeks, then her earlobes and neck. He whispered, "Jo, Jo," as he continued to hold her to his chest.

She was so overwhelmed, she didn't know what to say or what to do.

He lifted her chin to look directly into her amber eyes and asked, "*Is* time running out for us? Is it really running out?"

Knowing what he meant, but not sure how to answer, she said, "You leave on the weekend."

"I'm hoping that only means our *week* together will have run out, not that *time* will have run out."

"What are you saying?" Could he possibly mean he wanted to see her again after his vacation was over?

"Oh, Jo, I don't want to scare you off. You probably aren't completely over the loss of your husband and I don't ever believe for one minute that I could replace him, but I'm hoping this weekend isn't going to be the end of it for us. I want it to be the beginning. I want to keep in touch with you, and see you again and again and again."

When she didn't answer, he felt the wind go out of him. *She's trying to find the right words to let me down gently. Why did I have to blurt it out like that? Why couldn't I have just enjoyed what we have for a couple more days? She won't even look at me.*

Slowly she lowered her head until it was resting on his shoulder. She lifted a hand, stroking his cheek with her forefinger. When she tried to speak, her voice broke and she found herself sobbing into his shoulder. He tightened his arms around her and held her close, not sure if the sobbing was a good thing or a bad thing.

"Just hold me for a while please," she sighed. Her sobs seemed to diminish a bit and then she leaned back in his arms and looked at him. Again she lifted a hand to his face and moved her finger back and forth around his chin and then touched a finger to his lips.

"Stu and I knew each other during high school. We weren't sweethearts, just friends. We always seemed to be hanging around with the same people. Then he went away to university in Eastern Ontario and I didn't see him for years. I elected to stay home and take a business course in a community college, and then I accepted employment in a small law office. Shortly after he returned home, he began working for an engineering firm. They found themselves in need of some legal advice and he was the one elected to engage a lawyer. The law firm I worked for had an excellent reputation in corporate matters and when he came for an appointment, we renewed our acquaintance. He asked me out for lunch that same day and the rest, as they say, is history. I told you how we worked hard and built this lodge into what you see today. What I didn't tell you was that Stu was the love of my life. We were second nature to each other, I guess a certain amount of it comes from our long marriage, but we always just seemed to know what the other was thinking. I loved Stu like I know I will never be able to love anyone again. We were married for thirty-seven years and I never gave a thought to carrying on without him."

She took several deep breaths.

He didn't know whether she was waiting for him to say something but decided to wait a few seconds. Just when he was going to speak, she continued.

"There hasn't been a morning that he wasn't the first thing on my mind when I awakened, or a night that I haven't fallen asleep thinking of him and even talking to him — until this weekend."

What was she saying?

"After our first evening together, you and me, I felt guilty because I had spent a whole evening without thinking of him and the next morning I felt even guiltier because I had slept through the night without a dream or thought of him. I can't believe I've shown you the places around the lake, and talked about Stu so much without breaking down until now. We had a great life in all ways, days and nights. When he died, I was positive a part of me had died with him. I never expected I'd ever again feel a man's arms around me or a man's lips on mine, nor did I ever think I would want to."

Here it comes. She's going to let me down gently.

"Mike. I love being in your arms and I love the feel of your lips on mine. I want it to continue. I have to admit I am a little confused though. In all fairness to you, I'm not sure about these awkward but wonderful feelings. I'm not sure if I just love it because of the way it makes me feel again, or whether I love it because it's you. Do you understand what I'm trying to say?"

"I think so."

"Good. Because I'm not sure I do."

"I don't want to put any pressure on you. I don't want to frighten you away from me."

"I don't frighten easily. Mike, just have patience with me. You've awakened feelings in me I thought were dead and it's kind of taken me by surprise. I don't want this to end either but I don't know how much I can give you right now."

He hesitated, then after taking a deep breath he spoke barely louder than a whisper. "Since you're talking about fairness, I don't know how to tell you this except to come right out with it … dammit, this is hard for a man … but … I'm not sure I can … I've experienced a problem a few times and, well … I'm sure you're still young enough to want — no — to expect, to have certain needs filled. Shit, I don't … Dammit. Do you know what I'm trying to tell you?"

"Yes, I think so. Mike, maybe I *am* getting old but sometimes I just want to be held, kissed and caressed. And if it leads to more …? Well great. If it doesn't, I won't be throwing myself off the nearest bridge. My needs have changed in recent years, too. I need to feel cherished and loved more than I require a hot steamy affair. Of course, I'll never back down from a challenge either … but sometimes the race is more exciting than the win."

"Jo, my sweet Jo. How did I get so lucky? You are one understanding woman. If you say the possibility is there to continue to see each other after my vacation is over, I can survive for several months on that promise alone."

She turned to face him straight on and studied his face. "We'll see each other, Mike. The problem is that I don't know when. My season isn't over until the end of October and yours, I'll wager, goes till at least January or February. That's the time of year I hit the road again."

"Maybe I could hit the road with you. Would Barney be upset if I could manage it?"

"Barney doesn't even know yet that he's volunteered for the job."

Just then a knock sounded at the door and she could hear Cook calling that he had a hot pan in his hands. When Mike opened the door, the aroma of garlic-roasted spareribs preceded the chef into the room. He set the pan on the stovetop, lifted the lid and invited Mike to savour the "bouquet".

Jo stood, thanking him profusely. "I don't suppose you would like a few perogies for yourself."

"Well, I suppose they might go well with the spareribs for my supper if you have a few to spare."

Jo gave him a dozen with lots of butter and onions, smiling when she could almost see the drool running from the corner of his mouth.

She turned an element on and put a frying pan on it. Taking another dozen of the potato turnovers she dropped them into the pan with margarine and onions. Mike watched as she fried them to a golden brown, then covered them with more of the margarine mixture. Jo quickly put placemats and plates on the table while Mike got the flatware and napkins.

Jo asked if he wanted wine and he reminded her that he didn't drink, but told her not to let that stop her from enjoying some. She arranged the perogies and all their trimmings in various serving dishes while Mike set the whole roasting pan down on a hot-pad on the table. After filling tall glasses with iced tea from a refrigerated pitcher, Jo invited Mike to sit and enjoy.

***

"If I hang around here long enough, I'll soon reach two hundred and fifty pounds. Man, that was one of the best home-cooked meals I can remember eating in a long time."

"You can take some of the credit," she replied. "After all, you did most of the peeling, mashing, cutting, rolling and pinching."

"Be careful how loudly you say that, it makes me sound like I've been abusing you," he laughed.

She couldn't believe how many spareribs she'd eaten and decided to clean the plates off before anybody started counting bones. Finding out he had no room for coffee or dessert, she loaded the dishwasher, put the leftover ribs in a baggie in the fridge, and put the pan to soak.

Mike turned the evening news on and they sat together on the sofa to watch it. He commented, "There's a young rooky out of The Midwest that everyone is talking about. I wish I had more information on him."

"There must be something on the Internet."

He was thrilled with what she was able to pull up on the screen and, before they realized it, most of the evening had been spent at her computer.

"How did I ever, for even one minute, think I was living before I met you?" he said. "For a lady who knows diddly-squat about football, you've been more help to me in a couple of hours than all those so-called expert statisticians who do this for a living."

They rose and Mike walked to the door and opened it a few inches. "You know, I think the rain is letting up. Hopefully that forecaster was right and it'll be sunny tomorrow."

"I rather enjoyed sharing this rainy day inside, just the two of us." She sidled up to him and slid her arm around his waist.

Kissing her forehead and moving his arm around her shoulder, he mumbled agreement as she reached up and pulled his lips to hers. "Oh, Mike, you have no idea what your kisses do to this foolish old woman. Do you?"

"Old woman? Old woman? What are you fifty-four? Fifty-five?"

"I'll be sixty on my next birthday."

"Get out of town!"

"See, I told you I was an old woman."

"Well, you're the youngest looking almost-sixty-year-old I've ever seen. How come your body doesn't know how old it is? I believe it still thinks it's thirty."

"You old smoothie."

"Honestly, if you hadn't told me you and Stu had been married for thirty-seven years I never would have guessed you to be even fifty-five. That's why I was so intimidated by you. But now that I know you're practically ancient, I won't feel so bad about not jumping your bones. Why I'll even help you across the street at the next intersection."

"How can you change so fast you ... you ... Jekyll and Hyde? I'll fix you, you old fart. Tomorrow, if the sun's shining, we are crossing the portage into Second Lake and we'll see who's in shape and who's not."

He swept her into his arms and laughing, led her back to the sofa and gently put her down again. "If you don't stay off that foot for more than half an hour at a time, you won't be hiking anywhere tomorrow. Will you let me get an ice pack for it? Massage it for a while?"

"Promise you won't start kissing my toes."

"Why? I love kissing your toes. Your toes were made to be kissed."

"And I love you kissing my toes — too much. That's why you mustn't."

Mike got an ice pack and sat so her feet her were on his lap. "What about your heels? Are your heels off limits too?"

"If you don't behave, I'm going to have to send you home."

"Well then, we're going to have to watch another movie. Do you like westerns?"

She nodded.

"Good. I saw one out there I haven't watched yet."

He came back with a John Cusack movie which she had seen and knew it had an ending she didn't like either but she didn't say anything. She didn't get to see it anyway. It turned out to be her turn for falling asleep on the sofa. She vaguely remembered being carried to her bed and being covered with her quilt. A warm brush of lips on hers was the last thing she could recall.

In the morning, she once again awakened to the smell of freshly brewed coffee, but this time it was delivered to her in bed along with a glass of juice and some french toast. A bright yellow tulip lay along one side of the tray. His change of clothes indicated he had been to his cabin at some point. If his bed was still made again this morning, the cleaning staff would be having a heyday with the rumours. He set her mind at ease when he said the rain had stopped at about the same time as the movie ended, so after depositing her in her bed, he had moseyed on down to his.

He sat on her bed, drinking coffee as he watched her eat her breakfast. When she finished, she moved her tray to the night table.

"You're spoiling me, Mike. Who's going to do this for me when you're gone?" She rested a hand on the side of his cheek.

"Little lady, I wish I could do this for you for the rest of our lives."

"Oh, Mike." She sat up and reached for him and pulled him to her. They fell back but she didn't release him. "Just hold me. Maybe if you hug me enough and kiss me enough I might be able to store them all and recall them bit by bit over the summer. By the time they're all gone, maybe it'll be time to see each other again."

He stretched out beside her holding her so closely she could feel his breath on her temple. They lay like that for the longest time. Finally she realized she was prolonging the agony of getting up and starting another day. In the back of her brain niggled the knowledge this would bring them one day closer to his leaving. She reluctantly slid from his embrace and went into the washroom. She quickly showered and shampooed her hair. Wrapped in her white terry bathrobe and her head swathed in a towel, she went out to find him sitting on the deck. She poured herself another cup of coffee and joined him. Almost immediately she sensed he was avoiding eye contact. Had she said too much? Gone too far?

Finally, he shifted so they were facing each other. He leaned forward, took her coffee mug and put it on the patio table. With both of her hands between his, he looked at her. When he spoke, his voice was husky, almost breaking. "Jo. I have to leave tomorrow."

She couldn't believe her ears. "What? Why? I don't understand."

"My secretary called. She's the only one who knows where I am. She said the Network has been trying to reach me for a couple of days and they're putting some pressure on her to find me. They didn't know I was taking this vacation and they have to get some promos shot before the start of the pre-season broadcasts. Nadine hated like hell calling me, but they're unrelenting in their phone calls. Something about my contract stating I have to do these. She phoned my lawyer and he felt the wording is so ambiguous it's anybody's guess, but he advised her to try to get me back there."

A lone tear sat on her bottom eyelashes just waiting for gravity to make it fall. She felt her lip quiver as she moved from her chair and knelt in front of him, resting her head against his chest. He pulled her to an upright kneeling position and closed his lips over hers. The tear finally fell, followed by a flood burst. He picked her up and carried her inside and stood her in front of him. "Jo, baby, I don't want to go. Believe me I don't want to go."

"When did your secretary call you?" Her voice was barely more than a whisper.

"There was an e-mail message from her when I got back to my room last night. I called her at home. I hardly slept all night, sick at the thought of having only one more day with you. Oh, Jo, I know it's probably too soon for you to deal with this, but I love you. I love you more than I have ever loved anyone. Can you believe it took me sixty-six years to discover you, and now I have to leave you?"

"Mike, I wish I could tell you that I love you too. Maybe I do, I don't know. I just know that I love being with you. I am going to miss you terribly." She turned away from him and started to cry again. The towel slid from her head and down her back. He buried his face in her damp, clean hair and wrapped his arms around her, crossing them in the front. He breathed in the peach fragrance she used in everything, from shower scrub to body lotion to cream rinse in her hair. She leaned back into him and sobbed. "It seems like all I've been doing these past twenty-four hours is crying."

"I don't like to cause you so much heartache."

"You haven't caused me heartache, Mike. I think I've held back my tears for too long. It's time to let go."

"Jo. Let's get dressed and go into Thunder Bay, to your fancy restaurant. I do owe you a dinner and I never renege on a bet. We can stay overnight and you can take me to the airport tomorrow."

"What time is your flight?"

"I don't know. I haven't changed it yet. I thought I'd do that in town."

Hesitating for a moment, she finally turned her teary eyes to his. "Let's go for a boat ride this morning before we go to town. I want to show you something."

Jo threw on jeans and a hooded sweatshirt while Mike went down to see how the boat had weathered the storm. By the time she made her way down to the dock, he had the boat dried out as best he could and the motor was running. She instructed him to head to the west end of the lake when he guided the boat out of the bay. He realized this was the part of the lake they had seen from their vantage point at the top of the waterfalls. She sat in the front of the boat staring out at the shoreline, with down-turned mouth and the sparkle missing from her eyes. When she finally looked at him, he winked but it only made her mouth quiver, so he decided not to continue along that route.

When they reached a point about midway up the shoreline, she motioned for him to pull closer into shore. When the boat was barely crawling along, she switched to the bench next to his and told him to cut the engine and use the paddle. He rowed to where a small grassy area met sandy beach and stopped when she put a finger to her mouth in a signal to be quiet. It wasn't long before a lone Canada goose lifted off from the short grassy meadow. Mike saw moisture in Jo's eyes again and reached for her hand with a question in his own eye.

"This goose has been coming to this same spot for three years now, alone. Her mate must have had an accident or been shot."

"Why doesn't she join the rest of the geese?"

"This is probably where her mate met his demise. Canada geese mate for life. When one dies the other remains alone until it eventually dies too. When Barney first told us about her, I had to come and see her for myself. Last spring I felt akin to her and came often to watch her, knowing she was feeling the same loneliness I was. I, too, thought I'd mated for life."

She looked into his face, riveted her teary, copper-brown eyes to his azure-blue ones. "Mike, I'm not a goose." It was more a question than a statement. He moved closer on the seat beside her, and wound his arms around her. The top of her hair was wet again. It was his tears this time. He lifted her chin with his index finger and brought her lips softly to his.

"No, darlin', you're not a goose."

A half sigh, half sob escaped her and she smiled as she whispered, "Let's go back. I have a big date tonight with this retired football player and I have to get ready."

ELEVEN

The ride back was completed in silence. Mike marvelled at the beauty of the landscape while Jo's thoughts were lost in the beauty of the man beside her. He seemed to have such a keen understanding of her unspoken thoughts and feelings. Could she really be this fortunate, to have found a man who was so totally different from Stu, yet a soulmate? What had she done that the gods were looking on her with such favour? Mike had told her his feelings were not of a sexual nature, but of a more loving, companionable nature. *Why couldn't we have had a few more days?* she asked those invisible gods above.

There were a number of things that required attention because she was going to be away overnight. A trip to the city was never just a pleasure trip. It usually meant coming back with a vehicle full of supplies, along with trips to the dry cleaner's, the printer's, the accountant's, and Molly had mentioned that several of the tablecloths had been mended and patched to the point of looking tacky. This would all be dispensed with after Mike's plane left, so she may be required to stay in town a second night.

She also had to think about packing for herself. Jo had never stayed in a hotel with any man but Stu. *What does one wear to shack up in a motel room these days?* She sat up and then rolled back on her bed, laughing hysterically at the thought of herself, Jo Henderson, at age fifty-nine, being taken to dinner and then a romantic night in a hotel. She didn't know if her hysteria was caused by joy, wonder, or fear. She had only known the man a few days for cripes' sake!

She smiled maliciously, thinking that Barb would just about croak if she knew what was happening in Jo's life right now. No one knew except for herself and Mike and, well possibly — no probably — the staff. Even her kids weren't aware of what their mother was up to. She sat up with a start. *My God, what will they think? They must never know that I spent the night in a hotel with a man I've known for less than a week. I know what they'll think. They'll think I've gone stark raving mad. They'll think I'm suffering from dementia, or worse. Maybe I am. Oh goodness, what am I doing?* She sat rocking on her bed with her head on her hands. *I'm acting like a lovesick teenager, no — worse, like a desperate, love-starved, lonely old woman. I can't go through with this.*

Then she thought about Mike leaving the next day and taking his warm comforting arms, his beautiful blue eyes and those sexy, soft lips with him. She would miss his winks, his easy humour and his singing, his off-key singing … especially, his off-key singing. *This is going to be the longest summer ever.* Last year she hadn't wanted the season to end. She hadn't wanted to go back to the empty condominium and face the long winter days and nights alone. She had poured herself into the work here in the lodge, wishing she could extend the season some way. This year, October couldn't arrive soon enough. To hell with what other people thought. Life was too short, and getting shorter with each passing year. She was not going to allow this wonderful happiness, this silly madness she was experiencing with Mike, to slip through her fingers. With that thought, she jumped up and started going through her wardrobe again.

Thank goodness she had let Barb talk her into picking up this little "eggplant" coloured dress. She had laughed at the name of the colour when the salesclerk told her. In another fashion season, it would have been called something more glamorous like midnight violet, or stormy purple, but right now "eggplant" was in, big time. She hadn't thought about the kind of occasion for which she might need this slightly sexy number, with its bare shoulders and spaghetti straps, but she had been caught in a weak moment. It didn't take too much persuasion on Barb's part for her to ask the salesclerk to wrap it up. She'd probably been in one of her "I'm all alone now so what's the point" moods at the time and needed something to snap her out of it.

With the problem of her eveningwear solved, she now had to choose her nightwear. Everything she owned, she had worn with Stu and that would make her feel almost adulterous, whether anything happened or not. She started digging through her drawers and found a nightgown she had purchased to wear on her last trip to Mississauga. Upon her arrival, she had realized that she'd forgotten to pack a dressing gown so wore her more-respectable pyjamas while there. She used to laugh at her aunt who was always prepared for the "emergency": *What if the hotel catches fire and you have to run out wearing only what you have on? You must always wear something presentable.*

"This little ensemble is perfect — presentable and slightly sexy," she contemplated as she wrapped it in tissue and folded it carefully into her travel bag. As an afterthought, she placed one of her favourite peachy-scented sachets in the tissue. This time she remembered the dressing gown and a pair of almost-colour-matched slippers. Finally satisfied that she had everything she could possibly need, she zipped up her overnight case and pulled it to the door. She laid her garment bag over the top then made sure all her windows were closed and the door from her apartment to the lobby was locked.

Mike shook hands with Cook, then kissed Molly on the cheek, which sent her off blushing. Barney had already helped him load his things into the Explorer so, saying he enjoyed watching the American football teams and that he'd be listening for Mike every weekend, Barney wished him a successful television and football season. He then put Jo's things in the vehicle, and slapped a rear fender as they set off for town.

Making the airport their first stop, Mike discovered he had no choice of flights. He was very lucky to obtain a seat available on the only plane heading south the next day, at eight-thirty in the morning. Since it was an international flight, it meant having to arrive at the counter an hour and a half before departure. Jo groaned but didn't make too much of a fuss, knowing he was just as disappointed as she was.

When Mike asked her for directions to the hotel where they'd be staying, panic struck. It was only then she realized all the owners and managers of the better places were friends of hers and Stu's. Reluctant to spend the night with Mike at her condo, feeling there was still too much of Stu there, she was in a real dilemma. How could she check in asking for a double room with a handsome gentleman beside her? Even if he remained in the car, sooner or later someone would realize she had a male companion in her room. Mike recognized her hesitation, and mistaking it for shyness once again, immediately came to the rescue. He said he would feel better if they could get a motel where they could pull up in front of their room. That eliminated a succession of trips through the lobby making the chance of being recognized minimal. He didn't mention that she wouldn't have to run the risk of being recognized by anyone, and she was grateful. His credit cards were imprinted with his full name of Michael James Talbot, and that's all it seemed to take for anonymity.

Once their luggage was inside the room, Jo was overcome with a strange feeling of awkwardness. They were in a room with one bed, not two as she had anticipated when asking for a double. Not usually a bashful person, she felt a real sense of modesty all of a sudden. How could she possibly shower and change in front of Mike? He was still almost a stranger.

Coming out of the bathroom a few seconds later, Mike took one look at her and again got a good handle on the situation. "You know, I took a good look at that tub and shower, and as much as I would enjoy sharing, there is no way both of us will fit in there. So, I'll give you first dibs on it while I find a car wash somewhere and get the buggy cleaned up. If this restaurant is as fancy as you say, they won't want a mud-covered SUV in their parking lot. *No.* No arguments now." Holding up both hands in front of him as if fending off a dispute, he continued, "I know you are just aching for me to scrub your back for you, but I'm sorry, you'll just have to carry on by yourself one more time."

He pulled her close and kissed the very tip of her nose.

***

You are one lucky guy, old fella. He knew he had read her correctly. The scared look on her face told him she wasn't one to sleep around. *Thank God some women still have morals. Just take your time and give her some slack.*

***

Jo couldn't believe how easily she had been let off the hook but decided to make her shower a quick one, just in case there were no lineups at the car wash. When she passed the full-length mirror, she gave her body the once-over. *Well, Jo, this is one time you can be grateful for smaller breasts. They manage to hold their shape better than heavier ones. Too bad the tummy and buns are a little soft, but I guess, all things considered, your shape isn't too bad — for your age.*

She managed to have her underwear in place underneath her dressing gown and was almost finished applying her makeup when Mike returned. He quickly and unabashedly stripped to his shorts, grabbed a fresh pair from his suitcase and headed into the shower. Meanwhile, she finished her "toilette" at the vanity just outside the bathroom door. By the time he had showered, she had just finished slipping her dress over her shoulders and was attempting to get the zipper closed. He moved behind her and planted a kiss on her bare shoulder as he took the zipper and easily slid it up. She leaned back into him as his arms found their way around her waist.

"You smell delicious," she whispered.

Suddenly, she experienced flashback memories of him starring in a soap commercial on television many years before. He had been so strong and virile looking then, she recalled, but decided the years had been more than kind to him. The almost-white hair, and creases in the corners of those blue eyes, had enhanced his good looks.

He leaned and spoke softly in her ear. "If we don't leave this room soon, we won't be eating dinner at all."

She looked up and kissed him under the chin, drinking in the scent of his aftershave lotion. He caressed her lips softly with his own and joked, "I'm quite anxious to get this gambling debt paid and get you off my case."

Giving him a soft elbow to the mid-section, she informed him, "Excuse me. I believe I'm the one that's all dressed and ready here. You're right, you do have a debt to pay. And while I think you have a very enticing chest and midriff, I really don't think undershorts are appropriate attire for the restaurant. Just maybe it's you who should get your butt in gear."

The restaurant she had chosen overlooked the city lights and the harbour. They could see the brightly coloured sails of the boats out in the protected harbour just beyond the breakwall. It was still early in the season and the waters of Lake Superior were very cold, but many sailors enjoyed getting their boats into the water by the Victoria Day weekend in May. In the background, keeping his vigil at the entrance to the harbour, was the dark rock formation known as the Sleeping Giant. This peninsula, which contained a large provincial park, was many kilometres long and formed a natural harbour for the numerous ships arriving in the port daily. When the rays from the setting sun caught the cliffs at various angles, the colours of the sheer rock could range from black to deep purple to a rusty brown and right through crimson.

The restaurant was located in a former mansion near a garden park and scenic lookout in an area of the city that was populated with large homes and estates. They were seated in what was formerly a small sunroom off one side of the main dining room. It was furnished in a Victorian style with a wood-burning fireplace in one corner. A fire was currently lit, and the flames cast a romantic glow onto their table. Jo had requested this particular room, knowing that the alcove was small and contained one table, ensuring their privacy. She and Barb used to enjoy this room. Here they could catch up on all their personal gossip without being overheard. There were no memories of dining with Stu at this restaurant as he had always felt uncomfortable with the formality of it. He was more a steak-and-potatoes diner so preferred a more casual setting where suit and tie were not a prerequisite. So Jo sat back feeling no guilt when she stared at Mike with unabashed admiration. What a dashing figure he presented in his grey suit and white shirt. Were those miniature gold footballs on his dark grey tie?

Of course they were. She couldn't help but wonder if it was a gift from someone. From the admiring look in his eye when he had swung her around in the motel room, she knew her dress was a hit as well.

Sitting across from him now, she could sense his eyes on her and looked up. He was appraising her from the top of her hair, down over her shoulders to where the table broke his view. "Your dress has given the colour of your hair a new hue. What do you call the colour you're wearing?"

"Eggplant." After the look he gave her, she was having a hard time keeping a straight face.

"Egg what?"

"Eggplant."

"Spell that for me please — in American."

"E-g-g-p-l-a-n-t."

"That's what I thought you said. What the hell kind of name is that for a colour?"

"It's very in this year. I'm not sure I can wear it well. I really don't think reddish-brown hair and eyes go well with eggplant." Her shoulders were shaking with silent laughter.

"Jo, if any colour doesn't look well on a woman as beautiful as you, it deserves to be called … What was that again? Oh yes, 'eggplant'. In fact, if any colour doesn't look well on you, it shouldn't be allowed to be a colour at all. It should be kicked right off the colour spectrum and sent out into cyberspace somewhere. Let it get a new name like zabalfar, or jiloritz."

"You are an idiot. An absolutely silly, jibbering, certifiable idiot."

"Make that an absolutely silly, jibbering, certifiable, *love-sick* idiot and I'll agree with you. But I'm your idiot, Jo, and you're stuck with me, I'm afraid."

"And a more lovable idiot I know I'll never find." She could feel a lump forming in her throat. She was relieved when their waiter brought their salads.

They ate their meal in relative silence, sharing the odd comment about the taste of the food, or to pass the pepper or the butter. When Mike eventually pushed his plate away, she commented, "This chef was born in Europe and trained in several cities there. After moving to Canada and prior to coming to Thunder Bay, he managed the kitchen in one of the major hotels in Montreal."

"I can understand why this is your favourite dining place. The only thing missing is romantic music and a small dance floor. I wish I could hold you close and sway the night away."

She understood and nodded. "If it's romance you want, there is a lookout complete with beautiful gardens only a few blocks away. The kids used to park there at night when I was a teenager. To 'look at the stars'."

He took her hand and whispered, "I don't need stars to feel romantic."

She tried to make this dinner with Mike last as long as she could, ordering dessert when she really didn't want any, lingering too long over coffee as if by staying here, she could put off tomorrow. All too soon, they had to leave. He squeezed her as he smoothed her wrap around her shoulders and thanked her for sharing this place with him.

"There are a few other places I want to share with you as well."

On the way back to the motel, she showed him the neighbourhood where she grew up, the elementary and high schools she had attended, and the church where she had made her first Communion and Confirmation, and also where she and Stu had been married. Down the block, where her childhood home was still situated, had grown a row of three huge willow trees. Only one was still standing. Pointing it out to him, she reminisced, "The kids in the block used to clamber up them every evening and shyly discuss 'grown-up' things. It was a private meeting place where the girls and boys could get together after the dishes and homework were done. Lots of secrets were shared in those trees, a number of first kisses, and more than one set of initials carved into the trunks."

They then drove by the neighbourhood park where the ice skating rinks were methodically fenced and flooded in the wintertime, one for hockey, and one for family skating. "We enjoyed the wintertime so much. I can't imagine growing up where there is no change of seasons."

When they arrived at the motel, Mike stopped her from turning on the lights when they entered the room. He wrapped his arms around her and kissed her so warmly and so longingly that he literally stole her breath away. Finally, gasping for air, she moved away from him and laid her wrap and handbag on a chair while kicking off her shoes. Swept again by a sensation of shyness, she wondered how she was possibly going to handle this. Knowing a car wash wasn't going to do the trick this time, she started undoing her pearls, watching in the mirror as he took his suit jacket off and removed his tie. Panic set in when she perched on the edge of the bed and Mike eased his long lean frame beside her. He kissed her temple as he put one hand on her neck then let it slide down over her bare shoulder. When he began kissing the warm skin where his hand had been, all she could manage was a whispered, "Oh my."

He slid the zipper down the back of her dress, his kisses following the widening display of smooth skin. She was sitting straight up with her hands folded demurely in her lap as if she were having tea with the president of her church group. Fully aware of the sensations in her lower abdomen, she was absolutely terrified to move. It had been too long between first dates — almost forty years.

Mike eased the spaghetti straps from her shoulders and continued kissing the curve of her neck, skimming his lips under her jaw line then softly tasting the sweetness in the hollow of her small, but inviting, cleavage. She gasped as he slowly eased her back onto the bed. While he caressed her neck and breasts with kisses, she closed her eyes and let all the sensations that had been buried for so long, surface. She felt his lips on her eyelids and forehead

She whispered, "Wait …" and slowly opened her eyes and kissed his mouth with a promise to be right back. Jo slid off the bed and grabbed her nightgown and some body lotion in her favourite fragrance, then hurried into the bathroom. Taking her time rubbing the peach-scented lotion into her elbows, knees and heels, she smiled when she found herself humming. With emotions warring between shyness and eagerness, she returned to the bedroom. Mike was already lying bare-chested under the covers of the king-sized bed, and the television had been tuned to a station playing romantic music.

Jo couldn't help but wonder if the bare skin continued beneath the covers and, if so, just how far. The small upshift at the corner of her mouth made it clear she'd let her imagination free.

"Now, what does that sly smile mean?" he asked, lifting the covers in invitation.

"You never know," Jo said softly, slipping in beside him. She didn't know if she was more surprised or disappointed. He was wearing pyjama bottoms.

She nestled into the crook of his arm, turning ever so slightly toward him to breathe deeply of his scent — that wonderful mix of musk and soap that made him so male. One sultry movement of her arm brought it against the sculpted nakedness of his chest and, almost unconsciously, Mike began to caress it, running his fingers along the length. Jo shivered.

She lifted her eyes and met his gaze. "What?" she asked softly, still tingling under his touch.

"This," he whispered and leaned to cover her lips.

Jo could not have given herself more completely. Her mouth left his to seek his eyelids, his ears, the strength at the edge of his jaw.

"God, Jo," Mike gasped, unable to hide his pleasure … not that he wanted to. But, if he let go, he would devour her, and he knew she wasn't ready for that. Almost, but not quite.

Still … he couldn't help himself.

Her head was now nestled on his chest where her lips still played. It would take a bigger man than he to push her away. He closed his eyes and let his hands find the softness of her thigh.

***

At the touch, she jerked slightly, not because she was startled but because she wanted so badly to let go and love him. But was she really ready for that? Could she give herself to Mike and not regret it tomorrow? And there was the nagging knowledge that he was leaving. What then? What if all she had were memories? Would that be enough to quell regret?

She raised herself to a sitting position, one hand resting on the bare skin of his belly. "Mike. When do you think we'll see each other again?"

"I don't know … Come here."

"Mike. I'm serious."

"So am I," he breathed, pulling her closer. "Come here."

"Mike … Wait. What if we never see each other again?"

He sighed and let her go. "OK. Let's try to make some plans."

The moment was gone.

He confessed that he certainly hadn't expected someone like Jo to walk into his life when he'd signed those all-exclusive contracts. That he was going to be broadcasting a game somewhere every weekend — and likely Monday nights — from the pre-season games starting in August until next January, was a given. In between were meetings, travelling, personal appearances, TV talk shows, and lectures and workshops with minor football leagues, high schools and colleges, and if he were lucky, some commercial endorsements of sponsors' products. It was a safe guess that little, if any, time would be left for a personal life.

"I can't see a break in my schedule until the end of January," he said, sadly. "The playoffs have to be a priority."

"I know. Maybe I can take a break. The lodge will close early in October but I have to stay there for another few weeks to take care of end-of-season details. That brings us into Christmas. I have to spend that with my grandkids. I always do."

"I don't want you to disappoint them," Mike said quietly. "You have trade shows in February and March, haven't you?"

"Until the beginning of March. That looks like the first free time together we'll have."

"Not if the contract isn't renewed … Or if I quit. Then I'll have a ton of spare time from the end of January on."

"Oh, Mike. Do you hear all the 'ifs'? My bones tell me that something is going to happen and we're never going to be together."

Mike couldn't bear it. He wrapped his arms around her, pulling her back onto the pillows where he held her so tightly it took away her breath. "Listen to me. Listen… I'll do everything within my power to make sure we're together. Always. You are my heart. You have to know that."

Jo couldn't help herself. She melted into his arms and felt the reassuring warmth of him. She sighed and closed her eyes picturing them together. Forever. While Mike held her close enough to make her peaceful.

***

In her dream, someone was kissing her toes. Try as she might to shake them free, the firm grip was inescapable. How could her toes be attached to her breasts? Impossible, yet there it was. With each kiss there was a distinct tingling. Her eyes shot open. Someone *was* kissing her toes.

"Oh Mike …" she giggled, her voice husky with sleep.

"Hey, sleepyhead. Time to wake up unless you're going to make me walk to the airport."

Suddenly, there was the crush of reality. "It's morning? It's morning! How did that happen? You were just holding me … Now it's morning?"

"It's morning. I wish we could go back to last night."

"We didn't …"

"Shhh. It's okay. It wasn't the right time. We both knew it."

"But …"

He kissed her into silence. "No buts, sweetheart. We'll have to give each other a rain check. I already showered so you have the bathroom all to yourself again. I hope there's somewhere in the airport we can grab breakfast."

His reply didn't give her any indication of his feelings about their lack of "romance". She wondered if perhaps he was relieved he hadn't been forced to perform. She immediately dismissed that idea though, realizing he had asked for their night together.

Jo jumped out of bed embarrassed at what an absolute washout he must think her. It was especially disappointing because she wouldn't be seeing him again for goodness knows how long. Grabbing her dressing gown, she headed to the bathroom. *Well you sure gave him something to remember you by, didn't you, old girl.*

"Did you say something?" he called out.

"Just talking to myself."

"That's a sign of old age."

"Thank you for that."

"Don't mention it."

After showering, Jo took extreme care with her makeup. She dressed in her best off-white linen pantsuit with a copper-coloured shell under the short-sleeved jacket. Putting on her small gold braided-loop earrings, she declared herself ready. There was no need for him to tell her how she looked in that colour, his expression did it for him. He pulled her close and kissed her ear while whispering huskily, "What do you call that colour? Carrot? No wait, I know, I know — squash!"

She grabbed a pillow and began hitting him with it. They started laughing so hard they had to sit for a minute to catch their breath. After a few moments, he checked his watch then loaded their luggage into the vehicle. Reluctantly, bothered by the empty feeling deep within her, she followed him out to the Explorer.

The airport was only a couple of kilometres from the motel. His luggage was checked through, his seat assigned and his boarding pass was tucked into his shirt pocket. There was plenty of time left for breakfast before he would have to pass through security. They took a table in a corner where he sat facing the wall and away from the early-morning crowd. Both sensed the need to keep the conversation light. Mike gave Jo the name and phone number of his personal secretary in case she ever had to reach him urgently. He said Nadine knew his whereabouts at all times.

"I'm not going to tell anyone about our relationship until the season is over. I don't want any rumours to leak about us because I know how invasive the press can be." He wasn't sure whether anyone would even give two hoots about him or his love life. On the other hand, he may have a successful television season and that always led to loss of privacy. "I will give Nadine instructions to treat your phone calls as a top priority, any place or any time. I promise to call at least once a week from wherever I happen to be. Time differences won't always make it easy, but I'll try my best."

Then it was time to go. Jo had promised herself she wouldn't cry, that she would make him leave laughing.

They walked to the security gate and moved to one side of the door. He held her closely, and then brushed her cheek with his lips and followed that with a very soft, tender kiss on the mouth. He headed away, through the door.

She called after him "It's rutabaga."

"What?"

"The colour. It's rutabaga."

When she saw his grin spreading from ear to ear, she turned and walked out.

TWELVE

The weeks dragged. Mike, true to his word, telephoned once a week and Jo counted each and every day between those phone calls. He confided he hadn't anticipated the gruelling schedule his job entailed and confessed that his age was definitely showing because he was certainly feeling the effects.

Jo, on the other hand, couldn't seem to find enough work to keep occupied. After her ankle healed, she tried to fill her time by designing and developing new flowerbeds, rearranging furniture, assisting Cook with the baking, all the while watching the phone. She grudgingly had to admit after several weeks that staring at a phone does not make it ring.

***

Mike's flight home had been a time of contemplation and soul-searching. He was embarrassed that their promised night of romance had turned out to be — nothing. When Jo had fallen asleep in his arms, he remembered how many nights he had seen her apartment lights on till the wee hours of the morning. Her injured ankle had kept her awake more than she would admit. When he had given her the news of his early departure for home, she had worked non-stop to complete all her chores so she could slip away for a night. Even though he knew she must have been near exhaustion, he had wanted to wake her and make love to her in that motel room. He had hesitated, however, in case he was not able to bring his lovemaking to the desired conclusion. Realizing his own fears were probably his worst enemy, he wondered what it would take to overcome this problem. Was he being fair to her? Should he have tried, even if it didn't happen? *Maybe I'm being selfish. Maybe I should just let her go.* Deep in his heart, though, he knew he couldn't. *Well, they have pills for guys like me. I guess I'll have to overcome my pride and visit my doctor.*

***

By mid-July, after her flower gardens were blooming in all their glory and Cook couldn't find room in the freezers for any more of her tarts, muffins and frozen pies, she decided to wallpaper her living quarters. She spent several days in the city choosing colour schemes and patterns. She brought enough wallpaper samples back with her to paper her entire apartment in a patchwork design and still have samples left over. When final choices were made, it took her almost another month to complete her decorating. Mike's schedule didn't allow the chat time that it had earlier in the season. He was being commissioned for a larger number of personal appearances, but she was happy for him. He had been worried that the younger public might be wondering "who in hell is Mike Talbot?" It would appear that he had etched his place in football history after all. Consequently, he was being well-received by all ages. She began watching the pre-season games just to hear his voice and to catch the odd glimpse of him. Barney tried to explain the game to her, but she didn't think she would ever understand the differences between defensive and offensive teams, legal and illegal passes, and receivers. She eventually gave up the struggle, deciding to just watch the game and allow the play-by-play announcers and colour commentators to keep her informed about the good plays versus the bad. She lived for Sunday afternoons and the sound of Mike's voice.

Summer at the lodge had all indications of surpassing the previous year in revenue. Barney, while not having Stu's business knowledge, had a genuine warmth and friendliness. The guests picked up on this and continually indicated to her what a treasure the man was. She was well aware that the staff was very efficient and that they treated the place as their own. With this in mind, she toyed with the idea of taking a short vacation. She knew she would be busy the last weekend of August right through Labour Day weekend. However, if she played her cards right, there was a distinct possibility of slipping away for a few days. After checking staff schedules, she decided it was do-able right after the approaching weekend.

She wished there were some way to surprise him, but she would have to wait for his call and enquire about his upcoming travels. Maybe, just maybe, if she asked the right questions, she'd learn the information she needed without making him suspicious. Mike usually called early in the week, but when she hadn't heard from him by Thursday, she was about to ditch the whole idea. Eventually, she remembered he had given her the phone number of his personal assistant. Jo knew this was meant for emergency purposes only, but she wanted to surprise him so badly she decided to give it a try. The worst that could happen would be that Nadine wouldn't, or couldn't, help her. If that were the case, she wouldn't be any worse off than she was at the moment.

To her delight, Nadine not only agreed to help her but also encouraged Jo to leave it in her hands. The woman returned her call within a few hours with instructions to book a flight to San Francisco for Saturday and she would pick Jo up personally at the airport. Jo wasted no time making the necessary arrangements even though she would have preferred leaving on a weekday rather than a weekend when the lodge was busiest. She wondered if the beginning of the week wouldn't be more convenient for Mike, too, as he always had the time to phone then. The staff all co-operated by shifting schedules, appearing delighted to do so. They didn't know where she was vacationing but those who had met Mike Talbot hoped he was the reason for the sudden trip. Jo felt like a young girl going to her first prom. She took pains choosing her wardrobe for the trip and made sure she allowed herself time in Thunder Bay for a hair cut, manicure and pedicure.

During her flight, she reflected on the few days they'd had

together. Goodness, had it only been a few days? What did she really know about him other than the physical attraction she felt for him? He seemed genuinely interested. He phoned even if it was just from an airport between flights. Was that really enough on which to base a relationship?

As her plane approached San Francisco airport and started final landing procedures, Jo's level of anticipation peaked. The wheels of the plane couldn't touch down fast enough. *Oh, Mike, I hope you will be as happy to see me as I am to be here.* Waiting to go through customs, she started experiencing cold feet. Why hadn't he called this week? What if this was the busiest possible time for him? Maybe he's the kind of person who doesn't like surprises. There are many people who don't. His secretary would know that though, wouldn't she? *Oh hell, I'm here and there's nothing can be done about it now.*

After collecting her bags, she looked around and saw a tall blonde in a business suit holding a card on which was printed HENDERSON. Jo approached her and they introduced themselves.

Nadine hugged her warmly as if they were old friends. "My car is in the parking lot downstairs." Once free of the airport traffic congestion, she explained the evening's events to Jo. "There's a small reception this evening in one of the hotel suites for the volunteer workers who helped at a fundraiser supporting one of Mike's favourite charities. He's going to be introduced and thanked, then he's free for the evening. I've got it set up for you to surprise him just prior to that. There will be a lot of media people around and they may want some of Mike's time, otherwise he's all yours."

After assisting her with the hotel check-in, Nadine left her with Mike's room number and told her the time Mike definitely would be in his room. Previously, Nadine had told Mike she'd call him at precisely 7:00 that evening. She had asked him to be there as she might have some personal exciting news to share with him. Mike confirmed he would appreciate some down time in his room before the party and would eagerly await her news, whatever it was. Nadine assured Jo that absolutely no one was aware of her presence. In fact, Nadine reminded her, she was the only one who was aware of their friendship

— period. Mike had been very protective of his privacy and relationship with Jo and had threatened Nadine with her job if the news ever leaked.

Settling into her bubble bath, Jo could hardly contain her excitement. She had chosen a cream-coloured, two-piece outfit for the evening. It was one she had bought for the wedding of Barb's daughter and remembered how comfortable and elegant she had felt wearing it. The dress was sleeveless with a halter-top, which was glamorous enough for a formal evening yet with the jacket, it was suitable for almost any occasion. So she was confident that all possibilities would be covered for this evening. Just as some women can wear black so well, Jo knew cream or ivory tones brought out the best of her colouring. She sensed her nervousness when she had to redo her lips several times. Anxiously, she checked her watch and took a deep breath when it showed 6:55 PM. Five minutes to make her way up nine floors to Mike's room and knock on his door at precisely seven o'clock. She anticipated the feel of his strong arms around her.

Slow down, heart. He'll hear you even before he opens the door. She rounded a corner in the hallway but managed to duck back when she heard voices in the hallway. Peeking out, she saw Mike standing outside his open door. A gorgeous young woman was facing him. Jo was surprised to see Mike grasp her arms and pull her to him with enough force to crush the breath from her. The startled look on the woman's face was soon hidden from Jo's view by the back of his head. He gave her a kiss so intense it was almost brutal.

Shocked, Jo spun quickly around and ran back down the hallway to the elevator. Once inside, as she gasped for air. The breath had been crushed from her as well. The elevator was moving and she had to press her floor button quickly. After slamming the door to her room behind her, Jo started hyperventilating. She perched on the edge of the king-sized bed and lowered her head between her knees. *Why, oh why, did I come here?* What was that horrible scene she had just witnessed? Was that woman the reason Mike hadn't called this week? There was no way she could face him after what had just happened. *Oh God. I've got to get out of here!* Breathing a little more evenly, she straightened up.

Thinking Nadine might find out what had happened and give Mike her room number, she quickly stripped off her suit and nearly tripped herself as she balanced on one foot donning her slacks. She slipped into a golf-style shirt and threw the rest of her things back into her suitcase. Jo remembered the reception was on a floor above Mike's, so she felt it was probably safe to take the elevator down. Repeatedly looking over her shoulder, it seemed to take forever to check out of the hotel.

She hailed a taxi and immediately went to the airport. Unable to get a direct flight through Minneapolis that evening, she was able to obtain a late flight through Detroit to Toronto. Wanting to put as much distance as she could between herself and Mike as quickly as possible, she purchased a ticket and was delighted that she was able to board immediately.

She didn't sleep on the plane. Every time she closed her eyes she envisioned the startled look on that woman's face and then the back of Mike's head as he kissed her. *What a foolish old woman you've been, Jo Henderson! Where in the world did you ever get the idea that a woman your age could possibly hold the attention of a man like Mike Talbot? He's surrounded by beautiful, exciting women all the time. Most of them half your age.* Then second-guessing took over. Maybe she should have waited until morning and given him a chance to explain. Maybe she was his sister ... *Yeah, right. All men kiss their sisters like that.* Maybe she was an old friend that he hadn't seen in years ... *She must have been a very close old friend to be kissed like that.*

The more she thought about herself and Mike, the more she realized how hopeless this relationship had been right from the start. He may have found her attractive when he first saw her, and he well may have needed a get-away vacation before he started his new job, but she realized now, his lifestyle and hers couldn't be more different if they were living on separate planets.

It's a good thing I never confided in Barb about this silly relationship. It's humiliating enough to have to face up to rejection myself without having to explain it to anyone else. Serves me right!

By the time Jo arrived in Toronto, shock and humiliation had changed to hurt and anger. To realize that Mike had been playing her was enough to wound her deeply, but to carry on the charade after he left was the thing that made her angry. Exceedingly angry. She may never know the why of it, but she promised herself it would never happen to her again.

She decided to stay in Toronto for a couple of days. She wasn't expected back until the beginning of the week anyway, so her staff would be none the wiser. She needed time to compose herself and lick her wounds. The apartment she sometimes used in Mississauga wasn't available at this time of year so she took a limousine to downtown Toronto and checked into the Royal York Hotel. As much as she always enjoyed seeing her grandchildren, this time she just wanted to be alone. Needed to be alone.

Jo took out her frustration by shopping, and treating herself to a whole day in Lorena's Spa. While unsuccessfully attempting to purge her pain in steams and wraps, the number of messages being left on her phone at home were piling up. The same male voice expressing his disappointment that she wasn't home.

***

Fans and admirers had hounded Mike mercilessly in his younger years, but at his present age he was surprised to find that groupies still existed. At first it had been rather flattering, then a bit bothersome, finally reaching a point of being downright intolerable. He was pleased with himself that he had been blessed with the foresight not to tell anyone about Jo. No matter how well-meaning friends can be, eventually they always let things slip and he, under no circumstances, wanted Jo's life interrupted by "inquiring minds". To the unknowing public he was still a very eligible bachelor.

Recently, a female sports reporter had been coming on rather strongly to him. She was a beautiful young woman probably in her mid-thirties. As she had already told him, she found him very attractive. *God, these women are getting bolder all the time.* It was reaching the point where every time he went anywhere, even to the smallest party, she was there. Sooner or later he would find her beside him, flirting, touching, and eventually hanging on to his arm. He wondered if men ever filed sexual harassment charges against women. He figured in his case, not only would it be laughed out of court, he'd be laughed out of every dressing room across the country. He could see the headlines, "Grey-haired Has-been Files Sexual Harassment Charges."

He always found himself in the position of trying to stay below her radar, even attempting, usually unsuccessfully, to hide behind crowds. She would always tease him, asking how long he was going to continue playing hard to get. When she showed up at the door of his hotel room before the reception, he recalled the words she had whispered as he left a press conference the day before. "Mike, I'm not going to be satisfied until I've tasted your lips just once. Who knows? You might enjoy it." She had winked as she walked away.

In frustration and anger, he had grabbed her and brutally kissed her. He meant to hurt her. He wanted her to know there was no love or tenderness in those lips she wanted to taste so badly. Then he pushed her away from him, telling her through gritted teeth, "Now, you've tasted these lips of mine, you bitch. Get out of my hotel and get out of my life or I will have you arrested for stalking!"

With that he slammed the door wondering how in the hell she had managed to find his room. He got through the remainder of the evening with a forced joviality and was relieved when the reception ended with no further appearance by her.

He realized afterwards, when he had time to think about it, what a foolish thing he had done. No, it had gone beyond foolishness. It had been downright stupid. What if her camera crew had been with her? What if somebody, anybody, had witnessed him kissing her? How could he have explained that?

He was staying overnight in the hotel and realized it was early enough to call Jo after the reception. Anticipating her smooth whiskey-voice, he started whistling as he punched in her number. More than a little disappointed when she didn't answer, he left a message telling her he'd try again the next night from Buffalo. At least they would be in the same time zone. God, how he missed that woman! The more days that passed when he was unable to call, the more he realized his decision not to renew his contract was the right one. He was counting the months.

The next morning he remembered that Nadine hadn't called at 7:00 as she had said she would. Whatever it was couldn't have been that important after all. Perhaps he should check with her, just in case.

When she answered the phone, she sounded surprised to hear his voice, then asked "Well?"

"What do you mean 'well'?"

"How did it go last night?"

"It went very well. I would say the evening was a complete success."

"Well it took some strategic planning but I'm sure it was well worth it. She seems like a great lady, Mike."

Mike hesitated then slowly asked "Who's a great lady?"

Perplexed, she asked "Did you or did you not get a surprise knock on your door last night from a certain lady who shall remain nameless?"

He couldn't believe his ears. "Nadine, were you responsible for giving that … that … woman my hotel room number?"

It was her turn to hesitate.

"Nadine?"

"Guilty. Are you saying you're not pleased?"

"I can't believe you would interfere in my private life like that. I've told you countless times what your loyalty has meant to me. I just can't believe you would arrange a cozy little assignation in my hotel room with a woman I've been trying to avoid. If you value your position with me, you will never do anything like this again."

***

Nadine was stunned, absolutely stunned. She had expected supreme joy on his part. She turned crimson from the humiliation of his wrath. And wrath it had been, no mistake there. Well, at least he hadn't fired her — yet. What in hell had happened? She probably would never know. What had caused him to be so upset with that beautiful, classy woman from Canada, the one with whom he had appeared to be totally smitten? Well, she hoped Mrs. Henderson was surviving this incident without any lasting pain. She couldn't help but feel sorry for her.

***

Mike tried unsuccessfully for several more days to reach Jo and then was drawn into a whirlwind of a schedule that left him no time for any thoughts about personal life. With every unanswered phone call he became more determined that his days on television were numbered. He assumed she must have taken some time off and driven into the city.

***

Jo was surprised at the number of times Mike had called while she was away. She assumed that Nadine had told him about her visit and he was calling to make excuses. *If you have such a full love life, Mike, why bother?* Determined not to give him the satisfaction, she decided he would continue to get her voice mail when he called. In fact, she erased all his messages without listening to them. *There is nothing you can say that will make the slightest difference. That chapter of my life is over and I am moving on without you and your phoney promises.* She instructed her staff to take a message if he should call the business number. They did so without hesitation, knowing Mrs. H. was not in the best of moods and too private a person to question.

***

After a couple of weeks, it was becoming increasingly clear to Mike that Jo was not accepting his calls. Perplexed, he decided to eat humble pie and ask Nadine to try to reach her. Nadine attempted to avoid a touchy situation by reminding him that he had made it quite clear she was not to get involved in his private life. She especially didn't want to get involved in any part of it that included "that woman", as he had called her.

"I'm not asking you to call 'that woman'. I'm asking you to get Jo Henderson on the line for me."

"Is this the same Mrs. Henderson that came to your hotel room and you threatened me with dismissal for sending her there?"

Silence.

"Mike, you're a great boss but please don't ask me to call this lady. She trusted me … and well, I kind of liked her."

Mike came out of his office, his colour absolutely ashen and sat on one corner of Nadine's desk.

"What in the devil you are talking about?" He was starting to feel sick to his stomach.

"Mrs. Henderson phoned me a few weeks ago wondering if there was any way I could help her set up a surprise visit with you. She said she was able to free up her calendar for a few days and was dying to spend them with you. Knowing how often you phone her, I had no idea that your feelings about her had changed. I checked your schedule and told her I positively would be able to set something up. She flew in and I even met her at the airport. The evening of the Harmer Boys' Club reception, she was to knock on your door at precisely 7:00 in the evening — that's when I told you I would call you with some good news. I reserved a room for her several floors below yours so you wouldn't run into her in the hallway, at least not until the appointed time."

"She never came."

"Mike. You read the riot act to me the next day for sending her to you."

As realization dawned, Mike turned white and sank into the visitors' chair by Nadine's desk.

Alarmed, she poured him a glass of water and knelt down beside him. "What's going on, Mike? What happened?"

Mike related the events leading up to, and including, the scene that Jo must have seen in the hallway outside his door.

"No wonder she's not answering my calls!" The sick feeling that had started in the pit of his stomach crept up his throat. He began to perspire and downed the water Nadine handed him. "Oh my God, what do I do now?" He held his head with the palms of both hands. "Can you check my schedule and see if there are even two days I'm free to fly up there?"

"I'll call her. I'm sure she'll understand. She was so excited about seeing you again."

Nadine looked up Jo's number and dialled. There was no answer.

***

Jo looked at the number on the call display and recognized it as Mike's office. She hesitated then picked up the phone and punched her message code. She heard Mike's secretary asking Mrs. Henderson to please call her so she could explain about a huge misunderstanding the night she was in Los Angeles. Jo cursed Mike for resorting to using his secretary for his dirty work. Well, no matter. Mike Talbot was history.

THIRTEEN

For the weeks following her disastrous *surprise* holiday, Jo went about her work smiling and chatting with guests as if she didn't have a care in the world. She had survived the loss of her husband. She was certain she could survive the loss of a summer fling. Jo was determined to put Mike out of her mind as well as her life. It was difficult, but soon she would be closing the lodge for the season and moving back to Thunder Bay. Barb had driven out and stayed for a weekend with her over the summer and nothing about Mike was ever discussed.

Recalling this, Jo started giving serious consideration to spending some time with Barb in Florida. It was sounding more inviting every time they spoke. She thought momentarily about Mike, who had, at one time, figured strongly in her winter plans and who still called with decreasing regularity. He was persistent. She had to give him that. His ego probably could not accept being ignored by a woman. She had an unlisted, unpublished telephone number in Thunder Bay. She was thankful she hadn't taken him to her condo, so he had no way of knowing where she lived. She had always used a post office box for her mail since she was in and out of the city all year round.

She had almost weakened and picked up the phone once or twice when he called. However, on these tempting occasions, she'd just conjure up the image of him in the doorway of his hotel room with that woman in his arms. It was enough to strengthen her resolve not to give

131

him a chance to weaken her with his charisma. She was still smarting from succumbing so easily the first time and blushed with anger and embarrassment every time she thought of it. She couldn't understand why he was being so persistent when he obviously had a busy social life. Once again she chalked it up to his ego.

Early in the second week of October, her last guests left and the staff set about winterizing the lodge. There were water lines to flush, freezers to bed down, and boats to be lifted from the water. After checking the generator and other equipment and cleaning her own accommodations, she departed. It was always a bittersweet time for all. End-of-season meant a well-deserved rest for everyone, but it was like saying goodbye to family members who wouldn't see each other for six months.

***

Barney, who was always the last to leave, was loading his vehicle and late getting to the phone when it started ringing. However, it only rang twice and stopped. It was very late on a Sunday evening and he remembered Jo had arranged for the calls from here to be forwarded to an answering service in Thunder Bay.

***

Mike decided to call once more in the hope of perhaps having Jo answer the phone. It was dinnertime on the west coast. He was in the Los Angeles airport leaving for a full three weeks of games and appearances starting the next day in Dallas. When she didn't answer her own phone again, he tried the lodge one more time but reached an answering service. He realized with a sinking heart they had closed for the season. Mike told the service there was no message, feeling that his connection to Jo had just been severed.

***

Jo arrived home and spent several days putting her clothes and other personal things away. Before long, Barb telephoned to arrange a lunch date for the purpose of catching up on gossip.

Several days later they were sitting at their favourite table enjoying the harbour view from inside the restaurant. A waiter who had been serving them for years arrived with menus and welcomed them once again. When Barb questioned a new soup on the menu, the waiter turned to Mrs. Henderson, "Perhaps you can critique it for her. I believe you sampled it the last time you were here for dinner." Jo assured them it was delicious, but decided on a salad for herself.

***

After cautiously scrutinizing her while they ate, Barb decided there was something different about Jo's mood, something she just couldn't put her finger on. Barb thought she detected a slight shadow creep across Jo's face when she teased her about another summer gone and no American fisherman winning her heart and stealing her off to Iowa, or Nebraska, or wherever they all came from. After several unsuccessful attempts at switching to another subject, Jo looked Barb right in the face and said, "As a matter of fact, a fisherman from Wyoming did steal my heart. However, there will be no sneaking off to parts unknown. Subject closed. I will not discuss it further. Let's just change topics please."

Taken aback, Barb knew her friend well enough to know that when Jo closes a subject, it stays closed. She sensed, however, that her friend was hurting and hoped that an opportunity would present itself for her to offer a shoulder, or at least an ear.

After commenting favourably on the soup, she wondered, "So, Jo, who has replaced me here in our favourite hide-a-way? Who's the new best friend that you're swapping gossip with?"

Jo, with a rather guarded look, replied, "It isn't anyone you know."

Barb deduced it probably was the Wyoming fisherman and the jerk may not just have stolen, but broken, her friend's heart. *The bastard,* she said to herself, thinking this poor woman could only stand so many tragedies in one lifetime. Then she silently wondered if Jo's boys were aware of this unhappy turn of events in their mother's life. Probably not. Jo usually played her cards pretty close to her chest.

Barb was determined to break the sombre mood she had inadvertently brought upon her friend.

"Why don't we stop by the casino, Jo?"

"My, my, you must be feeling lucky. I didn't think you liked that place."

"No, not lucky. I just get a masochistic thrill seeing how much of my money those machines can suck out of my pocketbook. I keep waiting for one of them to actually laugh at me when I turn my purse upside down trying to shake out cab fare."

***

Several hours later, after many ups and downs on several different machines, Jo felt Barb nudge her elbow. "Let's go have a glass of wine and call it a night. I'm exhausted. That vacuum cleaner had me for almost three hundred dollars, but I fought dirty and I climbed my way back. I'm up six dollars and that sucker is not getting it."

Jo laughed at her friend standing with her jacket askew, and wiping her forehead as if she had just survived a major battle. They always managed to have a lot of fun together. "Oh Barb, I hope you still want company in Florida. I can't think of anything I would enjoy more this winter."

"That's fantastic, Jo. I was beginning to think I had been replaced, not only at 'our' restaurant, but as your fun-loving companion-in-crime, too. I'll call you when I have all the details and then we can book our flights." Smiling, she hugged her friend and gave her an extra squeeze.

After several weeks at home, Jo once again packed her bags then headed to Southern Ontario to visit her family. She was excited about spending some long quality time with her grandchildren.

The oldest, Matthew, played minor hockey and John had said he was showing some real talent. Jo thought about her son John's hockey years. She had never been overly fond of the sport so attended out of loyalty rather then pleasure. It would appear her grandson was going to continue the family tradition.

After arriving in Mississauga and attending a few games, she realized, to her utter amazement, that she was actually enjoying them. Jo even helped her son and his wife by joining the car pool of parents driving their sons to the early morning practices. To add to her wonder, she resurrected her knitting skills, and before long, found herself sitting a couple of mornings each week in a cold arena, looping wool around her needles. She was actually producing something that was beginning to look like an afghan. She smiled as she noted that all four edges were, in fact, even.

One evening, she had to chauffeur both her grandsons to the rink for a game. John and Amy were attending parent–teacher interviews at the boys' school. She was sitting in the stands with little Sammy while the hockey players warmed up on the ice, when a man wearing a team jacket sidled along the row behind and sat down almost directly at her back. He swiped Sammy's toque from his head and ruffled the boy's hair.

"Judging from this sea of grey heads, it would appear all the grandfathers and a few grandmothers have been called into active duty tonight. It might be a good idea in future for the school board to check the hockey schedules before committing parents to an evening at the school." His dark eyes sparkled as he spoke.

Jo looked at his jacket and asked if he was a member of the coaching staff. "No. Just an honorary director. Of sorts."

She noticed he pronounced each word precisely and with a very slight accent. "What does an honorary director do?"

He smiled. "Well, I'm actually a used car salesman. My daughter and some of the other team parents believe that is all the criteria necessary to be appointed Director of Fundraising." With a laugh he continued, "In other words, I'm in charge of raffle tickets."

"What are you raffling?"

"A fully restored '55 Chevy."

Jo laughed, "Oh my goodness! I took my driver's test in my dad's '55 Chevy. An automobile of that vintage probably brings back memories for a huge number of the hockey players' grandparents."

"Surprisingly, people in their mid-thirties are scooping most of the tickets we have sold so far."

He introduced himself as Tony DeMarco and did some reminiscing of his own. "The car being raffled is almost identical to the first automobile I ever owned. I think this one is in better condition than mine was, though."

"Maybe I can buy a ticket later?" She smiled as she added, "With luck, I might be driving back home instead of flying."

Near the end of the first period, John, Amy, and Tony's daughter arrived at the rink. Jo recognized the woman as a friend of Amy's and remembered that the two young hockey players were quite good friends. Tony left his seat soon after everyone arrived, and during the break, Jo went down to buy a ticket for the car raffle. Business was brisk and she found herself waiting in line. As she watched Tony chatting with all the people, she could understand why the line was not diminishing. He seemed very proud of the prize and went into great detail describing it to anyone who asked. Someone suggested, "Tony. You should get yourself a helper or you'll never sell enough tickets to break even."

Tony nodded in agreement, looked over at Jo and asked, "What do you say, Mrs. Henderson? You going to help me sell these tickets for your grandson's hockey team?"

"Wow. Lay on the guilt. When you put it like that, how can I say no?"

Amy gave John a nudge when she spotted her mother-in-law behind the raffle table and remarked to him that Grandma appeared to be getting very involved in the Mississauga Missiles Hockey Team. "Perhaps we could talk her into staying the winter."

"I doubt that, Amy. Needless to say, the boys would love it, but Mom has plans to vacation in Florida with Barb for a while before she attends the outdoors shows in the States."

"Well, I'm happy that she's involved in something while she's here. She seemed rather pensive when she first arrived. I wondered whether the lodge might be too much for her without your dad."

"Mom's a survivor. Always has been. She would never let anything keep her down. When we were growing up and got to whining or complaining too much, Mom just repeated that old cliché, 'When life hands you a lemon, make lemonade.' She always had this thing about putting the past behind you and getting on with life. If the lodge was too much for her, she would sell it before letting it pull her down."

Jo found herself becoming as excited about the car as Tony was. When she was shown a poster-size picture of it, it brought back some happy memories from her teenage years. They had sold just over a thousand dollars' worth of tickets with many parents promising to come back, when their sales were interrupted by the sound of the horn announcing the start of the next period.

"Do you need help during the next break?"

"I will accept any help you are willing to give."

By the time they closed up shop later that evening, their sales had covered about half the value of the automobile. Tony remarked on how happy he was because the team was really relying on the revenue from the raffle to help with their expenses.

"Mrs. Henderson, would you be willing to take a shift on the weekend? At the shopping mall where we'll be putting up a sales table?"

After agreeing to meet him there first thing Saturday morning, she bade him goodnight.

Later at home, a smiling Matthew proclaimed, "Grandma, it's so cool you're selling tickets for my hockey team. Most of the other grannies don't even come to the games." He demonstrated his appreciation with a big bear hug that smelled like McDonald's french fries.

***

On Saturday morning, Jo made her way into the centre area of the shopping mall. There were several tables arranged by different groups hawking various fundraising items. Tony was already there setting up an easel with the poster of the car. He handed Jo a carpenter's apron with change in the pockets and gave her a supply of pens. They sat and chatted; the morning shoppers were slow in making their way to the centre of the mall.

"Mrs. Henderson, do you mind if I ask why a pretty woman like you is called by a man's name?"

"When you're given a name like Josephine, it doesn't take long before your friends shorten it. At first it was Josy and eventually just Jo. Josephine was my maternal grandmother's name."

She smiled later in the morning, when she realized he had stopped calling her Mrs. Henderson and was now referring to her as Josy. Obviously he wasn't comfortable addressing her with a "man's name".

Business picked up as the morning progressed and before they realized it, lunchtime had come and gone. Jo asked when her replacement would be arriving, as she wanted to get a bite to eat and then had some errands to run. As she was speaking, she heard someone calling Tony's name and apologizing for being late. Turning, she recognized a team mother with Tony's daughter close behind. Jo greeted the women, removed her apron, and reached for her jacket. Tony took it from her and held it while she slid her arms inside.

"Josy, I insist on buying you lunch. All the volunteers are reimbursed for their meal when they work on Saturdays."

By this time she was quite hungry and didn't need much persuasion.

Jo found conversation with Tony came easily. She guessed his years in the used car business had honed his personality into the friendly, easy-going person he seemed to be.

After a short while, he opened up about himself a little. "My wife died ten years ago. She suffered through a very long and painful struggle with cancer." He admitted sorrowfully, that while it was difficult to be without her, he was relieved to see her finally released from her pain. "Ours was an old-fashioned marriage arranged by our families, but we couldn't have been happier."

Jo then told him about Stu's accidental death, and explained that she usually came to visit her grandsons for a while every fall, usually staying through Christmas. Finally, after realizing how much time had passed, she stood. "Thank you very much for lunch, Tony. I enjoyed selling the tickets and if you need me, I'll be happy to help again at Thursday evening's game."

On Thursday morning Amy called Jo and asked if she would mind picking up Sammy from his karate class so that she and John could both see the start of Matthew's game. After being assured that Amy would take the first shift selling tickets before the game, Jo agreed. When Jo and Sammy finally arrived at the rink, the game was well underway. Just prior to the first intermission, Jo made her way down to the lobby and found Tony getting his cash box ready. He dismissed her attempts at an apology for not being there before the game, explaining he was happy she could come at all. The horn sounded to end the first period and shortly the rush was on. Tony seemed to know just about everyone on a first name basis and everyone had a joke or a funny incident to share with him. At one point, Jo noticed a very large man standing in front of them. He wore a full but well-trimmed beard and a Toronto Maple Leaf cap on his head. He was studying the poster of the car. Tony introduced him to Jo, adding that the man was in advertising and looked after all the promotion for his used cars. The man remarked on what a beauty the car was but expressed concern that something was missing.

"A name! She's got to have a name, Tony! That'll give her a personality. What do you think would be a suitable name for a classic beauty like that?"

Without hesitation Tony announced, "Josephine. Her name should be Josephine."

"Josephine," said Tony's ad man. "Perfect. I'll even throw in some free advertising and promotion. I hope you have enough tickets printed. You couldn't have picked a better name. What made you think of it?"

"It seemed to fit your description to perfection."

Choking down a laugh, Jo realized that her Italian sales companion was looking directly at her as he spoke and immediately realized what a wonderful compliment he had paid her. Before too many days went by, there seemed to be posters everywhere of the car bearing her name. Her grandsons were quick to tell their friends the car had their grandmother's name.

***

"A car? You have a car named after you? Tell me, do you come with a spare tire?" Barb found this hilarious. "My goodness, peewee hockey games, selling raffle tickets in malls, hanging around arenas. Jo, you sound so ... so ... 'Canadian Grandma'."

"I am a Canadian grandma, you idiot! Besides, Matthew and Tony are both glad that I am."

"Matthew and *Tony*? Did Sammy change his name?"

"No, of course not. Tony is the gentleman who gave my name to the car. He also takes me to lunch every Saturday in appreciation of the time I devote to the sale of raffle tickets."

"So … What does this Tony look like? Is he single?"

"He's single, a widower. He's pleasant looking, not too tall, kind of a stocky build. He has dark hair, which is greying a little at the temples, dark eyes and a very kind face. It's hard to guess how old he is. He could be my age but I would guess a few years younger."

"And?"

"And what?"

"And are you seeing him?"

"Yes, Barb. I see him every hockey game and every Saturday. I already told you that."

"I can't picture it. Grandma Henderson sitting with a kind-looking man at the hockey rink, selling raffle tickets. This is too much!" Barb started laughing hysterically.

"Put a lid on it, Barb, or I'll cancel my plane reservation to Florida. I could stay here and sell tickets all winter."

"You wouldn't."

"No, I'm just teasing. Actually the draw is a couple of days before Christmas."

"Then the romance is over?"

"There *is* no romance!"

***

After a month of hockey games and Saturdays at the mall, Jo realized that she and Tony had developed a real friendship. Then one Saturday, "Josy, do you think we might skip lunch today and make it dinner instead?"

Damn, why now, when everything is going along just fine? I hope dinner just means dinner replacing lunch, Mr. DeMarco.

FOURTEEN

Jo found herself hesitating, unsure of his intent. As pleasant as Tony was, she certainly didn't want to encourage another relationship. She was still hurting from the last one, for heaven's sake. She almost couldn't believe it when she heard herself saying, "Well, I suppose we could, just this once."

She promised herself that if she sensed he was reading more into it than she wanted, then Mr. DeMarco would kindly and gently be placed into history. Tony informed her that he usually went to Mass at 5:00 in the afternoon on Saturdays, therefore, he'd pick her up around 7:00 PM.

Jo was ready when he arrived at her suite and they went to a Chinese restaurant near the hockey arena. He seemed to know just about everyone that came through the door and introduced her to so many people, she forgot their names as soon as they walked away from the table.

"Josy, I apologize for the constant interruptions. Perhaps we should have gone somewhere outside the neighbourhood where I don't know as many people. I always enjoy this particular restaurant, though. I'm not aware of any other that serves better Chinese food."

After savouring the delightful flavour of their scrumptious chicken guy ding and mushrooms, and vegetables chow mein, Jo couldn't imagine anything better anywhere else and told him so.

Their conversation centred on minor hockey, but when Jo admitted to never having attended a professional hockey game, he offered to take her to see one of the Toronto Maple Leaf home games. "It's almost impossible to purchase game tickets, but one of my friends owns season tickets and has offered them to me from time to time. There is a good possibility they might be available for a game in January."

Jo thanked him but declined. "I'll be in Florida for most of January then I immediately have to return to Thunder Bay."

She noticed the smile fade from his face. His intense brown eyes held hers, while softly saying he was enjoying her company immensely. "This disappoints me. You are the first woman I feel comfortable sharing dinner with since my wife died."

"Tony, I am very touched by your kind words. I'm sorry, but I'm not ready for anything more than … than a casual friendship. I'm truly sorry. I don't want to hurt you."

He took her hand in his then slowly brought it to his lips. "I understand completely. I have been alone much longer than you. I hope we can continue to be friends."

She smiled and squeezed his hand. "Certainly. I'm enjoying our friendship."

When he took her home, he walked to the door of her building with her, kissed her hand again, and bade her goodnight. When alone in her suite, she sat down and thought about Tony's handsome face that framed those dark, romantic eyes. She wondered how, after having been closely united and so deeply in love with Stu for all those many years, she could find herself attracted to two men in such short succession. Did that make her a floozy? She didn't feel like one. She wasn't looking for a man. Hadn't been when Mike came upon the scene, either. Vulnerable possibly, but she wasn't going to accept anything more than friendship from any man, not for a long time anyway.

Jo hoped she hadn't hurt Tony's feelings by her slight rebuff. Admittedly, he was a charming man, polite in an old-fashioned way, and she really did enjoy calling him a friend.

The following Tuesday evening, she was very relieved when Tony greeted her with a big smile at the ticket table, and handed her several books of tickets. The sales had dropped steadily at the rink because most of the hockey fans were the same groups of parents who had already bought their tickets. There were still some newcomers, and some regulars who tended to wait until the last minute before purchasing, but for the most part, the major rush was over. Tony and Jo had more time to chat between periods, and he asked her all about her travel plans to Florida and about the shows where she did her promotions. He had never been to Northwestern Ontario so she enjoyed telling this eager listener all about the scenic countryside with the abundance of lakes, the fishing and the sunsets — oh, those glorious sunsets.

"You wouldn't believe the sky could turn so many colours. It just takes your breath away. After all these years, I am still awed by the splendour of it."

When they were closing up shop for the evening, he commented, "Perhaps I can talk my son-in-law into bringing my grandson to your resort. I think I would enjoy the three of us 'men' going fishing together."

"I promise you won't be sorry. Not with the fishing or the scenery."

On the evening of December twenty-second, the draw for "Josephine" was scheduled to take place at centre ice, between the second and third periods of the hockey game. The rink contained a full house, and they had peddled another several hundred dollars' worth of tickets that evening prior to the draw. When the second period was nearing the final two minutes, Tony asked Jo to accompany him down to the ice surface to assist with the draw. He asserted the car was named for her, she had worked hard selling tickets, so it was only fitting that she should draw the winning ticket.

"But Tony, you're the one responsible for the whole fundraiser. From the first idea right through all the successful ticket sales. That's not fair to you."

"Why don't you draw the ticket and I will read the name. Does that sound okay?"

"If that's what you really want."

"Listen. We're a team, you and me, through to the end. Grand-mothers and grandfathers have to stick together to help their grand-children."

With that they stepped onto the carpet leading to centre ice and Tony thanked all the people who had helped with the success of the raffle. He gave an unofficial estimate of the total ticket sales to thun-derous applause. He then announced that the real Josephine, Josy Henderson, would draw the winning ticket. He gave the drum several turns, opened the hatch, and Josy, after reaching well down to the bottom, handed him a ticket. Tony read the name and suddenly, whoops and shouts could be heard from a seat near the visiting team's blue line. It was only seconds before the lucky ticket holder bounded onto the ice. Tony slipped the keys into Jo's hand for her to present to the winner. It was a man, Jo guessed, in his mid-forties and wearing a Missiles jacket. When she handed him the keys and put her hand out to shake his, he gave her an enormous bear hug and placed a kiss on her cheek. They had to redo this scene several times for the various cameras that were flashing in their faces. Finally, Jo backed away, but Tony caught her arm and drew her in beside him while he completed interviews with several reporters. He told her they wanted to ask her a few questions, and she realized they were interested in two things. One was how it felt to have a car named after her, the other was how a grandmother from Northwestern Ontario had become so involved in the fundraising efforts of a hockey team in Mississauga, Ontario.

"My friend, Mr. DeMarco is responsible for both." She smiled at Tony. "I came to the rink simply to watch my grandson play hockey and before I knew it, I was charmed into selling tickets. To my surprise, he also chose my name for the car."

After a few more simple questions, the carpet was removed for the Zamboni to resurface the ice, and everyone returned to their seats. Tony asked, "Will you join me and some of the other fundraising committee members in a celebration after the game?"

"Of course. I would love to."

About ten of the helpers she had noticed around the rink and the mall went to a bar located closer to the city centre and drank beer, toasting their own success. Tony appeared to be the host and paid for several rounds. Jo, never a big beer drinker, didn't want to single herself out, so she nursed a glass of the light beer on tap. A couple of the reporters from the rink had joined them and Jo found herself really enjoying the camaraderie. She felt younger than she had in years and linked, in a small way, to this warm friendly group. Sipping away on an unwanted second draft, she noticed the respect and friendliness everyone showed Tony and realized that all these people had a very high regard for him.

One of the younger women came and stood by her, and after a few minutes of chatting, asked, "Are you and Tony seeing each other socially?"

Jo was surprised by her boldness, but realizing younger people are more open about relationships, answered that they were good friends only.

"Too bad," the woman commented, "I'm rather disappointed. Tony has been noticeably happier these last few weeks. He is such a nice man. All his friends hoped he had found someone special."

Jo was about to explain that she wasn't from Mississauga and that she would be leaving right after Christmas, but figured, in the end, it really was no one's business. The woman nodded and chatted for a few more minutes then moved on to a conversation with another woman. Tony had been watching Jo, smiling when she talked with his friends so easily. When he noticed she was sitting on the edge of the crowd, finally, he made his way over. "Are you ready to leave?"

Feeling bad about pulling him away from his friends, she offered to take a taxi but he wouldn't hear of it. "I think there's a rule about going home with the boy who brought you?"

She laughed and reminded him that the rule only applied to "girls" and by no stretch of the imagination could anyone mistake her for a girl.

"Ah. My dream would be to know you when you were a girl. You broke the hearts of many boys in high school, I have no doubts."

"I had to work so hard and concentrate so intensely in school just to get passing grades, my father didn't allow me to date much. When

I completed a college secretarial course, I started working right away, and still didn't have much time for learning the fine art of breaking hearts. I'm afraid I was rather plain and boring as a young girl. Not many boys noticed me. My friend, Barb, however … Now there lies a different story. She always had several on the string. When she got married, most of the eligible bachelors in town were left to mend their broken hearts."

"Those boys must have been either blind or brainless, Josy. I cannot imagine you ever being boring. Or so plain not to be noticed. I have a feeling there were plenty of broken hearts, whether you noticed them or not."

While they were walking out to the car, Tony asked Jo if she had any plans for New Year's Eve. After replying that she usually spent a quiet night at home, he took her hand and asked, "Will you come with me to a family gathering at my brother's home?" When he noticed the start of a slight frown, he added, "I know you want friendship only, Josy. That is all I am extending. It's just an informal evening but perhaps we could have dinner together first."

He really was a pleasant man. Gentle and kind. She had noticed that the young players at the rink called him by his first name, and he always had a word of encouragement or praise for each of them. Everyone had a high regard for him, and deciding to go with her gut instincts, she accepted his invitation.

Christmas was happier than she thought it would be. Her mind drifted only once in a while to a pair of blue eyes, wondering where the man who owned them might be spending the holidays. At one time, she and Mike had discussed the possibility of being together during the Christmas season. *Yeah. Like you ever intended* that *to happen, Mike Talbot.*

It was heartwarming being with her family and watching the young boys opening their Christmas presents. They had all gone to Mass the evening before, and later had listened to carollers singing their choruses outside the front door. Amy's parents were away this Christmas visiting her brother who lived in British Columbia, so they were a smaller group than usual. Jo couldn't help thinking how nice it was not to have to share the grandchildren this year. *What a selfish thought. You should be ashamed of yourself, Jo Henderson.* She smiled innocently. *But I don't really feel selfish, and I'm not ashamed.* She smiled triumphantly this time. Amy went all-out on the turkey and trimmings. Just when Jo thought she couldn't possibly bring her fork to her mouth one more time, her daughter-in-law backed in from the kitchen with plum pudding aflame. Jo decided she might have room for one or two small bites after all.

Much later, when she was pulling the covers over her in bed, she realized her idle thoughts had been on Mike and not Stu this day. Fraught with guilt, she mentally asked forgiveness from Stu and then turned her thoughts to Christmases past, when their own sons were small. Jo finally fell asleep remembering cutting down a Christmas tree on their own lake property the last year both boys had lived at home.

John and Amy had decided to go tobogganing on Boxing Day in the hills northwest of Mississauga. Matthew had a scheduled hockey game at 11:30 in the morning, which Jo decided to skip, thinking she could use the time to catch up on her reading. She had unopened newspapers from several previous days on her kitchen table. Her family agreed to pick her up later, on their way to the hills.

What the heck? There in one corner — a rather large corner — of the first page of the sports section, was a picture of her being kissed on the cheek by the winner of Josephine. The accompanying article told the story of the successful raffle and recounted some history about the team. Then it homed in on one Mr. Tony DeMarco, well-known used car magnate in the Golden Triangle. It explained how he had worked incessantly to help raise funds for the hockey team on which his grandson played. It continued to report how, in recent weeks, he and his friend, Josy Henderson, for whom the car was named, worked side by side to make this raffle an unqualified success. It mentioned the amount of money they had raised, and that every penny had gone to help the minor league hockey team, thanks to the generosity of Mr. DeMarco who had donated the car.

Jo read the article again. She was surprised to see herself in the news, but even more surprised by the disclosure of Tony's generosity. He hadn't mentioned to her that the car was a donation. In fact, she remembered him saying at one point that the sales to date had covered the cost of the car. She smiled at the use of the term "magnate" in reference to Tony. *How much of a magnate could a used car salesman be?* she wondered then decided that an inexperienced young reporter searching for descriptive words had probably written the article. Oh well, it was nice to see both the league and Tony receive some publicity, even if it was her picture they used.

Jo and her family enjoyed their afternoon on the toboggan runs. It brought back many fond memories from happier years when she and Stu had spent their leisure time in the winter enjoying outdoor activities with their own sons. Jo found herself participating in many jaunts out in the fresh air over the next few days. She even went ice-skating, which she hadn't attempted since her boys were very young. Then a friend of John's invited the whole family to his country cabin to enjoy snowmobiling for a day. The week seemed to speed by and before she knew it, New Year's was almost upon them.

Jo looked at her wardrobe and realized her choice of evening clothes was rather limited. Amy dropped by for lunch one day, and the two of them decided to choose something from Jo's closet that would be appropriate for New Year's Eve.

"Oh, Mother, how gorgeous! I've never seen this on you," Amy exclaimed holding up the eggplant-coloured dress.

"I've only worn it once."

"Really? Bet you looked smashing! Too bad it's a bit bare for this time of year or you would have knocked Tony's eyes out with it! What was the occasion?"

"I didn't buy it for a specific occasion but I did wear it once when I went out for dinner with a friend in Thunder Bay."

"Oh, Mother, you didn't waste this beautiful dress on Barb did you?"

"No. It wasn't Barb." Before Amy could ask any more questions, Jo lifted out the hanger with the cream-coloured outfit she'd worn that fateful evening in San Francisco. She posed holding it in front of her and turned for Amy's approval.

Her daughter-in-law nodded. "With your colouring, you won't need much in the way of accessories."

Jo decided if there were any unpleasant memories associated with this dress, she would exorcize them by enjoying New Year's Eve with another handsome man.

***

"We have dinner reservations for 8:00, Josy." Tony informed her the morning of New Year's Eve.

"I'll be ready. Why don't you come early enough to have a glass of wine before we leave?"

After taking great pains to ensure her hair and makeup were absolutely perfect, she chose matching topaz pin and earrings. That was the only colour she added. Carrying a cream-coloured evening bag and wearing cream shoes, she was pleased with her reflection in the mirror. Since she would be meeting Tony's family, she wanted to look her very best.

At 6:30 a knock sounded. When Jo opened the door, Tony was speechless. He raised her hand and kissed it in true European style, never taking his eyes from hers. Jo couldn't help but think how handsome he looked, his dark eyes were almost as black as his suit. He was not tall, probably around five feet nine inches, quite full-chested, thick through the waist, but with a flat stomach that gave him an appearance of great strength. His suit fit him well and appeared to be of very fine quality. She guessed his grey shirt and tie were both silk. She wondered how she had thought him plain looking when she first met him. His looks grew on you as you came to know the man within, she guessed. He truly was a very beautiful man on the inside.

Jo was hesitant in complimenting him, afraid to encourage him in any way. "That is a beautiful suit you're wearing. You look very handsome."

***

Unable to take his eyes from her, he realized it was going to be very difficult not to do or say anything that might frighten this gentle woman. He hoped with all his heart that after her holiday down south, she might come back to visit her grandchildren again. Tony was a patient man, but he knew his patience would be sorely tried over the next few months.

They stood for a few seconds staring at each other. Jo broke the tension by asking, "Do you prefer red or white wine?"

"Red, please. You look beautiful, Josy." He wanted to tell her so much more, how the soft colour she was wearing enhanced her delicate features, how the graceful lines of her dress followed the lovely curve of her waist and slender hips. It was because of his fear of losing her that he kept these thoughts to himself.

***

They enjoyed a leisurely dinner of prime rib roast and lobster tail at one of Toronto's finest downtown restaurants. The elegant table settings and quiet holiday atmosphere contributed to a hushed anticipation of the midnight celebrations. This was the adult counterpart of Christmas Eve for the children. The little ones look forward to the gifts they can expect under the tree the next morning, while on this eve, the grown-ups anticipate what the New Year will bring them.

Jo was quite surprised that Tony was able to get a reservation on such short notice. Once again, she enjoyed his ability of being a great conversationalist, and was surprised to learn that he loved the theatre. He was familiar with most of the major plays and musicals that were currently running in New York and Toronto. When she stated that one of her favourites had been a production of *My Fair Lady* at Stage West a number of years before, he mentioned that it was returning in the early spring and that perhaps they could see it together *if* she were planning to return. Slowly, the realization dawned that this man, who had worn a baseball cap and hockey jacket for the entire time she had known him, had another whole facet which intrigued her. She agreed to attempt a return trip east before heading back to the lake.

They left the restaurant well past 10:00 and travelled the short distance to his brother's home, situated in a nearby residential neighbourhood of stately, well-maintained houses. The house was decorated very festively on the exterior and the strains of Christmas carols could be heard coming from inside. They proceeded unannounced through the front door. Once inside, Tony helped her remove her coat and hung it in a closet at one side of the spacious foyer. Sure enough, just as the sounds that had permeated the windows facing the street had indicated, almost everyone was gathered around the piano singing. The song of the moment was "Silver Bells". They entered the living room hand in hand.

As soon as Tony was spotted, the singing stopped and one extremely beautiful, slender woman with silver hair, broke from the group. She smiled as she hugged him and kissed both of his cheeks. It was his sister Sophia, Jo learned when they were introduced, the eldest in the family. Then his brother, Giorgio, their host, who preferred to be called George, wandered over wanting to be introduced to the famous Josephine. Before she knew it, Jo was hugged and kissed by nine or ten different relatives and realized that everyone was calling her Josy. The entire group welcomed her warmly.

George's wife, Jean, who was not Italian either, declared with a wink, "Josy, you have no idea how happy I am to have another fair-haired female in our midst."

George laughed. "After twenty-five years of marriage, you are more Italian than if you had been born in the old country, but you're just too stubborn to admit it." He offered Jo a wink.

As the evening progressed, Jo realized what a truly loving, close-knit family they were. She was also surprised to discover that this was the first New Year's Eve Tony had shared with them since a few years after his wife had died. He later disclosed that he had found it too painful, since she had always enjoyed this evening so much. Jo was overcome with emotion when a woman, who appeared to be about the same age as Tony's daughter, whispered softly in his ear, "Welcome back, Zio," giving Jo's hand a squeeze at the same time. Jo was struck with how much thought Tony must have given to the invitation he had extended for her to join him this evening. Knowing how difficult it was for her to frequent the places that were special to her and Stu, she understood the emotional stress Tony must be suffering tonight.

They continued with the conversations and singing until midnight, when the large grandfather clock in the corner of the dining room started booming out the hour with great resonance and clarity. The time had passed so quickly, it took them all by surprise. Tony placed his drink on the table and embraced Jo in his powerful arms, black eyes looking into amber ones. He kissed her fully and gently on the mouth. A simple "thank you" escaped his lips as he took her hand in his and kissed it. She noticed the moisture in his eyes just before a cousin slid between them and kissed her after saying "Happy New Year," then sent her moving on to another, then another.

Once the initial celebrations and toasting were over, George asked Tony, "Will you do the honours this year?"

Jean whispered to Jo, "Their mother died on January first, sixteen years ago, and every year since then, one or several of them, always sings 'Ave Maria'. After that, we all drink a toast to their mother. The hymn was her favourite."

Tony hesitated saying the honour didn't belong to him since he hadn't joined them in many years, but they insisted. He took Jo's hand, pulled it through his arm and held it there firmly. Sophia keyed the first few notes on the piano and then Tony broke into a rich baritone that sent shivers through Jo. When he finished, she wiped the tears from her cheeks and realized there wasn't a dry eye in the room. She turned to Tony and kissed his damp cheek and saw the emotion smouldering in his dark eyes. He managed a smile as he brought her hand to his lips before he released it.

Jean stood up as she dried her eyes with a lace-edged handkerchief. "It's time for food. Everything is set up in the dining room. I'll just need a couple of minutes to set out the hot dishes."

The invitation had only to be issued once before everyone started moving toward the dining room. Jo held Tony back as she whispered, "I've never heard that hymn sung with such emotion and tenderness, Tony. It made my heart stop beating." She kissed him softly on the cheek.

A few hours earlier at the restaurant, Jo had vowed she would not even look at food at least until dinner the next day, but when she saw the banquet laid out before her, she realized how truly fickle her intentions were. The women must have been cooking steadily for a week to prepare all the delicacies that were so beautifully arranged on the table. Finally, around four in the morning, after eating and dancing and singing most of the night away, everyone agreed it was time to go home.

While Tony and Jo were working their way through the departing guests in the foyer, George asked Tony if they could meet to talk in the next few days, as a decision had to made in the very near future. The men agreed to meet three days later, and Jo and Tony kissed their goodbyes to everyone. When George held her in a warm embrace, he whispered, "I hope we will see you again, Josy. Soon. And often."

Then before she could give a reply, she was released from his embrace and a cousin was hugging George in her place and thanking him for the evening.

During the drive home, Tony was very quiet and seemed in a contemplative mood. Jo didn't push for conversation, it seemed he wanted to be left alone with his thoughts, but he did reach over and take her hand at one point, smiling at her as he did so. As they neared her building, Jo hoped Tony didn't have any expectations about coming upstairs. She was experiencing strong emotions and didn't want to have to deal with them. She was relieved when he asked what time she was leaving the day after New Year's.

"Will you let me drive you to the airport?"

"I was hoping I would see you again before I leave. Thank you for one of the nicest New Year's evenings I've enjoyed in a very long time. You have a wonderful family, Tony."

As he brought her hand to his mouth, he whispered, "You have no idea what this evening has meant to me. What having you by my side has meant to me. Thank you, Josy."

After escorting her inside the building and seeing her safely into the elevator, he kissed her cheek and left. As she rode the elevator to her floor, she was positive she heard bells. New Year bells? Or warning bells?

FIFTEEN

The next day, thinking — or at least hoping — that her mother-in-law would be sleeping in, Amy waited until almost noon before phoning to hear all about the big date. Jo felt herself once again wrought with emotion as she attempted to tell Amy about Tony's family, and the hymn he sang, and how comfortable she had felt in his brother's home. Amy remarked that Tony's daughter had often confided how much she enjoyed the family gatherings. Sylvia had also disclosed that theirs was a very close and loving family, and her wish had always been for the kind of marriage for herself that her mother and father had shared. She had confided in Amy that after her mother died, her father seemed to build an armour about him that was hard to penetrate. He appeared happy enough on the outside, but she knew he was suffering such terrible loneliness on the inside. And he would not let anyone in. He kept his pain within that shield and presented nothing but smiles and laughter for his daughter, her husband, and his grandson. Amy commented that anyone who knew Tony had nothing but the greatest admiration and respect for him. After concluding their conversation, Jo realized her emotions were in turmoil and she wasn't the least bit sure how she should deal with them.

Tony was a deeply caring man and she realized that he probably had the same principles, morals and sense of family that she had. He didn't excite her quite the way Mike had. He didn't have the same flirtatious, easy sense of humour that Mike had. That was one of the things she found she had really enjoyed with Mike, and what she now really missed. Mike could probably walk away from a relationship as easily as he walked into it. *Duh … That was exactly what he had done, wasn't it?* Whereas, Tony would not give his love away very easily. His would be a lasting kind of love, and while not as exciting, it could certainly make her feel very protected and cared for. One pair of eyes were blue and exciting, the other dark and passionate.

After finding herself weighing each man's flaws and perfections, she decided that Florida was the best thing for her. *I can't think about this right now. I just want to get away and have a fun-filled, relaxing-in-the-sun time with Barb.*

She had her bags packed and was all ready to go about half an hour before Tony arrived. Her suite was close to the airport freeway and she knew they had ample time. Her flight being an international one meant that she had to be at the airport well before her scheduled departure. They had agreed to allow enough time to share a late breakfast together in one of the airport restaurants after checking her bags through. True to his word, he delivered her to the terminal early, so they were soon sitting in a corner booth in a Seattle Coffee House near the security gates. Jo ordered quiche and coffee while Tony asked for the sausage and scrambled egg special.

She remembered sitting with another man in another airport. Was this her destiny to be always saying goodbye in airport terminals?

"Josy? Josy?"

She was lifted from her reverie by Tony's soft voice. He was handing her a business card.

"I have written my home number on the back. Keep it in your wallet. Please. Do you have a number where I might reach you — in case of an emergency?"

Realizing she had only Barb's cell phone number and not the condo phone, she gave him her own cell number. Smiling, she informed him, "Tony, you can call me even if it's not an emergency."

He returned the smile. "I think I might be able to come up with an emergency of some kind … If I try hard enough."

She was surprised to find herself dawdling and really not wanting to say goodbye. Determined, though, not to make any promises, she kept the conversation light, knowing that once commitments were made, she could not break them without hurting him. Finally, they walked hand in hand to the security gate and before he let her slip through the doorway, he took her hand and brought it to his cheek. Then he placed two soft kisses upon it and lifted her chin with his other hand. She looked at the sadness in his eyes and felt her own eyes growing damp. Removing her hand from his, she slid it around his neck and without too much thought, she was kissing him and sliding her other arm around his waist. Taken by surprise, Tony responded slowly. Then hesitantly parted his lips slightly and kissed her with all the warmth that he felt.

She turned quickly, not trusting her emotions, and went through the doorway without a word or a look back. Tony was left empty-armed but smiling. He went whistling through the concourse and out to the parking lot. Jo walked dazedly to the gate where her plane would soon depart. During the flight, she could feel Tony's lips, as if they were still pressed against hers. She was surprised at how much she had enjoyed the passionate warmth of them, and for the life of her couldn't figure out what had made her behave in such an irrational manner.

Barb met her at the airport in Tampa and they drove down the coast to the beach condominium they would be sharing for the next month. Almost instantly, Barb sensed something was amiss with Jo, but she wisely put off her questions until Jo was settled. When they were enjoying a drink on the balcony overlooking the bay, Barb commented. "You don't appear to be feeling well."

"Just tired from the holidays, and the flight. I had a busy time over New Year's. After a few days of sun and beach, I'm sure I'll feel like a new woman."

Barb knew her old friend better than that and wouldn't let up. Finally, after taking a deep breath, Jo looked at her friend and said, "OK. I can see you're not going to leave me alone until you know all the sordid details. Better pour yourself a tall drink. It's a long story."

She told Barb everything that had happened to her since Mike's first phone call to reserve a cabin until her parting kiss with Tony at the airport. Feeling like she had been through the ringer by the time she finished, she sat teary-eyed in front of her friend.

"I was on the verge of telling you to get a life, Jo. I thought perhaps you were starting to feel alone, that life was passing you by. Boy, was I wrong!"

"I needed this break, Barb. I really am in desperate need of some time to think and regroup. I was so hurt by Mike, I didn't think I would ever trust my heart to another man. Then, while I'm still licking my wounds, along comes Tony. I did not, I repeat, did not, need another man to further complicate my life. I really want to make sure that whatever my feelings for him might be, they are not in any way merely a rebound from the aftermath of Mike."

"This Tony sounds like a gem."

"Oh, he is. If I wasn't still hurting and so unsure of my feelings for Mike, Tony would have swept me off my feet. He's so … so … reliable!"

"Just reliable?"

"No. Not 'just' reliable. Although after Mike, reliability is a real plus. He's nice looking, kind, considerate. Seems to be financially secure. I believe he might be a man capable of great passion. You should hear him sing, Barb! Like an opera star. His family is warm and caring. A perfect man really."

"Then what's the problem?"

Joe stood up and looked out at the water, then sat and looked at her hands. "Mike. Mike is the problem."

"Mike? God, Jo, he sounds like a jerk."

"That jerk is under my skin."

"What are you gonna do about it?"

"I don't know. I'm hoping that time will cleanse him right out of my system. You have no idea how much he hurt me. I really cared for him. I still do, I guess." She stood up again and stared out over the balcony. "I can't blame him completely. I suppose it's a real 50–50 situation. Fifty per cent he's a jerk and fifty per cent I was a naïve, stupid woman. "

"You are not stupid, Jo. He's a predator. A predator who took advantage of a lonely widow. I say he's not worth the tears you're shedding for him."

"OK." Jo took a deep breath and looked Barb squarely in the eye. "OK. OK, I agree. Maybe he's not but just allow me some space … Please. I don't really want to talk about it any more. Or even think about it for a few days. I just want some time to relax and I'll deal with this when I'm ready. I came here to soak up the sun and enjoy a long vacation with my favourite friend."

Barb put down her drink, knelt beside Jo and wrapped her in a bear hug. "Take all the time you need, sweetie. In the meantime, it is now almost bedtime. We still haven't eaten and I'm starving."

After devouring a delivery pizza, they changed into their pyjamas and watched the late news on TV.

The next morning after they'd eaten breakfast on the balcony, Barb decided to show Jo some of the local scenery. Their tour ended with a shopping spree at a giant flea market. They tried on silly hats, bought some colourful T-shirts and giggled as they watched their "distinctive" features being drawn by a caricaturist. Jo found a poster advertising a '55 Chevy — coincidentally the same colour as Josephine — that she bought and autographed as "Josephine" to take back for Tony.

After a day of laughter with her friend, Jo felt much better when they returned and changed into their swimsuits and went down to relax by the pool. That evening after dinner, they strolled along the beach looking for an ice cream vendor.

For the next few days, they followed pretty well the same routine. Jo decided to sign up for scuba diving lessons, something that had been a life-long dream. She was going through brochures about a few classes being offered in the vicinity, when her cell phone rang.

Barb looked at her questioningly as Jo picked it up.

"Josy, it's not exactly and emergency but my stomach is unsettled and my heart is empty. I think I might be coming down with something." The deep, rich baritone voice surprised her.

"Tony, I'm sorry to hear that but I distinctly remember telling you that you didn't need to wait for an emergency."

"I didn't want to bother you too soon. I thought maybe if I waited a while, you might begin to miss me just a little, but then I decided if I waited too long, you might forget me."

"It's good to hear your voice. And no, I haven't forgotten you."

Barb smiled and went out onto the balcony, closing the door behind her.

"Did you have a good flight?"

They talked about her flight, the condo, the view from the balcony. "I'm thinking about taking scuba diving lessons."

"I used to scuba dive in the Tyrrhenian and Adriatic Seas when I visited Nonno and Nonna, my grandparents, in Italy."

"I wouldn't have pictured you as the water sport type."

"Really, cara? How did you have me pictured?"

"Oh, I don't know. More the vineyard or olive grove owner, I guess."

His laughter was warm and came from deep within.

"Tell me, Tony. How is the hockey going? Are our grandsons playing well?"

He gave her a play-by-play description of how their two grandsons had scored the only goals in the game the night after she left. There was a prolonged pause finally, and in that pause, she realized she didn't want the conversation to end. Grasping for straws, she reminded him, "Tony, don't forget your promise to take me to the dinner theatre when I return."

His heart skipped a beat when he realized she really was planning to return to Mississauga. "Josy, I'll buy the tickets tomorrow. Tell me when to expect you."

"Perhaps you should buy the tickets then tell me when to be there. Tickets aren't always available when you want them."

He laughed. "Therefore, I will get them for the earliest possible date."

"I thought the show didn't start until spring." She laughed at the eagerness he displayed in his tone.

"That's true. Unfortunately. It's sometime the middle of March.

Do you really have to wait until then to come back?"

"When I leave Florida, I have to return almost immediately to Thunder Bay. Once there, I have to pack up my gear to go to some of the outdoors trade shows back in the States again. A good part of my summer business depends on my attendance at these shows. It might be a good idea to buy tickets for around the end of March. I should be finished by then."

"Ah, bella. What am I going to do without you until then?"

"Well, if you play your cards right, I might be able to stay a few days in Mississauga between Florida and Thunder Bay."

"You tell me which cards I should play and I will stack the deck."

"Tony?"

"Yes, cara?"

"Will you call me again? Soon?"

"Perhaps in an hour or so?"

She could hear Barb close the door behind her as she came back inside so she hesitated answering.

"OK. If that's too soon, I'll wait until tomorrow."

"I miss you, Tony." She couldn't believe she said that! And what's more she realized she meant it. The silence on the other end of the phone was deafening.

"I am overjoyed. I will call you again tomorrow night. Goodnight, my love."

"Goodnight, Tony."

"Well. So much for taking time to think, girl."

"Oh Barb. He is such a … such a … nice man."

"Hmm. I would love to meet this … nice man."

"I'd like that, too."

Jo stared at the window. When had she become so impetuous? She had always been known for having both feet firmly planted on the ground.

***

Try as he might, Tony could not erase the smile. He finally gave up trying and sat contemplating the conversation he had just shared with the woman he was certain he loved. She had surprised him at the airport when she had put her arms around him and kissed him. He knew she was hesitant about opening her heart to him, but at least she was not afraid to show her emotions or her affection. Perhaps, with patience, he could win her over.

***

The following day, Jo received her first scuba diving lesson and was disappointed when she found out it took place in a swimming pool. Thinking she would immediately be out under the ocean, swimming with the fish among the underwater flowers and coral, she was disheartened.

She told Barb, "When I walked into the change rooms by the pool and looked at all those young faces and slender, well-toned bodies, I almost turned around and walked right back out. I was the only one there in a one-piece bathing suit, most had thong bikinis on. Talk about feeling like somebody's great-grandmother!"

"Come on. It couldn't have been that bad. You have a great shape — for your age."

"Thanks a lot. That makes me feel much better."

"You mean there were no retired executives, or Naval men there?"

"The pool was full of children. Not a grey head among them. And thank you, but I don't need any more men to distract me."

"Children?"

"Yes, children. Nobody there was over twenty-five. But, I felt good about keeping up with them. My breathing was perfect, and my swimming — even with that heavy gear — was excellent. No one had to help me out of the pool, and no one offered to fetch my walker, and no one — God bless them — tried to hand me a cane. The instructor did promise us that after several lessons we will go out into the shallow lagoon. Who knows? Before I hit sixty-five, I may actually go under the ocean."

Barb wanted to go for an early dinner so she could watch a made-for-TV movie later. Uncertain what time Tony might call, Jo agreed. She had given him the phone number for the condominium, so she left her cell phone at home and saved herself the trouble of carrying a purse. The ridiculously low price of shrimp in Florida always amazed her and she could never seem to get her fill. They ate again at an all-you-can-eat shrimp buffet, and then felt compelled to walk the couple of kilometres home to work off the calories.

When they arrived back at the condominium, there was a message from Tony, saying he had called before going out to a meeting. He was disappointed to miss her because he would be out of town for a couple of days, but he promised to telephone her again upon his return. On impulse, she called his number and left a message that she, too, was disappointed at having missed his call and would look forward to talking to him in a few days.

Friends of Barb's from Chicago phoned a couple of days later to inform her they were down in Florida for a few weeks and were planning on going out on their boat for several days. They said they would be delighted if the two women would join them. They absolutely would not accept "no" for an answer, and would expect both Barb and Jo at the dock the next day at noon. They further issued orders for the women to bring enough changes of underwear for at least three or four days. Jo was persuaded to go because of the promise of some scuba diving around the Keys. Some certified divers would be among the guests and they would assist Jo with her dives.

Feeling guilty about leaving before she could speak with Tony again, she phoned and left a message on his answering machine and promised to call him when she returned.

After four days filled with scuba diving, fishing and sun, they returned to their condominium. Jo was overwhelmed by the undersea experiences she had enjoyed. Saddened that the colours and indescribable beauty under the ocean could be enjoyed by only a precious few, she was determined to experience them again and again. Perhaps she could talk Tony into an undersea adventure. What in the world was she thinking? Laughing to herself, she pondered the difficulty of twisting Tony's arm into taking a Caribbean vacation with her.

The two women mutually decided to do nothing but relax and lounge around the pool for the next week or so. There was a message from John on the answering machine just checking up, and several more for Barb. She returned John's call that evening and learned that Matthew had injured his elbow and would have to sit out a few games. She spoke with Amy briefly and said to give Sammy a big hug for her.

By the time Barb returned her calls it was quite late in the evening and Jo wondered whether Tony might already be in bed. She realized that she really was yearning to hear his voice, so decided to chance a late call. She dialled his number and was relieved when he sounded wide-awake as he answered.

"Hi, Tony. I hope I didn't wake you up."

"Cara mia, you have my permission to wake me anytime."

"It's wonderful to hear your voice."

"Do you really mean that?"

Hesitating only a moment, she took a deep breath and answered softly, "Yes. Yes, I guess I do."

"I'll be counting the days until I can meet you at the airport."

Attempting to lighten the tone, she laughed. "In case you run out of fingers and toes to count with, I may have to come back a little early."

"Don't play games with me, Josy."

"Tony, I can't promise you anything, but I *do* miss you and I *do* want to see you again. Soon."

"That will be enough for me. For now."

"I had the most marvellous time the last few days. Can you believe this silly old woman actually went scuba diving in the Florida Keys? When my instructions began in that swimming pool, I wasn't prepared for the extraordinary beauty that exists under the ocean."

"So now, beautiful old woman, your life is complete?"

"Almost, I still have to climb Mount Everest!"

"Mama mia! From the depths of the sea to the top of the highest mountain. How is a man supposed to keep up?"

"I'm being facetious. I think I've had enough adventure for a while. You were away also. Did you take a vacation?"

"I was away on business. Someone wants to buy my business and I am considering his offer."

"Will you retire then? You seem too young to settle into a rocking chair."

"I think I've come to a time in my life when I would like the freedom to travel."

"Where would you go?"

"There are so many places I've not yet seen. The world is very large."

"My goodness, that sounds like you plan to be away months at a time."

"Possibly."

Jo felt a twinge of anxiety and hoped he wasn't planning on going anytime soon.

"You won't leave before I come back will you?"

"Would it make you come back sooner?"

"I promised Barb I would spend the month with her and I'm already cutting it short. Will you meet me at the airport when I do return?"

He laughed softly. "Do you say hello with as much passion as you say goodbye?"

Jo found herself blushing as she tried to explain to him that she didn't know what came over her that day.

"Cara, I like a woman who is not afraid to show her emotions. Of course, I will meet you at the airport."

"I'll call you when I know when I'll be arriving and give you the flight number."

"Josy. Don't ever be afraid to call me, whatever the hour. You've made me a happy man and I will sleep well tonight."

***

Someday I hope you will make me even happier, he thought and bid her a good night.

He lay awake for a long time, picturing those amber eyes and her short curly hair. He had been so in love with Angelina, he never thought another woman would ever interest him so. As soft and quiet as Angie was, Josy was vivacious and outgoing. Angie had been so timid, never would she have sat with him and peddled raffle tickets in a shopping mall. She would have cooked the whole hockey team spaghetti and meatballs, or donated some of her fabulous baking to a fundraiser, but to sit in public and sell tickets to people? Never! It wasn't that it was beneath her. She was too timid to attempt selling anything, to anybody. Josy on the other hand, was quite comfortable being around people, any kind of people, and any age. She was confident and outgoing. He had watched her with the volunteers and parents from the hockey team at their celebration after the ticket draw and he was amazed at how easily she managed to find common ground with everyone there. They all seemed to like her and she laughed quite freely with them. Her laugh was another thing he found enjoyable. It was so sincere and seemed to come from deep within her. *Face it, Tony, there isn't a thing about her that you don't find enjoyable.* Dare he hope that sometime in the near future, he might listen to her laugh and look into those beautiful eyes whenever he chose? Day or night? *Yes, my darling, Josy. I am determined you will be mine. Soon.*

SIXTEEN

The next day, Jo phoned the airline and moved her departure up by a week, which meant she had only one more week to enjoy with Barb. So much for thinking-time.

Her friend teased her about the abrupt end to her "long holiday with her closest friend". "I never thought I'd lose out to a Latin lover."

"I don't know about the Latin lover handle you've placed on him. He's never made any moves on me. You hear about Italian men not being able to keep their hands to themselves but he's been a real gentleman. He's respected my wishes about keeping our relationship on a friend level. Of course we're getting to an age where companionship is more important than … Well. Than anything, anyway."

"Do you want him to make a move on you?"

"I don't know. Sometimes I hate the thought of never again feeling the exquisite pleasure of a man making love to me and other times it just doesn't seem that important. I guess if it happens, great, if not … it's no big deal. I wouldn't think a man Tony's age has lost his sex drive. Maybe deep down that's why I'm afraid to encourage him. I'm not young anymore and I'm not sure I could satisfy, or keep up with a man with a really strong sex drive."

"You know, Jo, it's a bugger getting old. Especially if we're aging quicker than the men in our lives."

"I guess I should be happy I've even got a man in my life, but it frightens me, too. I think Tony is a man of very deep passion and I wouldn't want to disappoint him. Oh, Barb. I was quite content living alone. Why did I have to meet — not one, but *two* — men to complicate my life?"

When Jo arrived back in Toronto eight days later, she was surprised to realize she was very nervous about seeing Tony again. After much deliberation, she had chosen one of her very best pant and sweater ensembles. They were sage green and quite striking. She carried a soft leather jacket as she came down the escalator. She was confident she looked, if not smashing, then as reasonably close to it as she would ever be. Jo picked up her baggage at the carousel and proceeded through customs. When she spotted him standing in the concourse, he was wearing a black leather jacket over a grey turtleneck sweater and grey pants. His dark eyes were searching hers. Her breath caught. She realized what a truly handsome man he was. Wondering how she ever could have thought him only pleasant looking, she hesitated, then walked toward him slowly — almost bashfully — as if seeing him for the first time and not entirely sure how to greet him.

Sensing her hesitation, he didn't quite understand it. He slid one arm around her waist and she leaned into him. He kissed her forehead, whispering how much he had missed her.

She looked into those glorious, deep, black eyes, and whispered in return, "I didn't realize how much I had missed you until I saw you standing here."

Jo was sure she had felt his heart miss a beat. He carried her luggage to the sidewalk beside the arrivals driveway then he left her while he retrieved his car from the parking garage. After she was settled in the passenger seat, they left without another word spoken. Whistling and holding her hand in his, he glanced at her several times with a very distinct sparkle in his eye. When they arrived at her suite, Tony carried her luggage right into her bedroom and placed all the suitcases on top of her queen-sized bed. Only then did he slowly slide his arms around her waist and kiss her softly, at first on the mouth, then the slightly upturned tip of her nose and each eyelid. He waited for her to open her eyes before touching his lips to hers again, this time with more intensity. Jo's breath caught. This man's passion, she felt, ran much deeper than that displayed on the surface. Some element inside her changed as she melted into the pleasant feel of his soft, full lips. His kisses disarmed her. She could not remember anyone whose lips had felt better. *Not even Stu's.* She felt a twinge of guilt. Tony kissed her cheeks then her hands and still said nothing. He finally backed away still holding her hands. Taking a deep breath, he asked, "Would you like me to mix you a drink, cara?"

She nodded and pointed to the small liquor cabinet near the sofa. After handing her a rye and Coke mixed just the way she like it, he deposited himself in an easy chair. "Now, tell me all about Florida and the fun you had with your friend Barb."

They talked for a couple of hours. He was an attentive listener and seemed to share her absolute delight with her scuba diving experiences in the Florida Keys. She was thrilled with her newfound adventurous underwater skills. "It's nice talking to someone who can appreciate my experience. While Barb had been duly impressed, she was unable to fully appreciate or comprehend the feeling of being below the sea and swimming among the weeds, enjoying the colourful flowers and the numerous species of fish."

Tony not only understood, but added his own memories to the picture. Then he filled her in on how he had spent his time. "I didn't experience anything quite so exciting during the last few weeks. I was busy with business dealings most of the time. Fortunately, that is pretty well finished now."

"Did you close the deal on your used car lot?"

He raised an eyebrow as he smiled and replied that he had. Then with a slightly apprehensive demeanour, he rose from the chair and said, "Josy, I would really like you to come with me to my house. I want you to see where I live."

Now? She wasn't quite sure what his purpose was. Could it be he just wanted her to understand him better as a person? Maybe he lived more humbly than she and he wanted her to see what lifestyle he could afford, before they went any further. Whatever the reason, she decided sooner or later she would be learning where he lived anyway, and probably sooner was better than later. After assuring him she wasn't too tired, they headed down the 401 for Toronto. She could not recall his ever mentioning where he lived. She was surprised when they drove into a very exclusive area south of the 401 and slightly north of downtown Toronto. She was even more intrigued when he entered the underground parking garage of a very large and prestigious condominium building.

They floated upwards through many floors inside an elevator with wood and marble interior, the floor covered with a plush paisley-patterned rug. When the doors opened, they stepped into a large octagonal foyer with mirrors glistening on every second wall section. Sconces hanging with crystal prisms decorated the alternate walls, and small marble-topped tables were placed under each. When Tony switched on the lights as he ushered Jo inside, the effect was similar to entering an elegant wonderland. The sparkle bounced off each mirror, but instead of blinding light, it reflected softly with a glitter that was elegantly whimsical. She could not believe her eyes. The apartment was larger than most homes she had ever been in. The decor was exquisite and obviously, professionally done. She walked through a long wide hallway into a living room that commanded a view of the skyline of downtown Toronto and the CN Tower.

Tony watched as she stepped, speechless, through several of the rooms.

"Sit down, my love. I really need to talk to you."

"You must sell a huge amount of used cars."

He laughed then. A rich laugh that came from deep within. He moved around a large, heavy coffee table, and settling beside her on the sofa, lifted her chin with one hand. "Josy, my sweet Josy, I did sell used cars, that is true. However, I owned more than one location. In total, I had eleven around Southern and Eastern Ontario. I enjoyed it as a hobby. I love cars and I love people, so I was doubly blessed to have the opportunity of spending my days bringing one to the other."

"I might be wrong, but I doubt that even eleven used car lots could give you this lifestyle, Tony."

"You're right, they couldn't." He took a deep breath and settled back into the cushions. "I was born in Italy but my parents brought me to Canada when I was a fairly young man. My father started selling cars in Hamilton and eventually owned his own business. With his connections in the old country and in Europe, he eventually went into the sale of luxury imported cars. He was very successful, as was his brother who remained in Italy to manage the family vineyards. My grandfather owned a lot of land in Italy and was considered quite wealthy. My father and uncle were both killed in a highway accident in Italy while Papa was there visiting. My uncle had never married, so eventually when my grandfather died, my brother and I were the only male heirs to the entire family estates. My sister received a generous cash inheritance, so she and my brother-in-law have lived comfortably also.

At the time of my father's death, my mother went into her black mourning clothes and shut herself off from all activity outside of family and church. She spent the rest of her life cooking and making life as easy as she could for Sophia, Giorgio, our spouses, our children and me. My brother bought out my share of my father's car business and I went into used cars. I guess I have a little peasant blood in me, but I was never comfortable selling fast cars to the rich and famous. I am basically selfish. I get much more satisfaction from seeing a father of three get a good deal on a two-year-old family van, or a young fellow buying his first used pickup truck with chrome roll bars and lighted running boards. One car lot led to a second, then a third and so on. My brother did very well for a number of years, but soon people weren't able to buy expensive toys like they once had and his sales started dropping. He had an opportunity to sell his business and acted upon it. He took over the management of five of my car lots and we have both been happy.

"My family money has allowed me to buy the luxuries I have, and my own money allows me the privilege of enjoying them. We sold all the family property in Italy except for one villa in Umbria, which is where our families reside when we visit. Angelina and I lived in a very large home that was built on three levels not too far from this neighbourhood, before she became ill. When she could no longer manage the stairs, we moved here. Unfortunately, her suffering was too great by that time, and she did not have the opportunity to enjoy our new home for very long."

He paused and took several deep breaths. "After she died, my daughter, Sylvia, her husband, and my grandson became my whole life. They filled the emptiness and brought me whatever happiness God chose to send my way — until I met you, Josy. I won't ask from you any more than you're prepared to give, but you must know by now, my sweet, that I care for you. I care very deeply. After being blessed with a wonderful woman like my Angie, I never thought God would help me find another. If you're only prepared for friendship right now, then I will settle for that. Although, I believe you are capable of much more."

Jo sat staring at the floor for the longest time, not really understanding what she was feeling. She didn't know how to respond. Realizing Tony was waiting for a response, she raised her eyes to his and looked into the face of a man who was already deeply in love with her.

Too much was going on here. Disconcerted as well by the knowledge of his wealth, she was completely overwhelmed. "Tony, this is all so overpowering. No one ever told me that you were more than you first imparted to me, a used car salesman."

"A man doesn't brag about what he has."

"Some men do, but not a gentle man like you. I'm so afraid I will end up hurting you that I'm terrified of letting you get too close."

"And how would you hurt me, cara?"

"I've been hurt recently myself, by a man I thought loved me. I believe he might still be buried somewhere deep inside my heart. Until I'm certain he no longer dwells there, I'm afraid I can't give it to anyone else."

"That's fair enough. You're being honest and that's all I can ask. I'll have my work cut out for me, filling your heart to overflowing with love for me — so there will be no room for him. You won't prevent me from trying, will you?"

Smiling, "No, Tony. I won't stop you from trying."

After a long sigh and a determined shrug of his shoulders, he smiled. "Josy, I know you've had a long, tiring day. Where shall we go to eat?"

"I'm sure there must be a fantastic kitchen somewhere in this palace. Shall I fix something for us?"

"Another night, perhaps. I didn't bring you here to cook for me. Do you like Italian?"

"Oops, that sounds like a loaded question."

Laughing together, they left for Tony's favourite bistro. The leek-filled ravioli melted in her mouth and the mild flavour of the rolled, stuffed veal proved to be the best she had ever eaten, but the combination of easy laughter and the romance in the dark eyes across the table, provided the *pièce de résistance*. There really was a new easiness about their relationship. Jo believed it was because the walls were tumbling down, the secrets out in the open. They could understand, also, the deep love each had felt for their mates and how devastating their losses when their loves were taken from them.

After they finished their meal and relaxed with after-dinner drinks of Frangelico, Tony reached across the table for her hand. "You must be tired, my love, from travelling all day. It means the world to me that you chopped your vacation short and returned here. I know you haven't even spoken to your son or grandchildren. Forgive me for not feeling guilty about keeping you to myself." He kissed her hand. "May I pick you up for the hockey game tomorrow night?"

"Of course."

"It is an eternity since I've enjoyed the pleasure of your company at the hockey rink. I promise I won't ask you to sell any more raffle tickets."

He drove her home and after kissing her forehead, reluctantly turned and walked toward the elevator. The phone started ringing before Josy even had her coat off.

"So …? What happened?"

"What do you mean what happened?"

"When you ran into Mike. What happened?"

"I didn't run into Mike."

"Jo, he followed you into the airport, practically on your heels. I would have quickly followed you in and made sure you knew he was there but cars were honking behind me. I figured by the time I got inside, the two of you would already be talking anyway. Are you telling me that you really didn't see him? Didn't speak to him? Jo, he went through the door right behind you. He absolutely *must* have seen you."

Jo collapsed onto the sofa feeling like she had been kicked in the stomach. If Mike had recognized her and ignored her, then she had no alternative but to finally accept that it was over. She certainly had not given him the opportunity to explain by telephone, but if he had been right there. In person … "Barb, are you absolutely certain it was him?"

"Yes, Jo. I'm positive. I could hardly wait for you to get home and tell me what happened. I'm sorry. Maybe I shouldn't have said anything."

"That's OK. I guess it's clear now. The door on that part of my life just slammed shut. Actually, I'm glad that any lingering doubts I may have had are now permanently removed. Gone. Thank you and goodbye, Mike Talbot."

She wiped a lone tear from her lower lashes.

SEVENTEEN

"Where have you been? I've called several times. Was your flight delayed? Is Tony with you? Oh dear, I wasn't thinking about him being there. Have I screwed things up talking to you about Mike while Tony is there?"

"It's OK, Barb. Really. Tony just brought me home from dinner and he's gone. The phone was ringing as I came in the door." She hesitated for a minute, then "Tony told me today that he's in love with me."

Barb hesitated. "Do you have feelings for him, Jo?"

"I'm not in love with him, but I do care for him." Probably more than she cared to admit, she thought. *Cripes. How shallow is that? Crying for the one who left and the next minute talking about the love of a new one?*

"Are you going back to the lake?"

"Definitely. I'm not changing my life. Tony knows I'll be leaving soon for Thunder Bay and that I have a tour of outdoors shows before I open my business for another season."

"And he's OK with that?"

"He wouldn't ask me to give up my business, my resort. I think he would prefer I remain here and just let him look after me, but I'm not ready to alter my life for any man yet. Who knows, I may miss him enough to change my mind, but for now, it's business as usual."

"If I came to Toronto could I meet him?"

"I would love for you to meet him, Barb."

"I'll telephone first if I decide to come. I know your schedule is uncertain at the moment."

***

The next day, Jo called Barney and discussed the confirmed summer reservations with him, the vacancies, and the sportsmen shows that were booked. They discussed the possibility of cutting one of them since there weren't as many vacancies to fill this year. Unfortunately, the one they decided to eliminate was right in the middle of the tour, so it didn't really shorten her travel season at all. Barney informed her that the boat and motor maintenance was all under control. He added that he had been out to the lake the week before and checked over the lodge. As far as he could determine, everything seemed to be in order. They agreed she should call him upon her arrival in Thunder Bay, and they would make final travel plans. Jo knew she would have to start packing soon, but for some reason this season, her heart just wasn't in it.

A couple of hours at the beauty salon, including a thirty-minute massage, helped to ease all the tension from her system. By the time Tony arrived to drive them to the hockey game, she was feeling like a new woman. She was waiting for him downstairs when he arrived. Without a thought, she leaned over and kissed his cheek before fastening her seat belt. His dark brown eyes seemed to sparkle at the sight of her. He took hold of her gloved hand and continued holding it all the way to the rink.

When they arrived inside, John and Amy were surprised to see her, and even more surprised when they realized she had arrived with Tony. "When did you get back, Mom?" John asked.

Jo was embarrassed when she told him she had arrived the previous afternoon. John knew better than to ask who had picked her up at the airport, but he and Amy exchanged a knowing look and a nudge. Matthew was playing his first game since he had injured his elbow and he was determined to make up for lost time. He scored two goals that evening, and assisted on another. John asked Tony and his mother to come to the house for coffee after the game. He wanted to hear all about her Florida trip.

"Tony, I hear you're about to become a man of leisure." John spoke easily with Tony as he picked up some of Sammy's toys and made room for the man to sit on the sofa.

"I'll probably take it easy for a little while. Before too long, I hope to be doing some travelling."

"Will administering the foundation take up much of your time?"

"Hardly any. My lawyer and my accountant will be doing most of the paperwork. It's better having the administration done by outside parties."

"What foundation?" Jo asked.

"The team directors met with the players' parents last week and discussed what should be done with all of the money we, I should say you and Tony, raised in the car raffle. They, the boys included, decided some of it should go to assist kids whose families can't afford all the costs associated with hockey. They talked about setting up a fund to help underprivileged boys go to hockey school. Buy proper skates and equipment. When Tony found out—"

"John, there's no need to go into detail about things."

"Tony. Everyone needs to know how generous you are with the kids."

"That's not why I do it."

"We all know that. Anyway, Tony's matching the total, dollar for dollar, and a foundation is being set up. Everyone voted for Tony to be the administrator of the fund since he's about ninety-nine per cent responsible for the whole thing anyway."

"Why, Tony. That's a very admirable thing you're doing." Jo couldn't help being impressed. "Well, here's our star of tonight's game." She said this as Matthew entered the room in his pyjamas and stood up to give him a hug while kissing the top of his head. "You're not too old for your grandmother to kiss you are you?"

"As long as you don't muss my hair. How was Florida, Grandma? Did you go to Disney World?"

"No, Matthew, I didn't get there. I'm waiting for you and Sammy to join me for that one. I did go scuba diving though!"

"Cool! Did you see any sharks?"

Laughing, Jo told him the only dangerous thing she encountered was a giant fishing hook lying on the bottom of the ocean floor. "I have some gifts for you and Sammy that I'll bring another day."

"I bet none of my friends have grandmas who go scuba diving."

"Your friends' grandmothers probably have more sense," she replied, looking rather pleased with herself.

They said goodnight to the boy and drank their coffee while Jo told them all her experiences in Florida.

"I thought you were staying for another week or two. I was surprised to see you tonight," Amy said.

As Jo and Tony made eye contact, Jo quickly replied that she had a change of plans and decided to come back a week early. She couldn't help the flush she felt on her neck.

"You and Barb didn't have words did you?"

"No, no. I just felt I wanted to come back a little early."

Amy and John both noticed Jo slide her hand into Tony's and decided to let the questions drop. Later, after the couple had left, Amy asked John, "Do you think anything is going on between those two?"

"I wouldn't be disappointed if there is. I can't think of a nicer man than Tony for my mother to have as a friend."

"What if they're more than friends?"

"I guess that's even better. Mom and Dad had one of the greatest marriages a couple could hope for. They were so compatible and enjoyed each other's company more than anything. But he's gone now. And she's too young, too vital, to spend the rest of her life alone. I know she loved my father and that no man will ever take his place, but I think she still deserves some happiness. If a nice guy like Tony can make her happy, then I'm happy too."

***

When they pulled up in front of Jo's building, Tony asked if she would attend evening Mass with him the next day, Saturday. Jo hadn't been to church since before leaving for Florida and decided it would be nice to go together.

"My church is in downtown Toronto so why don't we come back to my place after and I'll fix dinner?"

"OK, but I'll cook dinner."

Tony didn't have to be coaxed so she gave him a list of a few groceries he could pick up for their meal.

While standing beside him in church the next afternoon, Jo was stunned again by the quality of his voice as he sang along with the choir and the congregation. When it came time to greet each other with the sign of peace, he took her hand in his and kissed it, wishing her peace and happiness. They then turned to the others around them and she noticed everyone called him by name. When they took Communion, even the priest repeated his name, so she realized he was a regular attendee at Mass. As they left the church, Tony introduced her to many of the parishioners as his lady friend. The priest winked as he commented in a loud stage whisper to her, "I hope we'll see you again … Soon."

Once again she felt like part of a family.

In his enormous kitchen, she prepared shrimp cooked in garlic butter, done the way she had enjoyed it in Florida, Mediterranean salad, green beans baked with sour cream and Swiss cheese. Seasoned, roasted potatoes completed the meal. It was a real pleasure to cook in such a well-equipped kitchen. The side-by-side full-width refrigerator and freezer were fronted with stainless steel doors, as were all the other appliances. The gas range was commercial size and accessorized by a tap installed on the wall, to fill large pots. She was not surprised, envisioning the large pasta meals his wife must have prepared for their family. While she cooked, Tony tossed the salad vegetables then set the table complete with candles. From his temperature-controlled wine cupboard, he chose a superb white wine. They ate at an intimate round table in the kitchen, rather than in the elegant formal dining room. While she tidied up the kitchen afterward, he loaded the dishwasher. They then retreated to the den with their parfait glasses filled with chocolate ice cream. After pouring liqueurs, he offered to teach her the game of backgammon. When she found Luciano Pavarotti in his CD collection, she insisted he play it.

With music in the background, a fire in the fireplace and sipping Frangelico, they passed the evening playing backgammon and gin rummy. Before she realized the time, the clock was chiming midnight and he faced a long round trip driving her back to Mississauga. When he gently grumbled that she lived so far away, she reminded him that Mississauga was relatively close compared to Thunder Bay where she would be residing for the remainder of the year. He wrapped her in his arms while whispering huskily how difficult it was going to be to survive the separation for such an extended period of time. He kissed her hair, eyelids and ears, then she felt his lips on the side of her neck. It felt delicious, too delicious. Time to stop it before stopping became an impossibility.

Easing herself from his arms, she didn't trust her voice and merely shook her head as she looked at the passion in his eyes. He leaned forward, resting his forehead on hers then slowly went to the closet and returned holding her coat open for her.

She looked at him when they were on the freeway and realized the silence had continued. "Tony, I hope I haven't made you angry."

"Cara, you could never make me angry. I know what a genteel lady you are. It's just that your beauty makes me feel like a young man again. A man with emotions that I must learn to control. Please forgive me."

"How you flatter an old woman."

"Old? You are nowhere near an old woman."

"I'm sixty years old, Tony."

"Sixty. I'm fifty-seven and here I sit, looking like an old man beside you. You have the vitality and appearance of a woman at least ten years younger."

"I'm sorry if you thought you were courting a much younger woman." She turned to him, hesitated, and then decided to continue with the thoughts on her mind. "At the risk of sounding very bold, the fact remains, Tony, that you are younger than I am … and, well … I've not been active sexually since before my husband passed away." Oh lord, maybe she shouldn't have started this … "What I'm trying to say is that I'm not sure I could keep a man happy… Sexually, that is … at my age … that is."

"I don't believe age is the issue. If a man is unable to bring enough pleasure to a woman for her to please him in return, then the problem is his, cara — not her age." He lifted her chin, turning her face to his. While looking her squarely in the eye as best he could while driving, he continued, "I promised not to pressure or hurry you, and I will not. When you are ready, I'm certain you'll make me as happy as I hope to make you. I think it such a waste of time this driving back and forth every night. However, if I must, then I will — forever if need be. I'm not a man who gives up easily. I repeat. I know you are a lady who has high principles and I'm a patient man. You already have my heart, cara, and some day, I hope to have yours."

***

He smiled to himself at the realization that whoever this other man in her life was, he may have won her heart, but apparently the winnings had not included her body. Tony intended to have both. He was a lucky man to have found such a beautiful woman, and one who did not give herself easily. From the way her breath had caught when he kissed her throat, he knew she was capable of passion. He started to whistle happily as he continued to drive.

***

Startled, Jo wondered why the sudden burst of whistling. Oh well, she was just happy that her rebuff hadn't hurt his feelings or made him angry. It would have been so easy to give in, but she still felt strange about going to bed with a man, any man. She recognized that Tony wouldn't stop at toe nibbling. *Oh, my gosh. What made me think of that?*

The next morning he called her with an invitation extended by his sister-in-law, for them to come for lunch around two o'clock, if she had no previous engagements. Jo was delighted as she had enjoyed New Year's Eve with them, and had hoped she might see them again. Jean had a meal prepared that was almost equal to the elaborate holiday meal. George's and Jean's son and daughter and three grand-children joined them, as well as Tony's daughter, Sylvia, her husband,

Steve, and Tony's grandson, Robert. As she listened to, and partici-
pated in, the conversations around the table, Jo felt as if she belonged
here. The discourse flowed as easily as the wine, and the hearty
laughter was warm and genuine. She could sense the love and the
bond everyone shared. They included her as naturally as if she had
been a regular companion at their table for years. A couple of times
she caught Sylvia looking from her to her father and smiling approval.
It made her feel wonderful, and somewhat relieved, to realize there
was no resentment apparent.

After lunch, Jo helped Jean clean up the dishes and put the food
away.

Jean watched Tony's beautiful friend scrape plates and cover
bowls with plastic wrap. She smiled, as Jo appeared happy even
wrapping garbage, all the while humming to herself.

"Do you always hum when doing unpleasant chores?"

"Hum? I never hum."

"Josy, believe me, you were humming."

Jo turned pink as she realized she must be guilty without having
noticed. It was true, she never hummed — except, as her family
always reminded her, when she was extremely happy or excited. She
relapsed into a quick remembrance of being teased unmercifully
when the star right-winger on the school hockey team asked her to the
high school dance and she hadn't been able to stop humming for a
week.

"If you say so, then I must have been. I didn't notice," she replied
with a sheepish smile.

***

Jean noticed the blush but didn't add to Jo's embarrassment by
disclosing that it was one of Tony's favourite songs she had been
humming. It was one he frequently whistled when he was happy.
Smiling to herself, she truly hoped this beautiful, warm woman might
be the trigger behind her brother-in-law's newfound contentment.
Tony was too young to be alone. He was much too full of love and had
such a passion for living life to its fullest, it had bothered her to watch

him spending his days and nights alone all these years. She had worried tremendously about him when his Angie died. Something inside him seemed to have been buried with her, and it frightened his whole family. Sylvia and Robert had been the only people able to make him smile all these years. When Tony had unexpectedly called on New Year's Eve to say he would be joining them for the evening and bringing a friend, their joy knew no bounds. Then, when he arrived with this sincere, beautiful Josy, the whole family hoped the black armband had finally been removed from his sleeve. As that evening had progressed, each family member had offered up silent, individual prayers in thanksgiving for Tony finding this delightful person. Jean watched Josy's graceful movements and charismatic manner, and felt with all her heart that she was exactly the miracle they had been praying for.

***

By the time they joined the men in the living room, the football game was already at half time. Jo was surprised to learn there were still games being played this late in the season. Tony made room for her to sit beside him on the small sofa. The half-time show was just being completed and the game resumed within minutes after she sat down. As soon as the play-by-play commentary started, Jo recognized the voice of the colour commentator. She stiffened, but tried very hard not to let her discomfort become apparent to the others. The smooth easy drawl emanating from the voice on the television sent her emotions exploding in a thousand different directions. She shivered and Tony put his arm around her shoulder asking if she was chilled. She shook her head but was visibly relieved when Robert asked if anyone wanted to play scrabble with him. Tony looked stunned as she virtually sprang off the sofa, leaving his arm embracing thin air when she followed Robert to the dining room table.

EIGHTEEN

Tony glanced at Jo in the car. "I appreciate you letting me watch the balance of the football game, even though you didn't seem to enjoy it."

Toying with the idea of telling him the reason for her discomfort, she thought it better not to bring Mike's identity into their relationship. If Tony ever inquired further, she would deal with it then. In the meantime, she merely commented, "Some situations bring back unwanted memories."

He mistook it for memories of her husband and never questioned her further.

At her door, she apologized for having a fair amount of business mail still to deal with that evening. "I'm sorry, Tony, but I'll probably be busy most of tomorrow, too. Why don't you come for dinner here tomorrow night and then maybe we can catch an early movie?"

He agreed after assuring her he understood. Once safely inside her door, she covered her face with her hands and burst into tears. She had really thought she was completely over Mike but the sound of his voice was just too much. She had avoided football games on TV for just that reason, but there he was, broadcasting the Super Bowl Game, which of course, almost every sports-minded male watched.

***

Tony knew it was more than the football game that had upset Josy, but

183

he had no idea what it might have been. He had turned it over in his mind a dozen times but couldn't figure out what had sparked that sudden rigidity and her all-too-apparent panic to leave the room. All he could hope was that it didn't happen again, and he hoped there wasn't a situation, or a person, at his brother's house that might be distressing her.

The next evening he telephoned before he came over just in case she still wasn't herself, but she seemed eager to see him.

***

She had broiled chicken thighs and prepared a rice casserole that was filled with various vegetables. Instead of wine, she had chilled tomato juice, which he found to be a really pleasant change. Their conversation was light during dinner and he helped her clear away the dishes afterward. He relaxed in an easy chair and read the Mississauga newspaper while she finished in the kitchen. All the while her gaze kept returning to Tony who appeared to be at home in her living room. She stopped once just to take in the ease with which he had pulled an ottoman over and lifted his feet onto it.

When she was through cleaning and everything was put away in the cupboards, Jo lowered herself onto the footstool in front of Tony then tugged the newspaper down so she could see him. "I've been thinking that I have only a few more days to share with you before I leave."

"I realize that, cara. I hate to think about it and I definitely don't want to discuss it."

"But we must."

He brushed the curls on her forehead with his fingers. "Why must we? Why can't we just bury our heads in the sand and enjoy these last few days? Any discussion we must have about your leaving can be done on the very last day."

She removed his hand from her forehead. While holding it in both of hers, she opened his fingers kissing them one at a time. Then she kissed his open palm and held it to her cheek. "Sweet, gentle Tony."

"If you knew my thoughts right now, you wouldn't think me so sweet." He leaned forward taking her face between his hands and kissed her forehead and nose, and then tenderly, her lips.

"I think this will be my last year in business." It was such a blunt, simple statement. She had given it a lot of thought the night before and during the day, and suddenly, there it was. "I am going to talk to my sons about selling the lodge."

***

Tony was confused. His eyebrows raised as if he hadn't heard her correctly. "And then what will you do?"

"Over the last couple of days I've been giving some thought to relocating closer to my grandchildren. Perhaps Toronto." She was looking at his chin.

He lifted her face until she was looking straight into his eyes. "And what will you do in Toronto, cara?" His voice was hushed, still thinking he was asking questions to which he may not want to hear the answers.

"I think it's time to look to the future. I've been living in the past, afraid to move on." She was looking directly into his beautiful dark eyes, inches away. "I've met this very nice man, you see. I'm quite certain he could make me extremely happy, but I have some baggage I have to get rid of. With a great deal of patience on his part, and determination and trust on my part, I think … together … we could bring me out of the past and into the present. If we can accomplish that, perhaps we could look at the future — together. The only thing that's holding me back is the possibility of hurting him. He really is a very nice man."

He was sure his heart had stopped, he couldn't breathe. Finally, all he could do was whisper her name. "Josy! Sweet, Josy!" She realized his eyes were watery and she ran her thumb under his bottom lashes to wipe the moisture away. "Josy, you must know by now that my heart is so full of love, there's no room for hurt in it. It's full to over flowing. Nothing else can possibly fit inside. I will open your heart, too, and my overflow of love will pour into yours. You'll see."

***

"Tony, we have two days and three nights left. That's roughly sixty-two hours." As she was speaking, she noticed a smile forming at the corners of his mouth. "What are you smiling at?"

"Continue, please."

"I was adding up all the time it takes to drive back and forth. I believe you had mentioned something about it yesterday. I started to think about all that wasted time. Not to mention all the gasoline consumed and air polluted, wear and tear on your vehicle, et cetera, et cetera."

He was holding both of her hands to his open mouth.

"It's really unfortunate you don't want to talk about it. Maybe we should bury our heads in the sand and talk about it on the way to the airport?" She withdrew her hands and started to rise.

"Cara, I don't want to waste time talking at all." He stood and pulled her the rest of the way up.

She smiled. "Let's go to a movie."

They went to a cinema at the mall near her building and when they arrived at her apartment once again, Tony prepared his own special recipe for hot chocolate, which they drank while watching the late news. Finally, without saying a word, he turned off the lamps and the television. He took her arm and tucked it under his and walked with her to her bedroom.

Nervously, she took a clean nightie from her dresser drawer and went into her en suite. She was shaking as she quickly slipped into the shower. While towel-drying her hair, she sat on the lid of the toilet and tried to breathe normally. *Oh my. What have I gotten myself into? Is it too late to change my mind? My goodness. Everyone is talking about safe sex these days. At my age I don't have to worry about pregnancy — surely I don't have to worry about anything else either.* She pictured in her mind an image of Tony — sweet, gentle Tony. *He wouldn't possibly be carrying anything. Or would he? He's sweet but he is a man after all. A passionate man at that.* She started to shake with laughter. *Where are these thoughts coming from?* She knew it was only a nervous reaction. Nerves. Yes.

Surely he would understand how uneasy she was. Her silent laughter stopped and she felt more confident. *He really is gentle. Thoughtful. Passionate. Latin. Lover. Patient. Passionate? Stop.* She was bordering on a panic attack. Maybe he would be content with just holding her in his arms tonight, in fact she was sure of it. He would understand. He said he was a patient man. Once he knew how nervous she was, he would be even more patient with her. She slipped on her peach-coloured nightgown and strode with a little more confidence into the bedroom, smiling as she slid in beside him. Oh, goodness, he was totally naked under the sheets. Now what? *Are naked men usually patient?*

When she started to speak, he covered her mouth gently with his lips. "Cara." His lips were nibbling her ear lobes. "We agreed not to waste time talking."

He stopped her mild protests with more kisses and before she realized how quickly it was happening, her body was responding to him and her nervousness was being replaced with … other emotions. He was so right. He was a man who could make a woman want to please him, ache to please him. He awakened in her a passion she had never felt before. He started softly with her mouth, and then gradually his lips caressed her neck, each breast. Oh, what those lips were doing to her breasts. Just when she thought her pleasure was at its peak, she was besieged with a new sensation. Not only his lips but now his hands were working a magic of their own. Tormented, she wanted him to stop, but realized she was holding his head so tightly to her breast, she must surely be suffocating him. With a smile, she accepted him, knowing in her heart that she had become the impatient one.

Sometime during the night, she awakened to a new urgency, a new desire. She could not believe how her body was reacting to this man. He lay spooned with her, his back curved into her stomach as she slowly slid her arm around his waist. With her fingers, she followed the thin line of hair growing down his mid-section, all the way from his chest past his navel. She continued teasing him with a light touch, until she felt a slight stirring where that line met a thicker mat of hair. When his hand covered hers and moved it lower, she kissed his shoulder and encouraged him to roll onto his back.

The next morning she awakened certain that some other woman had taken possession of her body. She couldn't possibly have behaved the way that hussy had. Where had this person come from who was posing as her? Embarrassed and unable to face him, she tried to remember what he had whispered to her sometime during the night, something about her being patient … something about good sex like good wine should not be rushed … Good lord, sixty years old and she was still learning about sex.

When she started to get out of bed his arm tightened around her. Pulling her to him, he whispered into the hair on the back of her head, "Never have I had such a night. You are a doomed woman, Josy, I will never be able to let you go now."

Barely able to control her blush she rolled over to face him. Kissing his jaw, she whispered softly, "Tony, I hope you won't have to."

"Cara, I'm happy we've shared the full pleasure of our passion before you leave. I promised you I wouldn't force you to any long-term commitment, and I will honour my promise. For now, I will be content to have you in my arms whenever I can. Just leave me with the promise, that if the man who holds the strings to your heart returns, you will tell me. I don't want you deceiving me because you are reluctant to come to me with the truth."

"I'm not a deceitful woman, Tony. You are a wonderful man and soon, I'm hoping, I'll be free of these strings that are wrapped around my heart."

The next couple of days passed too quickly. Amy came to help her package some of the things she traditionally stored at their house. That was one of the inconveniences of living in a shared apartment, when you check out you have to remove your belongings. John had tried unsuccessfully on several occasions to talk his mother into staying with them, but she liked her own space.

Watching the introspective expression on Jo's face while she worked, Amy finally offered a penny for her mother-in-law's thoughts. Jo was taken by surprise and was indeed tempted to confide in her. She hesitated though, worried about the risk involved of losing the young woman's respect. Finally, she opened with, "Amy, I'm thinking about Tony and worrying that I may have done him an injustice. He has expressed deep feelings for me but I'm not in a position to commit the same to him. He's very understanding and accepts, for now, that I can only give him half a heart. Even at that, I'm wondering if I'm making a mistake by encouraging him."

"Why are you hesitating? Because of Dad?"

Jo looked at Amy before lowering her head to stare at the floor. Amy mistook that as a yes and informed Jo that no one expected her to remain alone for the rest of her life. She was positive Stu would have expected her to get on with her life. She further confided John's own stamp of approval for a relationship between Tony and his mother.

"Amy, it's not Stu that's keeping me from loving Tony."

"Then what?"

"My darling daughter-in-law, let's leave this packing for now and I'll make us a pot of tea. I have a long story I want to share with you. It's a confidence that must be kept between you and me, though."

When Jo finished telling Amy about Mike, she felt like a load had been lifted from her shoulders. She was concerned, though, that Amy might not still hold her in the same high regard as she had previously. The young woman surprised her by setting her cup down and kneeling beside Jo's chair, then giving her a very long, affectionate embrace. "Oh, Mom, why didn't you confide in us? Why didn't you tell us you were hurting? Did you think we wouldn't understand?"

When Jo didn't respond, she continued. "I mentioned to John shortly after you arrived in the fall, that something seemed to be troubling you. I wanted to ask you about it then. I thought perhaps you were overworked, exhausted. But John assured me that you would not allow that to happen. When you got caught up in the raffle ticket sales and then started spending time with Tony, I thought perhaps I'd been mistaken." She hesitated then asked, "Have you figured out what you're going to do?"

"I'm going home to Thunder Bay and then to a couple of outdoors shows with Barney. I probably will come back to Mississauga for a break after that. I've promised Tony that I would, and then I'll open my business at the start of fishing season, as I always have … For this year, anyway. I will have to talk to the boys about future years."

"Do you expect to see this Mike again?"

"No. It's merely a matter of getting over him. He injured me very badly and as long as I'm still hurting, I don't think it's fair to make a commitment of marriage to Tony. Poor Tony. He is so patient with me. It all seems so unfair for him. That's the troubling part and that's why my conscience is bothering me."

"Maybe you should confront Mike and let him know exactly how deeply he wounded you."

"Oh Amy. I'm sure I'm not the first woman whose heart he's broken. Nor will I be the last. Men like that take it in their stride and move on. When Barb told me that he walked through the door to the airport right behind me, without even making his presence known to me, I realized then that I mean nothing to him. He probably was upset that I wouldn't answer his phone calls and didn't allow him the satisfaction of breaking it off. Because I feel so bitterly towards him, I can't understand why I still feel so melancholy when I hear his voice on TV or recognize him in a commercial. God help me! I'm a foolish old woman behaving like a wounded teenager."

"You do sound bitter."

"I *am* bitter. Anyway, until I can rid myself of these emotions from the past, I can't plan a future."

Again Amy gave her a warm hug, "Oh, Mom, I wish I could help you, but I guess you have to work this out yourself. Mike sounds like he's — or was — a very exciting man. Too bad it didn't work out. Think maybe you're mistaken about events?" She started to laugh softly then, as she looked at the older woman. "All this time I was feeling sorry for this poor lonely widow who leads such a sheltered life. I thought Tony was your knight in shining armour coming to carry you out of your misery. You have more going on than some of the single women my age."

Jo thanked her for listening and especially for not judging and hoped Amy understood better now why she was leaving Tony behind for a while and getting on with her life.

"But you are coming back before you go to the lake?"

"As soon as the shows are finished. But I won't be staying long."

They finished packing, and then Jo went home with Amy to have dinner and visit with the boys before she left for Thunder Bay.

***

The next morning, Tony arrived punctually to take her to the airport. They were very quiet, speaking only when necessary. Once her luggage was checked through and her seat assigned, they walked hand-in-hand down the concourse toward the security gate. She looked at her watch and suggested they had time for coffee. He sat beside her on the bench in the coffee shop while still holding her hand.

Playing with her fingers, he spoke in a deep voice. "I don't know why I have this overwhelming feeling of great loss. You are coming back aren't you, Josy?"

"We have a dinner-theatre date."

He laughed nervously, "Are you coming back for me or for the grand dinner buffet at the theatre?"

She winked at him. "You never know."

He brought her hand to his mouth and whispered, "I can't live without you, Josy. You are everything to me now. I will have to wait, I understand, but it will be difficult. You're going to grow tired of my incessant phone calls."

"Call anytime you want. Day or night. Especially at night when my work is done and I can enjoy a leisurely conversation."

"I hope some day you'll marry me. You know that."

"I can't marry you until my heart is whole again."

"I think your heart isn't receiving the right kind of medication. It needs gentle loving care morning, noon and night. Who is there better than me to give it that kind of attention?"

She wondered if there wasn't some logic to what he was saying. "You would accept a woman with a broken heart?"

"If you're that woman, I'd welcome your broken heart. I know I can fix it."

"I need time."

Putting his arm around her and pulling her to him, he whispered,

"I promised I would give you that time but I can't promise I'll be enjoying it, cara"

She kissed his lips. "If the time comes when I can offer you myself as a whole person, Tony, I would be honoured to be your wife."

"Not if, cara, when. And the honour will be mine." He couldn't speak. His throat tightened and his eyes filled.

Jo glanced at her watch and realized she had to leave immediately or miss her flight. He ran with her to the gate and gave her one last hurried kiss. "I'm going to work on getting rid of that 'if' business."

***

Barney had decided to drive to Minneapolis rather than fly, so Jo arrived before him. He had never been comfortable on a plane and he liked not being handicapped by the amount of luggage he could bring. Not that he carried a lot of wardrobe with him, but you never knew when you might find a bargain in a fishing rod or a boat motor. When he checked in at the hotel, he found Mrs. H. having a late lunch in the dining room.

***

Happy to see him, she gave him a warm embrace and a peck on the cheek. She felt total relief at having his assistance this year. They drove over to the arena and quickly found the location of their booth. Jo usually returned her confirmation to the show organizers early enough that she was pretty well assured of the same location each year. Barney brought the truck in through the loading doors and quickly removed all their equipment and advertising material, piling it into a neat stack in one corner of their booth. He left her there while he found a parking place in the lot outside. One advantage to having Barney with her was that he was able to bring all their supplies down, saving her the trouble of packing up and shipping everything. Jo knelt and started to unpack brochures from one of the boxes.

She had been working for a couple of hours when a large shadow dimmed the area where she was bent over her work.

"Hope all your wiring is hooked up satisfactorily, ma'am."

NINETEEN

Jo felt an explosion of goose bumps. She could see a grin spreading across Barney's face as he reached out his hand to shake the one of the man behind her. The exchange of greetings between the two gave her a few seconds to compose herself before she turned and looked right into the blue eyes she had been trying so hard to forget.

"What are you doing here?"

"Now is that anyway to greet someone? Especially someone who has been waiting for such a long time to see you?"

"Hello, Mike. Now, once more, what are you doing here?"

"I'm working here. And I happen to be free for the next half hour. May I buy you a coffee?"

"No, thank you. I'm busy."

"You go right ahead, Mrs. H. It's gonna take me a little while to get everything hooked up. You're kind of in my way at the moment anyway."

Mike stepped around the counter and took her arm, guiding her around the counter and out of the booth.

"There you see? You're in Barney's way. We'll just wander over this way and enjoy a soft drink or a coffee. Don't look at me like that. I'm not kidnapping you. I promise to bring you back within the hour."

He had a firm grip on her arm as he walked her hurriedly in the direction of the dressing rooms. After opening one of the doors, he motioned for her to enter. "After you, ma'am."

Once inside, she stood with her arms folded, looking at him with daggers, afraid to speak in case she fell apart. Determined never to give him that satisfaction, she set her jaw and waited for him to talk first.

"Tell me. Do I call you Jo, Josy, Josephine, or what?"

Stunned, she could only open her mouth and stare at him.

"You don't accept my calls, answer my mail, or even let my secretary talk to you. I thought you had disappeared from the face of the earth. Then — quite by accident — I picked up a Toronto newspaper lying on a seat in a New York airport and what did I see? A big picture of you being kissed by some hairy-faced guy and find out your 'friend' calls you Josy. He has even named a car after you. 'Josephine,' for Christ's sake! I didn't even know your name was Josephine!" He was unsure what he wanted to do more — shake her by the shoulders or wrap his arms around her and kiss her senseless.

Silence.

"Have you nothing to say after all this time?" He was trying, without much success, to smile.

"No."

"Jo, please give me a chance." He wrapped his arms around her and crushed her to him. She tried to push him away but he was too strong for her, and before she knew it her mouth was covered by his and her lips were betraying her. Before she lost total control of her senses, she finally managed to turn her head away, eventually pushing herself free.

"Why won't you take my calls?" A look of near panic on his face.

"I hurt too much!"

"You never even gave me a chance."

"To do what?"

"Explain."

"You owe me no explanations." Her eyes darted toward the door. She was finding it difficult to breathe, being in the same room with him. She couldn't — she mustn't — look at those blue eyes. Why did he have such an effect on her?

"You don't really know what you saw that night."

"I know exactly what I saw that night. I saw you passionately kissing a young woman. And don't try to tell me that she attacked you. I saw how surprised she was. It was totally you're doing, Mike. Not hers. Yours! Now. I have a show to prepare for, so please excuse me."

"That wasn't what happened."

"Oh really."

He reached for her arm but she pulled away. "Please, Mike, don't manhandle me."

Reluctantly, he released her. "All winter I've been hoping you would be at this show. I needed a chance to clear up this misunderstanding."

"I see. Then why did you ignore me in the Tampa airport?"

"What are you talking about?"

"Did you fly out of Tampa on a Tuesday afternoon about two weeks ago?"

"Yes."

"Ha!"

"Ha, what?"

"I was told you came through the front door right behind me. You were practically stepping on my heels yet you never even attempted to speak to me. Why?"

After a moment of deep thought, his face lit up. "I remember. So that was you!" He slumped into a chair. "I do recall coming through the door and thinking how that haircut and figure reminded me of you. Everything and everyone kept reminding me of you. I missed you so much that every time I turned around I thought I saw you. I was just about to peek to see if the face resembled yours when I heard an old friend call me. He calls me Mickey. Has for years. Apparently, I remind him of someone he once knew by that name. I can't believe I was that close to you. Let me see. If I recall you had on slacks and you were carrying a leather jacket." He dropped his head into his hands and muttered. "Christ! If only … Jo, if only I'd known."

Jo remembered hearing a man's voice calling the name Mickey. It was such a different name that it had stuck in her memory. Perhaps he was telling the truth … About that incident anyway.

There was a knock on the door. Someone called his name and informed him he was needed on the sound stage right away.

He stood and grasped her arms in each of his hands. "Jo. Can we go for a drink after the show? It will be the only chance for us to straighten out this mess. I'm taking a plane out to the west coast later tonight. Please? I'm begging you to give me an opportunity to explain."

She hesitated, then in spite of her misgivings, agreed. "I guess I owe you at least a chance."

Barney had the A/V equipment all hooked up when she returned. She finished unpacking the brochures and postcards. By the time the posters and pictures were hung, it was time for dinner and to change for the evening opening.

Barney proved to be a godsend. He conversed intelligently with the prospective customers about the fishing and about available rental equipment. She was pleased with the way the bookings were going, consequently, when closing time approached, her "sullen" mood had elevated to "pretty good". Mike came by and chatted with Barney for a few minutes.

"You don't mind if I steal Jo for the remainder of the evening do you, Barney?"

"I can't leave yet. I have to help Barney tidy things up a bit."

"You skedaddle, Mrs. H. It won't take me long and Mike said he has to leave town later."

Mike smiled his thanks, then took Jo's arm in his and walked her away, leaving Barney to secure everything. They went to a bar just down the street from her hotel where he ordered a soft drink and she asked for a glass of wine. They sat in silence for the longest time, Jo not wanting to initiate the conversation and Mike hardly believing they were actually together. He just wanted to consume her with his eyes. Finally, he broke the silence. "I've been sick since this thing happened. When you wouldn't accept my calls, I almost lost it. The only thing that kept me going was my work. Otherwise I would have fallen apart. My secretary was in worse shape than I was, thinking she was responsible for this whole misunderstanding."

"I travelled several thousand kilometres that day because I wanted desperately to see you again. I arrived outside your hotel room just in time to see you devouring some woman's tonsils and you call it a *misunderstanding*? A *misunderstanding*? The hurt and humiliation were devastating. I rushed back to my room and vomited, I was so upset. I couldn't get out of town fast enough. I even took a flight in a different direction to put distance between us. And you call it *a misunderstanding*. I don't think so."

He was ashen. "I didn't know for a couple of weeks that anything was wrong. When you weren't answering my calls, I thought perhaps you'd gone to visit your family, although I thought it strange you weren't picking up your messages. When Nadine and I finally realized the disaster that had unknowingly occurred, I went crazy. She couldn't believe what had happened either and tried to reach you, to explain. Jo, I don't understand how you could just write me off like that. Even criminals get a chance to come clean. Did I really mean so little to you?"

Jo felt a knot forming in the pit of her stomach. Could she have been so terribly wrong? No. She knew what she had seen. "You meant everything to me. That's why it hurt so much. It has taken me all this time to get over you."

"Are you over me, Jo?

She hesitated, then spoke softly. "There is someone else in my life right now. He wants me to marry him."

He looked like he had been kicked in the stomach. "Please tell me you're kidding about that, trying to make me feel bad."

"I'm not kidding."

He took her hands in his, his breathing visibly laboured. "Oh, shit. What have I done?"

"I don't know. What have you done?"

"Will you let me tell you?"

She agreed to listen. After finishing their drinks, they continued their conversation while they walked to her hotel. It was a beautiful late winter evening. The temperatures had gone well above freezing that day and there was still an unseasonably, warm breeze blowing.

He looped her arm through his and they walked slowly while he explained as best he could, the chain of events of that evening, and about how the woman had been stalking him. "Christ. I even heard the elevator bell and realized someone had been in the hallway." He shook his head in disbelief.

He stopped talking. They had walked right by the hotel. He grabbed both of her arms and held her close. "You can't marry this guy. I love you. I never, ever thought I would say that to a woman again. When I get back, we have to talk. You know hardly anything about me, about my life, my daughter, about … About anything." His tears of desperation were dampening her hair.

Josephine, what have you done?

"I'll have to take a cab to the airport. Soon. I can't have found you only to lose you again. Please don't get married until we have another chance to sort this out? Please, Jo? Promise me?"

When she hesitated, he looked at his watch and asked, "May I see you up to your room?"

He would be leaving shortly so she saw no harm in it. She was too unsure of her feelings at the moment to be spending any length of time alone with Mike Talbot in a hotel room. They took the elevator up and as her door closed behind them, he had her in his arms. She felt the old excitement coursing through her. When she helplessly slid her arms around his neck, she cried. Cried for what he had done. Cried for what she had done, and cried for Tony who had done nothing, nothing but love her — unconditionally. At sixty years of age, her life was a mess. Could she walk away from Mike and be totally happy? She thought not. Time. Once more, she needed time.

He held her, and kissed her, and whispered to her of his undying love until he could no longer delay his departure for the airport.

"What airline are you flying? It's very late to be heading west."

"It's a private jet that belongs to one of the sponsors. I have to be out on the coast first thing for a public appearance. It's arranged and everyone's waiting for me. Otherwise I'd cancel. I *have* to go. But I'll be in touch as soon as I can."

"Still as busy as ever."

"I was all set to give it up but when you walked out of my life I had to keep busy doing something. So I signed for one more year. God, if I'd only known you still cared. You do, don't you."

It wasn't a question. It was a statement. "Yes, Mike, I never stopped caring. That's what's hurt so much."

"What about this other guy?"

"He's not 'this other guy'. Tony is a wonderful, loving, caring man who doesn't deserve to be hurt."

"So you'd marry him rather than hurt him?"

"Damn it, Mike, I don't know. I really don't know. I was quite certain I could be happy with him, but now …"

"But now?"

Jo clung to him and cried. She kissed him long and hard.

"I'm afraid to even hope. Maybe I shouldn't go. I'll break my contract. I'll do anything to get you back into my life. I love you so much."

"No, Mike. I need time. Catch your plane and call me in a few days when I'm back home again." She wrote down her unlisted number. He kissed her and walked out the door into the hallway then turned around and took her arm once more.

"I can't go, Jo. I'm afraid you won't wait. I'm afraid this other guy, pardon me — Tony — will persuade you not to wait. I'm afraid you might … I'm just afraid."

Jo reassured him she would make no hasty decision, that she would wait until they could talk again. He kissed her hard and passionately and then pushed the button for the elevator. When it arrived he stepped inside and once more asked for her reassurance she wouldn't get married at least until they had another chance to talk. "Please just give me your word on that. I have this gut feeling I won't see you again."

"I promise."

"Jo … Do you love me?"

She stammered "Yes" as the door closed. Then he was gone.

Surprised at her outburst, she wondered, *Did I mean it? I'm not even sure. Oh, Mike. Why did you have to come back and confuse me?* Her thoughts were a jumble of emotions.

When Jo went to bed that night she had a hard time falling asleep. After tossing and turning for hours she finally dozed off … and dreamed of Tony in a dark suit with a red rose boutonniere in his lapel. He was laughing and dancing with her. She realized it was a wedding, her wedding, and she was laughing also. He swung her around, pulled her close, but when she looked up at him he had blue, blue eyes. She woke up with a start and realized it was almost morning and that she had slept fitfully.

Knowing she wouldn't, or couldn't, go back to sleep, she turned the coffee maker on, then the television. Flicking channels, she caught part of a news flash and froze. A small privately owned jet had gone down just east of Los Angeles. It had crashed into the side of a mountain and burst into flames. There were no survivors. The plane was owned by Madison Food Industries and well-known football broadcaster, Mike Talbot, had been one of the seven passengers aboard.

TWENTY

Jo was still sitting, staring at the television when her phone rang an hour later. She was still sitting when, moments later, Barney knocked on her door and called her name. She was still sitting in the same position when the hotel security opened the door for Barney ten minutes later. The security man called for a doctor because Jo appeared to be in a state of shock.

After she was sedated and sleeping in her bed, Barney returned Amy's call. It was she who had called earlier in the morning after seeing the early morning newscast. He agreed to stay with her until John could make some arrangements.

Amy had hated to tell John about the relationship between Mike and his mother. She had hated breaking a confidence, but if Jo was as distraught as Barney seemed to think, then her sweet mother-in-law would need care and support from her family. When the dust settled, it was Barb who arrived later in the day and took charge of checking Jo out of the hotel. She then took her good friend home to Thunder Bay. The trip was completed in silence on Jo's part as were the days and weeks that followed.

During a short stay in hospital, John came and went and finally Jo was released into Barb's care, who then settled into Jo's condo with her. Barb had always admired Jo's strength and tenacity, so it completely unnerved her, seeing her friend in this almost catatonic state. After Stu's death, Jo had been courageous in the way she picked herself up and carried on. It had been brutal the way Stu had suddenly been stolen from her, his life snuffed out so abruptly. Now another catastrophe had snatched another love and another life from her. How much could one heart — and even more importantly, one mind — endure? Watching Jo sit stiffly and stare at absolutely nothing, made her wonder whether Jo was seeing something that no one else could. Sighing, she prayed a silent prayer that this woman she loved like a sister would snap out of her stupor and take charge of her life once again. In the meantime, she would continue to minister to her daily needs.

The time would come, though, when Barb would have to leave and more decisions would have to be made. Barney suggested that if Mrs. H. were not up to it, he would open the lodge and get it running. For the most part, their entire staff was returning so everyone was experienced and capable of carrying out his or her work without supervision. Most of them had met and liked Mr. Talbot and would understand why they had to carry on in the absence of their employer. Poor Mrs. H. had suffered a terrible loss from a tragic accident for a second time. It was all too much for her to bear.

John, Amy and Barb discussed two possibilities with Jo's psychiatrist. She could come and stay with her family in Mississauga and continue her outpatient therapy, or she could go into an institution for more rigorous therapy in the hopes that she would snap out of her lethargy. Jo had not spoken a word or shed a tear since the news had exploded so brutally through the television screen. As each day and week passed, her chances of fully recovering became slimmer. She was not eating well, only what Barb could force down her. With the addition of supplemental formulas, she was managing to obtain enough nutrition even though she had experienced some weight loss. Finally, after consultation with doctors in Thunder Bay and Mississauga, it was decided that she would go east and after a full examination, the direction of her therapy would be decided there.

Barb knew how strongly Jo felt about always putting on a "face" and looking her best even if she had nothing particular planned. So each day she helped her friend complete her toilette even though the sick woman seemed oblivious to the face looking back at her from the mirror. The day before John was to arrive for his mother, Barb had just finished fussing with Jo's hair, when there was a knock on the door. Thinking it was a neighbour, since the security buzzer hadn't rung, Barb opened the door without checking the peephole. There, standing in the hallway, was a man with a stocky build and dark brown eyes set into a round, gently handsome face. Barb knew immediately who he was.

Whether she should invite him inside or not was another question. John had made it quite clear that Tony was not to be allowed to communicate with Jo. That had not stopped Tony from calling almost daily, however, to enquire about Josy's health. It was too late. Jo's perch at the dining room table provided a clear view to the entrance foyer and as she looked up, Barb realized that Tony was seeing a forlorn little woman, very distant from the Josy he had known. He dropped his bag inside the door and walked slowly over to the table and knelt on the floor beside her chair. "Cara mia, I couldn't stay away a moment longer." Taking her delicate hand in his, he leaned forward and kissed it. Barb watched as he looked into Jo's amber eyes, the eyes he probably knew so well and saw that a single tear hung on her bottom lashes.

She still didn't cry. Just that one, lone tear escaped. Whether it was a tear of sadness or joy didn't matter, it was an expression of emotion, however slight. Barb moved into the living room to keep her distance from them as she waited to see how her friend would respond to this unexpected visitor. The relief was immediate when Jo did not react negatively at the sight of Tony.

Jo looked almost quizzically at him, as if trying to remember something. As much as he yearned to take her in his arms and hold her to him, he exercised control and merely pulled a chair close while continuing to hold her hand. Whispering endearments, he brushed his other hand through her curls and let his fingers outline her face. His thumb lightly worked its way across her upper lip then the lower one. "Josy, my love, my beautiful little love." He had almost forgotten that Barb was there until he caught her movement in the corner of his eye.

After reluctantly releasing Jo's hand, he stood and walked over to Barb. "I'm sorry. My manners are atrocious. But when I saw Josy sitting here I just had to touch her, hold her. I'm Tony DeMarco."

"I know who you are, Tony. Jo has described you to me many times and of course, I recognized your voice."

"I've been beside myself with the need to see her since the first day, but her son felt my presence might only increase her fragile state. When he told me they were thinking of institutionalizing her I knew I couldn't stay away another day. I had to see her. Even if from a distance."

"How did you get into the building?"

"Josy gave me a key. I don't know if Josy told you that we've discussed the possibility of getting married. I let myself in the front door, but didn't want to just burst in here without knocking. I'm relieved she didn't go into hysterics at the sight of me. Although she doesn't seem to recognize me."

As he spoke, he felt a soft hand slide into his. Jo had quietly moved to his side where she stood without saying a word. It took everything in him not to pull her close and smother her with kisses.

Barb didn't know what to make of Jo's reaction to Tony's presence. It was the first time she had given an indication of any awareness of anyone around her.

"Does John or Amy know you are here?"

"I was afraid they might not agree."

"But you came anyway."

"I couldn't stay away. I hope you understand."

"You love her very much."

"More than life."

Barb's heart went out to this lovely man who cared so much for Jo. She looked around for a minute, hesitating before she spoke. "I have some groceries to buy. I'll leave you alone with Jo but I'll be back shortly."

"Thank you. You must be Barb."

"I'm sorry. It's my manners that are atrocious."

She left then, satisfied that Jo was in caring hands. She didn't know what John's reaction would be, but she was compelled to react to a gut feeling. Now she could understand her friend's confusion and dilemma about her deep feelings for Tony, while still in love with Mike. This man certainly was a gentle individual and he obviously loved her very much. *John. Please don't choose the next hour in which to call*, she prayed silently.

When the door closed behind Barb, Tony turned and looked into Jo's eyes. They weren't the clear bright eyes that he knew so well. They were dull and unfocused. *Oh, my poor sweet. How you must be suffering.* Again he brushed her hair from her face and feathered his fingers over her cheeks. She didn't let go of his other hand and she didn't take her eyes from his face. She was like a child staring at a kind stranger.

Barb returned an hour later carrying a carton of milk. Tony smiled to himself and wondered what she had busied herself with for the hour. It certainly hadn't been grocery shopping. "Barb, I wish to thank you for allowing me this time with Josy. I'm extremely grateful. She has forced me to do all the talking, unfortunately," he smiled, "but I've enjoyed just sitting with her. The phone rang a while ago but I thought it might be prudent not to answer it."

When Barb checked the call display she saw it was John's number.

"It was John. I'll have to return the call or he'll wonder where his mother is. Tony, I'll have to tell him you're here."

"Of course."

"Can I fix you something to eat first? You probably haven't eaten."

"Certainly." He looked in the direction of the phone. "Anything to delay that phone call."

Barb laughed. She liked this man. Then she turned the stove on to heat soup for them to eat.

When she received only recordings, even on John's cell phone, she realized how busy he must be trying to get all his work done before coming to fetch his mother. Tony fed Jo almost all of her lunch himself to make sure she ate. "My poor Josy is just a shadow. It worries me to see how much weight she's lost."

"She's on so much medication she rarely makes it through a day without taking a nap after lunch. Do you want to settle her in her room? She seems to sleep better in there."

Tony removed Jo's shoes, helped her stretch out on top of her bed and tucked an afghan around her. As he was pulling the door shut behind him, he thought he heard her say something. Barb caught his hesitation at the door and started to move toward the bedroom. Tony went back to kneel beside the bed.

"I didn't stop him." It was barely a whisper.

"What are you saying, cara?"

"I didn't stop him. And now he's ..." Then the tears came. Heavy, convulsing tears.

Barb hurried to the room but stopped inside the door as she watched Tony gently handle Jo. He sat on the edge of the bed as she continued to sob. She was having trouble breathing so he pulled her to him and enclosed her in his arms, rocking her like a baby. He held her tightly, encouraging her to cry it out. Barb watched for a few moments then, as she closed the door leaving them in private, the phone started ringing. She noted the call display as she picked up the receiver. "Hello, John."

***

Jo was exhausted from her own crying and she finally fell asleep in Tony's arms. Once again, he laid her gently on the bed and covered her. He sat for a long while, watching the sobs escape even in her sleep, then quietly left the room. She slept right through dinner and awoke in the early evening. Lying, staring blankly at the window, she was unaware of her own shivering. Tony came in a short while later and asked if she wanted to eat something. She turned to look at him when he knelt down beside her, but didn't answer. He noticed her shivering and suggested she put on a sweater. She still didn't answer as she raised herself up to get out of bed. She walked into the living room and moved again directly to the window to stare outside. Arms folded in front of her, she continued to shiver. Barb brought a sweater for her and was about to help her with it when Jo took it from her and hugged it to herself. Tony took it and eased it over her arms, then buttoned the front. All the while Jo remained staring out the window.

He stood beside her and wrapped his arm across her shoulders, surprisingly she allowed herself to be drawn in close. Tony wondered what her beautiful, sad, golden eyes were seeing. Something was drawing her to the window even though she didn't seem to be concentrating on anything in particular. He wished he could climb inside her head to see how he might ease the turmoil there. He loved her so, his little *tesoro*. He scanned the evening sky hoping to see something, anything that might be drawing her, but to no avail.

Barb, in the meantime, reheated stew and set a place for Jo at the table. When the bowl was filled with the nourishing food, Tony suggested to Jo that she make an honest effort to eat. Allowing herself to be led like a child to the table, she sat and ate the whole bowl. Barb offered sliced cheese and she ate that, too.

"I'll make tea." Barb put the kettle on.

"Hot chocolate." She was looking at Tony when she spoke. He seemed startled, but then remembered he had made hot chocolate the night they had spent together in her apartment.

"I'll be happy to make it," he responded when Barb looked quizzically at her friend.

Barb felt there was a significant breakthrough in the offing and that it was entirely related to Tony's presence. She was beginning to feel that not only was she a third wheel, but that she might actually be hindering Jo's progress. "Tony, do you mind if I slip out for a short while? There are a few things I should have picked up for Jo before she leaves tomorrow."

"Do you think I mind spending time alone with the woman I adore? I can't thank you enough for allowing me this opportunity. You go and do whatever you have to and I won't complain however long it takes."

***

When the hot chocolate was ready, Tony brought a cup to Jo in the living room and turned the television on.

"Don't!" she cried out.

"Don't what?"

With obvious shortness of breath, she stood up holding her hands over her ears, turning her back on the television.

Realizing her trepidation, he quickly turned it off.

"I'm sorry, cara. Do you not like that program?"

There was no answer although she seemed to calm down once the television was turned off.

"Can I get you anything?"

No response.

He guided her back to the sofa, all the while whispering endearments. He continued to talk to her as if she were listening attentively. He told her about his work with the foundation and how well their grandsons had played during the hockey playoffs. She drank her hot chocolate in silence. When she had finished, he took her cup and placed it in the kitchen sink. He returned to the living room to find her standing at the window again. After sliding an arm around her, he asked, "What do you see?"

Just when he thought she was not going to answer this question either, he heard a faint whisper, "The sky." Her eyes became shiny from unshed tears.

"What do you see in the sky, cara?"

Not answering, she looked straight ahead somewhat forlornly. *Star light, star bright, first star I see tonight. I wish I may, I wish ... I wish ...*

Unaware of her unvoiced thoughts, he waited for her to answer, unsure whether to draw her out further. She solved his dilemma by turning quickly and walking toward the kitchen. She poured soap into the sink and after filling it with hot water, proceeded to wash the dishes from her late dinner. He took a towel and dried them, all the while keeping up idle chatter about whatever came into his head. He told her about his sister giving piano lessons to a neighbour's child and how his brother had gone to Italy for a vacation. She finished washing the dishes, then began to polish the stove and refrigerator and cupboard doors with an unnatural fervour. She seemed obsessed. He watched for a while then took her by the arms and suggested she might want a break.

Laughing lightly, Tony turned her to look at him. "Cara, I'm worn out just watching you."

She put the towel down and paced the length of the kitchen and dining room. It was then he realized she was avoiding going back into the living room.

"Would you like to go for a walk? It was a beautiful day today and I'll bet it's still warm."

She turned and pulled her jacket from the front closet. He remembered how she had been shivering earlier and found a hat for her to wear. He left a note for Barb in the event she returned before they did, then arm in arm, Tony walked with the woman he loved down the hallway to the elevator. It was warm outside just as he had predicted. She slid her hand into his and they headed up the street. They walked in silence for a while before he tried unsuccessfully to have her respond by asking her to show him where she shopped for groceries, and where her drugstore was located.

"Does your hair stylist have her shop near here?" When she finally did respond, it was by pointing rather than telling. Afraid of overdoing it on her first outing, he soon steered her back in the direction of her building. The apartment was still empty when they returned more than forty-five minutes later.

Tony knew that John was coming the next day and would be taking Josy to Mississauga. She would eventually be placed in a nursing home. He wished he could prevent that from happening. He knew that John and Amy had their children to worry about and that Josy needed constant care, but it broke his heart to think of his Josy in a care facility.

"Are you tired?"

She nodded.

"Do you want to go to bed?"

She nodded.

"Would you like me to prepare a nice relaxing bath before you slip into your nightgown?"

Again she nodded.

When Barb returned, Jo was soaking in bubble bath while Tony was turning the bedding down for her. When Barb asked how the evening had progressed, she was pleasantly surprised to learn that Jo had agreed to go outdoors. Feeling Tony had made greater strides in a half day and evening than she and the doctors had been able to accomplish in several weeks, she wondered about the wisdom of John coming tomorrow. He had not been pleased to learn that Tony had gone against his wishes by visiting his mother. In fact, Barb knew that John was quite angry. If only they could get Jo to speak — about anything.

Jo soon opened her bathroom door and emerged wrapped in a terry bathrobe. Tony asked if she would enjoy a cup of hot chocolate. Without answering she walked straight to her room, closed her bedroom door behind her, put on her nightgown and climbed into bed. When Barb and Tony checked on her a little later, her pillow was damp and tears still nested in the hollow of her eyes.

Barb commented to Tony how relieved she was that Jo was showing signs of emotion. Until Tony's arrival she had not responded to questions with any type of emotional or oral response. She had not indicated in any way whatsoever that she had heard what was being said to her. Tony said he was not surprised, considering that in less than two years she had lost so tragically, two men she loved deeply.

After hearing how gently he spoke of Jo's losses, and realizing how it must upset him to see her so obviously affected by Mike's death, Barb couldn't help but think how fortunate Jo was to have someone care for her so passionately. If only her friend was able to comprehend it.

With the knowledge that after tomorrow he may not have access or opportunity to visit his sweet Josy, Tony asked Barb if it would be possible to sleep on the sofa rather than move to a hotel. Other than risking the further wrath of John, she didn't see any harm in it. Actually, Barb felt that if Jo should awaken during the night, she would be comforted by Tony's presence. She offered him the guestroom where she had been staying but he declined, saying he would be perfectly comfortable on the sofa.

As it happened, Tony was roused during the night by a slight sound. When he opened his eyes, Jo was sitting on the floor leaning against the sofa, the back of her head just inches from his face. He moved slowly and kissed her hair, afraid to touch her in case he frightened her. She turned, and kneeling, stared intently at his face.

"Your eyes are brown."

"Yes, they are."

"They were blue."

"When?"

No response.

"Are you sure it was me?"

"We were dancing at our wedding. We were laughing and twirling, but when you spun me around, your eyes were blue."

"Dancing at our wedding?"

Barb thought she heard something and came into the room amazed to hear a two-way conversation. She saw Jo kneeling by Tony talking to him. *Talking to him! Wonderful!* Not wanting to interrupt, she backed away, her eyes quickly filling with tears. When she caught the next exchange she knew in her heart John was wrong. Tony should have been here from the beginning.

"I was all alone."

"Ah, sweet Josy, if you had looked inside your heart you would have known you were never alone."

"I waited for you but you never came."

"I'm here now and I will never leave you unless you want me to." He slid off the sofa and sat beside her on the floor pulling her close to him.

Barb crept quietly back to her room leaving the two of them sitting on the floor holding each other. She wished she could stop John from coming. It was a totally unnecessary trip.

In the morning when she awakened, she found Tony and Jo reclining side by side on the sofa, feet up on a hassock, sound asleep. His arm was wrapped securely around her. She hurried to the kitchen and started the coffee, then went to have a shower. When she came back to the living room, Tony was awake motioning her not to awaken Jo who was sleeping more soundly than she had in quite a long time. She wondered whether Jo had taken her medication last night, as she didn't remember giving it to her.

A short while later, she could hear Tony's voice as he chatted with Jo, then he wandered into the kitchen. He wanted to shower and shave while Jo got dressed. Barb surprised him by throwing her arms around him in a very warm hug. "Thank you for being here".

He revealed to her it had damn near killed him, not being here. "It was only John's strong warning that I would do Josy harm by coming that kept me away." They wondered what John would decide to do when he arrived later that day.

Jo ate her breakfast in silence once again. She appeared to be rested and her pallor seemed less pronounced, probably from the walk in the fresh air the night before. But when Barb told her that John was arriving later that day and probably would be taking her back to Mississauga with him, Jo's jaw tightened noticeably and she put her toast down.

Barb took her plate away.

"Would you like to play backgammon?" Tony asked.

No response.

"Do you want to watch television?"

"No!"

"I'll put some music on. I brought Luciano Pavarotti with me." He went to the CD player and inserted the disc he and Jo had enjoyed together. She sat stiffly in a chair, leaned her head back, closed her eyes and appeared to listen to the music. Long after it finished though, she continued to sit with her eyes closed.

"How about going for a walk with me? I have to pick something up at the drugstore."

Without speaking she stood. As they were going out the door, Barb heard her ask Tony, "Can we go to church?"

She seemed to be kneeling forever in the nearby church, while Tony watched and wondered what was going through her mind. *What is she praying for? For her lost love? For some well-deserved happiness? Does she realize what has happened, or has she closed it out?* Finally, Jo crossed herself and sat back in the pew. She put her hand through Tony's arm and seemed more relaxed than she had been at breakfast.

They took their time walking back to the apartment. John was there when they arrived, very upset that Tony had taken his mother outside the apartment. Barb had spent the short time she was alone with him, trying to explain the positive effects Tony's presence had on Jo. The men shook hands but John's demeanour was not as friendly as it had always been. He was not happy with Tony. *What if his appearance in her home had sent his mother really off the deep end? The man had obviously put his own need first and not considered his mother's well-being at all.* John was not going to let anyone interfere with the course of treatment the doctor had prescribed.

John hugged his mother but received no response in return. He had to admit she looked better than the last time he had seen her. She still had that vacant look about her but something had changed. He couldn't put his finger on exactly what it was. He asked Tony and Barb to excuse them while he talked with his mother. Jo put her hand in Tony's and held onto his arm with the other one, keeping him standing fast. Tony saw the look on John's face and gently removed Jo's hand, saying he would be in the other room.

John tried to explain in the simplest language he could. "Mother, I really want you to return to Mississauga with me and stay at our house for a while. The boys were asking about you and Amy wants you to come as well. I've already purchased an airline ticket for you to return with me today."

Jo sank onto a kitchen chair and stared once again into space. John asked her what she thought about this plan but received no reply. He called Barb from the other room.

"Would you help Mother pack some clothes and cosmetics, please? We'll worry about the rest of her things later."

"John. I still think you should reconsider. Maybe a couple of weeks with Tony ..."

"She will leave with me. Today."

Barb didn't argue further.

"Jo, do you want to take any of your favourite jewellery? How about some pictures?"

Jo didn't respond except to take an envelope from her night table drawer. She then walked to the living room and picked up the Luciano Pavarotti CD, putting both items in her purse.

John, in the meantime, talked on the telephone with her doctor and received assurance that he was doing the right thing. He then turned to Tony. "Thank you for your concern about my mother. I know it can't have been easy for you. However, the family will handle her care now."

Tony took it as a dismissal and donned his coat. "May I say goodbye to her, John?"

"I don't think so. It would be best not to upset her before her trip. I'm not sure how she's going to react to the plane ride."

Realizing the inference to the fact that Mike had died while travelling by plane, Tony didn't argue. He would have liked to be with her in case she was frightened but he knew John was doing what he thought best.

"Perhaps I can see her in Mississauga after she has had a chance to settle in?"

"I'll let you know if the doctor approves. At this point, I don't see that happening for a while."

Tony smiled at Barb, nodded at John, picked up his small valise and left. Barb caught up with him in the hallway and hugged him tightly before he stepped into the elevator.

"John, I really wish you would reconsider about Tony. Your mother seemed to respond to him in a way that she has to no one else."

"The psychiatrist here has warned me that my mother's state of mind is very fragile right now. He feels that keeping her sedated and free of any stress for the time being is the best thing for her. When she's had time to heal a bit, the doctor in Mississauga will establish a treatment program. She has had two severe shocks in the last two years and to force her to confront the latest one prematurely might cause irreversible damage. He explained that her mind is like a broken bone that has to heal to a given point on its own. Once that point is reached, therapy can be started to strengthen it and make it completely healthy once again. To start treatment prematurely could be disastrous. He wants her to relax and start the healing process stress free. Allowing Tony into the picture right now might be adding that unwanted stress — might only be confusing her more. I'm not happy that Tony came here when he knew I was against it. I only hope his visit didn't set her back. I'm not an ogre, Barb. I feel badly about Tony. He's a nice man. I'm only trying to do what's best for my mother."

Surprisingly, Jo boarded the plane without any visible sign of concern or anxiety. She had allowed Barb to hug her but had not responded in kind. She had not asked about Tony nor given any indication of being aware that he had left. She followed John to her seat and held her purse very tightly with what could only be described as a smug smile.

TWENTY-ONE

When they arrived in Toronto, Amy and the boys were at the airport to welcome them. It was the first time Amy had seen her mother-in-law since Mike's accident and she was taken aback by how thin she was. How could she have become so gaunt in merely weeks? Then she realized it wasn't just weight loss but hollow eyes and pale colouring that was adding to the effect.

"Mother, I'm so happy to have you back with us. Matthew and Sammy could hardly wait for your plane to land. We're going to make sure you get lots of tender loving care — hugs and kisses are the boys' specialty."

Jo allowed herself to be hugged and kissed, then her luggage was loaded into the family van. She stared vacantly out the window as they drove the short distance to her son's home.

Several weeks passed and there was no visible change in Jo. Amy had arranged a month off to be home with her, but try as she might, she was totally unsuccessful in getting her to respond verbally. It was increasingly difficult to have a normal evening in their home. The boys wanted to watch TV in their free time, but Jo had to be kept from the family room whenever the set was on. They could not go out for an evening together and leave her alone. John and Amy realized, that as much as they wanted to keep her at home, her condition was not improving.

One day, Amy drove with Jo to a large mall near their home in the hope that Jo might enjoy trying on some clothes and getting her hair

216

done. One of Jo's prescriptions had to be refilled, and while Amy was at the back of the drugstore at the prescription counter, her mother-in-law wandered to the magazines nearby. It took only a few minutes for the pharmacist to count the pills and put them through the computer. When Amy turned to collect Jo and proceed to the beauty salon, Jo was nowhere in sight. Amy went up one aisle and down the other, feeling the panic that a parent does when she loses sight of her child. It was evident she was not in the store so Amy went out into the concourse of the mall hoping to catch a glimpse of amber hair. Nothing. She went back to the cashier and asked if she had noticed Jo leave. The woman had been extremely busy and hadn't noticed anyone.

Amy then searched through the nearby stores to no avail. She didn't want to alarm John with a phone call but she was reaching panic stage. She guessed Jo wouldn't know her way home and might be terrified when she, herself, realized she was lost. Amy finally relented and placed the call to John. He met her in the mall security office within a half hour, and they watched a video from the drug store camera of Jo leaving the store and turning left, into the crowd in the mall. John sent Amy home in the unlikely event that his mother found the presence of mind to phone. The kids were due home soon anyway. He had a picture of his mother in his wallet and decided to start asking at the stores if anyone had seen her. He and Amy agreed, if they hadn't located her within an hour, they would phone the police.

When John called to see if Amy had heard anything, she suggested they try calling Tony. It was a long shot, but one she felt they should take. Tony had called regularly inquiring about Jo, hoping each time that he might be allowed to visit her. John kept putting him off, telling him that when she showed significant improvement, he would discuss it with her doctor. John reluctantly agreed to the call and said if she would do that, he would notify the police. There was no answer at Tony's place, so Amy phoned his daughter, Sylvia, only to learn that he had been out of town for a few days and was not expected back until the next evening. When asked if there was a message she could pass along, Amy said not, feeling it best not to alarm and upset him as well. They would have located Jo by tomorrow evening she was sure.

The search continued all night without success. She had disappeared completely. No one remembered seeing her. John was beside himself, while Amy expressed concern that Jo was long overdue for her medication.

Early the next morning, they decided to call Barb and tell her what had happened. They were surprised when she suggested trying some of the churches. Then she relayed to them how Jo had asked Tony about taking her to church. With a spark of hope, John jumped in his car and drove to several churches in their area and in the area of the mall, but with no luck.

While he was still out searching, Amy answered a phone call at home. It was from a priest at a Catholic church in downtown Toronto. A woman had been discovered sleeping in one of the pews and she seemed to be extremely confused. She was able to give them John's name and that he lived in Mississauga. Amy assured the priest from the physical description that it was her mother-in-law, and that her husband would get there as quickly as he could. How the hell did she get all the way to downtown Toronto? And why? The priest had said she looked vaguely familiar but couldn't recall her having been a parishioner there, and her name was not one he knew.

When he arrived and observed how forlorn and pathetic she looked, John's anger and frustration turned to relief and concern. He hugged her tightly, thanking God that she was safe. He called her doctor from his cell phone and was told to bring her to his office right away. He wanted to take a look at her to make sure she was physically all right.

When Jo was once again safe at home, Amy fussed over her and poured a warm bath, encouraging her to soak for a while. Later she prepared a bowl of hot oatmeal and helped Jo eat some of it before tucking her into bed. Jo slept most of the day. John, in the meantime, caught up with his brother in Nakuru, Kenya and asked if he could possibly come home for a month or so to help with their mother. Mark readily agreed and promised he would be home within the week.

Tony called the following evening, upset that something had happened to his Josy. John assured him that she was now home safe.

He did not tell the man that she had been missing all night, or where she had been located. Tony asked again if he could be allowed to see her and John as much as told him — politely, "don't call us, we'll call you."

If Jo was aware that her younger son had arrived on the scene, she showed no outward sign of it, neither pleasure nor surprise. Mark, on the other hand, was visibly shocked at the physical and emotional state of his mother. John had tried his best to keep him apprised of everything through e-mails, but Mark was not prepared for how thin and old she looked. He agreed to be her companion during the day so Amy could return to work. He realized how little he had seen of his mother in recent years and witnessing her in this ghastly state weighed him down heavily with guilt. The two brothers discussed Jo's future and decided if there was no improvement in her condition by the time Mark was due to leave, they would have no alternative but to find her a good nursing home and sell the lodge in Northwestern Ontario. The out-patient treatments did not seem to be working, and it was becoming apparent that her present condition might be long term.

Try as Mark might to help his mother, another two weeks passed and Jo continued her silence. Once in a while, a one-word response, usually "no," would escape but for the most part she spent her days sitting, or standing, staring out the window. Mark took her to scheduled therapy sessions and as the spring warmed he took her for walks outdoors. He and his mother had had a special connection while he was growing up. She always seemed to know his thoughts and he always uncannily anticipated her reaction to his ventures. At times he wondered if she wouldn't enjoy spending time camping out with him in the wild. She had an affinity with the skies, and some of the sunsets he viewed from far-off mountaintops would make her heart sing.

"Mom, when you're well again, I'm going to make a point of inviting you on one of my excursions. We'll watch the sun go down then lie out under the stars. Sometimes, when I'm alone up on a mountain, the heavens seem so close I swear I could almost touch them. Every once in a while I wish I had someone to share the beauty with me."

Jo looked at him without responding.

He knew that the man named Tony called regularly to enquire about her progress. John informed Mark that Tony had been a friend of Jo's while she stayed with them the past fall and winter.

"Tony's grandson plays hockey on the same team as Matthew, so they struck up a friendship. Mom got involved selling raffle tickets for a car and they had dinner a few times. Tony mistook Mother's friendship for love. I feel his presence only confuses her. The man she had obviously been in love with was Mike. She was crushed by his death, Mark, and she'll have to successfully overcome that hurdle before dealing with Tony. I can't seem to make Tony understand this though. I realize it's hard for him to accept, but I have to put our mother first. It isn't easy as we were quite good acquaintances, and his daughter is a close friend of Amy's."

One day while they were out walking, Jo stopped suddenly and asked Mark what day it was. Stunned by hearing her put several words together and actually initiating a conversation, he replied, "It's Saturday, Mother."

A sense of urgency surfaced in her next question, "What time is it?"

"It's almost two o'clock. Why?"

"I want to go to church."

"You want to go to church *today*? Saturday?"

"Yes."

"OK. We can go. I have to confess, Mom. I haven't been inside a church in a long time."

They walked home quickly, Jo almost breaking into a run. She went directly to her room and sorted through the clothes in her closet. John and Amy were out with the boys at their karate lessons and had planned to visit a farm near Waterloo for the afternoon and evening. The parents of one of John's co-workers owned a small horse farm and had issued several invitations to the Hendersons. They decided to take advantage of Mark's availability to baby-sit Jo. Mark hoped his mother wouldn't need any help getting changed or applying her makeup. He was visibly relieved when she came through her bedroom door, dressed in a nice suit and with makeup and lipstick evenly applied.

"What church are we going to, Mother? Is it within walking distance?"

"Tony's church."

"Tony's church?"

"Yes.

Oh … Oh. Now what? "Can we not go to a church near here? Just the two of us?"

"No."

"Do you know how to get to Tony's church?"

"No. Tony will take us. Call him"

"How will it be if we meet him there."

"Promise me he will be there."

Oh Lord! What was he to do now? The first time his mother speaks to him she's having him make promises he probably can't keep.

"Promise me!"

He prayed a silent prayer for forgiveness by his brother. "OK. I'll see if I can find Tony's phone number."

She hesitated only momentarily, then smiling coyly she removed an envelope from her purse and gave it to him. Inside he found a business card with a phone number penciled in. He dialled it, hoping Tony wouldn't be home, thereby letting him off the hook.

"Hello?" a rich baritone voice came through the earpiece.

"Is this Tony?" When Tony responded affirmatively, Mark continued. "This is Mark, Jo Henderson's son."

"Yes?" Tony sounded hesitant.

"My mother asked me to call you. Surprisingly, she wants to go to church today. More specifically she wants to go to your church."

There was dead silence on the other end of the phone. "Tony? Are you there? I realize it's an intrusion and that you probably have other plans, I am just trying to appease my mother. If you can't make it on short notice, I'll understand."

"Josy asked you to call me?"

"Josy? Oh. Yes, Josy. She did."

"There isn't time for me to come and get her. Is it possible for you to bring her?"

"Yes, but —"

"This is too good to be true. I'll give you directions and I'll wait for you outside the front door."

"Tony, please don't read more into this than what might be there. When you see her you'll understand."

Mark couldn't help but notice the marked improvement in his mother's eyes when she was all dressed and they were on their way. He wondered if this was the church in which his mother had been found the night she went missing. She seemed to be drawn like a magnet to it if it were, and, he had to concede, this Tony might be more important to her than John said he was. He parked the car and helped her step out of the passenger door. They proceeded across the parking lot. His mother's step seemed to have a new spring to it instead of her usual plodding along with her head down. A dark-eyed, stocky, well-dressed man was waiting on the front steps. A smile brightened his face as they approached.

He held his hand out to Mark but his eyes were on Jo. "Ah, cara, it is so good to see you."

Jo didn't answer except to take hold of his arm. Tony nodded to Mark and they went inside. She knelt, her mind apparently buried deep in prayer. Finally, she crossed herself and sat back in the pew, sliding her hand into Tony's. When they stood for the entrance hymn, Mark was very surprised when that rich baritone voice he had heard on the phone, erupted into song. He sounded like a trained opera singer. Obviously, he was a regular attendee, as he knew and sung all the responses without the aid of a missal and Mark couldn't remember the "Gloria" sounding so "glorious". When it was time for Communion, Tony stood back and let Jo precede him up the aisle. The priest recognized her when he placed the Communion host in her hand and made the connection when Tony stood behind her and followed her back to their seats.

Mark saw a change in his mother's face as she walked back down the side aisle and she once again knelt in her place in the pew. She looked less haunted, almost at peace. After Mass, Tony invited them to join him for dinner at a nearby restaurant. Mark didn't want to push his luck with his brother so declined the invitation. Tony walked with them to the car, shook hands with Mark who smiled warmly and nodded in return. Tony held Jo's arms with both of his hands, "Thank you, cara, for joining me at Mass."

His lips lingered as he softly kissed her forehead. She didn't respond other than to lift her eyes to the level of his tie. He opened the car door and helped her inside.

Emotions ranging from ecstasy to absolute agony, raged in his heart. He couldn't have been happier to see his lovely Josy whom he missed so much, at the same time hating how sad and grief stricken she appeared. Dare he hope that Mark might be the answer to his prayers?

TWENTY-TWO

"You're wrong."

"You haven't been here, Mark," John shot back at his younger brother. "It's been over two, almost three months and Mom still won't look at anything on TV. We made a decision to live normally and allow the children to watch it in the family room but she practically runs from the room when the set is turned on. Until recently, she would have a panic attack if anyone went near the television. You see how she won't talk to anyone and mostly just stares out the window or at the floor? Her doctor says she is in very deep mourning and seems unable to pull herself out of it. I know it's hard to think about her loving someone that deeply when she seemed to have no difficulty getting over Dad's death. He says it's probably the combination of the two deaths in relatively close succession. Plus the fact that they were both very sudden. I talked to him about Tony and he feels she may see him as a replacement for the men she lost. Like a mother who loses her child might turn to someone else's to replace it."

"It wasn't like that. You should have seen her face light up when she knew he was meeting us at the church. On the way back from Communion, she looked … Well. Almost happy."

"Well then, we'll just take her to church more often if that's what makes her happy. She's never even mentioned church before."

"On the contrary, I believe she was trying to tell us something when she found her way to that church last month. Didn't you say she asked Tony to take her to church in Thunder Bay? And I don't think she just wants to go to church. I think, no … I damn well know, she

224

wants Tony to be there with her."

"We'll see. I'll talk to her doctor again."

"Her doctor could be wrong, John."

"And you're an expert all of a sudden?"

"No. No, I'm not. But I am kind of looking at this from the outside in and maybe I can see something that those of you who have been so involved, can't. Can we give it a try? Let's see if she asks again next Saturday. Maybe you could come, too."

Every day Jo asked what day it was. When Friday came, she asked if she could go to church the next day. Amy offered to go as a family to the neighbourhood church. Jo said no. Mark looked at John and he nodded agreement. Mark made the phone call and Tony was ecstatic that he would see his Josy again.

Mark talked John into coming and it ended up a family affair. When they strung out in the pew, Jo let everyone else in so that she and Tony were sitting together by the aisle. John had to admit that his mother did seem to brighten when she knew, once again, that she was going to church, and even more importantly, that Tony would be there. She held the man's hand all through the service and seemed very much at peace when she came back after receiving Communion. Again the invitation was extended for dinner and was declined. Tony would have to have patience.

Mark left during the following week, but extracted a promise from John that he would continue to take their mother to Tony's church. With his own promise in return, to try to come home again over the summer months, he left to continue his research on the other side of the world. He was very happy to receive a return hug from his mother before he and John drove to the airport.

"Thank you, Mark," was all she whispered.

Still reluctant to have Jo placed in a care facility, they arranged for weekday home care. A few weekends after Mark had left, John and Amy decided to attend a soccer match that Matthew's team was playing in in Owen Sound. They made arrangements for the homecare giver to extend her service through the weekend, Friday afternoon until Sunday evening. When they were preparing to leave, Jo asked if it was Saturday yet.

Hoping that she wouldn't know it was approaching the weekend, they replied that it was not. They had been taking her to church every Saturday and she seemed to be responding favourably, but this trip was important to the boys, and a respite that they needed as well.

"What day is it?" she asked.

Before John or Amy could respond, Sammy in his young innocence blurted out, "It's only Friday, Grandma."

"Phone Tony," she said to John.

"Mom, we won't be here to take you this weekend."

"Tony will take me."

"You can't expect him to come all this way and back again just to take you to church. We'll take you again next weekend."

"Tony will take me." She sounded very sure.

"We'll take you next week, we promise."

She disappeared into her bedroom. When she came out she had his card in her hand and went to the phone. John was about to stop her, but Amy held him back. They watched as Jo dialled the number and waited while it rang. Realizing this was the first time she had made any attempt to do something for herself in months, they held their collective breath waiting to see what the outcome would be.

"Hello?"

"Will you take me to church?"

"Josy, is that you?"

"Will you take me to church tomorrow?"

"Yes, cara, I will take you to church."

"Will you come for me?"

Through tears, "Yes, Josy. I will come for you."

She hung up the phone without any further exchange. "Tony will take me." With that she returned to her bedroom and closed the door.

John immediately went into the den and called Tony. He explained to the man, that they were going out of town and that this was strictly his mother's doing. Tony asked John's permission to take his mother to dinner after church. After a long hesitation, John gave in, not without some misgivings. He asked Tony to call him on his cell phone after his mother was safely at home again. Then he told the home care worker that his mother would be out for several hours on Saturday if she wanted to have dinner with her own family.

The next day Jo was ready and waiting by early afternoon. When Tony arrived a little past four o'clock, he was happy to see Jo dressed and looking somewhat healthier. While driving the car, he chatted to her about everything he had been doing in the past couple of months. When his questions to her went unanswered, he continued talking to her as if she understood and was responding. He was so happy to have her to himself, sitting beside him, even if she wasn't talking. It was enough that she had phoned him. If only she knew how much that phone call meant to him.

After church, he asked if she would like to go for dinner but she walked to the car without answering and without looking at him. Tony was hoping she might have happy remembrances at a nearby restaurant where they'd dined before, but she appeared not to notice. It was difficult continuing a one-sided conversation, but he could suffer anything just to keep her with him a while longer. When his suggestions about items on the menu were returned with a blank stare, he ordered for both of them. They ate in one-sided silence and eventually it was time to leave. It was a beautiful evening for a walk, but he knew John would be waiting for his phone call.

He closed the passenger door and went around to the driver's side. Glancing across at her, he noticed she was crying softly, a few tears had found their way down her cheeks. "Josy, what's the matter?"

"Thank you. You're nice."

He wanted to crush her to him and not ever let her go. "I wish I could be nice more often. Better yet, I want to be nice all of the time, cara. I believe everyone is trying to be nice to you, perhaps you just don't realize it."

She shrugged and wiped her eyes with his offered handkerchief. That was the end of it. When he brought her to the front door and opened it, she turned wet eyes toward him and said, "I heard you". Without another word, she went inside. Having no idea what she meant, he left and made his phone call to John from the car.

On Sunday evening when her family arrived home, they found their mother fully dressed in a nice outfit and her makeup complete. John asked Maggie, the caregiver, if they had been out, but she replied they had not. She went on to explain that when Jo got up Sunday morning, she had eaten a full breakfast, went into her bathroom and came out showered and face made up. Around noon, she had gone to her closet, chosen the outfit she had on, then sat and listened to a Luciano Pavarotti CD several times over. After an afternoon nap, she had gone back to staring out the window.

When John asked his mother if she had been to church the day before, she nodded.

"Did you come home right after?" he asked, hoping to draw her out.

She just shook her head.

"Where did you go?"

"We ate."

"Where?"

"Somewhere."

"Did you enjoy yourself?"

She nodded and went into her bedroom. Every day the following week, Jo showered and got dressed without help. She took time to put on makeup and style her hair but she was still unresponsive to verbal communication so her therapist couldn't draw anything more out of her. The following Friday she stood in front of the calendar on the kitchen wall and simply stated, "Today is Friday."

Amy was peeling potatoes for supper and stopped to look at Jo.

"Yes, today is Friday. It's wonderful that you didn't have to ask, Mother."

"I'll phone Tony."

"Mom, we'll take you to tomorrow. We enjoy going to church with you."

"I'll phone Tony"

"Tony certainly has a beautiful singing voice."

"I better phone him."

"Will you tell him that we'll meet him there?"

"Yes." She went to the phone and dialled his number without looking it up. Amy wondered if some of her memory was returning. "Tony?"

"Yes, cara. I've been hoping you'd call."

"Tomorrow we will all come."

"You don't want me to pick you up?"

"Yes I do, but John will bring us."

Tony wasn't sure what this last statement meant. Did she mean she would rather he came and got her? He didn't want to interfere in John's plans so he let it pass.

"I'll look forward to seeing you again, Josy. Maybe we can all go for dinner after Mass?"

"No."

"You don't want to?" He was jolted by her quick negative response.

"Yes, I do."

Tony wasn't sure what she meant by her mixed answers. "So you want all of us to go for dinner then?"

"Just me."

"Will that be OK with John?" Tony was smiling.

"It's OK with me."

Tony wanted to sing out loud. He knew he had to clear it with John in spite of what Josy said, but he had high hopes.

There was a click as Jo hung up the phone.

"What's OK with you?" Amy was surprised that Tony could get more than one sentence out of Jo. The only response she got was a shrug, with a sly look of … What? Was that a hint of a smile? God, her mother-in-law hadn't smiled in months.

The next day it took Jo forever to get dressed. She kept changing her mind about what she wanted to wear. Finally, she was ready and looked almost like her old self. Even John noticed how her eyes seemed brighter and more alert. And did they have a touch of eye shadow and mascara on them? It was a beautiful Saturday and Jo wore one of her spring suits that hinted at the colour of celery. It seemed to bring out the colour of her amber hair and eyes.

When Tony saw her, he beamed with pleasure at the sight of her. "Aw, Josy, my beautiful Josy. What an exquisite outfit you are wearing."

Jo put her head down and slid her hand into his. John realized at some point during the Mass that he was singing the responses, too, and that he was actually enjoying bringing his family to church. But why did it have to be so far from their home? Even the boys were singing and had stopped giggling when shaking hands at the sign of peace. When Mass was over, Amy was surprised when Jo started to walk away arm-in-arm with Tony. John told her it was OK, that Tony had cleared it with him the day before. She smiled thinking that maybe Jo's son had finally recognized that Tony brought out her best. Or could it be that this return to religion was having a profound effect on him? She slid her arm into John's and walked away arm-in-arm.

Tony took her to the same restaurant, thinking it might be more comfortable for her. This time she looked at the menu herself and asked for a chicken dish he remembered she had eaten last winter. He commented again on how beautiful she looked. "Are you feeling better, Josy?"

For a moment he thought a shrug was all the answer he was getting. Then she slowly answered, "When I'm with you in church, everything seems to be clear."

He took her hand. "Josy, I am so happy you are looking and feeling better."

Their dinner came and as they ate, he watched her and wondered whether she would ever truly be his. Jo didn't add much more to the conversation but she seemed happier on the drive home this time. When they arrived at John's, Tony kissed her cheek and thanked her for the most wonderful evening he'd had in a long time. She hugged him around the middle, the way a child would, and went quietly into the house.

***

"I want to go home."

"You are home." John was startled by her statement, which came out of the clear blue, a few days into the following week. They were eating dinner and Amy had been talking about her day at work.

"I want to go to my home."

"In Thunder Bay?"

"No. The lake."

He caught himself, almost commenting that she must be insane to think she could go to the lake. She seemed more normal these days, aside from not talking much. Where in the world had this idea of hers come from?

"You aren't well enough to stay at the lake by yourself, Mom. Maybe before the summer is over we can take you and stay for a week or so."

"I want to go now."

"You can't go now. Who'll look after you?"

"Tony."

John almost choked on his food. "Tony lives here. He's not at your beck and call. Taking you to church is one thing, but you can't possibly expect him to drop everything and take you halfway across the country to stay at the lodge."

She cringed at the tone of his voice and he felt bad for sounding so short with her but sometimes she had to be spoken to as a child.

"If I asked him, he would."

"You're probably right, but you can't ask him. It wouldn't be fair to him, Mom. Besides, you need to continue your therapy and there are no doctors at the Red Sky Lodge."

She sat at the table picking at her food but did not argue further. A couple of weeks went by and John thought she had either worked out the impossibility in her own mind, or she had forgotten about it completely. Their weekly Masses continued and then the whole family started joining Jo and Tony for dinner. One extremely nice day late in July, Tony phoned to see if he could take Jo out for the day. Amy agreed without even asking John who had already left for work, and then she called Jo to take the phone.

"Yes?"

"Josy, I think it's a perfect day for a ride in the country and I know a place where we could eat lunch outdoors. Do you feel up to it?"

"Yes."

"I'm already on my way, I'll see you in forty-five minutes."

"Thank you."

He was there in less than forty, and she was sitting waiting. Amy cancelled the home care for the day and waited with Jo for Tony to arrive. She had noticed how Jo had brightened at the sound of Tony's voice and decided that she was going to make sure they saw more of each other.

Jo's beauty always overwhelmed him, even when it had been fragile, *especially* when it had been fragile. Pulling her to him, he lifted her chin with his finger, "Josy, there is a price to pay for this outing. We are not going anywhere until you smile for me."

At first she frowned at his request, then ever so slowly, the corners of her mouth turned up and her lips parted in a very definite smile.

"Oh, Josy, what that does for my heart." He kissed her lightly and took her arm as they headed for the door. Amy had the biggest smile of all as she watched them leave.

It was a wonderful, grand, glorious day. They visited craft shops in a nearby village, and ate lunch at a converted mill in a farming community a couple of hours northwest of the city. After walking through a Christmas store in another small town, they enjoyed sitting and eating ice cream at a sidewalk patio table. Tony hated the thought of taking her home.

All of a sudden she started to cry. Frightened by this sudden emotional change, Tony slid off his chair and crouched beside her, offering his handkerchief. She shook her head and wiped her nose and eyes with a tissue, then standing, she sniffed and took a deep breath. She starting walking again, he caught up with her and took her hand as they walked.

"I have to go home."

Tony's heart sank. "It's still early, cara."

"I have to go home to the lake, to the lodge. I can't explain. Every Sunday I ask God to help me get well again, and every time I leave church knowing that I have to go home."

He was surprised at the clarity with which she spoke.

"No one listens to me. When my mind gets cloudy I know I say silly things, so I say nothing. Then, when I'm OK and I say something, no one listens to me. No one talks to me like I'm normal. Except you."

"Have you told John about this?"

"I told him I wanted to go to the lake. He said we could go for a week later in the summer."

"And that's not good enough." He stated it rather than asked it. "Tell me, Josy. Is this something you have to do by yourself?"

"I can't do it without you."

It took a moment for him to realize that he had stopped breathing.

She started to cry again. "I can't seem to do anything without you."

They stopped in the middle of the sidewalk and he held her to him. "Why do you think that is, Josy?"

"That's the part I don't know. When I try to think about it, I get confused again. I just know that if I don't get to the lake, I will never get better. You're the only person I feel … I don't know … I don't know how to describe it. I have to go and you have to go with me."

"Then if John allows it, we will go."

"No, Tony. We will just go." With that she started to walk back toward the car.

***

"No, definitely not! Mom, you can't just go back there. I'm sorry, Tony. If you're encouraging this, then I'm going to have to ask you to keep your distance from my mother again."

"John, I have stood by and watched the struggle in your mother's mind for several months now. Whatever you're doing, or not doing for her, isn't working." He spoke softly and reasonably, not wanting to cause Jo any more anguish. "If this might help her, as she seems to feel it will, then why not give it a try? There is nothing to lose and possibly everything to gain. She wants to go and I'm willing to take her. Will you at least let her talk to her doctor about it?"

"And if he says no?"

Tony turned and looked at Jo. "What do you think, cara? Will you abide by the decision of your doctor?"

"Don't put the decision on her. Her condition is fragile enough without placing these conditions on her."

"Perhaps that's part of the problem. It is *her* mind, *her* condition, and it should be *her* decision."

"She's not responsible enough."

"Not responsible enough for what? For making her own decisions? Does she tell you that? Does she tell you anything? Do you listen?"

In spite of being angered by Tony's words, something stirred in John's gut, instinct possibly. "I'll abide by what the doctor agrees to, and nothing more."

"May I go with you and your mother to the doctor's appointment?"

"Why? Don't you trust me to present the problem fairly?"

"He may have some questions for me that you can't answer."

"Fair enough. There's still time to catch him in his office. I'll try to get an appointment as soon as possible."

Jo held on to Tony's arm while John placed the call. An appointment was arranged for two days later.

"I'm sorry, Tony, if I seem short-tempered with you. My mother is my first concern and it always seems that you stir up some kind of — I don't want to say trouble exactly, but … something — when you're around her."

"I understand, John. There's no need to explain. I think we both want what's best for Josy, but we don't seem to agree on what that is."

Jo walked with him to the door and kissed his cheek. All she said again was "Thank you."

She went straight to her room and closed the door. The next morning she was slower to shower and dress and she put on hardly any makeup. The day after that, John came home early to take her to the appointment. Tony arrived at the doctor's office minutes later and they all went in together. John noticed that his mother sat next to Tony, and that she took his hand as they sat down. John did most of the talking while the doctor looked from one to another. He asked Tony why he wanted to go with Jo.

"I'm in love with her. I want to make sure all avenues have been explored to bring her back to health. Josy seems to think she needs to go back to the lake before she can move forward. Personally, I don't really know, but I realize nothing that has been done to this point has helped her."

Then the two men were asked to leave and the doctor talked a long while with Jo. When John and Tony returned, the doctor said he could see no reason why Jo shouldn't be allowed to go to her lodge. He did recommend that her previous doctor in Thunder Bay be notified, and that she see him within a couple of weeks after arriving at the lake. When they stood to leave, he asked John to stay for a minute and he closed the door.

"John, I have not seen your mother's mind so clear as it is when she speaks about the lodge or about Mr. DeMarco. I think this might be a good thing for her."

"What did she tell you exactly? Can you tell me?"

"No, I can't. But she spoke with such wisdom that I wasn't sure this was the same woman I've been treating all these weeks. It's the first time I've gotten more than one- or two-word phrases from her. If nothing else, the fresh air and change of scenery might do her some good."

"Thanks, Robert. I'm counting on your experience in this situation. I can't help but think she's returning to a place that has strong memories for her of two men who meant a great deal to her. If it all comes crashing down around her, I hope this third man is strong enough to help her."

"This third man, as you call him, may be the only person who can."

TWENTY-THREE

The staff was delighted when they learned that Mrs. H. was returning for a visit. Molly had been keeping her apartment dusted and cleaned but she went through it again on the morning of Jo's anticipated arrival. John had phoned Molly and told her that a male friend of his mother's, a Mr. DeMarco, was coming to look after her, and would be staying in the guest room in the apartment. She made sure there were fresh sheets and towels for him. Everyone, including Barney, was happy but slightly apprehensive about her stay. John had warned them not to be upset if Jo didn't talk much, or not at all. They were nervous about her "condition" and hoped she would find some happiness here this year. Lord knows that the last couple of years had not been kind to her. They made a pact to see to it that nothing would upset her so she could just relax and get stronger.

When they pulled into the driveway, Jo felt a panic attack approaching. Her skin turned clammy and she found it difficult to draw her breath.

Tony stopped the vehicle. "Put your head down between your knees, cara, and breathe deeply."

She did as instructed and the uncomfortable feeling soon passed. Following her directions, Tony drove around to her private entrance where he parked the vehicle. When they climbed the steps to her deck, he was astounded by the view.

"It's no wonder you wanted to come back here to recuperate. I've never been an outdoors man, but I like your lodge already. You told me I wouldn't be disappointed by the scenery and now I see why."

After bringing their bags inside, he phoned John as promised and announced their safe arrival. A soft knock sounded on a door near the hallway and Jo let Tony answer it.

"Pardon me, mister. Would you tell Mrs. H. that Molly's here?"

"Come in, Molly." Jo smiled when Molly peeked around the door.

"Oh, Mrs. H., you're looking so good. A little thin, but Cook will have you fattened up in no time."

"Thank you."

"I readied the guestroom for the gentlemen and I wondered whether I could bring you anything before dinner?"

"Do you have any iced tea?" Tony did the asking.

"Yes, sir. I'll bring some in."

When she knocked again, Tony took the tray from her and said that Mrs. H. would probably rest for the balance of the afternoon.

"The flight and the drive have taken quite a bit out of her."

"I'll tell the others not to disturb her. I'll be back with dinner around 7:00. If you need anything before then, just ask." She left with a smile.

Jo went outside and sat on the deck where Tony brought her drink, then he sat beside her. Everything was as she remembered it. She looked toward the honeymoon cottage and felt a wave of depression sweep over her. If she tried hard to look between the shrubs, she felt she would see Mike standing on the end of the porch. A broken intake of breath could not be avoided. It did not go unnoticed.

"How many cottages do you have?"

With a start she pulled herself out of her reverie. "Twelve."

"Tomorrow, when you're rested, will you show me around?"

"Of course."

Sensing her mood swing, he tried to keep her busy answering questions. When their drinks were finished, he stood and reached for her hand. "Why don't you lie down for a while and rest, cara?"

She awoke to the aroma of fresh beer-batter fried pickerel. It was a comfort-smell which lured her quickly into the living room. Her table was set with place mat, napkin and cutlery, and Cook was transferring platters from a tray to the table. Jo watched as he laid the tray down and walked toward her with outstretched arms. After giving her an uncharacteristic hug, he held her chair and then with a flourish waved her to sit.

"Welcome home, Mrs. H."

Home. It was good to hear that word. She thanked him and sat.

After sampling the food, Tony exclaimed, "None of the finest restaurants in Toronto, or even in Italy, could touch this meal. I can't remember ever eating such splendid fish."

Jo smiled listening to Tony singing happily as he piled the dishes back onto the tray. The brief clean-up finished, he exaggerated the tightness of his waistband as he joined Jo once again on the deck. She knew by the shape of the clouds that they were going to enjoy one of the more beautiful sunsets. She watched Tony's face as the colours exploded in the heavens until even the trees and sand seemed red and pink. His eyes changed colour with the sky, and soon the dark brown seemed almost a deep purple. He pulled her close to him, and when the sun sank out of sight and the last pink faded into deep grey, he finally looked at her.

"Now I understand."

She smiled then, all on her own with no prodding. "Most think of the sunset as the end of another day. I see it as a promise of a glorious tomorrow," she said softly.

With her snuggling under his arm, he whispered, "Tomorrow's promise. What a beautiful thought."

They sat contentedly until the mosquitoes drove them inside.

"I'll prepare a warm bath for you, cara, with lots of bubbling crystals sprinkled in it."

After soaking for about twenty minutes, Jo noticed her skin wrinkling. She wrapped herself in a bath sheet and paddled on her bare feet to her bedroom. Tony came in later to tuck her in. He sat on the edge of the bed.

"Thank you, Tony. I couldn't be here without your help."

He held her hands in his and kissed them both. "It is I who owe you the thanks."

"For what?"

"For a very fine dinner, for a fabulous evening, for allowing me this time with you. Goodnight, my love."

The next morning she showed him around the grounds. "I can't believe Barney found the time to keep my gardens looking so wonderful. He even planted annuals in the colours he knows I like."

Barney, who had proudly watched her appraisal from the fish house, was happy to see her looking much better than when he had left her in Minneapolis. She was quiet and withdrawn, but John had told them to expect that. Circling around the honeymoon cottage, she gave Tony a tour of all the others.

He started walking toward the cottage she had been avoiding but she caught him by the arm. "Please don't go there."

He looked beyond her and realized this must have been Mike's cabin. In an attempt to lighten the moment, he picked her up and laughingly pretended to throw her into the lake. As they wandered back up the hill to her apartment, they speculated what Cook might have prepared for lunch.

She rested again during the afternoon, happy that he hadn't asked any questions about the honeymoon cottage. Later that evening, Tony asked if she had a VCR. Her alarm at turning on the television was evident until he told her he had a surprise for her. He went into his room and came out with two videos. She tensed as he inserted one of them into the machine. The television screen exploded with the colour of scenic mountains and green forests. The music in the background was Italian. "This is where my roots are, cara."

He had noticed her fists curling into tight balls when he turned on the set, but it wasn't long before her breathing returned to normal and her fingers relaxed. They watched for about forty-five minutes while he showed her where his grandparents had lived and the places he had visited. When a beautiful old church came on the screen, he said, "This is where my parents were married and my grandparents buried."

"Stop the tape for minute please, Tony."

She moved closer to the television screen and studied the picture. "Will you take me there?"

"Certainly, Josy. When would you like to go?"

"Someday." She shrugged.

"Someday soon, I hope," he replied with a sigh.

She settled back and continued to watch the film. Before he inserted the second tape, he made her the hot chocolate she so loved. She took his hand as the screen came to life with the ocean where he had scuba dived. The camera had scanned beautiful beachfront properties, island homes and resorts. When it was finished, she was tired and ready for bed. This time it was she who held Tony's hands and said good night with a kiss.

***

The sound of a door closing woke Tony in the middle of the night. He checked Josy's room and saw that she was not in her bed. Looking around, he noticed the screen door was ajar and looked outside to see her sitting on the deck. She was staring down at the cottage below. With her knees pulled up and arms wrapped around them, she sat like that for a long time, just peering into the darkness. He remembered how she had always stared out the window in Thunder Bay. Not knowing whether to interrupt her thoughts or not, he just continued to watch her. Finally, she lowered her head and sobbed. He let her be for a few minutes before he opened the door and stepped out. He pulled her to him on the settee and stroked her head as she sobbed in his arms. When her crying had subsided, he walked her back into the house and tucked her into her bed.

The next morning, she said nothing and he took his cue from that. He placed a bowl of oatmeal in front of her. "Make sure you clean it all up. Follow my instructions and just maybe I'll let you take me for a walk along the beach later."

They spent the next few days quietly soaking up the sun and walking the beach roads. He had asked her once about fishing but she refused, suggesting he go with Barney. Realizing she may want some time to herself, he agreed to spend a half-day out on the lake.

While they enjoyed the sunsets every evening, Tony noticed that Jo always appeared melancholy afterwards. They seemed to settle into a semi-routine and John called every night to make sure she was fine. After about a week, she offered to take Tony for a hike. They climbed to the lookout where she and Mike had gone the day of the storm. Tony was totally taken in by the scenery. He explained that after years of living in Southern Ontario, he had absolutely no idea that Northern Ontario had so much beauty. He had a preconceived notion that this part of the province was full of ugly bush, gravel roads and very remote fishing "camps". They enjoyed a picnic lunch at the top of the falls overlooking the whole region, and then took their time going back. When they were almost back at the lodge, she smiled at Tony. "I'm feeling quite a bit better. I think this hike in the hills might be just what the doctor ordered. Maybe it's that endorphins thing."

Pleased that her mood had lifted, Tony reminded her that she had a doctor's appointment in Thunder Bay the next day. They decided to stay at her condominium for a day or two so she could show him around her hometown. Again, she revisited places she and Mike had been to but found she was able to get through it all with no panic attacks. The doctor completed the routine check on her vital signs, then after a short question and answer period, he closed her file. "Considering the report I received from your doctor in Toronto, I'm amazed to see how well you're doing. All that the fresh air and outdoor exercise must be the right medicine indeed. Unless you notice an increase in your feelings of anxiety, I really don't see any reason for you to return. Keep up the exercise and make sure you get plenty of rest."

"Thank you, Doctor. I can feel myself getting stronger daily."

When they arrived back at the lodge, Jo noticed that a young couple was loading their vehicle, in the process of moving out of the honeymoon cottage. Molly went down after a while and stripped the bed and brought the towels and bedding up to be laundered. It wasn't booked until the following weekend, so she brought all the blankets and linens to be aired on the outdoor clothesline.

Several times during the afternoon, Tony saw Jo looking toward the building. Finally, he said, "Why don't you show me that cottage now?"

She looked at him and almost said no. He took one hand and lifted her chin. "Please?"

Nodding, she held his hand very tightly and walked down the path, hoping she would not fall apart. Tony asked if it had always been a honeymoon cottage.

She whispered a very brief, "Yes."

They wandered around to the front porch and found the door had been left open, which was very unlike Molly. Tony walked in ahead of her and turned to see her cautiously stepping inside the door. Asking her who did the decorating, he motioned to the new draperies and rug in front of the hearth.

"I did," she replied, remembering how worried she had been about what Mike would think of the old ones. The previous summer after he had left she had bought new drapes, quilt and rug as a surprise for his next visit.

"It's OK, Josy."

"What is?" she asked.

"Whatever you're feeling, it's OK. You don't have to be afraid of what I think. Talk about it if you like."

She hesitated, then began to speak about how she had wanted everything to be perfect for Mike. She talked about her ankle and how silly she felt about her clumsiness when around him. Before she knew it, she was pouring her insides out. Everything. She told Tony everything. She couldn't remember when they moved to the swing outside, but at one point she realized they were moving slowly back and forth on it. He noticed that her story didn't go beyond the walk she and Mike had shared outside of her hotel in Minneapolis. She didn't tell him how she had learned of his accident or the fact that he was dead. However, he sensed that she had unburdened a heavy weight this afternoon, and she seemed totally exhausted.

He helped her to stand and suggested a nap before dinner. During the walk back to her suite, Jo held his hand so tightly it almost hurt. Tony lay with her, cradling her in his arms until she fell asleep. She awoke almost at sundown and realized she was extremely hungry.

"I'll bring a tray from the kitchen, cara."

When she agreed, her voice was a bit husky and her throat was still dry from talking so much that afternoon. Her mind seemed clearer and she had less trouble focusing her thoughts. She freshened up and sat at the table where Tony had laid out cold chicken and a salad for them. After she had eaten everything on her plate, he smiled mischievously and went to the refrigerator. He came back with a big piece of fresh strawberry pie, which he said he'd stolen under the threat of death. "Cook chased me with a butcher's cleaver. He said it was meant for tomorrow's lunch."

From behind his back, he produced two forks.

It was almost impossible to stay away from her bed that night. He wanted to hold her and soothe her sorrows, but he was determined to wait until she was ready. She had progressed such a long way in a short time, he was not going to jeopardize everything just to satisfy his own selfish needs.

A week or so later, she asked, "Would you like to go for a boat ride?"

"I really hate to leave you alone again."

"I'll take us," she said.

"In that case, I can't think of anything I would rather do."

Barney was delighted when asked to get a boat ready for them. He noticed she didn't take any fishing rods, but at least she was going out on the lake. Jo took Tony to several places that she and Mike had never visited, then slowly she worked her way to the trapper's cottage and finally slowed right down. She inched her way along the shore where her goose lived. After several passes, she realized the bird was not there. An overwhelming feeling of loss took hold of her, and she experienced a melancholy that she couldn't explain. She revved the motor and left in a hurry, almost in a state of panic. Tony hung on to the boat with both hands and wondered what had frightened her. When they reached the dock, she quickly tied the boat and didn't hear Barney greeting them. She ran up the incline to the lodge to climb the stairs to her deck. skipping every second one. Barney looked at Tony who shrugged and followed Jo with his eyes.

"I have no idea what happened out there."

When Tony came inside, Jo was lying on the bed staring at the ceiling. He sat on the edge of the mattress and brushed the hair from her face, softly whispering words of comfort. She continued to gaze at the ceiling until the phone rang. Tony answered it and heard John's voice. "I just had a phone call from Mark. He wants to come back to Canada and to the lake. I think this news might really please Mom. She gave up years ago trying to get Mark to visit the lodge."

"Your mother is resting right now, John. Can I pass the news along when she wakes up? Do you know when Mark is expecting to arrive?"

"I'm not sure exactly when, probably in about two weeks."

Tony went into the bedroom to give Jo the news and found her sitting up sobbing. He sat beside her and held her hands.

"I'm sorry I'm being such a drag, Tony. I wanted to see the goose, but she ... but she wasn't there. I'm sorry ... I'm so sorry."

Jo tried to explain to him about the goose and how she had stayed alone after her mate died. She couldn't get it all out without breaking down and crying. Now the goose was gone.

"I wonder if she died of loneliness and heartbreak? Do geese have feelings do you think, or only instincts?"

Tony couldn't answer her questions, but he was grateful humans weren't geese because they would have missed out on so much happiness.

She remembered someone reassuring her that she wasn't a goose, and now ... He was gone, too. A feeling of guilt took hold of her. She had tried to tell herself she wasn't responsible but sometimes it was so overwhelming that she found it too hard to deal with. She had no right to happiness. She had no right to be with Tony. If only, if only ... If only what? She couldn't remember. If only she could remember.

She barely touched her lunch. Tony felt inept in his attempts to help her. This goose business had really upset her. What a silly thing to set her off, he thought, but obviously there was something deeper at work here. He forced her to go for a walk that afternoon and tried to interest her in playing backgammon. It would appear they were almost back at square one. He was reluctant to have her take the medication that she abhorred. She said it only made her sleepy and her mind foggy. In the end he insisted and she gave in.

She was sleeping fitfully and he heard every time she moaned or moved in her bed. Finally his own weariness overtook him and he fell sound asleep. He didn't know what woke him, the light from the window or the sense of Jo standing in his doorway. She came and sat on his bed, took one of his hands and kissed it.

"I'm sorry for being so much trouble."

"You are never too much trouble, my love."

"I've not been easy to understand these last few months."

"You've been through a very difficult time. How do any of us know how we would have reacted?"

"I had a dream again last night."

He took hold of her hand and kissed her palm. "What did you dream about?"

"Two geese, mine and another. She found her mate. They were lifting off the water in perfect synchronization."

"You didn't happen to hear if she called him by name did you? Was it Donald? Oh no, that's a duck, isn't it?"

She looked stunned at first that he would make fun of her, then she realized he was trying to lighten her mood. "I can't be certain but I think she called him Tony. I know he definitely called her Josy."

His heart skipped a beat. "And what do you think this dream means?"

Her eyes filled with tears and she turned away.

"Josy, my sweet. I always seem to make you cry." He sat up and put his arms around her.

She felt his hairy chest against her own bare skin above her nightgown. It felt so marvellous.

"You don't make me cry. Remembering makes me cry. That's why I don't like remembering."

"Perhaps if you face your memories head on you can challenge them, deal with them, then put them behind you once and for all."

He wasn't sure if she understood. She sat now, staring at

something just over his shoulder. "I know the exact instant that Mike died."

"And how do you know that?"

"I was dreaming about you and me." He didn't interrupt as she once again described the scene of them dancing at their wedding, ending with the fact his eyes had been blue, not brown. "It startled me so much, I woke up and couldn't get back to sleep. I tried for a while and then I made coffee. I watched the blinking lights of a plane in the night sky outside my hotel window for a long time, until it disappeared. Then I turned on the television. They said he died instantly, and I realized why I had seen his blue eyes in yours. I don't remember what happened after that. I feel so guilty. I was dreaming of you and me getting married, being so happy — at the exact moment he died." She repeated in a whisper, "I was happy and laughing while he … while he … died."

"My poor, poor Josy. How you have suffered!"

"Tony?"

"Yes, my love."

"Now I know why I had to return here. I had to come back before I could move ahead. The goose didn't die. She's soaring with her love. I didn't love Mike. I didn't know it until I came back here. I was unbelievably infatuated, but not in love. He was exciting and funny, handsome and famous. He was everything I needed or at least wanted at that time, but it wasn't love. I could have stopped him from catching that plane. If I had asked him to stay, he would have. I let him get on that plane … No, I *insisted* he get on that plane even when he wanted to stay … And he died."

"You didn't force him on the plane. The choice was his, not yours. He could have chosen to stay with you and he didn't. It was God's will, not yours that put him on that plane."

"I know that now. But I had to come back here to realize it. I had to be reassured again. I'm not a goose. I *can* love again. And I do. Oh, Tony. I do love you."

Tony wondered if he was the one dreaming now. He pulled her closer but she pushed him away. "We have to wait."

"Wait?"

"If you hold me, I won't want to stop until we're in bed. We must wait."

"Until when?"

"Until our honeymoon."

He moaned. "I think I took you to church one too many times."

"Tony?"

"Yes, my love?"

"Do you think we could go to Italy for our honeymoon?"

"And when would that be, Josy?"

"I can't wait much longer. My sixty-first birthday is fast approaching."

He jumped out of bed, then realizing he was naked, he pulled the sheet in front of him. "I better not let you see this naked body. You might be overcome with temptation. Almost sixty-one. That old decrepit heart of yours might not be able to handle it." She started to laugh. He hadn't heard her laugh in months. His own heart almost couldn't take the excitement. He crushed her to him and kissed the top of her head. With his eyes lifted upward, he offered a silent "Thank you."

Mark arrived and before long realized he had missed the lake more than he thought. He also missed his father. He and Tony went fishing daily and he quickly became very fond of the older man. It was not the same as fishing with his dad, but it was enjoyable. He helped Barney with some of the chores as he had done with his dad as a young boy. His father had always hoped that he might take over the management of the lodge one day. However, he encouraged his son even when they learned Mark's destiny would take him to the far reaches of the world. As the days passed, Mark realized that everything he had been searching the globe for was right here, where his roots were.

"How would you feel about giving up the management of the lodge, Mom?"

"Why?"

"I realize now, that this is where I belong. I haven't been back because I didn't think I could stand it here without Dad. I've been wandering around the globe looking for something that always seemed to elude me. I now know that I was looking for the peace and happiness I get when I come here. I don't want to interfere with your plans though, so I have to know how you feel about retiring."

"The reason I haven't wanted to retire is because I hated the thought of ownership being turned over to strangers. It was a dream of your father's that one day you would be operating the lodge with the same love and devotion he had for it. I will gladly turn it over to you. On one condition."

"What would that be?"

"That I could come back every year for a visit and watch some of our glorious sunsets."

"I wouldn't have it any other way."

TWENTY-FOUR

M ark flew with Tony and his mother to Toronto.

"There they are." Sammy was waving and jumping up and down. "Grandma, we're over here."

Behind him, John, Matthew, Sylvia and Robert were waiting at the baggage carousel. They rode in two vehicles to John's house where Amy and Steve were waiting for them. John and Amy were astounded by the change in his mother. She seemed positively radiant and glowing with health. Tony had warned them though, that while she appeared to have returned to her old self, she still was quite fragile and had to be handled with care. Everyone was nervous about her staying alone in her suite, but she insisted she was capable of taking care of herself. Tony had hoped she might come to stay at his place, but she insisted on being on her own.

"The bride should not be staying at the groom's house before the wedding." She had been adamant about that.

Understanding that she may have to prove to herself she was capable of independence, he didn't push the issue.

Two days later, they were at his church, and like all engaged couples about to be married, they were running through a wedding rehearsal. Barb had agreed to be the matron-of-honour and George was the best man. A small wedding reception was planned at George's. After the rehearsal, Tony took the wedding party — the grandchildren included — to the restaurant he and Jo had enjoyed after church on Saturdays.

Sammy climbed onto his grandmother's knee with an inquisitive look on his face. "Grandma, when you marry Robert's grandfather, will he be my cousin?"

"I always have a hard time understanding these things, but I think you might be called cousins — once removed."

"What does that mean?"

"I think it means you can call him your cousin, if that's what you want." She hugged him and ruffed his hair.

They were married at three o'clock in the afternoon. Tony was dressed in a black silk suit, and Jo in a soft yellow, short-sleeved, two-piece outfit. She carried a small bouquet of yellow roses with soft rose-coloured ribbons and lace. Mark gave her away as Barb looked on, smiling. George smiled also as he stood beside his brother. The two older grandsons took very seriously their job of ushering the small group of guests to their seats. John and Sylvia each gave a reading. The bride and groom exchanged traditional wedding vows and at the appropriate time, Sammy proudly produced the wedding rings, dropping only one of them.

At five o'clock they were back at Mass with their families surrounding them. Jo looked totally at peace, happy with the world as she strolled back to their pew after Communion.

Tony's sister, sister-in-law, and daughter had prepared the food for the reception. Amy had helped decorate the house and arrange the table settings. It was a traditional multi-course Italian wedding dinner, and the toasting and dancing went on until after midnight. At one point during the evening Tony stood, lifted a glass of wine to his Josy, wrapped his free arm around her shoulders and sang "I Have But One Heart". The women cried and the men cheered.

The newlyweds returned to Tony's condominium after the reception. With lights turned low, they waltzed through the rooms to Luciano Pavarotti singing the drinking song Mario Lanza had made famous. Tony spun Jo around and around, looking at her with the most wonderful, darkest brown eyes, eyes that took her breath away.

Slowly, he danced her into the bedroom, kissing her, tasting her forehead, her cheeks, her neck … until he found his way to the front of her throat. His fingers shook as he undid the back of her dress. He tried to keep his breathing steady but he knew it betrayed his passion, a passion that increased when she loosened his tie and opened his shirt. Shivers overtook him when she placed her lips on the hair that covered the upper part of his chest, began tracing the skin under his ear on the way to his mouth.

He picked her up and gently placed her on the bed. She gasped as he nibbled one of her breasts. His hand gently worked its way, inch by tantalizing inch, over the soft curve of her stomach. His tongue eventually abandoned her breast and began flirting with her belly button, teasing, teasing …

"Look at me, cara."

She turned her eyes questioningly to him.

"I want to see those golden eyes of yours catch fire."

This man absolutely made her body tremble. Everything she'd wanted in life, he gave her with a touch. Every word she'd ever longed to hear was there when he whispered her name. She knew she would love this man with all her soul and all her desire for the rest of her life. He took his time entering her, watching, as the flame caught and grew brighter and brighter until it finally exploded into a starburst of fireworks. He brushed each of her eyelids with his lips and smiled as he whispered his love.

"I must be the luckiest woman alive. Tony, I didn't know my body had a life of its own until I met you."

Satiated, she lay on her back, twirling the fingers of one hand around the curls of dark hair on his broad chest. He watched as her breathing slowed and her eyes deepened to their natural amber once more. Just when he thought she might drift into sleep, she smiled.

"Tell me again about the places we'll visit on our honeymoon."

He kissed her ear lobes and told her about the mountains and the ocean beaches. He nibbled on her breasts and described the vineyards; caressed her belly and told her about the magnificence of David. He promised to show her the splendour of the mountains and to carry her through fields of flowers.

A month later they returned from Italy and Jo couldn't remember being more content in her life. They had gone scuba diving several times in the sea near his grandparents' former villa. They had ridden in the gondolas through the canals of Venice and had toured vineyards and monasteries in Umbria. After lingering in mountain villas and seaside resorts, they had watched sunrises and sunsets in Tuscany. Most importantly, they had been content just being together.

After a couple of weeks at home, Jo decided it was time to pick up the few things of hers that remained in the suite she had rented from her friend. She stopped by the post office in that neighbourhood to pick up her mail and to give them her change of name and forwarding address. In the stack of mail waiting for her, she noticed a manila envelope with a Montana return address on it. When she arrived at the apartment, she opened her other mail first, but her eyes kept returning to the yellow envelope. It had been sent registered mail and insured. It was an insulated envelope and it felt like there was a package inside it. For some reason she was reluctant to open it. When all her other mail had been opened and read, she finally picked it up. She could not help the feeling of trepidation as she shuffled it back and forth, from hand to hand. After holding it a few moments, with shaking fingers Jo cut open one end, then dumped out the contents. She was right, there was a package with a smaller envelope attached to it. Her name was written on the front. A long letter, handwritten in a feminine script and folded in half, fell on the floor. She picked it up and eyed it with an unexplainable apprehension.

The salutation was simply, *Dear Mrs. Henderson.* She looked at the last page for a signature and saw that it was signed by Shannon Talbot Wilson. She dropped the paper as if it had burned her fingers, and sat staring at it. Finally, she picked up the first page and started reading.

> It was a long time before I was able to bring myself to go through my father's belongings. His sudden death was such a shock to me that I suffered a deep depression for several months, and then needed professional help before I was able to pull myself out of it.

However, now I am feeling stronger and able to deal with his affairs.

I know that my father was a guest of yours in Canada for a while in the spring of last year. I also know that he was deeply in love with you, and had hoped that someday he and you might have a life together. Dad was a very private person when it came to the people close to him, so I was not aware at first there was a woman in his life. I was very surprised and somewhat delighted to learn that he had opened his heart and finally allowed the love of a woman to enter again. Between what he had told me and what I have learned from his secretary, you appear to have made quite a difference in his life in just a short time.

Dad was so unhappy for so long that I thought I would never see the dad I knew as a young child, ever again. When you came into his life he changed, and I was delighted to see him smiling and trusting, and actually loving again. You know that he was a non-drinker and led rather a reclusive life for so many years. The last time I spoke to him, he told me he still hadn't told you why. I don't know why I feel the need to tell you all of this now, especially since he is gone. However, even without us having met, I sense a bond with you and would like to share some understanding of what, and who, my dad was. You really did make a difference in his life.

My dad was an all-star football player in his younger years; of course you would already know this. He was so good looking and such a successful athlete that everyone presumed he had the world at his feet. He met my mother early in his football career and they fell madly in love. She was a beauty queen, Miss Texas, when she was twenty years old. They got married when she was twenty-two and he was twenty-five. I was born two years later. Being the wife of a football player, or any professional athlete for that matter, is not an easy life. The teams are always on the road and even when they're home, their time is not their own. My mother soon found that she was alone more than she was with her husband. Having a young child kept her from traveling with Dad. He tried very hard to be with her as much as he could, but he seemed to always have obligations to fulfill, whether to sponsors, fans, or club owners.

My mother started finding solace in a bottle when feeling lonely. This went on unnoticed for a few years, then it reached the point that she was unable to conceal it from my dad any longer. When he learned of her drinking problem, he cut back drastically on his public appearances to be with her more. He felt extreme guilt and took the responsibility for driving her to alcoholism. My mother eventually gave up the bottle, and she and Dad seemed to be happy again. I was delighted to have my daddy home more as well. My mother got pregnant again and soon I had a baby brother. His name was Tommy and we did everything as a family. We went to Disneyland in California, my parents bought a cottage on a lake in South Dakota where my mother, Tommy and I used to spend most of our summers. My dad joined us when he could, but mostly we were together only during the spring in our house in Texas.

When Tommy was about five, my mother started drinking again. My dad tried everything he thought possible to help her to stop, but she said the loneliness was driving her to it. He was transferred to Green Bay and after a few more years, my dad finally decided we were more important to him than anything so he retired from football and started a career in television. He was home a lot more and spent a lot of time with Tommy and me. I thought those were the happiest days of my life. The only problem was that my mother didn't stop drinking this time. She then said she felt guilty for making Daddy give up his career and spent her time drowning her sorrows. I don't know how many times Daddy had to bring her home early from parties and family picnics, so we finally quit going to them. It seemed like they were always arguing, our happy home wasn't so happy any more. He begged her to get professional help but she refused. Then real tragedy struck. One day while I was spending some time with my grandparents, my dad came home and found my little brother floating in the swimming pool and mother passed out on the patio with a bottle in her hand.

I don't think I ever saw my dad smile again. My mother was admitted into a detoxification center after facing charges for my brother's death. My dad and I went to live at my grandfather's for a while. My dad quit his job and purchased a ranch where we moved together. I loved our life on that ranch in Wyoming, and my dad gave a good imitation of being happy. My mother eventually died from complications caused by alcoholism. She never did get over my brother and her responsibility for his drowning. My dad didn't even go to her funeral. He took me to Texas, but it was my grandparents who actually took me to the service.

My dad never touched alcohol after my brother died. He gave me everything he could, except real happiness. He tried, but the face he presented to the public was not the face of the man I knew at home. I eventually went away to college, married, and came home often for short visits. I loved him so much and wished so badly, that he could find someone who could make him happy. I had just about given up hope; he was in his mid-sixties after all. Then he met you.

At first I didn't know what, or who, was responsible for such a positive change in him. I thought it was the new job and getting out into the public again, then late last summer he told me about you. He was like a high school boy talking about the new girl he had a crush on. He started to smile and laugh, and even sing and whistle again. I couldn't believe the change in him. I just thought, whoever this Jo is, she's got to be an angel of some kind.

Then I know something happened and he was upset. He was like a man with a mission, but he wouldn't talk about it. All I know is that he repeated a number of times that he was the most stupid man on the face of the earth, that if he lost you it was through his own stupidity. Then in March, he called me from the airport in Minneapolis. He was very excited and all he said was, "Shannon, I found her again and this time I'm not letting her go. As soon I get home, I'm quitting my job and I'm going to spend the rest of my life making her as happy as she's made me. She loves me. Do you hear that? She loves me."

Of course, as you know, he never made it home. Mrs. Henderson, I just want to thank you for making my dad so happy in the last year of his life. God knows he deserved it. I found this box and the envelope among the things his secretary gathered from his office. She said he had commissioned a jeweler to make it for you last summer and was keeping it until the next time he saw you. Neither she, nor I, have opened the envelope so I don't know what is in it. Again, I'm sorry for not passing this along sooner, but I've only recently been able to go through his belongings. Please take comfort in knowing that he loved you more than anyone, ever; more even than me, I'm afraid, as I was unable to make him smile. I hope someday I might meet you so that I can see the love of my dad's life.

Yours sincerely,
Shannon Talbot-Wilson

Jo was trembling by the time she finished reading. She sat staring at the smaller envelope attached to the little box. The tears streaming down her face were making it difficult for her to see.

She stood, walked to the window and stared out for the longest time. Finally, hands shaking once again, she slowly opened the flap on the envelope that had her name neatly printed on it. She lifted out the little enclosure card on which he had written *For Life*. Jo opened the box and gasped as she saw the exquisite design of the brooch. The sapphires, her birthstone, were fitted into a setting of two beautiful geese, flying in perfect unison.

The box remained firmly in her hand as she slid to the floor.

TWENTY-FIVE

It was dark in the room and she could hear voices in the distance. When she found herself covered in sterile white sheets and surrounded by a metal rail, she realized she wasn't in her suite at all. Where was she? She tried to sit up but the room kept spinning around her.

"Mrs. DeMarco, you're awake." A nurse stood at the side of her bed and immediately took hold of her wrist to take a reading of her pulse.

"Who are you? What happened? Where am I?" She realized now that the room wasn't going around at all. It was perfectly still, it was her stomach that was spinning around and around. When it started to churn, the nurse quickly placed a tray under her chin and encouraged her to bring it all up.

"Your husband and the doctor are right outside. I'll let them know you're awake."

Jo lay back and closed her eyes hoping to stop the motion. Someone took her hand again. She opened her eyes and looked into the grey eyes of a doctor who also took her pulse. Confused, Jo wondered why everyone was so interested in her heart rate. She heard a chair being pulled up, and slowly moved her head to look toward the other side of her bed. There, taking a seat, was a concerned-looking Tony.

"Cara mia, you gave us quite a scare."

"Where am I?"

"You're safe and secure my love. You're in the hospital and I think it might be wise for you to remain here for a day or so. You've had quite an unsettling experience, and I don't think you're quite strong enough to deal with it."

She was trying to remember. *What happened? What was he talking about?*

The doctor spoke softly, "Mrs. DeMarco, I've given you rather a strong sedative and it probably would be best for you just to relax and let yourself sleep for now. When you're feeling stronger, we'll talk."

Jo attempted an argument, but she was extremely drowsy and confused. Tony enclosed her hand in one of his and stroked her cheek softly with the other. She found herself drifting off into a dreamless sleep. The next time she woke the room was brighter, but the light was still subdued somewhat. She lay for a long time without moving, trying to get her bearings … trying to remember. She allowed her eyes to roam around the room without moving her head. Finally, she realized her hand was being held and she turned her head. There was Tony sitting in the chair, sleeping with his head on the edge of the bed. She pulled her hand free and stroked the back of his head. Sweet, loving Tony. He woke with a start and smiled when he saw that she was watching him and caressing him. He placed her hand in his again and held her palm to his mouth.

It started with a tear, then a barely audible whimper. Finally, deep uncontrollable sobs. She tried to turn away from him, but he wouldn't allow her to. He moved to sit on the edge of the bed and stroked her hair, all the while soothing her with soft, loving words. He encouraged her to let it out of her system. His beard was rough. She had never felt his cheeks unshaven, he was always meticulous about his grooming. She couldn't ever remember seeing him with his hair uncombed or his shirt undone. She realized he must have been here all night and wondered how long before that. When her sobs subsided, she felt an irresistible urge to latch onto Tony and hold him as tightly as she could. Her world was falling apart for some vague reason she couldn't quite understand, and she feared she would lose him, too, if she let go.

With her arms wrapped around him, she clung tightly and begged him to hold her as well. She was crying again, almost hysterically, and wished she could understand what was happening to her. He kissed her cheeks, shoulders and neck and assured her he wasn't going anywhere. The doctor came in again and asked her to lie back so he could examine her eyes. She wondered how he could possibly look into her eyes when they were so swollen and full of tears, but she allowed herself to be lowered to the pillow. The doctor lifted her eyelids and shone a light into each one. He took her pulse and made notations on her chart.

"Mrs. DeMarco, I want you to remain with us for observation for another twenty-four hours. If we feel you're strong enough to go home at that time, I'll release you, but you'll have to receive outpatient therapy. I understand you've been a patient of Robert Allen's before, so we can arrange for him to see you again, if you like."

"Doctor, why am I here?"

"You experienced a rather traumatic experience and maybe it's just as well if you let it go for the moment. Obviously, you aren't quite ready to deal with it yet. As your memory comes back, we'll help you. Your husband said he feels quite confident you would be more comfortable at home, but I think another twenty-four hours in hospital won't hurt."

"Just don't give me any more medication. I hate it. It confuses me."

"We'll see how you do today."

"Cara, if you'll allow me some time to go home and freshen up, I'll return quickly and stay with you until bedtime. I'll bring the backgammon board if you like."

"Don't be too long. Promise?"

He took her hand and brought it to his mouth. "I promise."

After Tony left, a nurse came and helped her into the washroom where she had a shower and change of hospital gown. She wouldn't look in the mirror because she knew she looked like hell. True to his word, Tony was back before noon and brought her travel makeup bag and a housecoat for her. They laughed together as she attempted to apply lipstick with a shaky hand and ended up with lopsided lips. Jo tried valiantly to concentrate on backgammon, but found it impossible. Instead, Tony found a newspaper and read several interesting articles to her. When the afternoon had passed and her dinner tray was delivered, he went down to the cafeteria and forced himself to eat a bowl of soup.

Sitting at a long table all by himself, he ran his hand through his hair and realized he had to face the question of their future together. *Oh my Josy. What are we going to do? I thought you put Mike behind you, and now this. I can deal with a real threat, but I can't compete with a ghost. Are you going to be fighting your feelings for him the rest of our lives?* He half-heartedly ate his soup then stood, and with a heavy sigh, went back upstairs to face his sad-eyed bride once more.

Someone had brought a book cart into her room and she was flipping through a magazine when he came back. When she didn't notice him inside the doorway, he took the time to study her fragile beauty. If only she could love him half as much as she must have loved Mike. He would settle for that. At the lake she had professed her love for him and only an infatuation for Mike, but obviously she was still confused. Her feelings for Mike apparently went much deeper than she would admit even to herself. He wondered if he would have to share her with a ghost indefinitely.

She turned then and saw him. "You look sad. Was your supper that awful?"

"No, my love. I'm sad because I have to leave you here again tonight."

"What happened? What did I do to end up in here, and why can't I remember?"

He sat and thought carefully before he spoke. Taking her hand in his, he said softly, "You have some demons from the past that you're having trouble dealing with. When you are strong enough, I hope we can face them together and put them behind you once and for all. For now, know that I love you, and I will be here for you no matter what."

The next morning, the doctor was in before breakfast was delivered. Jo reminded him of his promise that she could go home that day. He pulled up a chair and lowered his large frame into it. He looked at her thoughtfully and appeared to hesitate before he questioned her.

"Tell me, Mrs. DeMarco, prior to waking up in this room, what is the last thing you remember?"

Jo thought for a full minute and remembered driving her car on her way to her old suite.

"What street were you on, do you remember?"

"The radio was playing and I was driving down Winston Churchill Boulevard."

"And then what?"

Struggling to remember, Jo attempted to recall something, anything, after that. Did she arrive? Was she in an accident? Why couldn't she remember? Would she be kept here if she couldn't remember? Frustrated, she willed herself not to shed the tears she could feel building. Goodness, all she wanted was to go home.

"Mrs. DeMarco, I see that you slept the night without any sedatives and even though you're having short-term memory loss, I'm going to allow you to go home with your husband today. I will set up an appointment with Dr. Allen, and he will arrange suitable therapy for you. You are alert and able to take care of your personal needs, so I see no reason to keep you here. Mr. DeMarco, I understand, is available to care for you at home. The nurse will notify him that you can leave and I'll release you into his care."

"I don't seem to have any physical injuries, can you at least tell me why I'm here?"

"Dr. Allen will discuss your emotional trauma with you as the treatment progresses, so I don't want to get into that with you. I can tell you that your injuries are not of a physical nature, rather a psychological one. You've experienced a shock, which you are choosing at the moment to forget. Robert Allen will help you remember it, face it, and overcome it as you get stronger."

Still confused, Jo realized she would have to settle for a half explanation. She hoped it wouldn't be long before she understood completely. "Thank you. May I get dressed now?"

"Of course, but I see the breakfast trays out in the hall. I hope you'll make a good attempt at breakfast before you leave. I'll tell the nurse to call your husband. Good luck, Mrs. DeMarco. Your husband tells me you are quite a remarkable woman. He's as anxious to have you home as you are."

She watched him leave the room and wondered what awaited her. What couldn't she remember? She dressed quickly before he changed his mind.

Tony arrived within the hour, all smiles, and from the look on his face, Jo could almost picture him breaking out into song. Wouldn't that be a treat for the nurses and patients, to hear his rich baritone singing, "Oh What a Beautiful Morning". The thought made her smile, which eventually grew into a full-blown giggle.

"That makes my day already, cara, to see you smiling and laughing. Am I really such a funny sight this early in the morning?"

"No, Tony. You are a wonderful, grand, beautiful sight this early in the morning. Please take me home, darling."

They drove along the 401 in relative silence, holding hands and smiling. Tony did break into song, keeping company with Frank Sinatra on the radio. Once inside their apartment, with the door closed behind them, Tony swept her into his arms and kissed her long and hard. She wasn't sure exactly what was happening in her life, but she clung to him and prayed that nothing would come between them.

For the next couple of days, Tony didn't let her out of his sight. They went for long walks, and Jo found she could finally concentrate on card games and backgammon. They cooked together in the beautiful, well-equipped kitchen. They laughed. They kissed like young lovers. Tony couldn't seem to pass her in a room without embracing her and dancing a step or two with her. She thought her happiness was going to make her heart burst. What, she wondered, did she have buried in the recesses of her mind?

On Friday, Tony drove her to see Dr. Allen. They went into the office together and chatted with the doctor for a short while before Robert asked Tony to leave the room. He wanted to talk privately with Jo. Tony squeezed her hand and kissed her cheek, then went to wait in the outer office.

Jo found that her palms were damp and she was getting uncomfortable. She had a hanky in one hand and inadvertently started folding the lace edges into little pleats. Dr. Allen said nothing for a minute or so, simply watching the movement of her hands. Then he asked her why she was here.

Surprised, Jo replied, "I thought you were going to give *me* the answer to that."

Let me rephrase that, "Why do you think you are here?"

"Because something has happened that I don't want to deal with. It seems I've blocked something from my memory and I understand you're going to help me remember."

"Do you remember coming to this office before?"

"Yes."

"Do you remember why?"

"Yes."

"Why were you here before?"

"Because someone I cared about was killed in a plane crash and I fell apart. You helped to put me back together again."

"Are you still 'together'?"

"I think so."

"You think so. But you're not sure?"

"Dr. Allen, I'm not sure why I'm here. I'm not sure if I'm completely over Mike's death. I'm not sure if I will ever be completely over it. I'm not sure if I will ever be completely *together* but I'm managing."

"Managing ... what?"

"Managing to get on with my life. Managing to put the past behind me."

"Jo, you lost your first husband in an automobile accident a while back."

"Yes."

"Did you love him?"

"Yes."

"Did you fall apart and need to be put back together when he died?"

"I ... Not exactly."

"What do you mean not exactly?"

"I was devastated, I wasn't sure I could carry on without him. I missed him terribly. But I had a business to run and managed to get through it."

"When Mike died, were you devastated?"

"Yes."

"Did you still have a business to run?"

"Yes."

"But you didn't manage to get through it."

"No."

"Why is that do you think?"

"I don't know."

"You don't know why one death was so different from the other?"

"No. Yes. Maybe."

"Maybe?"

"I think when it happened the second time, it was too much for me to deal with."

"Both men died in tragic accidents."

"Yes."

Her palms were getting damper and she had run out of handkerchief to fold.

"Is this why I'm here? Does this have something to do with Stu or Mike?

"Tell me about last Monday."

"I don't remember too much."

"Tell me what you remember."

"I remember driving along Winston Churchill Boulevard, and then … nothing."

"Did you stop anywhere along Winston Churchill Boulevard?"

"No. I don't think so."

"What were you thinking as you were driving along?"

"I was thinking … I was thinking about …" She twisted the hanky in her hands and got up and paced behind her chair. "I don't know what I was thinking about."

"What kind of day was it?"

"It was bright and sunny."

"Did you have your radio on?"

"Yes."

"What was on the radio?"

"A call-in talk show. A woman was talking about growing an herb garden in a small balcony."

"But you don't remember what you were thinking about."

"No. Yes. I was thinking that … I was really interested in what she was talking about, so I hoped she would finish before I had to get out of the car."

"Where did you have to get out of the car?"

"I don't know … I was going somewhere, I remember … I remember I had a stop to make … Where was I going?" Jo was wringing the hanky tighter and tighter, and pacing faster. She stopped, out of breath, and perspiring noticeably.

When she volunteered nothing further, and several moments had passed, the doctor stood and walked around his desk. "Jo, I think we've talked enough for one day. I want to see you back here on Monday. You've done well, and now I want you to go home and rest."

Jo thanked him. She didn't know what for, though. On her way out the receptionist gave her an appointment card for the following Monday morning. Tony was waiting and slid a hand under her elbow as they left.

The next few sessions were pretty well a repeat of the first. After two weeks of talking, Dr. Allen decided it might be time to take this one step further. He would talk to Jo and Tony about it at her next visit.

TWENTY-SIX

Every day they walked and enjoyed the beautiful fall weather. The trees were just beginning to turn colour and the air had that fresh feel to it. Jo asked Tony if they could plan a weekend dinner for their families. Jo loved to cook, and after some thought, Tony agreed. It might give her some real pleasure and what could it hurt? Their families were delighted and accepted the invitation.

They had fun visiting the market gardens and bought fresh produce from the local farmers. They were paying for their greens when Tony noticed a bin near the cash register. "You know what would be nice that I haven't had in a long while?"

"What's that, Tony?"

"Eggplant."

Jo dropped her change purse and the coins went rolling all over the ground. She was embarrassed but grateful as it gave her time to compose herself. Tony didn't notice her discomfort and bent to help her pick up the loose change. *Smarten up, Jo. It's only a vegetable. Pull yourself together.* But she knew it was more than a vegetable, it was also a colour. She straightened up and asked him to pick out some nice ones for her to stuff and bake.

The dinner went over without a hitch. Tony was beaming with pride at the delicious meal his Josy had prepared. The dining room table seated fourteen easily, so all of them, his brother and sister and spouses included, were able to sit around a beautifully set table. Jo had taken great pains with her makeup and hair. She didn't want anyone thinking she looked like a crazy woman — even if she was one. She wanted this to be special for Tony. It was the first time the dining room and formal china had been used for company since his wife died. If he could handle it, then so could she. Jo watched him sitting at his place at the head of the table. She watched the interaction between him, his family and his grandson. She watched and gave thanks for the close-ness and love growing between her grandsons and his. His daughter and her daughter-in-law had always been close, now they were like sisters. He and George slapped each other on the shoulder, in good humour, when repeating stories from years past. Their sister looked at her brothers with such pride. Jo wondered how it could possibly get any better than this.

After everyone left, Tony helped her clean up and put away what the women hadn't already washed. He watched her placing the last of the crystal back in the china cabinet, and he thought his heart couldn't hold much more without bursting. She turned and saw him watching her and she felt something warm engulf her very being.

She walked to him and put her arms around his neck. After kissing him passionately on the lips, she placed several more gently on his cheek. She stepped back, still holding him and said, "Tony, I don't understand what's going on in my head right now, but I do know what's going on in my heart." She took his hand and placed it on her chest. "Do you feel it beating? It's beating for you, and only you. It has taken a long time, but you've shown me how to love. I can't ever remember being more content in my whole life. Even my beautiful sunsets at the resort never gave me this same kind of contentment and sense of well being that I'm feeling right at this moment. I love you, darling. No matter what happens in the future, with my therapy, my brain, my health, please know that my heart is yours and it always will be."

Tony was finding it difficult to breathe.

"I told you that whatever happens, I will be here for you. Cara, I love you so much and part of me wants you to get well, to remember, and then hopefully forget. Another part of me is so terrified of what will happen, if, in remembering, you find you don't or can't love me after all, and I end up losing you." He sighed, and pulled her close. "My sweet, sweet Josy, I couldn't bear it."

The next day, she and Tony entered Dr. Allen's office together. He looked from one to the other and noticed their hands were intertwined. He hoped that whatever the future held, their love would get them through it. They seemed to have so much going for them. He marvelled that they seemed to have this special bond that usually comes from years of togetherness, even though they were newlyweds.

"Jo, Tony, I feel that after this many sessions, we should have made more progress with the memory loss. My theory is that either you have buried it so deep, Jo, that it will take something stronger than talking to find it, or your psyche just doesn't want to deal with it all. Now, there are two routes we can travel. We can either let the therapy end here, and hope that down the road your memory may be triggered and return on its own accord, or we can look at an alternative approach such as hypnosis. Either way there is an inherent risk."

He went on to explain the dangers of another traumatic shock, if and when her memory might be restored by an unexpected event such as the one she experienced. He explained it could be something as simple as a familiar voice, or a remembered occasion. Then he explained the risk involved with hypnosis, and its possible effects on the brain as well. When asked, his recommendation was to hypnotize Jo and attempt to take her back to the events leading up to her memory breakdown. The reason for this choice was that it would be in a controlled environment, with him present and able to help her overcome any difficulties.

If left to a chance recovery, there was no guarantee when this might happen or how she might react. With the possibility of her being alone again, she may not be able to deal with it. However, he wanted them to go home and think about it. The ultimate decision had to be Jo's, but sometimes talking it out helped.

Jo decided no further discussion was needed. She wanted to get it over with and behind her. She wanted them to get on with their lives. Dr. Allen was to make the necessary arrangements as soon as possible.

He explained that if this were her final decision, he would call her within the next day or so with an appointed time.

Tony called Dr. Allen the next day with a question he needed answered. He wondered why the doctor could just not show Josy the pin and the letter to perhaps jog her memory. The doctor explained that because it had had such an effect on her when she originally saw it, it may just put her completely over the edge and do irreparable harm. It would be much better for her to remember with the help of hypnosis. He cautioned there was still some risk, but not as much as confronting her with these items without warning. With hypnosis, he could walk her through the events leading up to the discovery, but could interrupt the procedure at any time if he felt she were experiencing difficulties. The appointment was set for the following week.

Tony and Jo were drawing closer to each other with every passing day. Jo looked forward to the following Tuesday with eagerness as well as apprehension. Tony was quite confident that their love would be strong enough to help her through this.

They were walking through a park-like area about half a kilometre from their condominium, enjoying the sound of the crisp leaves under their feet. A small stream ran through the neighbourhood and in the middle of the park a man-made dam forced the water to form a large pond before it trickled out the other side. Tony stopped to talk to an older man who was sitting on a bench. The baby carriage in front of him had caught Tony's eye. Always making a fuss over babies and children, Tony leaned over the carriage and cooed to the little one inside. Jo smiled and kept walking. She could hear a dog barking just up ahead and wondered if someone might be throwing sticks into the water for it to retrieve. When Tony finished his "conversation" with the little one, he continued along the sidewalk that curved around toward the pond. Jo was staring at the pond with an expression Tony had never seen before. When he was close enough to see what had caught her attention so intently, he noticed two geese gliding across the water. A lone tear was making its way down Jo's cheek. Suddenly the dog started barking again and the two birds took flight. They lifted off the water and as they glided by at eye level in front of Jo, their profiles were in perfect unison.

Before Tony realized what was happening, Jo had dropped to her knees, unable to catch her breath. He rushed to pick her up and hold her close, cursing as he reached into his empty pocket for his cell phone. As he looked around for the closest exit, she struggled away from him and started to run, sobbing. He ran after her and caught her wrist in an iron grip and swung her around to face him. Her look of absolute panic frightened him. "Where are you going?"

"I have to go to my old apartment."

"Why?"

"There's something there that I need."

Tony's heart fell. He was going to crumble.

"What's there, cara? What do you need?"

"A letter. I have to read it again."

"I don't think that's a good idea. Let me call Dr. Allen and take you to his office."

"No, Tony. I must get that letter!"

He took a deep breath, hesitated, then with sagging shoulders he placed her arm under his. "Come, I will take you home. The letter is there."

When they arrived at the apartment, Tony opened the safe in his den and pulled out the envelope. As he walked back to the living room, he was positive he felt the way a man must feel going to the gallows. He wanted desperately to call Dr. Allen but didn't want to risk Josy's taking flight. He handed her the envelope and she grabbed it like a starving woman grabbing a piece of bread. Tearing the envelope in her haste to get at the letter, she read it twice. When finished, she stood and walked over to the window. Tony helplessly watched her, afraid to move.

She stared through the glass for the longest time. When she finally turned, her cheeks and the front of her blouse were damp with tears. God, what had he done? He had lost her for sure, he knew. He could feel it in the pit of his stomach and in the emptiness of his heart.

Then she smiled. He was sure he could hear her laughing softly. She came over and threw her arms around his neck and kissed his cheeks, then full on his mouth. She must have lost her mind completely, he thought. Dr. Allen was absolutely right, this was too much for her. He should call him.

"She thanked me. His daughter thanked me for making her dad happy. He died knowing happiness."

"Are you all right? Please. Sit down. I'm going to call the doctor."

"I don't need a doctor, Tony. I don't think I will ever need him again. I was not responsible for Mike's death. I was responsible for his happiness. Tony, if he had lived, I would have made him miserable. I would only have broken his heart. He soon would have realized, as would I, that I didn't really love him."

Jo stopped and thought for a moment. "He was exciting, and he made me feel exciting. He came along when I was still hurting from Stu's death and he lifted me out of my depression. He was handsome, exciting, romantic and wonderful, and he said all the right things. I was overcome with the fact that a popular man like Mike could find me attractive, and actually fall in love with me. I was caught up in the exhilaration of it. He loved me, and in doing so, made me think I loved him. When I saw him again at the sportsman's show, and later at my hotel, I should have realized that I didn't really love him. If I did, there would have been absolutely no hesitation on my part. I really am a terribly foolish woman. I was like a teenager who realizes the high school football hero wants to take her to the prom. She is star struck and thinks she loves him, but it's the excitement that she's in love with. It's not real.

"Reading his daughter's letter again reinforced how shallow our relationship really was. I knew nothing about the life he had before we met. All I knew was that he had played football in his younger years. I didn't know that he had lost a son, or a wife. I barely was aware that he had a daughter. Isn't that sad? What kind of a relationship is that? He knew very little about me, except that I had lost my husband and operated a lodge. Given time, we would have come to know each other better, but I know that I wouldn't have had the same feelings for him that I have for you."

She picked up the little box and took out the pin. Turning it over and over with her fingers, she looked up at her husband. "When I saw this, all I thought was, There are *not* two. One is dead — and I'm responsible. I'm the one that killed it. I thought, if only I had stopped him from getting on that plane he would be alive. What bothered me was that he offered to stay, *wanted* to stay, and I told him to go. He went. Only to be killed. All I could focus on was that I could have prevented his death. That I had sent him to it. *Now* I realize I didn't kill him. He got on that plane thinking I loved him. In his mind there were two geese that were going to be mated for life, him and me. If he hadn't boarded that plane, he would have lived only to die inside. The first time I read the letter, I was upset and wondered how she could lay this guilt on me. Doesn't she know I'm guilty enough, without her adding to it? Now I'm glad she wrote. I'm not glad he got on that plane, or that he's dead, but I now know why God does things the way He does. I've been praying for understanding. Praying to be let out of this prison in which I've been trapped, and now I am out. After years of loneliness and grief, God chose me to give Mike a little happiness in the end. He chose me to be the conduit of his happiness. In doing this, He gave Mike's daughter some peace of mind as well. She will never know how sad a turn Mike's life *might* have taken.

"When I saw those two geese at the park today, I realized there are two, still two. Only they're a different two. They're you and me, Tony. It's all in God's plan. Now I think we can finally get on with *our* lives and find our own happiness."

Now it was Tony who was holding back tears. "Josy, my love, I've already found my happiness — you!"

She looked at the pin again, then clutched it to her heart. "Do you realize that he and I spent only four days together? It seems incredible that a man, whose physical company I had only shared for four days, could create such turmoil in my life. Even though I was not in love with him, Mike did mean a lot to me and I hope you won't mind if I wear this pin sometimes."

"I will pin it on you myself. He was special man. He had to have been to make such an impression on you in that short period of time. Obviously, he preferred to spend your brief interlude together laughing and loving, rather than by talking about the past. I can understand how he must have been enamoured of you from the first moment he laid eyes on you, just as I was. You're right. Eventually Mike would have shared his painful past with you. With only a week to win your heart, he spent his time wisely. I, too, wish his life hadn't ended so tragically, but I'm happy now that you know his death was destined by God and not by any action on your part."

Jo stared in bewilderment beyond Tony's shoulder at the large windows facing west and south. "Tony, I've never seen the sun set so beautifully behind those buildings. You can actually see the colours reflecting off the office towers. The buildings seem to have a glow all their own. Why have I never noticed that before?"

"Perhaps, my darling, the clouds that have shaded your view are finally disappearing."

"What I see most clearly is that you've been more than patient with me. You've been a saint, Tony. Another man would have thrown up his hands and written me off long ago."

"I'm not a saint but not a fool either, cara."

"Most people love the sunrise thinking it the most beautiful way to start a fresh new day. As you know, I've always loved the sunset, the perfect ending to another day and the promise of a bright tomorrow. The more glorious the sunset, the more glorious tomorrow's promise. Tony, darling, I have never seen those buildings look more spectacular."

Tony took the brooch from her and pinned it to her sweater. He wrapped an arm around her shoulders and urged her toward the window.

"I understand the sunsets on the beaches in the Caribbean are spectacular, too. Why don't we plan a holiday on one of the islands, maybe enjoy some scuba diving?"

Jo remembered how she had been secretly amused once at the thought of trying to coerce Tony into just this situation. That had been during her Florida vacation with Barb. It seemed like a lifetime ago. It was. Mike's lifetime ago.

"Josy?"

"Sorry. I was lost in thoughts of beaches and sunsets." She lied, somewhat guilty about once more allowing Mike into her thoughts. She shook it off. "I've never been to Hawaii. How does a Pacific island vacation appeal to you?"

Tony squeezed her shoulder as he turned her slightly. He kissed the top of her head then whispered in her ear, "If that's what you want, we'll go there first. I think I told you once that I wanted to travel the world after my business was sold. I remember saying there are so many places yet to see, but what I didn't tell you, cara mia, is that I intend to make love to you in every single one of them."

Her eyes glowed mischievously when she lifted her gaze to his. "It's nice to know, darling, that your dreams and mine are the same." Her kiss told Tony what he already knew, but she whispered it anyway. "It really doesn't matter where we are, as long as we're together."

EPILOGUE

No more tears. She was determined there would be no more tears. She and Tony had enjoyed eleven glorious love-filled years together. Well, ten and a half, really. There had been nothing glorious about the last six months. A kind and gentle man, he had suffered a death that was anything but kind and gentle. His cancer, which had started in his colon long before he noticed any symptoms, had spread into his organs and was at stage four before his pain was enough to make him see a doctor. Tony had few faults but his reluctance to have regular check-ups was one that always worried Jo immensely. Now he was gone. She was angry with him, with his foolishness, when they first learned his fate. He could have prevented this. A religious man, he just reminded her that the day of his death is God's will. One way or another, when your time comes, it comes.

"On the day you are born God has already determined the day you will die, cara. It's what you do between those two days that He has given you free reign over. So we all must live life to the fullest. Enjoy and appreciate every single day."

He had taught her well how to do this. In their eleven years, they had travelled to and enjoyed many, many countries around the world. They never missed an opportunity to spend time with their children and grandchildren. In fact, they took their families on many of their travel adventures. His large extended family had become her large extended family. She would continue to live the life-lessons he had taught her.

Tony was buried next to his beloved Angie. They had agreed on this.

When her time came she would be buried next to Stu. She had thought it would be harder to walk away from the cemetery. Having six months to prepare for this day may have made it easier. No, that's not true, *she thought. Tony had made it easier.*

"Cara, you must lay me next to Angelina and walk away. Take our family home and feed them well. Sylvia and Jean will help you. I want lots of funny stories and singing. I want to be remembered as 'Tony, that nice guy from the hockey rink'."

Jo hoped the nice guy from the hockey rink saw all the Mississauga Missile hockey sweaters in the pews. His obituary had not only appeared on the obit page in the newspaper, it had also appeared on the sports page.

She reached for the pool pole and pulled the plastic glasses to the edge. Then took them and her own glass into the house, the house they had bought on the waterfront in Oakville. They had decided to move into a house that would facilitate pool parties for the grandchildren and large barbecues for their extended family. The dining room table, fully extended, held a buffet large enough to include cousins, nieces and nephews for various holiday celebrations.

A family man. She had been fortunate. After three deaths and two funerals, all fine men, she knew she would live the rest of her life with her memories.

She loaded the dishwasher with the last glasses and plates, turned off the kitchen light and started upstairs. The light was on in their bedroom, her bedroom now. She must have left it on this morning without noticing. When she rounded the doorway, Jo realized it wasn't a lamp left on, it was the sun setting. The doors were open to the balcony and she slipped through just as the sun rested on the open water of Lake Ontario. The red reflection on the dark water was Tony's promise of a glorious tomorrow. She was smiling when the phone rang.

"Hi, Jo. Just wondering if you're okay."

"Yes, Barb, I'm perfectly fine."

"What are you doing?"

"I'm just saying goodnight to a nice guy from the hockey rink."

Praise for *Fire in the Foothills*:

I've enjoyed the book so much that I'm on my second reading — a thing I rarely do. I'm now looking forward to the next one.

— Gill Foss, Ottawa, author of *Windows in Time*

There is no doubt but that your book is one of the best I have read. Your people are real and several times I had tears in my eyes.

— Joyce Fee, Peterborough

Praise for *The Wilderness*:

This romantic/suspense will make your heart beat a little faster and the pages turn a little quicker, you won't be able to put this book down.

— Mari-Lou Jorgenson, Thunder Bay

I just finished reading your new book *The Wilderness* and could hardly put it down. Ended up finishing it at 3 AM. Great characters and really exciting! Congratulations.

— Joan Shouldice, Ottawa

CPSIA information can be obtained at www.ICGtesting.com
Printed in the USA
LVOW11s0453240415

435861LV00003B/110/P